LIKE THE WIND

Vijitha Yapa Publications
Unity Plaza, 2 Galle Road, Colombo 4, Sri Lanka
Tel. (94 11) 2596960 Fax (94 11) 2584801
e-mail: vijiyapa@sri.lanka.net
www.srilankanbooks.com
www.vijithayapa.com

ISBN 955-8095-81-8

First UK Edition 2003
First Sri Lanka Reprint April 2005

Cover Design by Thushari, www.chandicraft.com

Printed by Tharanjee Prints, Maharagama

LIKE THE WIND

by

Daisy Abey

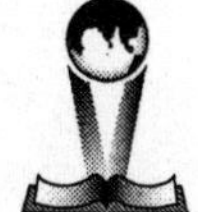

Vijitha Yapa Publications
Sri Lanka

By the same author

Poetry Publications
City of Leeds
Letter to a Friend
Under Any Sky
In Exile
Silent Protest
On Pennine Heights

About the Author

Daisy Abeygunasekara (nee Wimalagunaratna) was born near Matara Sri Lanka and was educated at the University of Peradeniya from 1960-1963. In 1965 Daisy migrated to the UK where, for three decades, she worked and raised her family. She worked for Zurich Insurance and then for seventeen years with the homeless in the inner city, helping vulnerable people with psychiatric and addiction problems, many of whom had been in prison or worked as prostitutes, to regain their lives. Now she devotes her time to writing. The sadness of separation from her homeland, juxtaposed with the experience of urban poverty in the West, has combined to make her one of contemporary Sri Lanka's leading writers.

For Isabel and William

ONE

Fragrance of blossom on the tall mango tree in the garden and the smell of damp grass mixed together filled the sky to the stars through evening clouds. The fine raindrops touched the mango leaves with a cracking sound. The full moon in a corner of the sky was washed away by faded sunshine; the hills, wrapped in the invisible touch of the night's darkness have entered the world of sleep with the retiring sun. A cool breeze blew across the ripening rice fields and entered the open house full of the scent of mango flowers. Finally the daytime tropical heat cooled and the flames blew in the wind. The evening silence echoed with the sounds of the approaching moonlit night. The changings, wavings, movings of the days and nights increased the tension in Rupa's mind. She could hear her mother's voice.

'How hard we've tried to arrange someone suitable for this child. I can't remember how many people have visited this house since the day she came home from university, there must have been dozens. It's all so pointless. We just waste time and money on matchmakers. They don't care whether it is a man without arms and legs, as long as a marriage can be arranged and they get their commission! I have no idea what's going to happen. Either the men aren't happy or she won't agree with the proposals for one reason or another, there's always something, Venus and Mars in the wrong place, the horoscopes don't match! This man is fat and short that one thin and tall; dark or light skinned, whatever nothing's ever right! Hmm.... We can never give the kind of dowry some of them ask. Money isn't something that grows on trees or you find under rocks. You remember that Morris Agent in Galle? When his son was proposed for Rupa, the very first thing they asked from the matchmaker was how much money she had in her bank account!

They try to wipe their dirty hands on our faces. I'd like us to live our life the way we want, not at the behest of some shark or other. In the end that man managed to marry a semi-literate bitch with a family in Colombo 7 completely loaded, as you'd expect with an address like that and a big house for the dowry thrown in! It's not easy to do anything with the girl either, I don't want to ruin our family reputation, I want to walk out of the front door without being covered in shame. If caste and wealth is not a problem, then some-thing else rears its ugly head. You have to have some luck in this world! Family customs must be followed when the girl gets to the right age. I know what she'll say; she doesn't want to live with a businessman, not at any price! I'll only be too happy if the whole thing ends without a major crisis.'

Dikwelle Hamine raised her voice. Loku Mahatmaya was inside the house pounding betel leaves. He dropped two pieces of dried black tobacco into the mortar and crushed them hard with the pestle, pretending to listen to his wife's angry voice. The betel mixture turned to a coarse brown powder but still there was no sign of Dikwelle Hamine stopping.

'Can't you see, she refuses anything even before it reaches her ear! She hasn't even seen these people from Kegalle. Thank god they are a respectable family. No problem about caste either.'

The sound of her voice was so loud that it drowned even the pounding of the betel nuts.

'Can you hear me? You wouldn't believe this. Yesterday morning she asked the matchmaker not to bother to bring any more men to this house. He's furious about it, I mean, a young woman like Rupa should have some self-respect. Isn't she embarrassed to argue with the matchmakers? When I was a young woman when a matchmaker came to our house I used to hide in my bedroom, behind the wardrobe. Bringing up unruly children doesn't give any hope for their poor parents!' Dikwelle Hamine washed the fresh brown rice. This season there had been a bumper harvest. She put the fingers of her right hand into the water to check the level, emptied out some to the line of her middle finger, lifted the aluminium pan with both hands and placed it on the burner. Before she placed the pot on the lapping flames she put together the palms of her hands and for a second bent her head, in the ritual gesture of prayer that prefaced the cooking of a meal.

Loku Mahatmaya and Dikwelle Hamine had lived in their house since they married thirty-five years ago. Everybody knew the house as 'Maha Gedara'. It was the ancestral home, the land passed onto from generation to generation. Long before Ceylon, the 'Pearl of the East,' became part of the British Raj, a vast area of land was gifted by the king of the county to Loku Mahatmaya's great great grandfather, the headman of several villages, a loyal follower from the hill country, the centre of the kingdom. Those days rural parts of the country were mostly tropical jungle and travelling could only be done by walking or by bullock-carts jarring along narrow rutted lanes. No communication system existed. The present house 'Maha Gedara' was built a hundred and twenty years ago, since then the house had been greatly extended with six large bedrooms. It was in a small village surrounded by a range of hills, there were only five houses in the whole village.

The hillside land was used for growing cinnamon, rubber and coconut. The morning sun appeared through the tropical forest beside the hills and covered the lowland paddy fields. The sound of running water through rocks in the narrow canal, the blaring call of peacocks, owls, bats and the howl of the fox broke the silence of the village. The white washed house was built of local stone and roofed with tiles hallmarked 'Clay hills', long fermented clay baked in kilns three miles away. The narrow road to Maha Gedara falls through acres of lush green paddy fields and crimson croton hedges. In front of the house there was a portico with lattice windows covered with overhanging scarlet bougainvillaea. As you entered the parlour you caught the smell of decades old ebony and satin furniture and scent of jasmine from the shrine in a corner of the long dining room flowed like fresh spring water. There were two storerooms always filled with bags of rice and flying dust-like moths. The kitchen was enormous with a grey cemented floor. The two-storey house had a balcony overlooking cinnamon land, the home of peacocks dancing at dawn with the rising tropical sun.

There was no electricity, the house had to be lit with oil lamps and water had to be drawn from a well. The cooking methods had not changed for centuries. Three stones positioned so that stalks and twigs could be laid across them and then set alight to heat the cooking pot.

Dikwelle Hamine added a handful of cinnamon stalks and some dried coconut palm leaves to the charcoal already starting to burn. She pulled the coconut scraper, which she used as a small chair forward and blew the fire several times. Patiently she sat by the fire and the bubbling rice pan, watching how the smoke gathered in swirls then crept out of the metal grilles of the windows. Dikwelle Hamine was quiet; perhaps she had at last stopped talking and was getting on with the evening meal. The sound of the mortar and pestle had stopped. Loku Mahatmaya emptied the well ground betel mixture with his fingers and put some of the mix into his mouth. He cleaned the betel stained mortar and pestle with a piece of cloth and pushed it into a corner. The mortar and pestle belonged to Loku Mahatmaya's father, a Village Headman who died many years before. The Village Headman was responsible for keeping law and order and for the general wellbeing of the locals. Only recently had he found these items in the loft hidden in a brass vase covered with dust and cobwebs. Loku Mahatmaya came out chewing betel leaves and sat in an armchair in the long sitting area near the storerooms.

'It's not necessary to talk about this matter all the time! I think you should leave Rupa alone, let her do what she wants. Why don't you mind your own business? Children these days are like that. They are stubborn and only do what they want.' Dikwelle Hamine did not hear him. He got up and looked round then he walked into the front garden. He spat betel juice into a mound of sand and covered the red patches with his feet.

The evening sun was moving towards the western sky behind the hills, floating clouds turned red and then dissolved into a dark screen. The woodlands with tall trees were already plunged into darkness. Loku Mahatmaya folded the sarong he was wearing and tied it in a knot. As night approached the wooden gate at the bottom of the sloping garden had to be closed. If he forgot Handaya, the black cow with a moon shaped white patch on its forehead and Ratti the brown-red cow, they would ruin the young banana and coconut plants. He watched the rain-washed blue green tender leaves of banana plants unfolding as a mother watches a baby. Loku Mahatmaya paced towards the gate along the brown gravel path, through the flowing darkness of the night. Ratti and the week-old calf were still grazing in the grassland beyond the barbed wire fence. The pot of rice was well cooked and steaming. Charcoal under the burner was turning to ash. The mouth-watering smell of Dikwelle Hamine's cooking was spreading all over the house and into the garden. She poured the squeezed coconut milk into a clay pot and mixed chopped onions, chilli and ground cumin to prepare a curry.

'This is a shame to our family, is no one suitable for her? In the end rumours will spread to every village about our daughter running away from home. Whatever happens its us who will have to face the shame. It's only me screaming and shouting day and night like rain falling onto a tin roof! All I do is talk to her father like playing a vina to a deaf elephant!' Dikwelle Hamine started to talk again but soon she realised that her husband was not sitting in the parlour. The kitchen door was still open and mosquitoes had begun to enter the house whispering in her ears. She slammed the door, stirred the coconut milk in the pot a few times and poured it slowly into the bubbling yellow plantain curry.

Dinner was almost ready. Only a little water was left at the bottom of the copper tub. No sign of Loku Mahatmaya in house or garden. She served the boiled rice, ash plantain curry and fish fry into the 'Johnson and Johnson' dishes and put them on the dining table. The dinner and tea set with deep blue floral spray design was a gift from her parents with the dowry when she married. It was so precious to her she'd never thrown away a cup or saucer, even when it was cracked or lacked a handle. She covered the food on the table with a wicker food cover until Loku Mahatmaya came home. No one eats before then; it was a custom of Maha Gedara. When Loku Mahatmaya sits at the table first she serves her husband

and then Rupa. If a poor neighbour who helped with the housework or any servants were there they were invited to eat. The servants had their meal in the kitchen, sitting on a bench. Dikwelle Hamine never sat at the dinner table with Loku Mahatmaya. She waited until everybody had finished eating and then had her dinner with Tilakawathie. Tilakawathie was a girl who grew up at Maha Gedara. She arrived when she was six. Her parents were too poor to bring up their family of eleven and Dikwelle Hamine had volunteered to adopt the girl.

TWO

There had been no rain for several weeks. At times the sky was heavy with swirling, thickening clouds, which soon dissolved into a blazing red sky. The evening sun slowly moved towards the tall treetops and was ready to sink into the horizon. The hot clammy air stuck your clothes to your skin. Rupa could hear her mother's voice flowing like broken waves from the kitchen to the room where she was reading. Streaks of her mother's anger, tropical heat and a slight headache began behind her forehead, swirled round her head and turned to utter discomfort. The portico was shaded with the evening's dim faded light. If the windows and fanlights were not closed at nightfall the mosquitoes would get in and infest every corner, hovering and buzzing overhead. These tiny flying insects with their needle-like stings even managed to creep inside the mosquito nets, which covered the beds. Soon they turned to round red bubbles. When they were squashed red bloodstains appeared on nets, beds, curtains, face, arms and legs. Itchy stinging irritations made the night unbearable. During hot dry periods the mosquitoes bred in ditches; at night they swarmed into the houses smelling blood.

Rupa remembered her childhood. She had no one to talk to so she talked to herself. 'I had heard my mother's story too often. I never disobeyed when I was young. When I was nine I was ill with typhoid and could not go to school for weeks on end. I still did not understand what illness was, every morning I cried I didn't want to miss the lessons at school. I had a friend called Dingihami, who came from a very poor family. I gave her some of my colouring pencils and tiny packets of beads, which we used to make bangles and necklaces with. My uncle had a grocery store and on our way to school we went to his shop to buy coloured beads and sweets.

Sometimes I was given so many I had enough to share with my friend. She had an unforgettable smile and gleaming eyes and used to hide her beads in a matchbox. Some days after school she came with me and my mother gave her ginger biscuits and tea. Together we made a water lily pond near the paddy fields. We made clay figures and dried them in the hot sun. I remember how we secretly drank pond water from a coconut shell. We had no idea that drinking such water could make us very ill. I lost contact with Dingihami after I left the village school. She married the man of her choice but sadly he became an alcoholic. She never came back to the village. There is a rumour that her husband was also a drug addict and left her altogether. I think she may still be alive, living in poverty somewhere.'

It was a struggle to concentrate on reading. Rupa closed the book and put it on the bed. She remembered how worried her parents were when she was ill.

'It's not worth telling these children not to play in muddy water. I always ask you not to let them play out in the fields. You must point out just how easily they can catch infections.'

Loku Mahatmaya was not happy with his wife. In his view she was entirely responsible for looking after the children and keeping them away from ditches of foul water.

'You are not allowed to go to school until you feel better. The doctor told you to stay in bed until your temperature goes down. I only can give you rice and vegetable soup, orange juice with glucose and king-coconut water.'

Dikwelle Hamine refused to give her anything to eat. Rupa felt so ill with the fever she could hardly speak or even open her eyes. But the smell of her mother's cooking was so tempting she felt like stealing some food but it was only a thought. She was frightened and she could not move out of her bed. The soup tasted sickening and the coconut water was undrinkable, but orange juice and glucose drinks prepared by her mother were delicious and the sweet taste stayed for hours on her tongue.

Rupa remembered one day when she was seven how she had disobeyed her father.

'Don't you want to go to school today? It's nearly seven o'clock. Time to get up, get ready quickly.' Loku Mahatmaya was angry.

'I prepared some milk-rice for breakfast today. Rupa can eat some before she goes to school.' Dikwelle Hamine looked through the kitchen door and said aloud.

'I don't want to go to school today daddy.'

'Why?'

'I feel tired. My tummy aches.'

A few minutes after her father came in with a furious face and she thought he would thrash her, so she threw the bedding aside and got up very quickly.

'Pig.' She murmured. Loku Mahatmaya did not hear. She put some pink tooth-powder on to her palm and ran to the well to get washed. Only Rupa knew why she didn't want to go to school that morning.

In the village school the blackboards had to be re-inked by the children. The ink they used was a mixture of charcoal powder and the sap collected from a shrub called palaini which grew in hedges up to eight feet high and when you cut its fleshy bark a creamy sap came out. It was the day that the blackboard in Rupa's classroom had to be inked. Although the inking was done by the older boys, every child in her class had to bring either charcoal or palaini sap. Rupa could not take any charcoal because her mother only used cinnamon stalks in cooking. The day before Rupa wanted to go across the paddy fields to collect some palaini sap from the overgrown hedges, but her mother said 'Don't go under those bushes and hedges child. The sun is very hot today and in the mid-afternoon reptiles are thirsty and come out to the canal for a drink of water. Palaini hedge is notorious for cobras. Yesterday afternoon I saw a snake creeping along the bund towards the hedge. Pythons like to coil round tree trunks and branches, palaini stems are thick and cool.'

Rupa listened to her mother. She thought the hedge along the paddy fields was a kingdom of venomous reptiles. She remembered how a snake killed their family dog Boola while he was running through the hedges after a rabbit. The dog lay dead, saliva bubbling out of its mouth. Going to school without at least a piece of charcoal was so embarrassing Rupa thought. She would get a black mark on the teacher's list. If she could pretend that she had a stomach upset, everybody would forget to talk about blackboard inking.

The first day after the inking their class teacher did not write anything on the board, it must be left for twenty-four hours to dry. The children were allowed to play all day. The girls played in the grounds in front of the headmaster's house, the boys played ball games and tug-of-war in the main playground. The girls played 'the wolf game.' Mr Wolf wore a red and green woven straw hat and a brown apron while he was hiding behind the large gnarled mango tree. The rest of the girls hid in corners, under bushes and trees. Finally Mr Wolf had to hide somewhere no one knew. The girls came out of hiding and started to sing and dance hand-in-hand in a chain.

We are not afraid of Mr. Wolf
Wolf tails, straw hats, wolf tails, straw hats.
Are you giving us sweet mangoes?
Mr. Wolf, Mr. Wolf
We are not afraid of Mr. Wolf.

'Mr. Wolf' suddenly burst out of a bush and started to chase the running, screaming girls.

Although Rupa wanted to play the role of Mr.Wolf she dreaded going to school that day, but her father made her go with a note to the teacher explaining why she was late. The teacher accepted the note with a smile. Calling your father a pig isn't very nice. The headmaster reminded the children in morning assembly that they must obey teachers and parents. The fear she had in her mind had to be cleared so when she went to the temple with her mother she knelt down in the shrine and prayed for forgiveness. Rupa felt that she had woken from a childhood dream of fragrance and colour. The unbroken ear-piercing cry of cicadas came from the woods. She looked out of the window and saw her mother walking down the path towards the well, a pail in her hand. Her father must have gone to put the cow and calf into the byre. Tilakwathie was picking jasmine in the garden. The sky was covered with a single layer of black clouds from which issued fine drizzle, the beginning of torrential rain. The man who lived in a mud hut at the chena up in the hills and his wife were going home along the bund in a hurry. He was carrying a large bag of groceries on his shoulder while she bore a wicker basket on her head.

'We went to the grocery shop in town. Hope we could get in before the rain falls. Our daughter is at home on her own.' He stopped for a minute to talk to Dikwelle Hamine; he smiled and showed his brown betel stained teeth.

'It's getting dark quickly. The paddy fields are dry and we could do with a good shower. Get home as soon as you can. When it's thunder and lightening you must stay indoors! I only came down to the well to draw some water. Remember to pray for safety when a storm comes.' Dikwelle Hamine urged.

From the window Rupa watched her mother coming back with a pail of water. She walked up the steps slowly looking very worried. Loku Mahatmaya put the calf into the byre and fed Ratti the cow with a kneaded mixture of rice flour in a palm leaf. Ratti shook her head, rolled her eyes and looked at Loku Mahatmaya.

'Eat everything, my daughter.' Gently he stroked the cow's head. Ratti put her rough tongue out as she chomped happily.

The latest proposal for Rupa was brought from Gunapala, who owned a coconut plantation at Kegalle, the son of a well-known businessman called Jayasena Mudalali. Gunpala's education ended when he was seventeen and he joined his father's company in Colombo. It was a fresh February morning when Kapurala the matchmaker walked into Maha Gedara through the curtains of tropical mist as the sun appeared in a silver-pink sky. Dikwelle Hamine stood under the gardenia tree on a carpet of scented ivory flowers. Kapurala was welcomed with smiles. He was invited in and sat on a teak bench at a corner of the portico lit with rays of sunshine flashed through the shaded grilled windows. Loku Mahatmaya sat in an armchair.

'Surely you must have heard of Jayasena Mudalali? Even a child in the street in Kegalle would know who he is. Gunapala is his only son. One day he will inherit all his father's wealth. Neither money nor anything else is a problem for that family. We must concentrate on this matter.' Kapurala the matchmaker drank his tea.

'That's right Kapurala, we are looking for somebody exactly like that. The only problem is Kegalle is very far from us and travelling is not all that easy.'

Loku Mahatmaya was delighted.

'Travelling from Matara to Kegalle is not a great problem these days. They only travel by car anyway. They have everything and Mudalali's business is based in Colombo. Gunapala recently bought a new car.'

The matchmaker became extremely loquacious.

'Whatever it is I think we should try to find out a bit more about that family, caste and all the rest.'

'I wouldn't dream of bringing a proposal from someone of a different caste! You must be joking Loku Mahatmaya. They are only looking for a girl with good manners and some ability, someone who can run that enormous house. I think they are perfectly right to expect someone intelligent to take on such great responsibilities! It's a beautiful place. To be honest I am a bit reluctant to walk on those red polished floors. It's like walking on glass! Mahogany, ebony, teak and satin furniture everywhere and no end of servants and helpers; you'll only believe me if you see it with your own eyes! Miles and miles of coconut plantation; you can see neither the beginning nor the end! And nobody except his own son to inherit the lot!'

The matchmaker continued. Loku Mahatmaya touched his chin with his left hand and stayed silent for a few minutes, lost in thought.

'What can we do now? We want to do everything according to our family tradition, from the start. I want things to be perfect. We can't plan anything now. They haven't even visited us yet!'

While Loku Mahatmaya was talking to Kapurala, Dikwelle Hamine stood by the parlour door and listened in silence. She was astonished to hear about the wealthy family from Kegalle.

'If Loku Mahatmaya and Dikwelle Hamine have no objections I certainly can go ahead with this matter. I am not a matchmaker who puts anybody into any kind of trouble. If I say something it is firm like the sound of that gecko on the wall. I never expect too much for myself in the way of money or gifts. I'm happy to accept what is given. I don't demand an agreed commission.'

'All right then. We must fix a date for them to visit here.'

'I am going to Colombo tomorrow to see Jayasena Mudalali. I'll try to arrange a date convenient for them. They have all kinds of other commitments.'

Loku Mahatmaya agreed with the matchmaker.

'I'll be back within a few days.' Kapurala the matchmaker was still sitting on the bench looking round. Loku Mahatmaya handed over some money and said:

'Keep this for your bus fare to Colombo tomorrow.'

The matchmaker put the money in his pocket, folded his faded black umbrella with white patches under his arm and left with a wide smile.

Dikwelle Hamine was delighted to hear about a proposal from such a wealthy family. Her face shone like a new moon shining through darkened clouds. She said to her husband, 'Don't worry about the distance to Kegalle. If money, a house and land are no problem, it really doesn't matter wherever we live in this world.'

Dikwelle Hamine thought constantly about the happy moment when her daughter became a member of such a wealthy family! Cooking, housework, sewing, whatever she did, she did with renewed interest and became even more talkative. She dreamed of visiting her daughter, to a house with servants in the middle of enormous coconut lands. She thought about what she would take when she went to visit Rupa. People from the hill country don't get fresh fish from the sea so she thought of taking some fish bought straight from the fishermen on the beach and also Rupa likes home made sweets. One day she said to her husband, 'Our house will be empty without Rupa. We will have to visit her often although Kegalle is a long way away.'

The atmosphere at Maha Gedara had changed over a few weeks.

Loku Mahatmaya was relieved that his wife no longer worried about Rupa day and night and was kind to her instead of always grumbling. Rupa could not believe the change in her mother.

The nearest post office to Maha Gedara was about two miles away. The postman only went round the villages twice a week. The village postmaster kept aside any letters for Maha Gedara and every morning Loku Mahatmaya went to the post office by bicycle to check his post.

It had rained all night after a long drought and the trees and the paddy fields had washed off the dust, drops of rain glowed like crystal bubbles. Sunken undergrowth of mimosas opened pink powder-puff flowers, the shrunken canal was flowing fast increasing the water level to the rim of the bund; frogs were croaking, crows cawing and blue peacocks dancing on mango trees. Fresh breezes blew from the hills and spread a green silk veil over the whole village. The bridge over the canal was narrow.

Dikwelle Hamine watched in silence the white waters gushing, carrying leaves and weeds swept on to the banks.

Loku Mahatmaya came home pushing his bicycle along the gravel road where the cracked earth had turned to a ditch in the few hours of rainfall. He started talking to Dikwelle Hamine from a distance. The daytime heat was rising, skin penetrating burning air boiled the sweat and blood and the sun shone like a sparking fire in the cloudless sky. Loku Mahatmaya pulled a white handkerchief from his shirt pocket and wiped the sweat dripping down his forehead.

'I met the matchmaker today on my way to the post office. Remember that Jayasena Mudalali's family he was talking about? They are coming to visit us next week.'

'Next week?'

'Yes, on Monday afternoon. Kapurala will come here sometime today to discuss any problems.'

'We have to get ready then, we may not live at their level but we are not a family that doesn't know how to entertain. Don't forget your great great grandfather's relationship to the king of the country.' Dikwelle Hamine was always very proud of their family history. She believed that what matters is not life style, but keeping the legendary ancestral threads of customs rock solid and pass them on to future generations.

It was a sunny February morning when the wind swept across the ripening paddy fields. As the vast stretched fields turned yellow the air, the clouds, the earth, the trees and the hills were reflected in the mingling sunshine. It was a world of confusing colours. Maha Gedara garden was washed with the fragrance of gardenias and white jasmine. The hedge was bursting with deep pink wild azalea blooms. Crackling sound of the wind blown grass and grains appeared in the fields and vanished in a rhythm of waves and interludes. Delicate yellow and blue butterflies touched the rose nectar, the song of peacocks adding a tremulous echo. Dikwelle Hamine's whole being was suffused with delicious sensations of good things to come. The day they had so long awaited had finally arrived.

The guests were due at two in the afternoon. Dikwelle Hamine was getting ready, making sweets for afternoon tea. Fresh palm treacle was brought from a neighbouring village, rice flour was roasted and nuts chopped the day before; she made treacle slices, cutting them into oblongs, milk and cashew nut toffee and ripened red and yellow bunches of bananas were ready on the store room table. The only other occasion when Dikwelle Hamine prepared so lavishly was for the New Year festival. She kept flowers, sweets, milk-rice and king coconut water on a table in the storeroom, hoping the angels would come through the window on New Year's Eve and enjoy the food and drink.

A few days before the guests arrived Loku Mahatmaya asked two workmen to clear the gardens, path, flowerbeds and the gravel road between the fields and the house. A woman called Ranhami lived in a tiny house near Maha Gedara. All his lifetime Ranhami's husband had helped Loku Mahatmaya's family farm the paddy fields. Their house and the compound belonged to Loku Mahatmaya having originally been built and still being maintained by Maha Gedara family. Ranhami made a long handled soft broom with coconut palm leaves, cleared up and swept cobwebs from every corner of the house. Tilakawathie polished the brass, copper and silverware using star-fruit juice spread on a soft cloth. Dikwelle Hamine asked Rupa to help herself to fruit and sweets from the storeroom.

'The garden looks beautiful. Are you getting ready for a wedding?' Rupa asked smiling.

The workmen levelled the ground, spread gravel and sand, tidied up flowerbeds and pruned the shrubs.

Loku Mahatmaya leaned against a king coconut tree and watched their backs bent as they patiently tilled the dry crumbling soil.

Dikwelle Hamine spoke to Rupa, happiness lighting her face.

'They are coming from a long way away. We must entertain them to the very best of our abilities. You must make sure you smile at everyone and speak politely. I'll arrange the table. You have to offer them a glass of water from a tray and invite them to sit down for tea.'

Offering a glass of water is a ritual. The guests only touch the glass, a gesture that signifies acceptance of an invitation for tea or for a meal. Rupa could not remember any other occasion when her mother was so full of delight.

'Why do we have to get all dressed up and offer all these formal invitations you keep on about? Why don't we just casually ask them to have something to eat and drink in the normal way? I think its better if you do these things yourself, mother. I don't know these people. I have never even seen them before! It's like acting in a play.'

'You mustn't say that, we have to do everything according to tradition. Don't forget our family history and our special relationship with the king of the country! We don't want to hear the slightest adverse comment. If anything goes wrong your father will be furious.'

'Nothing wrong with cleaning the house or clearing the gardens! I don't understand why everyone has to go to so much trouble. They'll come, eat, drink and go back. We don't have to care what other people think about how we live our lives. It's better if we live as we usually do, mother. What's this you always go on and on about, this relative of ours and a king of the country? We don't have kings anymore!'

'You never listen, do you? I am telling you about the history of our family. The downfall of the Old Kingdom of Ceylon happened when the whole country finally went under British in 1818. Our last king, Rajasinghe, was a close relative of a great, great, great grandfather of your father.'

'We live in the present, mother, not in history.'

THREE

Lowering clouds threatened rain in spite of bright sun earlier in the day. Dikwelle Hamine put her fingers through her soft silky hair and looked up. A squirrel was munching a deep yellow papaya fruit, holding the broken peel between its paws. 'I hope it's not going to rain. If it rains heavily the gravel road across the fields will flood and their car may not be able to pass through the mud.'

'It's been like this every morning for the last few weeks, but then the sky clears and the sun comes out in the afternoon' Loku Mahatmaya looked at the sky and wiped the fine raindrops from his arms and face.

Dikwelle Hamine had changed the curtains and even the doormat was free of dust. Maha Gedara stood like a fortress waiting to hoist the welcome flag.

The ivory chair covers with red, blue and green designs of birds, flowers and animals had been cross-stitched by Dikwelle Hamine when she was young. White crocheted door hangings, appliquéd with blue peacocks were taken out of the wardrobe for this special occasion and as she held them out the scent of moth balls and rose petal pot-pourri flowed across the house like a meadow-swept wind. The clock seemed slow and the breathless sun lingered among the green cloud of the tropical forest. Two o'clock in the afternoon was a long way away.

It was eleven when Loku Mahatmaya came to the kitchen with a telegram in his hand. 'Not very good news. The visit has been postponed.' He waved the telegram in the air.

'Cancelled? Why is that?'

'They don't say!'

'Due to unavoidable circumstances visit postponed until Friday next week – Jayasena Mudalali.'

Loku Mahatmaya read the telegram aloud and the cloud over Dikwelle Hamine's face was even thicker and darker than the cloud overhead. She sighed. 'Hmmm... I know they are the people with a thousand and one responsibilities, it must be some serious trouble. Kapurala the matchmaker hasn't been here yet either.'

Loku Mahatmaya fell into deep silence.

When Rupa heard that the visit had been cancelled she felt mixed feelings of anger and sympathy. She was pleased that she did not have to get dressed up and play the role of an over-controlled puppet. Her parents had been getting ready for this meeting for days on end. The whole situation would have been different if her parents were wealthy business people. She did not like the way they had been let down. Rupa knew that her mother would never accept the possibility of her 'family values' no longer being taken into account of and only money mattered.

Finally the visit was re-scheduled for two in the afternoon the following Friday. Everyone at Maha Gedara got ready with smiles, milk-rice and bananas on the table. There were large brass vases of coconut flowers on both sides of the front doorstep. Rupa was dressed in just the way her mother wanted and sat in a chair in the dressing room. She had goose pimples all over her body. She could see herself clearly in the mirror in the ebony wardrobe, wearing a sea-blue silk sari with a silver embroidered fall and a matching blouse. Her long hair neatly combed back was knotted in a 'special style'. She wore a pair of high-heeled black shoes. She remembered how happy she had been wearing the same sari on graduation day at the university and she thought to herself, 'I spent so many hours reading and studying in this room. This same ebony wardrobe in front of me stood against the wall in the same place, at the same angle all that time. It was a gift to my mother from my grandparents along with her dowry. Its position was changed only once a year when the cement floor was cleaned for the New Year celebration. Dressed up lavishly and sitting in your own home like a model in a showcase is not what I want! I feel like a scarecrow in the middle of the paddy fields. These clothes and shoes are so unsuitable! I don't want to wear this kind of clothing at home, it's much better if I could wear my red skirt, a floral white lace blouse discoloured by sweat under the sleeves and have my hair tied with a blue ribbon! I'm not used to wearing high-heeled shoes. I like to wear my usual pair of rubber slippers. It reminds me our village fair, the folk dancer with long false wooden legs. I don't have his skill, I feel uncomfortable I might slip on the polished floors or on the gravel path. I feel like changing to a dress but if I do that mother will be furious.'

Rupa sat for two hours. It was four in the afternoon. Then there came a dull humming sound as a vehicle approached. It was the sound a vehicle makes when it turns round the double bends of the hillside road, which runs through the rubber plantation.

'Get ready quickly, I think they are coming!'

Loku Mahatmaya was excited and panicky. Dikwelle Hamine rushed out of the kitchen, drying her wet hands on the fall of her cotton sari. The shiny black Morris stopped in front of the house.

Jayasena Mudalali, his wife, their daughter and Gunapala got out of the car. The driver parked under the avocado tree. Both parties folded their hands and bent their heads in the customary ritual of greeting.

'Do come in, please take a seat.'

'Thank you.' Then there was a sudden silence followed by a hive of noise. They all sat in the lounge, everybody laughing and talking nervously. The heavy rain and traffic delayed them; they described the long journey from Kegalle to Matara in every last detail. Gunapala looked round, Rupa was sitting down in the dressing room until her mother called her. Kapurala the matchmaker was sitting in a corner chewing betel, his eyes bright like polished marble. He joined in with the guests' conversation and laughed nervously, unsure of what was likely to happen.

Jayasena Mudalali was wearing a tweed suit. He was almost bald with a faint line of hair round his head. He seemed full of himself and walked up and down the lounge and then the portico, from time to time looking round. His wife was wearing a golden shiny sari with matching gold jewellery. Their daughter was dressed in an elegant red and yellow hill-country style Kandyan sari, gold bangles and blue and crimson jewelled rings which shimmered and tinkled when she moved. She said nothing. Gunapala was tall, fat and dark skinned. He wore a black suit, striped shirt and a tie with black spots. His white teeth shone when he laughed. He looked at his shiny black shoes while he was talking. Rupa suspected he was unduly proud of his new suit and shoes.

When Rupa held the tray and invited the guests for afternoon tea her hands trembled. While she was serving treacle cakes to Gunapala she dropped a few slices onto the floor where they broke into bits. The dog, lying under the twelve-foot long dinner table, grabbed and gobbled down the morsels. Gunapala's sister, a married schoolteacher, began a conversation with Rupa. Fearful and occasionally shaking, Rupa found it impossible to behave normally but everybody else seemed satisfied. After they said goodbye and finally departed Rupa felt relieved. Dikwelle Hamine, Loku Mahatmaya and Kapurala were talking animatedly about the guests and how successful the meeting had been.

To Rupa's amazement no one discussed with her anything about the meeting, although she heard mother and father talking about the wealthy, respectable family and their new Morris. Dikwelle Hamine thought Gunapala a smart young man and had no objections to accepting him as a member of her family with its long history related to the Sinhalese kingdom.

Two weeks passed quietly and things had changed at Maha Gedara once again. Tension in and around the house began to rise like soaring tropical heat. Dikwelle Hamine watched impatiently as hopeful mornings turned to evenings of despair. They had heard nothing from Mudalali's family, not even a letter. Dikwelle Hamine had in her mind that they might refuse the proposal after all.

One morning in the third week Loku Mahatmaya heard someone at the door clearing his throat. It was Kapurala the matchmaker waiting for the doors to be opened for the day. His folded umbrella was in his hand.

'Do come in Kapurala, I have not seen you for a while.'

'I've been so busy, I didn't even have a single minute's rest. I was away in Colombo. It was raining heavily when I came home from there yesterday. Last Monday I went to a huge wedding. The bride was given away with an enormous dowry and she was from a wealthy family. Furniture, cutlery, crockery, gold, silver, money in the bank, you name it, everything was there! To everybody's surprise the bride was given a fifty-acre rubber plantation into the bargain. I won't tell you about the windfall I had as a matchmaker.'

He laughed, touched and scratched his grey moustache.

'Who was the bridegroom?'

'Surely you know Loku Mahatmaya? It was in the papers. He's the son of Dr. Perera and he came back from England two months ago.'

'I can see you are a busy man.'

Kapurala was a messenger of good fortune for the Maha Gedara family. Dikwelle Hamine came to the portico with a welcoming smile. Kapurala was almost whispering at Loku Mahatmaya's ears. Dikwelle Hamine could not hear him.

'I went to see Jayasena Mudalali about that matter. They are willing to go ahead with it but there is a slight problem. When the girl is not a beauty this is something that always happens. They talk about the dowry. I didn't keep quiet either. I reminded them that our girl is a well-educated talented person. These things can be sorted out, perhaps some kind of compromise! Not to worry at this stage, I must go now.' Kapurala stood up briskly.

Dikwelle Hamine called him.

'Kapurala don't go yet, have some breakfast. I made some hoppers this morning.'

'I am on my way back to Colombo. I'm sorry, I don't have much time as I am already late for my journey.' Kapurala opened his faded black umbrella and left in the rain.

'What did he say?' Dikwelle Hamine was inquisitive.

'There seems to be a problem. They expect a lot for the dowry. We just don't have that kind of money!'

I think you should calm down and think carefully. We mustn't turn our backs on such a good proposal. Can't we do anything about it? The paddy fields are ready for reaping. We may be able to use our whole income from that.'

'Utter rubbish! Give them everything we possess including our daughter! Are you going to beg on the streets for our living for the rest of the year?' Loku Mahatmaya was furious.

Rupa felt helpless again. Her mother and father were arguing about the dowry day and night. Constantly she thought to herself.

'I don't think my mother understands how I feel about all those things with me in the middle. Those people are greedy. They value money and wealth more than a woman. If they are so rich and own such a successful business why are they trying to grab even more? Mindless sharks! I don't know why my mother wants to give me away to such a ruthless family with an unaffordable dowry thrown in. Don't my parents love me? It's alright to criticise my looks but Gunapala is hardly a handsome man. Does he have to listen to everything his father says? I wouldn't even give them one of my puppies! I think my mother is crazy trying to hang me round somebody's neck! Don't my parents know me? We should keep what we have and tell them to get lost.' Rupa tried to keep away from her mother and sank into her own world.

'The life we had at the university was beautiful. It was a world within a world and so much better than the so-called 'real world' I am landed in now. I think Kumara loved me, we were so close to each other. Once I had left the university we just lost contact. I don't think I can ever forget him. I think both Kumara and I may have had to face the same unexpected problems. We liked the country life and respected traditional family customs. We had so little real experience and all the confusions about background and caste, it was impossible to break away! I have no idea where he is now. The only thing I know is that he is from Kandy. We didn't write to each other during the holidays because we didn't want our parents to become suspicious of a secret relationship. It wasn't something acceptable in our families.'

Rupa told her mother that she had no wish to marry Gunapala anyway.

The atmosphere at Maha Gedara heated up again to boiling point, burning breathless air spread like a volcano about to erupt. Loku Mahatmaya and his wife hardly spoke to each other or to their daughter. It was a minute by minute ticking silence, which filled the house, crept through windows and doors and could blow up the whole village.

Rupa found it unbearable to live in the same house with her mother, she felt like a cat on a hot tin roof. She thought that if she was away from the house, at least for a while, it might help to calm her mother down. Day by day the memories of Jayasena Mudalali's family began to fade from everyone's mind and settle beneath the fragments of dust at Maha Gedara. Dikwelle Hamine remained silent although she had not forgotten the lost fortune. Loku Mahatmaya was glad to see things getting back to normal. Like clearing an arena after a folk drama Rupa tried to clear her mind until the next act began. Visits to Maha Gedara by Kapurala the matchmaker became rarer until they abruptly ended. One night after supper Rupa suggested to her parents that she should stay with her sister for a while. Rupa's father thought it was a good idea. Her mother burst into tears, a sudden emptiness overwhelming her utterly.

Rupa's sister, Rukmali, had been married for five years. She lived with her husband and their three-year-old son called Damit, in a five-bedroom bungalow on the outskirts of a small town four miles away from Maha Gedara. Her husband owned a small tea and rubber plantation and Rukmali worked in the local bank. Women from the village plucked tea leaves in the morning and in the afternoon bagged-up tea leaves were taken by lorry to the regional tea factory for processing. Rukmali only visited her parents at weekends. It was the following Sunday when her family visited Maha Gedara and Rupa returned with them. She spent some time every day looking after her sister's son. She felt immediately that her life had become lighter and happier than during all the time she had been at home since she left the university. Watching the beauty and harmony of a child's world released the pressure, which had built up in her mind.

One afternoon Kapurala the matchmaker appeared at Maha Gedara out of the blue. The door was closed and Tilakawathie was watering the garden. Dikwelle Hamine was in bed with flu and Loku

Mahatmaya was out feeding the cows. Trees and shrubs withered in the heat and the cooing of wood pigeons and wild fowls blew like waves from the sun soaked woodlands. Tilakawathie asked him in and gave him a cup of tea. When Loku Mahatmaya arrived home half an hour later, to his surprise Kapurala the matchmaker was sitting on the bench chewing betels, a muffler round his neck and folded umbrella at his side. Loku Mahatmaya sat in the armchair.

'Have you been busy again Kapurala? Unfortunately my wife is ill and our girl is away.'

'Needless to ask! May is the month of several auspicious dates for weddings and I had to be present at various celebrations and ceremonies. I have some good news for you Loku Mahatmaya. It's a perfect match, believe me, I'm telling you like that gheko on the wall nothing could go wrong, caste, education, wealth are no problem.'

'Who are they Kapurala?'

'I don't have to go into much detail. You'll find out yourself, surely everyone knows the son of Dr. Silva. He has just finished his education at Harvard and he is back home now. I saw him yesterday. Very, very smart looking young man. The family is only looking for a pleasant girl with an educated background; even mentioning a dowry would make them laugh! He owns a house in Colombo and is hoping to find a top job in the city. If I remember right, as chief executive at an oil company, he can speak English, French and Sinhalese as easy as drinking water! Just imagine Loku Mahatmaya having a well-educated good mannered young man as an additional member of your family! That's all we want.' He struck his umbrella on the floor to emphasise his point.

'All right Kapurala, come and see us again next week. Hopefully my wife will be better by then. By the way, try to find out as much as you can, then we can fix a date straight away for a meeting.'

Kapurala went away holding his umbrella to cover his bald head from the burning sun.

Dikwelle Hamine had sent a message to Rukmali to come home with Rupa the following Saturday morning. Dr. Silva's family were to visit the Maha Gedara family that afternoon.

'I am sick and tired of all these meetings. I wish our parents would get on with their life and leave me alone! It's like an identification parade, holding trays with glasses of water, invitations to sit at the table, all dressed up and most uncomfortable at that, just the way mother wants. The whole thing is like a play! I don't want to go home, I'll stay here with little Damit, you can go and see them if you want.'

'Don't worry about it,' her sister replied.

'We can always ask them to postpone the visit if necessary. I'll ask one of my friends to find out about Dr. Silva's son.' Rukmali felt considerable sympathy with her sister.

'Mother believes everything that Kapurala the matchmaker says. He's a cunning liar who makes up stories on the spot. He may have said all kinds of things about me! I hate the sight of that man. One day I told him not to bother bringing any more proposals. Mother was so angry she didn't speak to me for a week afterwards!' At least Rupa could talk to her sister about what was going on in their family and they could laugh about it.

A friend of Rukmali who worked with her in the office happened to be a distant relative of Dr. Silva's family.

'Deva is my father's cousin's son. We don't see them very much except at the New Year, but my father knows them very well. Deva's mother died many years ago and his father brought the family up with the help of friends and relatives. But there's something I must tell you. It's true that the son had his higher education in America but he is seriously mentally ill. To my knowledge he spent a long time in a psychiatric hospital while he was abroad and I don't see him being able to do any kind of work anywhere. I'll say he's a really nice person but only when he is well!'

Rukmali was amazed to hear her friend's story. When she told Rupa the truth about Deva, Dr. Silva's son, Rupa said, 'Thank God for that, I hope I don't have to go home now. I'm so pleased your friend found out these details, otherwise mother would have believed that matchmaker and we'd be going through the same old routine all over again! God only knows what would have happened.'

Rukmali spoke to her parents and the meeting was cancelled 'due to unavoidable circumstances' and Rupa never wanted to see Kapurala the matchmaker ever again.

FOUR

The incandescent sun appeared through the deep emerald hills of the tea plantation shadowed by acacia cascading with magenta-pink blossoms, making shapes and swirls over the awakening earth. Near Rukmali's hillside house were yellow green paddy fields and beyond them stretched red and blue water lily marshes, cool at dawn but soon burning with the midday sun. It was a Saturday morning. Rukmali and her husband had gone to a wedding. Leela, a sixteen-year-old village girl who looked after Rukmali's three-year-old son Damit and Rupa stayed at home. The bungalow had a veranda and a sun lounge at the front. The house was open all day and only at dusk were the doors closed. Rupa had her lunch later than usual while Leela and Damit played in the front garden under the mulberry tree.

'There's someone at the door!' Leela ran to the kitchen, Damit followed her and fell over three times each time getting up and rubbing his knees.

The bungalow had a large sitting room and a dining room with a line of latticed windows and fanlights. The bedrooms were at the back and there was a square enclosed compound with a corridor between the main house and the kitchen.

'Is it someone we know Leela? It doesn't matter, ask them to come in and sit down. I'm just washing my hands, I'll be there in a few minutes.'

'We don't know who it is. All we know is there's a car.' They ran back to the front door to ask the visitor to come in. Damit fell over again and started to cry in earnest.

Rupa cleared away the dishes and went to the front door. Rukmali's house was always very busy and Rupa was used to people coming and going when her sister was at home. The visitor stood by the front door. He looked tired with beads of sweat on his brow. Rupa vaguely remembered seeing him somewhere in the past. 'Please come into the lounge and sit down.'

'No thank you. I must go back soon. Is Rukmali in?' He wiped the sweat from his face with a handkerchief.

'I'm sorry my sister is not at home today. They won't be back until this evening. They've gone to a wedding. Is there a message I can give her? Please do come in.'

He sat on a wicker bench in the sun lounge.

'It's much cooler here' he smiled and said:

'I am Aruna. I came from England the day before yesterday. A friend of mine who lives there sent a parcel and a letter with me. She insists I meet Rukmali and talk to her.'

'What is your friend's name?'

'Chandra.'

'I know Chandra very well. Didn't she go to England about two years ago?'

'Yes, she is a close friend of mine. She and her husband live near me and often come to visit.'

'We went to the same school, but she was in a higher class. I think my sister was in her class.'

'I'll leave the parcel with you. If I get a chance I'll try to come and see your sister again. Are you Rupa?'

'Yes. Would you like a cup of tea?'

'The weather is too hot to drink anything warm but I don't mind having some water.'

Rupa brought him a glass of cooled water from the fridge. 'How long are you going to be in Ceylon, Aruna?'

'I came here for a four-week holiday. I must go back before my college starts in October. The main reason I am here is to see my mother who's very ill.'

'How is she now?'

'She's been paralysed for sometime. I don't see her getting any better in her old age.'

'When did you go to England, Aruna?'

'Three years ago.'

'Have you settled there permanently?'

'No, I want to come back as soon as I finish my education.'

'That's a good idea. So many people who go abroad these days never come back home. They decide to stay abroad for the rest of their lives.'

'I must go now Rupa.'

'Thank you for the parcel. Do please come and see my sister sometime.'

Rupa went out to the garden with Aruna when he left. His white Peugeot was parked under the mango tree. Leela, the girl who looked after Rukmali's son and Damit were trying to fly a red and blue kite. Little Damit pulled the string and ran across the garden jumping and laughing. Aruna waved to her as he started his car. Rupa stood until the car traversed the winding orange gravel road and passed out of sight on the bend, then she waited for the wind to blow the kite high while Damit sat on a little hill staring in wonder.

Leela ran up the path with a smile and said, 'Tha The Granny is coming.'

Rupa saw an old woman walking up the sloping path slowly with a basket in her hand. The old woman lived with her husband in a chena near the tea plantation. Everybody knew her in the village as 'Tha The Granny.'

'You are right Leela, it is Tha, I haven't seen her for ages. Let's go down and meet her.' Damit waved his hands in the air and jumped in excited anticipation. Damit sat in his tricycle and Leela pushed it along.

'Be careful Leela it's very slippery on the path.' With great difficulty the old woman humped her heavy basket. She looked at Rupa.

'How are you Tha? Can you recognise me?'

The old woman rested her basket on the ground, tightened her long green wrap-over skirt and stared.

'Goodness me! So this is our little madam! I haven't seen you for years and years. You look very skinny now! Don't you eat well?'

'How is your husband Tha? Does he still grow millet and vegetables in the chena?'

'We are getting too old, little madam. He hasn't got the strength to do much these days. He has arthritis and our millet is mostly abandoned to the wild animals. It's not worth growing anything; at night the wild boars and rabbits destroy the lot.'

Tha The Granny put her basket on the kitchen floor.

'I brought some wood-apples and honey mangoes for you. I can only find these fruits under the trees on weekends and during the school holidays, otherwise the children crawl through the fence to pick the fallen fruit.

'I love honey mangoes Tha.' Rupa picked up a yellow mango and savoured its sweet-and-sour odour.

'I had a message from your sister yesterday asking me to come round as they have to visit some relatives and may be late getting back. She wants me to cook something for your dinner.'

'I am so glad to see you, Tha. Don't bother much, while you cook something little for dinner we'll go down to the fields to fly the kite. We won't be long and don't worry we have to walk slowly with Damit.'

'That's all right,' Tha The Granny said. 'But be careful when you hold baby Damit and make sure you lock the front door before you go.'

They ate the honey mangoes as they walked down the gravel path while the old woman prepared the evening meal.

The daytime tropical heat mellowed, the margins of the fields were overshadowed by coconut palms, by rims of hills and nipples of rock which opened the door to a deep blue sky, a pink horizon, a magical blend of afternoon colours. They walked through orange-green crotons and scarlet bougainvillaea until they reached a hedge of twenty-foot high bamboo, which formed the boundary of the tea plantation and the paddy fields. There was a yard wide watercourse in between where the wind blew the flowing, crackling bamboo leaves. For a short distance they went along a woodland path covered in leaves. Rupa put her right foot on a plank and jumped into the field through a gap in the hedge, Leela handed Damit over to Rupa and with difficulty jumped over.

They walked to the middle of the fields and as the wind blew in gusts they watched the red, blue and yellow kite rise in ascending spirals.

'Look! The kite is going towards the lily marsh, now it's moving faster and faster!' Leela's eyes were gleaming and little Damit was waving with excitement.

'The lily marsh is always very windy,' Rupa said. They watched the kite, their hearts glowing with the delicious meadow-swept scent of felicity, until a strong wind sucked the kite away. It wiggled like a snake, then the string broke and it disappeared from sight. The paddy fields stretched endlessly until at last the sun began to descend and with it came the cool evening breeze. A flock of parrots flying towards the nesting hills faded on the distant horizon.

The water for the paddy fields came from a stream, which flowed down a deep valley, where it turned to a small waterfall between two rocks. A fountain of spray and bubbles crept under a narrow footbridge before merging into the watercourses of the paddy fields. Leela suggested that they went to watch the waterfall. Damit was tired and had fallen asleep on Rupa's shoulder. Crows were flying to their nests on rubber trees before dark while a hawk fished alone in the shallows, circling round and round then swooping suddenly on its prey. Rupa agreed to see the waterfall on their way back. They walked home slowly along a winding footpath. Rupa's mind was deep in thought about the visitor who had come to her sister's house at lunchtime. They saw Tha The Granny coming towards them.

'I just came to see why you are so late. Your dinner is ready. I was worried and wondered where you had gone with baby Damit.'

'Damit is all right. We took some food and drink for him and he enjoyed flying the kite. We are lucky the weather's so windy. We went to see the waterfall that's why we are a bit late. Is my sister home yet?'

'No they're not back.'

They walked into the house. The sun had suddenly sunk over the horizon with a pink and grey blue afterglow behind the hills slowly fading and the full moon above brightening the tall trees.

'You must be very tired and hungry now, little madam, I've put the kettle on. Would you like something to drink?'

'Let's have a cup of tea Tha.' Rupa sat on the bench in the kitchen. The old woman made some tea.

'There's a car turning round the corner. They're coming back.'

Leela shouted and ran to the garden, Damit followed her.

Tha The Granny had prepared the evening meal. For a while everybody was talking and listening to the details of the wedding Rukmali and her husband had attended, all about the bride, the guests, the jewellery, the colourful clothes and the food. Rukmali had brought Rupa a small individually made wedding cake in a gold-ribboned box. A silver horseshoe was printed on it and the couple's names were in gold. Rukmali asked Tha to stay the night.

Everybody sat down to the evening meal feeling as if they had all been to the wedding. Rupa told them in great detail about Aruna's visit.

'What a shame I wasn't here when Aruna came today! Chandra, my friend who lives in England, has sent me a parcel with Aruna. There's a beautiful teddy bear and a toy car for Damit. I would so much like to know how they are getting on in London. I wanted to write to them but I never had their address.'

Damit was playing with his new red car, pushing it along the floor, trying to load a doll onto it, making sounds like an engine with the brown teddy bear by his side.

'Aruna told me that Chandra insisted on seeing you. I asked him to come again before he goes back to England.'

'When is he going back?'

'I don't know exactly, he's come for a four-week break to see his mother. He didn't even stay for a cup of tea.'

'Listen to this Rupa! Chandra has sent me a letter, I'll read it to you.'

'Dear Rukmali, Aruna has decided to come to Ceylon for a short holiday to see his mother who is very ill. He is a good friend of ours. He is fed up with living in England on his own and he is looking for a suitable girl to marry. We know him very well, he neither drinks nor smokes. He isn't prepared to go to the trouble of formal visits, you know what I mean? Although he likes entertaining lavishly he finds formal 'do's very uncomfortable. He doesn't care about caste or dowry and if you know anybody suitable just talk to him. We mentioned Rupa to him!

Please do write to me. Chandra.'

Rupa couldn't believe it. Her face turned red as she listened and they all laughed. After a long day's excitement everybody felt tired, little Damit had fallen asleep holding his new teddy bear. Rupa went to bed early.

Doors and windows were closed as the night opened wide. The distant vistas of the rubber plantation were covered in velvet darkness with not a single star in the sky. The humidity and breathless air hovered under a full moon hidden among the sudden clouds. The ceiling fan in Rupa's bedroom flapped monotonously, constantly distracting her. She switched the fan off; it slowed down, turned round one final time and then came to rest. The whole house slept while Rupa listened alone to the crackling of heavy rain, rhythmically pounding on the roof tiles. The threads of memory loosened like a cotton-reel unwinding, her home and her life at the university stitched to her mind with tassels of brilliant colour. She didn't know where she was going. She could not stop thinking of Aruna and about her past, the visit by Gunapala in the presence of Kapurala the matchmaker and how her mother had tried to increase the dowry by selling the new season's harvest. And then there was the Harvard educated Deva, with his psychiatric problems! In spite of such bitter memories she loved her parents and her home Maha Gedara.

Although she wanted to marry Aruna and start a new life in England away from everything she had some anxieties still. She only knew about London in the vaguest of ways: Big Ben, The River Thames and the shops in Oxford Street.

She desperately wanted to see Kumara again. They had been very close to each other while they were at university. They never expected such a sudden end to their relationship. She would have to wait until the wheel of fortune turned round and she could meet him again. She remembered how they spent time studying in the university library and the timeless evening walks together near the River Mahaweli. The library was a fortress belonging to the goddess of wisdom. The trees with scarlet and orange blossoms and petal strewn grass created the confetti of their freedom. The whole campus was their private heaven. She remembered an evening when they were sitting on the wall by the Kandy Lake in front of the Temple of the Tooth. She could still feel the cool breeze around the silent lake while the carillons of the temple bells echoed and the sound dissolved into the still water.

'We have to go home in two weeks' time when we finish our final exams and say good-bye to university life. What are you going to do Rupa?'

'I haven't thought about my future Kumara. The four years have gone by like a day. I remember how sad I felt when I left school, a day just like today. When I think about leaving the university and our leaving each other I feel some sort of sadness tainting the future.'

'Rupa I think your parents may have already been looking for someone, sorting out an arranged marriage for you. They may want their daughter to marry someone of the right caste and all that goes with it.'

'It's all nonsense Kumara. I have no intention of marrying in the near future.'

'Let's put it this way then, if I send a matchmaker to your house proposing a marriage with you what would your parents say? They just wouldn't accept me with no caste and no horoscope. You know what that means? We'd be marked for life as though we both had some terrible disfigurement from birth.'

'Why do you have to send a proposal to my home? You can ask me now!'

'Would you like to live abroad Rupa?'

'Not on my own.'

'Let's go together somewhere away from here, where no-one cares about caste.'

They both thought that they were only joking, holding hands, feeling some unearthly happiness and laughing as if they had broken all the threads and strings of the history of family traditions. They promised to meet at the graduation.

When graduation day arrived the final results of sleepless nights and days of hard work were reflected in the students' faces overflowing with relieved smiles and the endless laughter of freedom. It was a beautiful day. The sun was kind and cool. The university was a field of celebrations. The trees were glowing with cascading pink, blue and yellow blossoms. Kumara was not there. Rupa was hoping to see him on that day. She felt the whole world was empty. Day by day fear of hopes ending and uncertainty haunted Rupa's mind.

Rupa spent that night waking and then falling into a poignant world of vivid dreams. She felt her enigmatic experiences were overshadowed by a cloud of confusion. She felt desperate but why she did not know, but she did know she wanted to be with Aruna. The following morning she felt as if she was convalescing after a long illness. She stayed in her room feeling exhausted. Rupa fell into a deep sleep. The book she was reading had fallen onto the floor. It was just after midday when she was woken by a sudden sound. But it was only the cat jumping from the roof onto a sheet of aluminium used for drying coriander seeds in the hot sun. Nobody was about. Everywhere was silent. A crow flew by the window cawing. Damit, Leela and Rukmali had gone to the well down the hill for bathing. Rupa went out of her room and sat in the sun lounge.

It had not rained for sometime. The purple orchids by the window had withered. The sun had moved to the middle of the cloudless blue sky. The sand in the compound was burning in the hot sun. As midday approached the heat began to rise. There was a distant sound of temple bells chiming. It was a full moon day. Leela and Damit came back after bathing running and full of excitement.

'The elephant keeper has brought the elephant!'

'Where is the elephant?' Rupa asked.

'There it is, in our coconut land, tied by a heavy metal chain to a coconut tree. Are you coming with us?'

'I don't mind.'

They went to see the elephant. The she elephant named Seetha was eating tender yellow palm leaves. The elephant keeper appeared through the bamboo hedge with a huge bundle of leaves and branches on his head for Seetha's dinner.

The mahout had been working in the forest with the same elephant moving timber for thirty years. Some days when he had finished work, he brought the elephant home. He lived with his wife in a tiny palm thatched hut by the main road. He always kept the elephant near his hut for the night, tying it to a coconut tree or a jackfruit tree in Rukmali's land.

'We came to see Seetha. Are you on holiday today?' Rupa asked.

'Yes, full moon day is always a holiday. Soon I'm going to take Seetha for a bath.'

'Where do you take her?'

'I always take her to the river for bathing. When it's a hot day she likes to play with water, spraying it into the air with her trunk.'

They watched the elephant for a long time.

'Kida, elephant.' He touched her thick wrinkled skin. She kneeled down, turning the trunk round. When he held some leaves in his hand she stretched her trunk, took the leaves and put them into her mouth one huge bundle at a time. Then he fondly stroked the elephant and gave her some bananas and a fresh coconut. She tramped the coconut, crushed it and put the bananas into her mouth a few at a time. After eating she lifted the trunk up in the air and trumpeted. It was so loud Damit covered his ears with his fingers. She was getting ready to go to the river for bathing the mahout explained.

'Daha, elephant,' he said aloud. They watched him going on the howdah, along the main road then turning at the bend and disappearing towards the river.

When they came home Rupa recognised the white Peugeot parked under the mango tree. Aruna was talking to Rukmali and her husband.

'When did you come Aruna?'

'About ten minutes ago.'

'We went to see Seetha the elephant.'

Rukmali interrupted and announced, 'Damit is very excited when Seetha comes to our land. He even talks in his sleep about elephants.'

'How is your mother now Aruna?' Rupa asked.

'Not much different. It is not easy to treat some illnesses in old age.'

They all had afternoon tea together. Rukmali went into the kitchen and Tha The Granny was there to help with cooking. Aruna was invited for the evening meal. Rukmali's husband was in the sun lounge working out the workers' wages on the tea plantation. Rupa and Aruna were in the lounge on their own. Rupa sat in the chair near the sewing machine.

'I started to make these curtains weeks ago. I still haven't finished.'

'Are you going to finish them tonight?'

'No, perhaps tomorrow.'

While Aruna was telling Rupa about England she listened to him as a child listens to a fairy tale. He told her about snow in winter, luminous arcades and shops, Piccadilly Circus, New Year celebrations, Trafalgar Square, under-ground railways and London life.

'Foreign students' lives in England are not very easy, Rupa. We have to study, live on a very limited budget and there are no servants.'

'Surely it must be easier than here? Cooking, washing and other things are much faster in a developed country with modern facilities, aren't they?'

'It's not quite as simple as you think, here we can get someone to help us whenever we want to, there we spend a lonely life and its easy to get completely fed up and want to give up and come home. I'm lucky I have my house there.'

'How did you manage to buy a house while being a student Aruna?'

'When my father died I was only nine and he left a large sum of money for my education. I took that money to England and I used some of it to buy a house.'

'That was a very bright idea Aruna! Do you live on your own there? It must have cost you a fortune to buy a house in England?'

'It's a three bedroomed house and it only cost me three thousand pounds, I bought it on a mortgage. I have let out a room to two university students but only for a year.'

'Honestly Aruna I can't imagine what the houses in England are like!'

'They are much smaller than most houses in Ceylon. There are bigger houses with large gardens out in the country, but mine is a town house with a medium size garden.'

'Are you intending to sell the house when you return?'

'I might do.'

Aruna told her that he was lonely and wanted to get married to someone who could adapt to the stressful life of the west.

FIVE

After Aruna left that evening Rupa felt empty and confused, all her thoughts entangled, mixed with the prismatic colours of her possible futures which at times changed into complete numbness. She did not want to be a burden on her middle-aged parents, watching them grow older, bound tight under immovable family traditions. She felt like leaving home and living in an unknown place, a den in the forest perhaps, eating wild fruit, leaves and yams, talking to wild animals and birds. Soon she realised that she was looking for a fantasy solution to her built-up real-life tensions.

The following day was Sunday. Dikwelle Hamine and Loku Mahatmaya came to Rukmali's house. In spite of several messages Rupa had not been home. So they thought it was time to go and see her. Kapurala the matchmaker had been to Maha Gedara several times with proposals but they had to tell him that Rupa was away and that things had to be delayed for a while. Rupa was pleased to see her parents. They had brought a huge bunch of sweet bananas, mangoes and oranges, all home grown and some freshly made treacle slices. Rukmali and Leela prepared lunch. They all sat together for the meal, although Rupa still felt uncomfortable. Afterwards Dikwelle Hamine sat in the lounge and spoke to Rupa. There was an air of tension.

'Would you like to come home with us today Rupa?'

'Not today.' Rupa said. 'I'll try to come home some other time.'

'You have to realise Rupa, you are not a child anymore, you are twenty three now and I was saying to your father that it's time for you to get married. Everybody in the village is asking me why you can't find someone suitable.'

'I don't care what the people in the village are saying about me. I've had enough of listening to Kapurala the matchmaker. He lies. You still believe anything he says. I don't want to get married yet.'

'People think that it's our fault that we keep you at home until you're beyond the suitable age for marriage. You mustn't forget your religion and family background. There's no need to tell you about our caste and all the rest.'

'You've started again, mother, about our family relationship to a king. I know all these things you talk about. If you are a Buddhist you must marry a Buddhist not a Hindu Tamil. I don't understand why we have to believe all this rubbish blindly. Mother I am sorry but I can't accept the caste system. It's unnatural and silly.'

'How dare you speak in such a way?' said Dikwelle Hamine. 'You're a disgrace to our family. You'll accept the next bridegroom Kapurala brings and I'll hear no more of this nonsense.'

Rupa felt the ship she was on board was caught up in a violent storm and about to be wrecked. She was drowning in an endless sea, helplessly trying to swim. Visions of Aruna flickered in her mind. Suddenly she was being carried on the crest of a wave and landing on shore shivering and wet.

Her father interrupted. Damit was pushing his car on the floor.

'Your mother is right. We want the best for you. You are young and just don't understand these things.'

'No it's you who don't understand and your generation with traditions that no more than disguise a form of slavery and servitude – they're finished! Freedom to choose the person you want to marry is what young people want. That's what I had an education for, leaving me to make my own decisions.'

Dikwelle Hamine burst into tears, but more in anger than sorrow. Rupa's father put out his hand reassuringly and touched his wife's shoulder.

'Do not take on so,' he said. 'She's young, she has got wild ideas from the university, she would soon see sense.'

'We were fools to pay for all that education.' Dikwelle Hamine snapped angrily and then a final silence.

There was a sudden crack of thunder and the heavy incessant rain of the monsoons lashed against the house.

'It's raining heavily now, after this morning's unbearable heat.' Rukmali came into the lounge carrying a tea-tray. 'It turned cooler and darker suddenly. I made some coffee.'

'We must go home before dark. If this rain doesn't stop our paddy fields will be flooded.' Loku Mahatmaya announced. Dikwelle Hamine poured a cup of coffee, added sugar and mixed it in, looking unhappy but trying to smile as if nothing had happened.

Rupa went to her room. She knew that in Eastern society when a girl grows up and reaches a certain age she has to get married and leave home. If this doesn't happen everybody gets disappointed and family disagreements start, but she just couldn't accept an arranged marriage of the kind her parents wanted. She felt she had been abandoned in a fortress surrounded by enormously strong iron ropes of religious belief and social customs. She felt that she was dying of an incurable illness. When she thought about her unknown future, walking through the streets of London, in a society where nobody knew of her existence she felt immediately better. She started to think about London.

The morning after, Rukmali and her husband had gone to work, Leela was playing with Damit and Rupa sat in the lounge. She had heard the birds sing as they landed on the branches of the mango and mulberry trees in the garden. Then there was the sound of a car stopping. It was Aruna who had come to see her. They both seemed to be relaxed and happy, talking, joking, laughing, eating bananas and biscuits and drinking fresh orange juice.

'Rupa, I wanted to talk to you about something very important. I'm going back to London in a few weeks time and I'm so much behind with everything I intended to do while I was here.'

He sat next to her on the settee. She was very quiet.

'Rupa, I don't know where to start. It's true we haven't known each other all that long but from the very first day I met you I thought you were the woman I have been searching for.'

Rather nervously he extended his right hand.

'I'm very taken aback Aruna. All last night I was thinking about you and about your life in London. I couldn't wait until you came today.'

'I would like to marry you Rupa. What do you think?'

'I'm in a state of shock. I'm not sure whether or not you are joking. I can't believe you are proposing, I'm just a village girl!'

'Rupa, although I'm being educated abroad I haven't forgotten my country. I never wanted to marry an English girl. I always wanted to find the right village girl and have a quiet life somewhere in the country.'

'That's what I always wanted Aruna. I never wanted to marry in the way my parents suggested.' Rupa put her head against Aruna's shoulder and said, 'But it's impossible for me to believe that things in my life could change so suddenly.'

'Would you like to go to England? We can live in the way we want, I feel so lonely on my own, Rupa.' There was a sudden feeling in Rupa's mind that she was going to be his wife very soon, it crept through her mind tingling and spreading all over her body.

'Living in England! It's like a dream, my parents will be very worried.'

'I don't want to live in England permanently. When I finish my education I might work there for a while and then we'll come back. Living in a foreign country is not like living in our birthplace. Freedom in another country is very limited: we are always foreigners!'

'If you are going back so quickly it may be very difficult to arrange things, especially a wedding just the way you want.'

'My college starts in two weeks time. It doesn't really matter. The most important thing in my motor engineering course is the practicals. I have just finished them. I don't think there will be any problem. They know that my mother is ill. Speaking for myself I don't want an elaborate wedding. It doesn't make much difference either way. What I really want is to get you there as soon as possible.'

'You don't know what my parents are like, Aruna. They wouldn't let me leave without a wedding involving the whole village.'

'All my mother wants is to see me happily married.' Aruna said.

'She is in her last few months of her life, paralysed in bed. I am sure Rupa she'll be very pleased to see you.'

They went out that evening; life seemed so enigmatic, walking through the monsoon washed country lanes, with the fragrance of fresh woodlands and the glowing blue light. Their lives seemed charged with a new fierce power and changed forever. When he kissed her goodbye that night she felt her first sexual awakening. She was delirious and slightly fearful.

Things seemed to have changed at Maha Gedara once again. Everybody had forgotten their usual arguments. Kapurala the matchmaker was disappointed and bitter. He spoke of the 'damaged characters of university educated girls' and how they turn their backs on poor parents. He started to gossip in the village grocery shop and post office and spread rumours that Rupa was wandering off at night with corrupted men from abroad! But all in vain and he never returned. Rukmali was pleased to see that her sister seemed happy at last. The family and the whole village were preparing for an elaborate wedding. Dikwelle Hamine was stunned but finally she accepted Rupa's decision. When Loku Mahatmaya spoke up in favour of her she said, 'It's better than running away from home I suppose, at least without darkening our names and our family's dignity.'

SIX

A two mile stretch from the main road to Maha Gedara was cleared so that giant yellow bamboo arches could be built across the road. The pandals were decorated with red bananas, oranges, cascading palm flowers and huge bunches of golden coconuts. The villagers were preparing for street parties.

A marquee was erected in the garden glittering with emerald and yellow leaf designs and a crescent moon strewn with colourful grains was placed at the entrance to the stage where the couple were sitting. There were two swans embossed with beads and white rice on either side. Huge brass vases of coconut flowers were placed on both sides of the wide entrance hall and there were flowers in every corner of the house. A six-foot high silver oil lamp with eight wicks was ready to be lit at an auspicious moment and flowing scented white jasmine garlanded the lamp. Storerooms were filled with best quality rice. Pineapples, bananas and vegetables arrived fresh from the hill country. A large area beyond the garden was made into a car park.

Rukmali and her family came to stay for a few days before the wedding. Master chefs and caterers were ordered in for the occasion and it was their task to prepare the wedding feast for guests and villagers numbered in their hundreds.

This was a day when everybody was given a lavish meal, even stray cats, dogs and crows. Dikwelle Hamine was tearful now Rupa's wedding day had finally arrived.

The ceremony was scheduled for eleven in the morning and visitors started to arrive at nine. Glamorous ladies in Cashmere silk and embroidered red, yellow, blue, green, pink and crimson silk saris wearing gold and silver necklaces, bangles and rings sat chattering with smiling curious eyes awaiting the couple's arrival.

Coloured balloons, silver decorations, yellow pineapples and water lilies garnished the marquee.

As the crowd gathered, the warm air grew thicker and thicker and mixed with the scent of perfumes. Maha Gedara and its surroundings seemed a very Eden. The bride was dressed in a white lace sari embroidered with sequins and beads, sparkling gold jewellery and a long train, a crowned queen.

There was car parking space reserved for the bridegroom's party nearer the house and as they arrived the excitement became near panic.

The bridegroom was wearing a deep blue suit, garlanded with magenta temple flowers. By the doorsteps his feet were sprinkled with water and he was welcomed by a young relative. Cocktail fruit drinks were served with traditional music in the background, ladies straightening their wrinkled saris and nervously touching their necklaces. The marquee was like a buzzing beehive. Precisely at eleven the bride arrived with her father. A hundred pairs of eyes focused on the couple as they ceremoniously exchanged rings. Then the groom put a gold necklace on Rupa's neck as she smiled.

According to custom a villager chanted blessings over the couple's bowed heads and six girls wearing long bright pink dresses joined in a chorus of wedding songs. After the blessing the couple ritually fed each other with a slice of milk rice.

The bride's uncle helped Rupa down from the stage, holding her hand while the registrar waited for them, sat at a table. The couple made the usual vows as husband and wife and signed the register, witnessed by an uncle and the Village Headman. Then Rupa and Aruna shared the task of lighting the symbolic eight wicks of the great oil lamp with a single blue ribboned candle. While the ceremony was going on the caterers got ready to serve specially fried and boiled dishes of rice, vegetables, fish, meat, salads, cutlets and popadams all beautifully laid out.

There was a huge wedding cake, decorated with red and white roses; after the meal the couple cut the cake. Individually wrapped gold, silver and pink tasselled cakes, matchbox sized cake boxes with the name of the couple printed on were handed to the guests who by now were seated. Now it was two in the afternoon and Rupa was tired with smiling. The couple sat on a settee in front of a huge display of pink and white carnations.

The soft cool sunshine of that morning soon started to warm up and through the day the heat glowed with a fierce red tropical glare, the sun a distant red simmering globe in a cloudless sky. The marquee was hot and the guests started to cough and sweat. The ladies' thin blouses were wet and stuck to their skin. By mid-afternoon a vortex of fast moving clouds began to swirl and everywhere was suddenly dark, overshadowed by lowering clouds. It only took ten minutes, then there was a crack of thunder and a burst of monsoon rain poured down as if there was a hole in the sky.

Everybody rushed to shelter, the marquee, the house and even the kitchen and stores were soon desperately overcrowded. Within half an hour the whole scene was washed out, rain beating on the roof tiles like incessant drums. In the mêlée the electric generator had broken down and people gazed at each other through the soft darkness. Suddenly a woman screamed and pushed herself through the crowd. The pleats of her sari came undone and fell to the floor unnoticed. A wet frog had jumped into the marquee. Some guests tried to get to their cars, their new clothes soaking wet but the rain slashed onto the windscreens in the gale-force wind. Rupa had somehow become separated from Aruna and suddenly she felt very frightened.

SEVEN

The monsoon storm swept across the whole country. Trees had fallen on the road, the fields were flooded and schools closed. The coconut land near the bridge was under two feet of water. Nilwala, the river of blue clouds, had become turbid, flawed, swirling and forming whirlpools. Rupa and Aruna sat in the balcony of the hotel room and watched the water level increase rapidly. It was frightening; the river was roaring and gushing so violently. Rupa was shaken. Aruna put his arm around her and brought her closer to him, which made her feel secure. Within a day or two when the monsoon would subside, the fields would be greener, the air softer and the sun would shine unceasingly.

Two weeks after the wedding Aruna went back to England.

'Don't worry Rupa, when I am in London I'll be so lonely I won't rest till you get there.' He said as he kissed her good bye at the airport.

She watched him disappear into the crowd filing into the departure lounge. Rupa knew she had to make a new life as Aruna's wife in England. She decided to spend as much time as possible with her parents during the short period before she left.

After the wedding was over Maha Gedara was quiet again. Dikwelle Hamine lost herself in housework and said nothing to anyone but from time to time she sighed. Loku Mahatmaya looked thoughtful as he sat on the cement steps staring out at the paddy fields. Dikwelle Hamine complained of backache and found it difficult to bend down. The cooking and housework was done by Tilakawathie with some little help from Dikwelle Hamine, who sat in the kitchen and chopped onions and cut vegetables while Tilakawathie did the rest. Rupa could not understand why her parents were so unhappy. Was it because Rupa was getting ready to go abroad? Or was it because she hadn't married a man of her parents' choosing?

Dikwelle Hamine talked to her husband with some feeling about their daughter's marriage. She sat by the ancient Singer sewing machine while Loku Mahatmaya was pounding the betel mix but her voice rose above the sound of the shuttle to-ing and fro-ing.

'Don't you see how she is abandoning her birthplace? We don't know what kind of man he is, do we? Not even God in his heaven knows it! We had to make all the arrangements for such a big wedding, but we don't know if their horoscopes match! Who knows what he may be doing in England?' Dikwelle Hamine considered it an eternal misfortune for the family that Rupa did not want to marry Gunapala. Her disappointment was manifest and Rupa felt it keenly.

'It's not worth talking about, it's over and done with.' Loku Mahatmaya said. 'We have to accept things as they are. Not like our days when someone went abroad and we never expected them to return. Remember that doctor son of the grocer in town? He was in Russia for months and now he's back. I saw him the other day, looking very well.'

Whatever his wife said Loku Mahatmaya had not forgotten the unaffordable dowry that had been demanded and his immense relief at not having to pay it. Aruna expected nothing and Loku Mahatmaya was secretly delighted.

Dikwelle Hamine's eldest brother was a wealthy businessman in Colombo, his business connected to exporting timber. Rupa stayed with her uncle while she was sorting out her passport and visa.

Three months had gone since Aruna had left for England. She noticed that during the last few weeks her room has become unusually untidy. She had pushed her books to one side and she laid her handbag, underwear, skirts, blouses, soap and talc on the floor. The half-packed suitcase was by the bed and the hand luggage was near the wardrobe.

'I'm glad you are home before dark.' Dikwelle Hamine said as she entered Rupa's room.

'I only just noticed my room is in such a mess. I pushed all the carrier bags under the table. I'll tidy up the room properly tomorrow.'

'It's unusual for you to let your room get untidy. Did you manage to sort out your passport?'

'Yes, but with great difficulty. I had an interview at the British High Commission this morning. They asked me all kinds of questions about where am I going to live, do I have any relatives abroad and are we going to live in rented accommodation? Can my husband support me as a student? Who is paying for my air ticket? Am I intending to work there? Have I got any savings? One thing I thought to myself was when they come to our country we don't even ask them to get a visa!'

'Have you booked your ticket?'

'Yes, for the thirtieth of next month. Only six weeks left.'

Dikwelle Hamine burst into tears but refused to speak and quickly went out, drying her eyes with her sari. She returned with a cup of tea for Rupa and a few minutes later Loku Mahatmaya joined them.

'We are going to Matara tomorrow. Your mother wants to buy a sari to wear when we go to the airport. Do you want to come shopping with us?'

'It's not necessary to buy new clothes for the journey. The New Year is near and everything is very expensive. You'll need a lot of money to buy the Cashmere silk sari that mother wants. I can't come with you. I had a letter from my friend Padma. She may be coming here tomorrow.'

'It doesn't matter. I'll go shopping with your father. The thirtieth of next month is a Friday. It's an auspicious day, even for weddings. We had rain in time this season and the paddy fields are in flower. Until the reaping begins they have to be left dry and we are not all that busy. We have plenty of time to get ready to go to the airport with you when you leave. I feel that the long-term bad luck our family had has finally gone. First I fell ill and then nothing went right for a long time. Rupa is happy now and I'm better. Have you heard that even the God Vishnu turns into an elephant and eats bamboo when his star is not good?'

The atmosphere at Maha Gedara was mute. Because of their own burgeoning grief Rupa's parents were more understanding. The following morning Loku Mahatmaya and Dikwelle Hamine left home early to catch the first bus to Matara. They would have a half-hour's walk to the main road. After her parents had gone Rupa felt the whole house empty and bleak. Tilakawathie was cooking in the kitchen and the smell spread all over the house and made Rupa realise how much she would miss her mother.

Wisps of sound from passing bees and perfumed air from the woods mingled and poured in through the window grilles. The morning sky was an explosion of colour. Prismatic lines of light flowed into Rupa's room lighting up phantom specks of dust. The shrubs called bormbu grew in the scrub and the heavy scent of their flowers was everywhere. Rupa remembered that the ripening of rice in the fields and the flowering of bormbu in the woods were simultaneous and the smell brought back all sorts of memories.

'I remember coming home from school with books, slate and pencils in hand, throwing them on the table, washing my face and hands and running straight to the dining room. My mother would sit with me while I was eating and ask me to eat a lot if I wanted to grow up quickly.

My friend Dingihami often came to see me in the late afternoon and we would go to the woods to pick wild berries and flowers. We ate as much as we could while we picked them, our lips turned scarlet with the rich red berries. I tucked my skirt into my knickers while I went fruit picking and used the folds of my skirt to carry fruit back home in. We never remembered how cross our mothers would always get when our skirts were stained with blackberry juice.'

Rupa saw her past like a stream of dreams flowing from an unknown shore, then away and gone forever. The dreams filed into her mind one by one like brief scenes from a play. She could not fathom why she entered into the marriage so suddenly. She had never wanted to add any unnecessary weight to her parents' life. Gunapala was a strong man, you could see his muscles bulge beneath his dark shiny skin while Aruna was thin and tall and always tired looking.

'We were born with freedom and marriage is a tangled up binding,' she thought. She remembered the time spent with Kumara at the university as free as air. She felt closer to Kumara than ever before. Rupa felt like a lost child, her feet weary from walking, seeing no end and then at last finding an oasis. Any hope of meeting Kumara again had faded and Rupa felt sad and confused.

In the short time Aruna was with her they had spent visiting friends and relatives. Sometimes she wished she had gone to England with her husband. At the airport Aruna's sisters had sobbed, tears running down their cheeks. Rupa felt uncomfortable in the middle of a crowd of unknown relatives. When she remembered that she must leave her parents and get used to living in a foreign country her anxiety returned. As long as Rupa could remember she had slept upstairs at Maha Gedara in an enormous satin bed with a tall bedstead. During the New Year period Rupa's mother used to keep home made sweets and bananas in cane boxes and put them under her bed. The smell of ripening bananas and treacle sweets was the most poignant odour of her childhood. Scarlet blossom in the hedgerow trees was a sign of the approaching New Year. Rupa remembered how she had played hopscotch using cashew nuts with shells together with the children from the village. Every year Rupa's friend Dingihami gave her a bag full of cashews. The wicker bag smelt dusty, rusty and smoky. It was kept on a kitchen shelf and sticky with accumulated cooking oil. Dingihami's parents lived in a mud hut roofed with a thatch of cadjans, dried coconut palm leaves.

Rupa went to school with Dingihami and they sat in the classroom next to each other. One day as they were coming home from school they couldn't believe their eyes to see a bulldozer and a steamroller on the road. Nobody had ever seen such an enormous vehicle. Six men were doing road works, laying tarmac on top of the red gravel. Thick smoke was swirling up from the huge tubs of boiling black tar. Groups of children gathered round and watched the bulldozer turn like a cranking metal giant and then the steamroller levelled the tarmac. They walked into the rubber estate holding each other's shoulders in a line. They jumped onto the fallen brown nuts from the rubber trees and cracked them as if the steamroller was crushing the stones. They forgot to go home. Rupa only realised that they were late when she saw her father coming towards her looking angry.

Two butterflies were hovering above the hibiscus. Rupa suddenly remembered her blue dress with yellow butterflies, which she wore at the university. The campus was surrounded by hills, the halls of residence and lecture rooms were scattered round and the River Mahaweli flowed along the valley at the bottom. The Hilda Obesekara residential hall with seven wings was situated by the river. She remembered how she watched a storm, standing against a pillar on the first floor long corridor. Broken tree branches and the ruins of palm thatched huts were caught up in the wind and carried away by the roaring angry river as it twisted and turned in sheets of turbid foam. Within a few days the heavy rain had stopped and the river was calm. During dry periods the river shrunk and turned to mere ditches, a white sand bed with projecting rocks scorched by the sun.

Rupa sat on the steps, sunken in deep thought, both doors open, waiting for her friend. She could hear the sound of a flute from far away. Sardiris the village farmer was sowing millet in his chena. His son Martia had taken his father's midday meal, sitting in the hut and playing his flute. The sound came from distant hills and it reminded Rupa of the headmaster's whistle in the village school. The school playground was like a moving sea with rolling waves. When the headmaster blew the whistle at eight in the morning everybody was quiet apart from an occasional whisper. The children walked into their classrooms in lines. Everybody had to stand up and say 'Good morning' when the class teacher arrived. Then they sang a hymn and the school day began. When the whistle blew at one in the afternoon everybody rushed to go home but nobody was allowed to leave until the final whistle blew ten minutes later. Some days when a lizard in the citrus hills made a long drawn-out whistling sound everybody rushed to sort out their bags, slates and books. The song of the lizard was similar to the headmaster's whistle with its rather reedy note. Rupa was shaken when she woke from her reverie. 'There's only one bus working today. The other one has broken down in and all the remaining passengers tried to squeeze into our bus.'

Rupa's friend Padma had walked in and put her handbag on the table in the sitting room. She wore a green sari with long braided hair.

Rupa had never been abroad before and she had no idea how long she was going to be away. Two days before the wedding on their way home Aruna stopped his car by the road where a few houses could be seen among coconut trees.

'This is our village Rupa. That distant building over there across the river is our old school. The temple is very near the school and in those days the head priest was my uncle. We went to the temple during break and picked fruit. We used to bath and swim in this river.' Aruna said.

'We were always told that anything belonging to the temple should only be used by monks who lived there,' Rupa replied.

They sat on the trunk of a tamarind tree, which had fallen in the storm. 'Rupa, we went to school by a bullock cart. Those days the roads were not tarmacced and when it rained the roads turned to muddy ditches.'

'We walked to school Aruna. There was a short cut through the citrus hills. Everybody in the village knew who we were, my father had asked them to keep an eye on us.'

'I'll take you to our temple one day.' He took her right hand and then suddenly kissed her. At the soft touch of his wet lips, she felt a strange sensation spreading all over her body.

They spent their wedding night at Aruna's house.

'Rupa, my father died many years ago and my mother was too ill to come to our wedding. She's delighted to see us here today. It's pointless going to a hotel or guesthouse for a night or two.'

'Newly married couples like their freedom. The honeymoon is as important as the wedding.'

'The waiters in the rest houses are very nosy and interfering. You know what they do? They look through keyholes. We'll spend our proper honeymoon in England Rupa.'

It was the night they were waiting for. They were alone together at last. The doors were closed behind them and the room was their own. They spent the night covering themselves with a thin cotton sheet breathing each other's warm air and he gave her himself for ever. She felt she was entering a world she didn't know existed.

The morning after the wedding the couple left for Kataragama at an auspicious time for the ritual ceremony of the temple. They drove along a dusty road, the shrubs in woodlands on both sides withered, dried, blackened or died. They saw a herd of deer crossing the road looking for water. A solitary wild elephant, known to be dangerous, broke the branch of a tree and trumpeted in the distance. In the soaring heat water buffaloes covered in dry mud desperately looked for ditches to cool themselves in.

'They haven't had a drop of rain in this area for a long time. Look at those cassia plants beside the road Aruna! The yellow flowers are completely covered in dust. The earth is crumbling and cracked. People who live in these remote areas must be having a very difficult time,' Rupa said.

'They are used to this life Rupa. During the rainy season they cultivate the land, grow vegetables and sow some grains and wait for the harvest. They dry rice and millet in the hot sun and save some grains for the next season. Then they wait for rain again staring at the sky and live their lives according to changes in the weather.'

'Are there any dusty roads like this in England Aruna?'

'We don't have this kind of dry weather in England. The difficulty there is the winter months from November to March. Sometimes it's freezing cold.'

'Do you get a lot of snow in London?'

'Don't worry about it, we hardly see any snow most winters. I'll make sure you'll have a warm house when you go there.'

The temple of Kataragama is a place of worship for Hindus, Muslims, Buddhists and even some Christians. The main deity is Skanda; the God of War, six faced and twelve armed who rides his peacock. The river Menik Ganga flows beside the temple and through the valley of the dry zone. The couple bathed in the river and changed into white clothes. They walked to the temple and poured coconut oil onto the burning wicks of the lamp, then they made their vows to the god. Rupa's eyes were bright with happiness. They walked bare-footed arm-in-arm on the scorching sand and watched the ritual ceremony of fire walking. They found it fascinating how men, women and even children walked bare-footed over the red hot embers.

Rupa was shaken and screamed when a cobra suddenly raised its venomous hood and stretched towards her, hissing. The charmer, who walked three times round the cobra said, 'It's only starting to dance. It has no poisonous teeth so it's quite harmless.' Although Aruna put his arms round her shoulders the fear in her mind did not go away.

A young woman carrying a two-year-old child stretched out her palms asking for money. 'We are very hungry,' she said. The woman was heavily pregnant and a four-year-old girl followed her. The woman's face was pale. She was wearing a dirty cloth and a worn out stained blouse and looked as if she would give birth at any moment. The child in her arms pulled his mother's blouse, trying to suck her breasts, which were full, but the mother looked weary with her terrible burdens. She was someone who couldn't plan beyond the day. Aruna gently placed a few coins in her palm. The woman smiled brightly. Her smile showed a row of betel stained brown teeth. Rupa took a packet of biscuits from her handbag and gave it to the child who trailed behind her mother. The child sat on the hot sand, opened the biscuit packet and ate the biscuits one by one.

EIGHT

A week before Rupa had to leave for England Dikwelle Hamine reflected sadly on her imminent departure.

'It's hardly a short journey Rupa is planning, all those thousands of miles! It's on the other side of the world where the sun and moon shine the opposite way round. Those countries are freezing cold and what will happen if she falls ill? We are not there to do anything for her!' She sighed.

'It's pointless just to talk and talk and mourn about something that's happened. You must accept reality. We shouldn't try to interfere when she's so completely set on something.' Loku Mahatmaya said.

'Don't talk like that! Only a mother can know how I feel in a situation like this. A mother's love is higher than the mountains in heaven. Sometimes I feel you are right, it's their fate and not even God can stop it.'

'Listen to me!' Loku Mahatmaya demanded 'I know those countries are cold, but people do live there. It can't be all that bad where English people live. If Ceylon were still under the rule of the British Empire we wouldn't have any of these terrible political problems, all the fighting and killing for land. I remember the day the white Government Agent at Hambantota District visited Kamburupitya. People had been gathering in the streets since morning. We had to walk five miles just to see him! Fortunately it was a beautiful January day. Needless to say he was riding a horse and looking very majestic.'

'I don't know how we are going to live in this empty house after she has gone. Rukmali doesn't come here often either.' Dikwelle Hamine could not think of a day at home without Rupa.

There were only two days left, Rupa's suitcases packed, her

name and her destination beautifully written on BOAC tags carefully attached by Rukmali. Everybody was getting ready to go to the airport. It was a five-hour journey from Matara to Colombo. The London flight was scheduled to leave at three in the morning in two days time. On the eve of the departure Dikwelle Hamine cooked the evening meal earlier than usual. Tilakawathie and the next-door woman, Ranhami, helped her.

Ranhami was talking to Rupa. 'We'll all feel empty after you have gone abroad. I brought you something very little. Try to come back soon with your husband. God bless you.' She gave Rupa a present wrapped in newspaper, with tears in her eyes.

'You shouldn't have bothered to bring me presents. You are doing enough for our family.' Rupa opened the parcel. It was a bar of sandalwood soap.

Dikwelle Hamine was washing the dishes in the kitchen and said to Rupa, 'Please go to bed early tonight. You must have a proper sleep before starting such a long journey.'

Ranhami was washing the clay pots and pans outside by the water tank. The glass chimney of the lantern hung on the wall darkened and the light grew dim.

'Don't try to wash the pots and pans at this time of the night Ranhami. Leave it until tomorrow and get it done when the sun rises.' Dikwelle Hamine asked.

'I've just finished the washing up. There's moonlight tonight.' Ranhami replied and kept the pots and pans in the 'pot shed' outside. Suddenly the two dogs began to bark and ran to the front garden. Someone flashed a torch and jumped over the stile in the fence. The dogs wagged their tails. It was Ranhami's son Dasa.

Rupa could not get to sleep. Moths, which got in through the open fanlights, were flying round the oil lamp chimney. They fell to the table dead or with a single wing, twitching. No one had remembered to close the windows and doors. The light in the kerosene lamps hanging from the sitting room ceiling was dimming because nobody had bothered to pump air into them. When the rain falls after a long drought those ground moths come out in colonies. Loku Mahatmaya spoke to Dasa while pounding his betel leaves.

'We are not going to be here for the next two days Dasa. Can you sleep here at night and be about during the day?'

'No problem Loku Mahatmaya.'

'Can you hear me Dasa? Remember to feed the dogs and remember they only eat fish with rice!'

'That's all right. Don't worry about it. We'll look after the dogs and as for the house, its nothing.'

Dasa was rough like a gypsy. He spoke in a loud harsh voice with a deep belly laugh. He was speaking to Loku Mahatmaya in the lounge and his voice echoed through the whole house. Dasa had lost a front tooth when he was twenty and the gap showed when he laughed. He had fallen from a coconut tree while trying to steel coconuts. He was known to the villagers as 'Chora Dasa' which means 'Dasa the burglar'.

Loku Mahatmaya was obsessively anxious about the dogs and reminded every new visitor that they must be fed during his absence. It was after midnight and still Rupa could not sleep. Rupa saw her mother moving the door curtain to check whether she had gone to sleep. Rupa closed her eyes, pretending a deep sleep. Dikwelle Hamine stood by the door for a few minutes and Rupa could hear her mother crying. Rupa had no intention of staying abroad for too long. She wanted to come back as soon as Aruna finished his exams. She noticed that during the recent months how worn-out her mother had seemed, wrinkles lined her face and hair turning grey. That night her father was very quiet at the dinner table. Occasionally he muttered to the dogs, sat on the floor beside him.

Rupa thought about the moment she would meet Aruna again and then she remembered the last evening at the university and her separation from Kumara. By now it was two a.m. and Rupa opened the window near her bed so a cool breeze could creep through the metal grilles. There was the unbroken silence of the woods, the hills and the fields, all washed over with moonlight. Bats fluttered among the branches of the tall jackfruit tree. Ripened jackfruit ripped open by the bats, their deep yellow juicy segments hanging over, gave off a sickly sweet-and-sour smell.

Dikwelle Hamine prayed before she finally slept, while the strong scent of joss-sticks still lingered. The journey had to be started from Rukmali's house at a time propitious to Rupa's horoscope. Everybody arrived at Rukmali's house around seven in the morning. Rukmali had covered the breakfast table with a choice selection of dishes, milk rice, fried onions, string hoppers, bananas and sweets.

'I'm not hungry, but I must eat a slice of milk rice at this very special occasion.' Dikwelle Hamine said.

During the journey from Matara to Colombo everybody was too tired to talk. The hundred mile long road runs along the white sandy beach through a canopy of coconut trees. The waves of the sea surge and break in an unbroken rhythm as they touch the shore. When their minibus drove past the fishing harbour near Matara they saw a faint line of boats on the distant horizon. Stilt fishermen were angling in the shallow waters, standing on poles like storks in a field, while the white frothy sea waves slowly moved and washed off the sandy beach. An enormous fishing net full of skipjack tuna and herrings was arriving and a group of fishermen were pulling the net ashore. Rough looking men and women shortened their long clothes to above knee length and stood on the shore, staring at the sea. They were arguing in bad language during the hours' long wait for the fish to finally arrive. Wholesalers in parked vans and market traders on bicycles were waiting for bargains.

'Look at that great black cloud moving upward from the skyline! When it's like this the fish in deep water move to the surface. I think the fishermen are doing well today. I bet it's a bumper catch!' Loku Mahatmaya's words broke the silence. Everybody in the minibus was dozing off shaking themselves and nodding their heads when the vehicle moved along the uneven road.

There were thick ropes running between the coconut palm trees. Toddy tappers climbing high and walking along the ropes while holding another rope were collecting coconut flower juice. They stopped at Kalutara Buddhist Shrine and made ritual offerings of coins and flowers. Dikwelle Hamine walked seven times round the large sacred Bo tree, knelt down and prayed for Rupa to have a safe journey.

They had the evening meal at Dikwelle Hamine's brother's house in Colombo then travelled out to the airport. As they reached the departure building Rupa felt uncomfortable with fear. There was little time left before check-in. Everything had changed in her life within such a short period. She felt sad to leave her home and parents. Rupa didn't know anybody except Aruna and Chandra in England. She felt tired and she wanted to return home with her family.

'We hope to come back soon.' Rupa said.

Loku Mahatmaya looked away and stayed silent.

'God bless you,' said Dikwelle Hamine. Rupa put her hands together, bending her head in the customary way and said goodbye to everyone. Rukmali tried to console her parents who found it so hard to accept Rupa leaving. They waved to her and Rupa waved back as she handed over her luggage and walked through the immigration check and into the departure lounge.

This was the first time Rupa had travelled abroad and she felt strange in an airport on her own. Passengers were speaking in an assortment of languages as they bought whisky and cigarettes from the duty free shops. Rupa looked at the glowing faces of tourists returning home. It was impossibly busy in Colombo airport that Saturday morning with constant announcements for passengers, arrival and departure delays and flight times. Some travellers read books and magazines or slept in the lounge, while others walked up and down, travel-bags in their hands, wheeled baggage trolleys or sat in cafés. Everybody else seemed used to travelling. Rupa felt quite alone among the unknown travellers, uncomfortable and anxious as she sat in the departure lounge until finally there was an announcement for boarding. Everybody panicked and rushed to the gates. Rupa followed on, not knowing what to do. Then in the aircraft an airhostess showed her to a seat.

'No smoking/Seat belts on.' The yellow sign flashed above her head. After a few words from the captain and crew wishing everyone a comfortable journey the plane at last took off. It circled the runway for ten minutes then finally it was airborne.

Rupa remembered home. She thought of her parents watching her leave. The engine thundered and the aircraft shook. 'God bless you.' Rupa remembered her mother's last words. How far from home was she now? 'My parents may be still looking at the sky,' she reflected. Minute by minute, hour by hour the distance between Rupa and her old home widened. She sat in a window seat feeling as if she was being carried away by some terrifying mythical bird to an unknown part of the universe. The aircraft was flying at thirty thousand feet, the roar of the engine quietened to a steady hum. Rupa felt slightly more comfortable when her blocked up ears slowly cleared. Airhostesses were walking up and down the aisles serving drinks.

Rupa looked out of the small window. Below she could see the sea at some distance joining the yellow, blue and pink smudged skyline. A huge wing stood out among the moving white clumps of cloud. Its flashing coloured lights brightened the otherwise empty sky. As the plane flew, hills, rocks, rivers and the sea swirled and shaped to make patterns of collage-like landscapes. The passenger who sat next to Rupa was a middle-aged European with a beard, very mature-looking with his head buried in a philosophy book. Travelling from Matara to Colombo airport in tropical heat, the long preparation for the journey and separation from her home had exhausted Rupa. She was shaken by this large creature with lightning wings and the growls of the engine carried her through an endless sky to a planet beyond the sea. Rupa finally fell into a deep sleep.

The airhostesses were serving a meal when Rupa woke up suddenly. Her head was leaning against the other passenger's shoulder and she felt immediately embarrassed. She thought of her parents, already in the minibus making their homeward journey. She worried in case the dogs had crossed the fields and hills and gone to the main road looking for her father. If they met with an accident or were killed by a poisonous snake her father would be heartbroken. The growing anxiety in her mind only subsided when she thought about meeting Aruna in a few hours. This was a very special day for Rupa, the day they were starting a new life together in England. For a moment she felt relaxed. She thought about the wedding day and night and the two weeks they spent together but she also remembered what Kumara asked her before they left university; 'Would you like to live a quiet life abroad with me Rupa?'

She felt so depressed she even looked around to see whether Kumara was travelling in the same plane.

The aircraft was moving at a steady speed and there was only two hours to go. Due to violent weather changes at high altitudes the plane shook when it passed through air pockets but apart from this Rupa's first journey by air was trouble free. The passenger who sat next to her did speak but she only just managed to understand him. The last few hours passed quickly and then the plane entered British air space. It was announced that the plane would be landing at London Heathrow Airport in twenty minutes.

NINE

It was just before dawn in England. At first it looked like a dark moonless sky with shimmering stars. The VC10 descended over London with its high-rise buildings, a myriad of flashing lights and long lines of yellow ribbon motorways. The view became clearer as the aircraft approached the ground. The River Thames flashed through the dawn light like a coiling giant reptile. Through the thinning clouds and green mist early morning London looked bigger and bigger. It was like a cartoon with long ant lines turning to match-box sized cars then moving vehicles could be seen underneath the towers and buildings.

'Seat belts on/No smoking,' the signs flashed overhead. An airhostess rushed up and down to wake the dozing passengers. Everybody began to chatter excitedly but Rupa felt uneasy because she knew nothing about the English way of life. She only knew that people there spoke English. England was a cold country she thought, soon at home it will be harvest time and her parents would be drying the new crop of rice in hot sun. There was a sudden rumble, then a sharp crack and the aircraft moved its nose down, making the surrounding area vibrate and then finally it touched down with a shuddering shake. Slowly it moved along the runway and then at last came to a halt outside the terminal. There was the announcement.

'Ladies and gentlemen, we have just landed at London Heathrow. The outside temperature at the moment is zero centigrade. Passengers are requested to remain in their seats.'

A few minutes later everyone was pulling out their hand luggage and travel bags, cigarettes, whisky and duty free perfumes, women brushing their hair and putting on make up, the aisles were tightly packed with standing passengers. An Asian man sobbed because his wife had fainted and had to be taken away in the airport ambulance. He didn't speak a word of English and someone from the Airport Authority waited outside to take him to his wife.

Wearing her blue cotton jacket Rupa felt impatient to see Aruna. He was waiting at the arrival lounge listening to the booming tannoy. The passenger in the adjacent seat to Rupa who had buried his head in a book for most of the journey now turned and smiled and wished her good luck. A hint of happiness tempted Rupa to smile back. The aircraft door opened and everybody got out quickly except Rupa who trailed behind the rest along the unending corridors and escalators, confused as to where she was going. She joined a fast moving queue at the Immigration check and realised that it was for British passport holders only; she was directed again to a long slow moving line of passengers. After half an hour's wait and a few questions from an Immigration Officer in a peaked cap she had her passport stamped 'To Join Husband' and Rupa was finally allowed in through the barriers.

London Airport was different to what Rupa had expected. She only saw Terminal One and it was not one enormously extended building as she had imagined. It was busy with continuous announcements over the tannoy for passengers in transit; men, women and children were rushing and pushing their luggage trolleys along the passageways. Rupa felt lonely and lost. When she went to the luggage hall she found the other passengers already collecting their luggage. She saw her suitcases on the shuddering carousel.

When Rupa came out pushing her trolley Aruna was waiting by the railings. His friend Chandra and her husband were there with a bunch of pink carnations. Rupa noticed the arrivals section was alive with welcoming smiles and kisses.

'We were worried! Everybody else who came in the same flight came through a long time ago.' Aruna said.

'Don't worry Rupa, you are here at last.' Chandra smiled.

'It took a long time for me to find my way out.' Rupa replied.

It was the day before the General Election. The whole country was waiting impatiently to know what was going to happen, a landslide victory was expected for Labour. People were talking about the decline of the welfare system, poor hospitals and bad schools. They went straight from the airport to Trafalgar Square to watch a Labour election rally. Rupa was tired but so glad she had got to England to be with Aruna at last. It was a cold bright morning. The sky was blue and there was a freezing, biting wind pushing at her thin clothing. Rupa was wearing a sleeveless floral dress and a cotton jacket, not realising how cold it would be. Aruna warned her how little England would be like the warm soft tropical mornings she was used to, even the sunshine seemed weak and powerless to melt the ground frost on the crisp white grass.

Rupa looked at the long line of immaculate black taxis drawn up in a line that moved slowly forward as the incoming passengers pushed their luggage onboard and scrambled inside. She wondered why they had not joined the queue and tried to get in. Aruna laughed.

'Did you think we were going by taxi? I have a car in the car park!'

They walked to the car park.

'Rupa I bought this car to go anywhere we like in England or Scotland to spend our honeymoon.' He kissed her as they got into his blue Peugeot. She had a gleaming smile on her face. They drove through the heavily congested areas of London along crowded streets. Rows of brick built or unpainted pebbledashed rather grim looking houses with sloping roofs seemed very strange to Rupa's eyes. She could not imagine what the inside of these houses would look like. She remembered the large whitewashed houses with red tiled roofs and the coconut palm trees slanted towards the sea, waving their elegant spiny leaves along the endless shores of Ceylon. At the end of a long cold winter most of the trees were still bare like upturned brooms standing under the sky and it was just before spring. Rupa wondered why London looked so dull and empty even when it was crowded and the sun was shining.

The election rally in Trafalgar Square was exciting even though they couldn't get very near. Mounted police were trying to control the disorganised, shouting crowd, yelling slogans and waving banners and flags. From a distance it seemed like a violent sea in a storm while Nelson's Column appeared through the clearing mist. She watched the luminous shop front displays in Piccadilly Circus and the huge shops in Regent Street and Oxford Street with great fascination. She hadn't expected Aruna to show her round London on her very first day.

When they came home Chandra and her husband were already there. Chandra had cooked rice and curry and the beautifully prepared meal was waiting on the table. Rupa remembered her mother's cooking at home but this was Aruna's home, a three-bedroom house with a long back garden. There was a privet hedge at the front and a hydrangea bush by the doorstep. When the meal was over and their friends departed, Rupa and Aruna were finally alone.

In the tropical dawn with its clamouring bird song and sunset skies with rampant colours were a daily routine. The irregular patterns of late sunrise and early sunset confused Rupa but somehow it didn't seem to matter. The doors and windows of their home were closed against the shivering wind and there was a coal fire in the lounge, the rest of the house kept from freezing by powerful paraffin heaters. They neither noticed nor cared about changes from day to night. Their bedroom walls were covered with sixties striped pink and blue papers and the carpet was pale blue. There was a fluffy yellow candlewick bedspread and the thick curtains in their room were tightly drawn.

TEN

A week after Rupa's arrival spring was on the way and the couple started their new life in London. Two parts of the same world seemed not far apart when looked down on from the sky but on the ground such vast changes in the way of life from East to West Rupa found hard to take in. The two-storey town house where they began their life together had a sitting room and a dining room downstairs. There was a door to the outside garden from the square kitchen with its Belling cooker and small hot water boiler fixed to the wall. There were two large and one small bedroom upstairs and a converted loft, which was used as a storeroom. A few weeks before Rupa's arrival the two students who rented a room for two pounds a week left and moved to a hall of residence.

The dark winter days were over and the next door neighbour was trying to start his rusty petrol lawn mower to cut the damp overgrown grass. The whirring of the mower broke the silence of that Sunday afternoon. The sun had hidden behind dark clouds all day and the wind was cold. Rupa and Aruna sat by the fire while the burning coal was glowing and the room was warmed. It was a world they had never known before.

'Rupa, I thought we could go away for a few weeks and enjoy our honeymoon. During the time I was in Ceylon, meeting you, getting married and everything having to be done in such a great hurry! I have taken so much unpaid leave I'm behind with my studies. I have to go back to work tomorrow but I'll try to get another week's holiday as soon as I can.'

'That's all right Aruna, the main thing is your final exam and when it's over we can go away somewhere with all the time in the world.'

'Rupa, this isn't the right time to go away on holiday anyway, its still very cold but it will be much better when we get some sunshine in a few months. Places in the North and in Scotland are even colder than it is in London.'

'I am so used to the warm sunshine in Ceylon I don't even feel like going out. Sometimes I go for a walk up and down the streets and come back quickly feeling cold.'

Aruna had to leave early in the morning and it was late in the evening when he returned. During the week he went to college where he studied mechanical engineering and on weekends he worked part time in a postal sorting office. The tail end of winter could still be felt although the daytime sun seemed slightly warmer. Houses still had to be heated. Rupa had no warm clothes except one long sleeved light blue dress, a couple of cardigans and some stockings Chandra had given her.

'Are there any shops around here Aruna? I feel a bit strange going on my own in case I don't understand what the people in the shops say.'

'There are a few shops down the street, a Woolworths and a Marks and Spencer. There's a big shopping centre in Croydon only twenty minutes away by bus.'

'Chandra is willing to go shopping with me sometime Aruna. It's her day off next Tuesday.'

'That's a good idea. We'll go and see Chandra tomorrow night and you can arrange a time to go shopping with her.'

Chandra was a plump woman with a round face and a kind mellow voice. She always smiled and spoke to everybody with no trace of anxiety. She entertained friends with both eastern and western style cooking. Rupa told Chandra that she felt uncomfortable speaking English.

'Don't you worry Rupa, if you don't understand what people in the street say. Do you think everyone in the street speaks Oxford English? You wouldn't believe me Rupa, I don't understand a word of English spoken by some people who work with me, but we manage,' said Chandra. What Chandra said had encouraged Rupa to go out on her own.

They saw Chandra on the following day and arranged to go

shopping on Tuesday. When she arrived that morning Aruna had gone to college and Rupa was waiting.

'I'm so glad you decided to spend your day off going shopping with me, Chandra. Apart from buying some milk and bread from United Dairies round the corner I haven't been to a shop since I came to England.'

Rupa was very excited about their shopping spree. Chandra told her that she had to get used to British money, pounds, shillings and pence. After a cup of tea they went shopping in Croydon.

What Chandra had told Rupa was true. The winter sales were over and the shops were full of new styles of spring and summer clothing and much else. Self-service was just starting to become popular in the early sixties and Rupa realised that her spoken English was not really a problem. She was surprised to see how quickly women with children walked along the pavements wearing high heeled shoes managing heavy shopping bags, pushchairs and prams.

'Rupa, you can buy anything in these shops! You can spend from a ha'penny to thousands of pounds.'

Rupa bought a bright red duffel coat with bone buttons from Allders. They went to several shoe shops but Rupa could not find what she wanted. She noticed that most English women's feet were thin and long and there were women's shoes up to size nine or ten. When Rupa tried to avoid the most fashionable shoes the saleswoman assumed that Rupa had some deformity and suggested she got medical advice. Chandra realised that Rupa was unhappy.

'Don't worry about what other people think about you. When you live in a foreign country you have to value your self confidence.' Chandra gave her two white silk roses, which Rupa realised were the height of fashion.

Aruna felt the freedom he had before would never be the same again. He had a wife at home and his lifestyle had changed.

'I don't like to be out all day leaving you at home Rupa, I'm not even free on most weekends. I have to work whenever I'm free, but hopefully things will get better in a few months time,' Aruna said.

'I don't like you having to work and study at the same time. I feel like finding a job. I'd also like to learn English.'

'We'll have to think about it Rupa.'

Aruna's final exam was only two months away. Rupa understood that she had to get used to a new country and it was not something she could find the answers to in a day, although she desperately felt that she should contribute something to the meagre family income.

ELEVEN

The days were longer for Rupa and she was more aware of her loneliness. Aruna left home early each morning and the sun had made its journey from dawn to dusk by the time he returned. Surrounded by a wistful emptiness, she looked at the darkening London sky. She remembered life at home. She thought often how her mother cooked meals and did housework while she spent most mornings reading a book or planting marigolds in the flowerbeds rich in orange soil at the bottom of the garden. The days she went for evening walks along the valley listening to the sound of creaking tree branches, gathering the wind fallen mangoes, had ended suddenly. Now she found it very hard to organise herself in an unknown country. Rupa could not understand the English life style and she was astonished to see their ways, how they managed to work, look after children, shop, cook and do everything else without servants. They were not friendly like the people in the East and Rupa found them reserved and uncommunicative. She only saw her neighbours occasionally, in the street or while she hung out her washing in the back garden. The people in the neighbouring houses lived all their lives away from everyone else. Jack, the old man who lived further down the street, had returned home after the war ended to find his mother had died of influenza. He married a war widow with two children but she left him after Jack became an alcoholic. Since then he had lived on his own with alcohol his only companion. Every Christmas he was given a huge bag of second-hand clothes by the Salvation Army, so he never needed to buy any clothes. Rupa discovered that English people living in country areas lived in the close communities she knew from Ceylon but here in the metropolis peoples' lives were cut off from families and neighbours. The middle-aged couple who lived next door to Rupa and Aruna worked at Scotland Yard. They spoke English with a strange incomprehensible accent. They had come to London from Glasgow three years ago looking for well-paid jobs. Rupa could make no conversation with her neighbours and she constantly agonised over her problems with spoken English.

It was mid March and spring had arrived. The frozen earth had started to melt, the wind swept, snow washed, blizzard blown skeletons of naked trees had finally woken. Withered grassland turned green and flower buds appeared in hedgerows. Woods and parks had suddenly begun a new life. Yellow daffodils along the riverbanks appeared through the damp morning dew and opened to the sun. The long nights were over and the shorter days gradually stretched out. A shivering, biting, threatening cold wind had turned to a cool breeze. The snow had gone and the clouds of mist and fog thinned and finally disappeared in the warm air. The loneliness in Rupa's mind had lessened. She felt a bounding sense of liveliness within her for the first time since she had arrived in England. Everything around was brighter; the air was warmer and the grass was greener. Aruna ended his studies, gave up the idea of further education and started working as a trainee engineer in a motor parts factory.

'It was with great difficulty I managed to get through my exams Rupa. At least now I've some engineering qualifications. I don't want to go on like this ever again. All I want is to find a job and earn good money.'

'I'm so glad everything is over Aruna, at least we can have some time together in the evenings and at weekends. Now I am beginning to see the differences between Ceylon and England. I still don't know anybody who lives around here. The lady next door says the same things whenever I see her, either the weather's freezing or warm and the days are gloomy or beautiful! She hurries off to work in the mornings and comes back tired at night and closes her front door as fast as she can if I'm in the garden. I feel so relieved you don't have to work and study at the same time. I'm not used to wearing leg warmers, gloves, boots and thick woollens. I feel better without them. I don't want to stay at home doing nothing.

I'd like to find a job and earn some money. I don't care what kind of work I have to do: nursing, cleaning, factory work or being a domestic, I don't mind.'

'Rupa, it's not necessary for you to find a job so quickly. I can easily earn enough for us both.'

'You're right in a way. I always think about the time I spent at the university studying for years on end. It was a waste of my education if I don't do anything worthwhile. After I improve my English, I may be able to study something in a university here.'

'Educated people are not the only ones who have a proper place in this world. Those days when my mother was young, all women had to look after children, do housework and live their lives as housewives.'

'I always feel that we must live in society as it is Aruna.'

'I intend to start my own motor parts business when I have some money. There's nothing wrong with further education, but I'd prefer it if you could stay at home and manage the housework.'

Aruna had taken two weeks' holiday. They visited the Natural History Museum with its enormous collection of ancient statuary and its displays of dinosaur skeletons and fossils. Rupa noticed there were some precious blue sapphires originally mined in Ceylon the 'Gem Country'. They visited the Planetarium and Madam Tussaud's wax museum with life-size statues of kings, queens, presidents and Prime ministers. They went down a flight of marble steps into the enormous basement with streaming red and orange flashing lights from the depth of darkness where the Chamber of Horrors with its ghosts and ghouls awaited them. Luminous eyes stared from gaping skeletal sockets. In the corner behind a crimson velvet curtain lay the horror of horrors – the tableau of a Byzantine torture chamber, complete with the arching bloodstained torso of a man suspended in mid air, slowly expiring as the steel hook on the end of a hawser bit through his belly. The tableau of the French Revolution had Queen Marie Antoinette's bloody head in a wicker basket beneath the smoking steel blades of Madame La Guillotine. When they went to Selfridges in Oxford Street and Harrods in Kensington Rupa could not believe her eyes. Although the prices were unaffordable everything was there. Aruna bought her a silk scarf, fluttering with crimson roses for half a crown. Rupa, beaming with joy wore it around her neck and tied a butterfly knot.

Rupa never forgot the day they went to Kew Gardens. Although it was bigger than the Botanical Gardens at Peradeniya, her memories of student days and the long walks and the time she spent with Kumara suddenly welled up in her mind. The gardens in Ceylon were a short walk from the campus and Rupa for a moment wondered if Kumara was there waiting for her. Rupa and Aruna met an old man with his wife, both walking with the help of sticks. He was limping and his wife held his arm. 'It's a beautiful day,' said the old man.

'Plenty of warm sunshine,' replied Aruna.

'Have you been to Kew gardens before?'

'No. This is my first time. I brought my wife to show her the spring flowers and the gardens. It's a wonderful place.'

The old man looked at Rupa gently nodding his head.

'We know every inch of the soil beneath our feet. I was born in the next village. My father worked all his life here. First as a gardener and then as a director. He was a happy man, you know what I mean! The gates are open to us now, but at one time these gardens were meant only for the leisure and pleasure of the Royal family.'

The old man smiled and continued talking.

'This is my wife Rosalind. Since we got married fifty-four years ago we've come here for walks almost every day. I can't believe how quickly some of these trees have grown. I remember them as young plants and how my father tried to protect them from wild animals. Now we are old, the plants have grown and in those days we were young and strong and we had plenty of energy left.'

The old man looked at his wife and laughed, showing his whiter-than-white false teeth, his caved in hollow cheeks. He was very frail; while he spoke he ran his fingers through his thin grey hair, occasionally wiping beads of sweat from his forehead. His wife was a shrunken old woman who wore a woollen coat, a blue scarf round her head, knitted gloves and black leather boots. She walked slowly over the damp grass. The old man kept on chattering as though he had inherited his father's job as curator.

'These gardens are very different today. Now people from everywhere visit this place. When we were young my mother brought us here for picnics and we spent hours, playing ball games. This is half term holiday week. That's why lots of kids are about. You don't have to go back to your country to see the tropical plants. Go and have a look inside those glass houses. There were no 'keep off the grass' signs. The gatekeeper didn't even bother with the penny admission charge. I think world belongs to the younger generation. You and your wife should try to make the most of your opportunities while you're young. That oak over there will stand for centuries to come'

Finally the old couple hobbled away.

Rupa looked at her watch. It was twenty to one.

'Aruna, I brought some sandwiches and a flask of tea. Let's go and sit somewhere.'

'There's a bench under that tree. We'll sit and have a cup of tea.' The Japanese cherry tree was covered with deep pink blossoms and the arching branches dipping to the ground had made it into a silky parasol. They sat on the bench.

'Today's very warm for spring. I feel very tired.' Aruna took off his black corduroy jacket and threw it on the grass near the bench. They ate their sandwiches and drank their tea, kissed and caressed. Aruna fell asleep, his head on Rupa's lap. When he woke up Rupa was stroking his hair.

'We could go to the Lake District for a few days tomorrow Rupa.'

'That's a good idea Aruna, have you been there before?'

'Yes, with friends. We could go for long walks by the lakes.'

When they went home that evening Rupa cooked a meal, washed up and cleaned the Belling then she packed their suitcases. Even the bedroom with its green curtains and yellow candlewick bedspread seemed brighter. The window was half open and the fresh spring air poured in. Their bed was soft and warm beneath the blue flannelettes.

The following morning they drove to the Lake District. As the hills, slopes and lakes passed through the thin mist, Rupa watched excitedly.

'Its amazing Aruna, so many lakes in the same place, perhaps millions of years ago this area was covered in glaciers and it was a kingdom of dinosaurs. When I think about these things, I just wonder who we are!'

They stayed in a guesthouse near Windermere. The next day they went to Grasmere, where Wordsworth was born in a tiny house with low ceilings. Although the poet had lived and died two hundred years ago the sound of his voice still echoed between the stone walls. Yellow daffodils danced along the valleys to the rhythm of the wind, like a mime in an open-air theatre. The trees, the hills and the meadows stood like vigilant night watchers of the past. 'Even for a few days, going away from overcrowded London is a relief,' Rupa said.

TWELVE

Autumn was slowly fading and winter on its way with longer nights. It was a Monday morning when a whistling wind tried to creep into their bedroom. Occasionally the long bay window shook as if the glass, dribbling with condensation, was about to crumble. Wearily Aruna tried to shake himself awake. He stretched and rubbed his eyes, pulling up the yellow flannelette sheets that were falling onto the floor. It was still dark. He thought he had woken from a nightmare and desperately wanted to sleep again. He looked at the Westclox alarm with its luminous red light on the polished teak bedside cabinet. Its rapid incessant tick irritated him. The clock showed half past five. Rupa was asleep. Their minds and bodies were entwined and they breathed the same air, cocooned in their intimacy. They were so close that Aruna felt they could never be separated. He put his arm round her. She was wearing a dusky pink thin night-dress. Like unborn twins being forced to leave their mother's womb and enter a world of woven blankets, Aruna had a strange apprehension indescribable and one he experienced only within the boundaries of their own home. Aruna and Rupa had only known each other for thirteen months but during that time their lives had changed beyond recognition. Had she adjusted to her new life in this strange foreign country, as well as to being his wife? Aruna felt uncomfortable about Rupa's seeming loneliness. Was there any way he could help her adjust? Had he burdened and buried himself in his working life? When Aruna got out of bed, the air in the room was cold and thick. He put on the convector heater and a warm yellow glow lit the corner beneath the wall-mounted bookshelf. He had rushed out to buy the convector when the old paraffin heater had started to flicker and give off a smell of burning a week before. When he went to the bathroom there was a slightly foetid smell of damp. Even the towel on the electric rail was cold. He went downstairs to make some tea. He placed a white enamel kettle on the Belling and watched the orange glow when the kettle started to hiss and steam came from the spout. Aruna's side of the bed had gradually become cold and when Rupa woke up she knew at once that he was no longer there and must be getting ready for work.

'You don't have to get up just yet, Rupa. Drink your cup of tea and stay in bed. The heating is on. You'll feel warm soon. I'll lock the door when I go.'

Rupa noticed that there was a heavy frost and a layer of ice had settled on the window. Outside there was a thick fog. She put on her pink towelling dressing gown and went downstairs with Aruna. Rupa stood by the polished oak door and watched Aruna pick his way along the icy path. Then she locked the front door, realising it was going to be a long day.

Every evening Rupa cooked a meal of rice and spiced meat or vegetable curry. Sometimes she made an English meal, pork chops with onions, boiled potatoes and vegetables. In the sixties it was fish and chips and curry was not on the menu. Rupa's next door neighbour hated the smell of curry powder and coughed hysterically when she smelt it and tapped vigorously on her kitchen wall. Rupa became panicky and burned incense to mask the odour, but then she thought the neighbours would start to sneeze and queue up at her door to complain.

Always she waited impatiently for Aruna's return. Aruna never knew what time he would be home. It seemed that sometimes he forgot he had a wife waiting at home. Slowly Rupa began to feel secure at least within the closed doors of their house. Privet and cypress lay outside the brick boundary walls and the wooden fence was covered with sweet honeysuckle. After Aruna had gone to work that morning a freezing wind shook every nook and cranny. The streets stayed empty, the skyline hidden behind the sloping tiled roofs of pebbledashed houses. Swirls of grey smoke poured out of the chimneys and dissolved into the cold air. The distant fractured wailing of an ambulance's siren approached. The tall white buildings of the local hospital stretched into the sky behind the houses. The melancholy sound of the siren seemed to haunt the air and mixed with the sighing wind. It was a quarter to eight. Rupa was still upstairs in the bathroom combing her dark hair, which fell over her shoulders. When she saw her face on the oval gold-framed mirror, she thought she had put on weight and that her complexion was slightly altered.

'Lack of sun and my own cooking, or it could be just the wrong shape of the mirror,' Rupa thought rather simplistically.

The doorbell rang once. Rupa was alarmed.

'Who can be ringing the bell at this time? Could it be the postman with a parcel or a registered letter?' She came out of the bathroom and looked at her front door.

'I don't think it's the postman. It could be a man selling home-grown potatoes, coal or fresh farm eggs. I'm not going to answer the door in case it's some conman trying to swindle me. I must be very careful,' Rupa said to herself anxiously. She looked out of the small bedroom window through the white lace curtains. The black wrought iron gate was closed and nobody was there. The doorbell rang twice again, this time louder. Rupa began to tremble.

'I don't usually open the door for anybody. If it's somebody I know, surely they would have telephoned. I must see who it is? Rupa slowly walked down the green-carpeted stairs, an indefinable fear in her mind.

'I shouldn't be frightened at this time of day, when it's broad daylight. No-one knows I am on my own here.' Rupa could see the vague outline of a figure in front of the door, wearing a blue coat.

'I'm sure it's a woman. Probably a Jehovah's Witness. I'm going to tell them I was born a Buddhist and I've no intention of changing my religion, otherwise they'll start to come here everyday trying to make me change my mind and it will be a terrible nuisance,' she thought.

Rupa opened the door to find their friend Chandra. A sense of relief flooded through her. 'I'm so pleased to see you Chandra after such a long time. Do come in.'

Chandra walked into the house smiling like a child. The scent of sandalwood came in with her and perfumed the whole house.

'Could you put this in the fridge Rupa?' Chandra handed over a large parcel wrapped in polythene.

'It's very heavy, what on earth is it Chandra?'

'I brought you some food. There's a bottle of mango chutney, a roast chicken and some fried veg for your dinner. Don't put that fruitcake in the fridge. Sorry I came so early without telling you. Has Aruna gone to work?' Rupa opened the parcel and put the cooked food in the fridge. Chandra had also brought some foreign vegetables, aubergines, aucra and sweet potatoes.

'Where did you get these?'

'A shop in Notting Hill that sells foreign food and all kinds of stuff.'

'Aruna leaves home very early. Thanks for the food Chandra. We'll eat it tonight.'

'I thought you might be at home on your own, that's why I came in the morning, just to see how you are.'

It was uncomfortably cold. Rupa brought down the convector heater from their bedroom. They chatted while the air slowly warmed. The coal fire had gone out and turned to a mass of black ashes over the iron grate. Rupa sat on the hearth and stirred them with the poker. Smoke poured out from beneath the grill. She emptied a shovelful of coal into the waiting fire.

'We're expecting a coal delivery in a day or two. If we run out of coal we can always buy some from the ironmongers down the street.'

'Don't worry Rupa. It's not necessary to light a coal fire, it's warm and cosy in here. Those convectors are very good.'

Chandra stood by the patio doors, drops of melted ice had made streaky patterns on the glass. Layers of night frost on the grass were softening under thc winter sun. Rupa made some tea and they sat drinking it on the beige leather settee.

'Are you getting used to life in England Rupa?'

'It's difficult to say. I feel very lonely and Aruna doesn't understand. He comes home in the evening tired and he's no time to talk to me or think about me. It's not worth saying anything to him. He just doesn't listen. He expects me to be here to keep him company. I wish I never got married and never came to England in the first place! The weather is cold, the house is cold, even the people are cold. I hardly go out and I don't know anybody around here except Aruna. All he wants to do is work, come home, eat if there's any food and then go to sleep. I don't like his temper either. Now he talks about working on Saturdays, to earn some extra money. Doesn't he love his wife?'

'Rupa, listen to me! It's not like living in the East. We just have to get on with living our own lives. I don't have much time to think about my husband or to see how he spends his day at work, but at the end of the day we are together and happy to be in each other's company.'

Rupa was quiet. 'Don't take these things so seriously Rupa. It's not a matter of life and death, problems have to be sorted out.'

There was a sudden squeal of car brakes. Chandra looked out to see what was going on. The road was slippery and a car driver who had tried to avoid a motorcyclist had skidded. Nobody else was around and fortunately no one was hurt. The cyclist passed, his engine roaring.

'These drivers don't realise how dangerous it is when there's black ice on the roads. It's like a waiting landmine,' Chandra said.

Rupa sat on the floor near the convector rubbing her cold hands.

'I don't like to live in this country Chandra. I feel like an alien from another planet.'

'Rupa, we have to cope with the way things are in England. You can't expect Eastern sun to shine in the West on a cold winter day! I'm sorry to seem so harsh you're just not in reality! Why don't you get out and go somewhere. Most people are ok. Get into a bus or on a train and try to find your way. I know Aruna, he may just be overloaded with his job. When you go out if you get lost, don't just ask anybody, ask one of those blue uniformed bobbies who walk up and down the streets!'

'I'd like to learn some English before I start to do anything else.'

'Why don't you go to Croydon Tech? They have day and evening classes for foreign students.' Chandra finished her cup of tea while she paced up and down the lounge talking non-stop. She explained to Rupa that Aruna was under enormous pressure, having to cope with his work as well as married life.

'I must dash off now Rupa, I've to work this afternoon. The quarter past twelve train from Carshalton goes to Victoria in half an hour, then I've got a ten minute walk from the station to where I work.' Chandra put her green bag over her shoulder and left in a hurry. She waved at Rupa and shouted, 'Look after yourself, I'll be in touch.'

Rupa closed the front gate and walked in feeling a different woman. She didn't have to make a meal that evening. The roast chicken and fried vegetables in the fridge would do fine. She just had to cook some potatoes.

Rupa piled the washing up in the kitchen sink and turned the convector off. She looked at her face in the mirror on the wall, brushed her hair quickly and rushed out wearing her red duffel coat and black shoes. She didn't even know where she was going. Rupa got into a 109 bus. The conductor was a middle aged West Indian. He came near Rupa rattling his ticket machine. He wore a navy blue uniform with a bright red London Transport badge on his pocket with his number on it.

'Tickets please,' he said in his strange accent.

'West Croydon,' Rupa replied.

'One and six, please.'

Rupa handed over a green pound note to the bus conductor. The double-decker crept through the traffic, passing lines of rain washed trees and drenched houses. At the roadside leaves had fallen and gathered under the hedgerows like roosting ducks. Hidden birds' nests were exposed to the cold wind of day. The conductor rushed up and down the bus, his ticket machine clacking incessantly. The bus stopped at a junction of five main roads. 'Five Ways! Five Ways!' Called the conductor. Most of the passengers got off, leaving the bus almost empty. There was a driver's change over, then the bus set off again. Rupa had never travelled in a London bus before. She felt frightened and confused. The bus went through an area where there were few houses to be seen. There was an industrial estate with factories and vast concrete yards where heavily laden lorries and trucks constantly reversed in and out of wide-open steel gates. Clouds of black smoke poured out of the tall chimneys swirling and rolling into the stormy sky. The air was misty and murky and daylight had already begun to fade. There was an enormous statue of a black bull in metal with huge horns on the top of a tall building. The bull with its bent head and straining loins faced the moving traffic. The factory made stainless steel cutlery. Finally the bus arrived at West Croydon. Rupa got off but felt unsure of her destination.

She did not know which way to turn. Croydon was much larger than Rupa had expected. She felt disorientated and considered going straight back in the next 109. She looked around for a policeman. There was a young woman sitting on a bench waiting for a bus. She had a bottle of coke and a newspaper and looked vaguely student-like.

'Is Croydon Tech anywhere near here?' Rupa asked.

'I've heard of that college. I'm sorry I don't know much about this area,' the woman replied.

Rupa wandered aimlessly along the busy high street. She passed Marks and Spencer, Woolworths and Allders. Men loaded with shopping bags, women with prams and pushchairs and satchelled school children were pushing towards the car parks, trains and the bus station. Rupa walked down Wellesley Road, she did not know where she was going. A man in a black suit was walking towards the station.

'Is Croydon Tech near here?' Rupa asked reluctantly. He looked at her and smiled. 'Yes, it's only five minutes away. Can you see that Midland Bank, over there with the yellow sign? The tall building next to it is the Croydon Technical College. There's a bookshop by the main entrance as you enter the building, you'll see the enquiries office on your right. You can't miss it. That's where I work.' The man explained then hurried away.

Rupa felt both nervous and excited. She walked past the bank and went up the steps into the college building. An elderly woman sat at reception. She put her gold-framed spectacles on the table and looked at Rupa curiously.

'Can I help you?'

'I'm a foreign student. Can you give me the details for English classes?'

'Do you mean information about English for foreign students, the examinations that are set by the Cambridge board?'

'I think so.' Rupa had never heard of the exams.

'We're enrolling new students over the next fortnight. Can you fill in this application form and return it to this office as soon as possible? You can post it if you like. We'll send you all the details and the timetable, after you get your acceptance.'

Rupa felt relieved in the college atmosphere with its meandering mass of students. She went to the bookshop at the entrance and bought a map of Croydon, Wallington and Sutton. Rupa didn't need to ask anybody the way back and a 109 was stood in the bus station. All the way home, she studied the map of Croydon, noticing nothing, her whole being for that time at least taken over by the prospect of being a student once again.

That evening Rupa waited impatiently for Aruna. The coal fire was sputtering and glowing in the lounge while the convector hummed non-stop in the bedroom. Everywhere in the house the air was warm; outside it was beginning to freeze, the earth and grass had grown white crusts of stubble as the frost settled. Roast chicken and fried veg was laid on the table while the potatoes were browning in the Belling. When Aruna finally opened the door he felt enveloped by the warmth. Rupa was busy in the kitchen wearing a blue checked pinafore with a triumphant smile on her face.

'I could smell your cooking as far as the garage Rupa. I thought it was Mrs. Smith next door cooking their supper.'

'We're having roast dinner tonight, the potatoes will be ready soon.'

'Roast dinner! What are you roasting?'

'We're having chicken, potatoes and fried veg.'

'Lovely! I can see you've done some shopping today.' Aruna

looked at the vegetable rack at the corner of the kitchen and said 'Aubergines! Where on earth did you buy them?'

'Chandra came here this morning. She brought us some food for dinner. There's a cake in the bread bin, she baked it last night.' Aruna opened the purple plastic bread bin and there was the fruitcake with marzipan and icing on top.

'Did she come on her own?'

'Yes, she'd taken half a day off and she came to see me.'

'I don't know how she manages to do all these things, cooking, baking, visiting and working,' Aruna said.

They sat down for dinner. Rupa was unusually chatty.

'Goodness me Rupa! You look so happy tonight. I can't believe the difference Chandra's visit has made to you.'

'I've something to tell you. I went to Croydon by bus.'

'Did you go with Chandra?'

'No, on my own! I went to Croydon Tech. They gave me an application form. I'll have to post it tomorrow.'

The whole time they were eating Rupa talked avidly about her future studies and her bus journey.

'That's a good idea Rupa. I realise you get lonely after I go to work. You'll feel better when you're busy. When are they starting the classes?'

'In four weeks' time. They're short of students so I don't think it's going to be a problem for me.'

Aruna felt a great sense of relief because Rupa had finally found something to do, but as the days went on and her talk of studying became something of an obsession he began to wonder about their future together.

THIRTEEN

How many years had gone by since Rupa had been a student? She tried to work it out. Searching her memory, blotting out the last three years. She remembered the days and evenings she had spent with Kumara with a poignant melancholy. She started the one-year English course at Croydon Tech with glowing delight. The four-mile journey from home was not a problem for her. Some days she travelled by train, some days she went by bus. She had a flexible timetable and went to some day and some evening classes. Rupa's lifestyle changed suddenly. When Aruna came home Rupa had sometimes gone to college and the house was cold.

Aruna had to do some extra work at home, light the coal fire or move the large metal bin to the pathway so that the dustbin men could empty the rubbish on Wednesday mornings. Rupa made sure there was some food in the fridge or in the oven; if Aruna came home feeling hungry he could always find something to eat. Some days Aruna went to meet Rupa straight from work and they brought some fish and chips. The oily cod or over-sized sausages with soggy chunky chips wrapped in newspaper saved Rupa the trouble of cooking and washing-up. The tense atmosphere had gone and they enjoyed each other's company on those cold evenings.

At college Rupa studied English, British Institutions and the British Way of Life. The last topic interested her most, how English people live, their social customs, food, clothes and their 'classless' class system. She realised that people who lived in other European countries had a life style in many ways different to the British. Rupa's tutor was Christopher Hunter, a tall Yorkshireman with a moustache. Hunter's sense of humour and his fluency attracted Rupa on the very first day. His voice echoed with the tinge of a Yorkshire accent, touching Rupa deeply. Hunter seemed to have a great dislike of the South in general and for Londoners in particular. When he described the relaxed life style and the friendly neighbours in the North, Rupa listened to him like a dog listening to his master's voice. The course was meant for all foreign students. There were Germans, French, Polish and South Americans but Rupa was the only Asian in the class.

Day by day Rupa secretly enjoyed the growing intimacy with her tutor. It was only a seed, which has to be sown and to grow in her mind, a hidden wild flower open to the sun and fading away unknown and unseen. Would it ever become a flood in a hurricane, or a seabed earthquake? Was it an all night dream to be followed by a dawn of despair?

'Many people who migrate to England want to stay in crowded London. They don't know about the other towns and cities. People in the north live in a caring community and there is plenty of open space for children to play. Working in coal mines, in weaving mills and in iron and steel foundries is very hard. I must stress that there is a growing problem in the industrial towns like Halifax where unemployment is beginning to bite, factories are closing down for good. When we were young we played with children who lived in the nearby streets. We used to walk miles and miles along country lanes breathing in fresh air and climbing the hills. We played ball games in disused railway yards until dark when our mothers called us for supper. Children who grow up in London don't have this wonderful freedom unless they belong to rich families. Whatever the problems they have the southerners still prefer to live in their stressful uncaring society. That morose looking man, who sat next to you in the train this morning burdened with his own problems, how typical he is! We talk, we smile and we help others. If a breathless old man is running to catch a bus, the driver doesn't speed away as fast as he can, he stops and waits. Someone will give him a helping hand while others offer him a seat. I've never seen that kind of friendliness in London.'

Rupa was astonished to hear Hunter's story.

It was 'discussion day' in Rupa's class. Anyone could talk about anything. Hunter expected the students to discuss aspects of social life and the culture of their own countries. The French talked of their vast cultural heritage while the South Americans earnestly lectured the others on the history of Maya Civilisation and contrasted it with the current problem of vast numbers living in shanty towns. The Germans tended to boast about their 'economic miracle' and complain vociferously about the division between East and West Germany. Rupa talked about arranged marriages, the caste system and the place of women in Eastern society. Finally it was question time.

'I always thought everybody in England had the same arrogant attitude to 'lesser beings', the stuck-up way they keep themselves to themselves. If they do deign to speak they're so boring, forever going on about holidays or how much they've blown on kitchen extensions! Why can't they just be friendly? If I face my next door lady in the street or in the back garden she's either late for work or late from work. Sometimes if we walk on the same side of the pavement she crosses the road double quick to avoid me! She's some kind of office manageress. I still feel very insecure living in England. Do you really mean what you say Mr Hunter, I mean about the North being friendlier?'

'You seem to be a bit confused Rupa. It takes time to make sense of all these impressions. You've got to live in a society for a while, experience takes time to accumulate and evaluate properly.'

A Polish student interrupted.

'I agree with Rupa, English people are arrogant. They regard the Royal family as an asset to the country and they're still proud of the British Empire, even though it's on its way out. If working class people live in such poverty, why do they spend such a lot of money keeping the Royal family in palaces and yachts and polo ponies?' Everybody laughed including Hunter. Czernowski, a passionate Pole, warmed to his theme.

'I think the time will come to reform these centuries old institutions. I've no special objections to the Royal family but when you contrast their lives with those of the men who work down the mine, covering themselves in grime and with all the dangers of gas and collapsing shafts they have to work so hard for so little! At the end of the day they have to wash all the dirt away and nobody begrudges them their beer! If you are born in an aristocratic family you know nothing about the struggles of the poor just to survive, but they are the same flesh and blood as the rest of society. It's nice to see a member of the Royal family about on a special occasion but society will change in the end.' Hunter nodded his assent and wound up the discussion.

Rupa's fear gradually faded. She enjoyed her vibrant student life style and at times even forgot she was married to Aruna. She learned how people who live in different parts of the country speak in a wide range of dialects. Customs had changed little for decades in the more far-flung areas of the country. Women from the South dressed fashionably, working in offices and spending their money on expensive household gadgets and holidays abroad but most women in the North remained housewives and left the bread winning to their husbands. There were about three to four children in the average northern family. During the summer holidays the children who lived in back-to-back terrace houses played in the narrow back streets, while mothers watched them with the baby in the pram outside.

Hunter regaled the class with his tales of the North and they listened spellbound.

Most of the foreign students who had come to England for further studies had found accommodation and colleges around London. Rupa noticed that some of the Asians who had settled in the early sixties had established their own business while Africans and West Indians were stuck in relatively low-paid employment. The friendly atmosphere in Croydon Tech made Rupa feel more secure, her nostalgia and isolation lessened as the weeks went by.

The Friday evening class was not popular among most students. They preferred to meet a friend in a pub for a drink with fish and chips or a 'Ploughman's Lunch'.

Fine rain turned the settled snow into slippery slush. When Rupa arrived at seven she was the only student in the class. Hunter sat reading 'The Guardian'. Rupa was wearing her red duffel coat and a green knitted scarf, her shoulder bag full of books. She walked in with a strange uneasy feeling and they exchanged smiles. The cold wind blew along the interminable corridors and the doors to the classrooms had to be kept tight shut.

'Are we having the class today Mr Hunter?'

'The weather's not good. I had hoped that at least a few people might turn up. Perhaps we'll have a short lesson and let everyone go home early.'

Rupa took off her damp coat and hung it up in the cloakroom. She handed over her essay 'Remembering my own country' and Hunter corrected it on the spot. The room seemed filled with an eerie silence, Rupa tried to read a page in the textbook but her mind refused to focus. Hunter called her. Rupa moved her chair and sat next to his desk, feeling her heart beating.

'I'm very pleased with your essay Rupa. You've pointed out very clearly the cultural values of the East as you see them. I've always admired politeness and hospitality, the best qualities of the East. Women there have an especial beauty of their own. Their long flowing dark hair, beautiful faces soaked in the tropical sun, midnight blue eyes and fragile smiles are quite unforgettable. There are a lot of Asian families living in Leeds and Bradford but sadly the new generation, their sons and daughters, often grow up influenced by corrupt Western values. I suppose it's inevitable. When these Eastern women come out of their front door wearing rainbow coloured saris, deep velvet salwars, glittering bangles and gold necklaces I feel an immediate sense of celebration. Rupa you have these qualities and I hope you'll never try blindly to become westernised. You've got rock hard determination and that's what you need to survive in the West.' As he looked at her she blushed. Then she looked down to avoid any eye contact. She felt as if she had fallen from a star. She was quite unaware of her desperation when he touched her. She felt numb and then a bubbling pain in her mind covered her vision. For a moment they were very close to each other, his wet lips, her soft skin; she felt distracted by his hypnotic power.

A minute later three more students arrived. Hunter finished the class early. Rupa couldn't believe that he was attracted to Eastern women and their culture.

Drizzling rain had turned to powdery snow mixed with flakes. Through the snow-washed glowing darkness Rupa went home that evening feeling like a bird which had lost its sense of direction. By the time Rupa arrived home the fallen snow on the pavements had begun to freeze.

'You're early today Rupa, there was a mile long traffic jam and I only just got back.'

Aruna was busy trying to light the fire, kneeling on the hearth, moving the coal with a poker, his hands covered with coal dust.

'The weather's getting worse, not many students turned up so Hunter sent us home early.'

Rupa went upstairs carrying her heavy bag wet with snow. As she took off her coat she felt the sudden cold air of the bedroom and started shivering. She rushed to the kitchen, opened the wall cupboard, then the fridge, twice shut the larder door loudly. Rupa made a quick meal, fried noodles with pork and eventually the house began to warm up. She was quieter than usual and Aruna didn't fail to pick up on her changed mood.

'I just can't believe the difference since you started going to college, Rupa. You don't complain about loneliness anymore or about anything else. No more tears of homesickness either. It makes me feel better I'm not guilt-ridden anymore if I'm late home from work.'

Rupa began to speak English with some self confidence: to the old Irishman at the greengrocer's, to the middle aged postman who had moved south after twenty year's work in a northern quarry, to the Scottish milkman who rang the doorbell early every Saturday morning to collect his week's money. They spoke a kind of English which, no-one easily understands, not even the natives, Rupa realised.

Whatever else occupied Rupa's mind her thoughts kept returning to Hunter, to the kind of man he was, even his dress habits. Hunter seemed to prefer denims and short-sleeved check shirts. He wore a woollen pullover and a dark overcoat on cold days and Rupa had never seen him wear a suit. She remembered their moments of closeness and a secret glow brightened her whole being.

A year had gone by and summer came with its long hot days. It was the end of term and Hunter was leaving to start a new job the following term as a lecturer in English at Leeds University. Rupa felt like the young student of centuries ago in the East, who had to stay with his teacher until he finished his education and by then be fluent in six languages. Those students had to begin long hazardous journeys home, days and weeks of eating wild fruit and carrying their drinking water in gourds, the hollowed out marrow-shaped dried vegetables.

On the last day of term, when Rupa went to wish him goodbye, she remembered her last day with Kumara. She stood by Hunter in silence but with tears in her eyes. When he looked at her she saw a deep sunken sadness on his face.

FOURTEEN

Slowly the weeks withered in moments of despair and melancholy. Dikwelle Hamine watched the calendar on the wall. Although it was the first week in April, the front page on the calendar had yellowed with dust and cobwebs and still showed January. She tore off the first three pages and April shone with a gloss of scarlet blossoms on leafless native trees. She remembered it was only two weeks before the Sinhalese New Year and now it was three years since she had seen her daughter. Dikwelle Hamine walked down the front steps and looked at the hedgerow behind the paddy fields. The hum of the New Year was in the air and the red blossoms had opened to the evening sky. Buzzing bees colonised the mango tree quilted with large clusters of small yellow flowers perfumed with musk. With her hand she swept away the dust and sat on the cement step.

'Soon the honey mangoes will ripen and another New Year will pass without my seeing Rupa. She says nothing in her letters about making a visit home.' Dikwelle Hamine sighed. The crisp blue airmail letters from England came every week at first but then less often.

The nights bright with stars flowed towards Maha Gedara from every direction. The heavy rain, which had poured down for days, had finally stopped and solid black trees canopied the still sky. Slowly the sun departed leaving the emerald blue of the hills covered in a thin veil of tropical mist. With a golden glow the white canal coiled round the shadowed fields. Loku Mahatmaya was wearing a short-sleeved shirt and a faded blue towelling cloth over his shoulders to shield him from the sharp wind. His body seemed to shrink with age, his skin wrinkled with darkening veins. He looked at the sky, his watery eyes trying to pick out the

'Milky Way'. Finally he looked at his wife who was sat on the step anchoring her chin on her right palm in a stalwart silence.

'The storm moved to the north east today. It said on the wireless that there was a cyclone in the Bay of Bengal sweeping towards Ceylon. There have been floods and villagers left homeless while families with all their herds were swept away like dried coconut husks in a hundred and sixty miles an hour wind. Everyone in the post office and in the grocery shop is talking about it. There are news bulletins all the time on the wireless bringing more bad news.'

Dikwelle Hamine abruptly switched her attention to her husband but stayed silent. A flock of mina birds flew over their heads and she felt the air move as they flew to their nests over the darkening horizon.

Tilakawathie walked down the path with an aluminium pail in her hand to draw some water from the well, her long shadow following her.

'I had this strange feeling that they weren't going to come back as quickly as they said. After all it's their life and it doesn't matter what they do as long as they sort themselves out,' said Loku Mahatmaya, plucking an overgrown mimosa from under the jasmine bush. He stared at the thorny weed with its pink flowers, then threw it aside.

'We're getting older and this house is too big for us. After Rupa had gone abroad I expected Rukmali to come home more often, but she seems to be coming less and less. I know she has got to do a job and look after that child but I hope at least they'll come to see us on New Year's Day.' Dikwelle Hamine sighed again.

'You're right, Rukmali's so busy and that child is always sick. First whooping cough, then measles and now a cold. They only believe in English medicines and they spend a fortune on them. Can't they try some native herbal medicines? They're quite harmless and soothing. I must visit them in a day or two. Usually they're at home on Saturdays unless they've taken the child to the doctor's. There's a bottle of honey in the cupboard upstairs. Remind me to take it when I go. Ginger and honey's good for coughs.' Loku

Mahatmaya pulled another handful of weeds and began to make a pile in the corner of a flowerbed.

On the top of the calendar it said 'ABN Drapery Stores Matara' in gold edged lettering. They received one every year. When Rupa was away at college Dikwelle Hamine used to mark the holidays in red ink.

The following morning Loku Mahatmaya and Dikwelle Hamine went to the ABN Stores to do the New Year's shopping. It was a small shop in a parade, no bigger than a corner shop in England with floor to ceiling glass cabinets and long glass topped tables where the owner could open out great rolls of fabric and display them to customers. The shop was full of brilliantly coloured fabrics with the latest designs, 'Lady Hamilton', crepe georgette, Manipur and Cashmere silk saris, lace and taffeta gowns. The shopkeeper welcomed them with a wide smile.

'Just the right day you had decided to come here, Loku Mahatmaya, our New Year stock only arrived this morning. Do please take a seat, Dikwelle Hamine.' He pointed her towards a chair.

Dikwelle Hamine, wearing a green sari and a pearl necklace, sat and waited for the shopkeeper to show her the latest line in saris. A minute later his son came in bearing a silver tray with a bottle of 'Elephant' brand portello and two fine blue glasses. She accepted a glass of the purple drink. Dikwelle Hamine always wore imported silk saris and lace blouses on special occasions but she preferred cotton saris at home.

'This is a top brand! Only forty rupees a yard, of course I'll give you a good discount.' The shopkeeper pulled out some lace material with a white floral pattern and spread it on the table.

'Make it three yards then,' said Dikwelle Hamine.

She added some dress materials for Tilakawathie and a pink cotton blouse with white lace edgings for Rupa, just in case she paid a sudden visit. All the poorer neighbours who helped the Maha Gedara family got some kind of clothing as New Year presents. As they came out of the shop there was a procession and the streets were filled with the incessant hooting of the cars, jammed bullock-carts, blaring of drums, tablas and flutes, clowns, puppets and native dancers. The New Year celebrations had already begun.

On New Year's Eve Dikwelle Hamine put some milk rice, sweets, fruit and king coconut water on a table decorated with coconut flowers and left the store room window open overnight. At night she lay awake listening to the sounds of the wind, swooping bats and pouncing owls, imagining they were the wing-beats of angels. New Year's Day was quiet. Rukmali and her family came briefly and stayed for lunch, but they had to go back early because Damit was poorly yet again.

'I hope one day Rupa and Aruna will come back and live in this enormous house,' Dikwelle Hamine said to her husband as she opened her ebony wardrobe to hide away Rupa's unopened New Year gift. The fragrance of sandalwood scented pot-pourri poured out, filling the entire room.

During the last few years, the situation at Maha Gedara had changed, clearly showing signs of their struggle to survive. The Agricultural Land Reformation Act had become effective giving the rice farmers more rights than ever before, the landowners being allowed a proportionately smaller share of the crops.

'It's just not fair. These rice lands are ours and we've inherited them from our ancestors. Now the government is trying to grab them from us and give them away to someone else. Years and years of good relationships between landowners and farmers seem to have come to an end and now its business, nothing but business! Even in the days when we had British governors we always had some kind of justice.' Loku Mahatmaya was furious but resigned. He had decided to keep the larger part of his rice land for himself and have the work done by paid workers without a tenant farmer but this meant he had to spend a long time involved with farming. Sowing, growing and reaping became a part of their daily life and at those busy times Dikwelle Hamine, Tilakawathie and the next door woman, Ranhami, made a mid-day meal and also made afternoon tea with biscuits for everyone who helped in the paddy fields. Huge earthenware pots and copper pans were used in cooking. Afterwards pots full of delicious food covered in banana leaves were carried off to the fields by strong men. A meal with boiled rice, fish curry and vegetables was served and they all sat under the shade of a breadfruit tree and tucked into their mid-day meal while the sun burned relentlessly in the cloudless sky. In Loku Mahatmaya's memory everything was done by the farmer and his family. The Land Law unreformed for centuries and the social customs that went with it were beginning to change, some disappearing altogether. The daily life of the village, unaltered for centuries, came under threat and Loku Mahatmaya found it hard to accept that it was no longer the world he had always known.

Loku Mahatmaya remembered when the rice lands were looked after by stocky middle-aged farmers, whose help was invaluable, especially through the difficulties of the annual harvest. The new crop was brought into the house at an 'auspicious time', after the rice was measured in the fields and the farmer's share handed over. It was a day of celebration when everybody smiled. There was a palm thatched hut in a corner of the fields, the floor covered with straw, with a beautifully woven mat on top. A temporary shelter built by the farmer to protect him from the sun while he tended the growing crop and at night it kept off wild boars and rabbits. Scarecrows stood amid the stalks waving in the wind and frightened away the parrots which came in waves of multicoloured rain to eat the ripening rice.

On the last day of harvesting the farmer's wife or his mother gave everyone a treat. She boiled a huge clay pot full of water over a log fire and made tea in it offering it to everyone in enamel mugs with sweets, treacle cakes, jaggery, cashew nuts and bananas. Under the tropical sun everyone supped the strong black tea and shared the relief of another harvest home. The refreshing smell of drying hay blew across the fields and filled the sky from end to end.

When Podi Appu the old farmer retired after working for forty-five years in the paddy fields belonging to the Maha Gedara family, Loku Mahatmaya reluctantly agreed to pass on the tenancy to Podi Appu's eldest son, Sira. The old system of trust was changing: when the tenant farmers were ready to retire, by tradition the tenancy passed to their eldest sons but those were the days when everyone clamoured for the passing on of tenancies to be backed by the force of law. In this case Loku Mahatmaya knew that to allow things to take their natural course would be a disaster. Sira was lazy and vain and a chronic alcoholic to boot.

'All he does is guzzle that toxic home brew, smoke marijuana and talk about the next general election, insulting land owners and swearing at everybody. The other day I met Sira in the street. He was so drunk he could hardly stand up. The postmaster told me that Sira was boasting about the vast rice lands he'd just inherited.' Loku Mahatmaya was anxious and Dikwelle Hamine tried to calm him.

'Don't go over the top about that young man! He's notorious, a loud mouth that no one in the village likes! I feel sorry for his family with four kids; you know Sira's wife's heavily pregnant again and she must feed those little mouths, at least with some rice porridge.' Two weeks later it was with relief that the village greeted the news that Sira had been killed in a drunken knife fight.

Maha Gedara was situated on the nipple of a small hill and there was a narrow orange road at the bottom, parallel to a canal that stretched to the nearby village. The road meandered through coconut, cinnamon, rubber and rice lands for about a mile, finally joining the tarmacced main road, which ran to the small town five miles away. About a quarter of a mile distant from Maha Gedara began the rain forest, layered with large and small tropical plants and undergrowth, self-seeding jackfruit and mango trees growing in the wilderness. A fresh-water stream flowed through the valley with emerald rocks and rows and rows of bamboo lining the banks. The stream supplied water to many of the villagers. There was a small dam, which directed the water to the rice fields. 'The White Sand Valley' was an area in the middle of the forest where a hidden footpath led to a village some distance away. The whole area was covered in lustrous silver sand and marble rocks that shone in the sun like great diamonds. Goraka was a species of fruit tree that grew wild in the area. The sour green fruit with juicy segments turn deep red or orange-yellow when ripe. The segments were dried in the hot sun and used as an ingredient for cooked fish, the flavour being rather like tamarind. Bats, giant red-necked squirrels, grinning monkeys, together with the wind and rain combined to drop these fruits to the ground. During the season it was a common scene in the mornings for glamorous women, after a swim in the stream, to collect the fallen fruits in their wicker baskets and emerge from the white path into the deepening sunlight. Their dark knee-length hair blew in the meadow-swept wind, heavily scented with wild flowers. During the day the birds sang on the wild banana and mango trees and at night the same trees provided a paradise for bats and owls. Fireflies circled in the darkness. At sunrise the night bats hid from the daylight and slept on fruit trees, their heads swinging down.

During recent years, under the government's rural development scheme, the rain forest was destroyed and pine trees planted. The thirsty new roots grew quickly, absorbing the dampness of the earth and soon all the underground springs had dried up, leaving only a trickle of water in the stream. Although the monsoon rain filled the canal soon it was all gone again. When the dry season arrived the earth's crust began to split and crumble, turning the grasslands yellow.

Dikwelle Hamine grew vegetables in a small plot attached to the Maha Gedara gardens. April showers were on time that year and she watched her aubergines, sweet potatoes, artichokes and runner beans grow with their lush green foliage. Then came the thundery rain, followed with masses of edible mushrooms appearing everywhere, their heads pushing through the cracks, making a pockmarked valley. Dikwelle Hamine's home-grown vegetables were more than enough for the needs of the Maha Gedara family and their neighbours. On Fridays some stallholders from the village market came to buy vegetables. What money she earned from selling her crop Dikwelle Hamine collected in a moneybox, an old English Crawford biscuit tin decorated with the faded picture of a kilted Highlander playing the bagpipes.

Dikwelle Hamine and Loku Mahatmaya never missed their yearly visit to Dondra Fair. First they went to the Buddhist temple in Dondra and then they went on to the fair. It was a huge annual gathering, attended by thousands from all over the country. The night before Dikwelle Hamine emptied the moneybox and counted out all the copper and silver coins. There were circles and parades of stalls filled with pins, buttons, toys, cutlery and crockery, incense, moth-balls, socks and pants for girls and boys. Fruits, nuts, hats and mugs, cobblers, barbers, tailors, sweet soft candyfloss, ice cream and rainbow coloured balloons. Musical chairs, singing, smiling, buying, selling, calling and whistling; jingling bells and dancing women. Sounds from the milling crowd reached the clouds, echoing and re-echoing to amuse the sky-gods.

Rupa was only seven when she went for the first time with her parents to Dondra Fair. Rupa's father bought a delicate red rose made of crab shells, which she wore on her hair. When they passed a toy stall Rupa stopped and started crying for a squeaky rubber doll with deep blue eyes. All she had at home was a worn and torn rag doll. With a wink, the stallholder gave her a six-inch plastic doll to stop her crying but one leg was missing. When Rupa asked for some treacle sweets her mother said, 'You mustn't eat sweets sold on these open stalls, you'll get tummy ache.' Dikwelle Hamine spent all her money on aluminium pots and pans. When they went home Rupa's friend Dingihami waited at the gate with a sunflower smile. Rupa gave her an egg shaped balloon and played with her new mouth organ. The green balloon burst then Dingihami cried. They made a bamboo stick flute and played on the moonlit sand, using the fields, the valley and the meadows as an open air theatre. Rupa's excitement kept her awake and it was hours before she finally slept. At midnight the evening goddess appeared in a shiny silk dress with a golden train, a diamond and ruby hair band and a harp in her hand. Rupa and Dingihami sang under the stars and danced hand-in-hand. The dusky pink bangles of the goddess, the sounds of their melodies mixed with the waves and the tides filled the night sky to the Milky Way. When Rupa woke up in the morning her rag doll was lying next to her pillow. There was a small parcel on the table wrapped in brown paper. She opened it and was amazed to find a blue tin of 'Evening in Paris' talcum powder and a soft toy dog. She smiled to see these gifts from her father and dabbed some talcum on her face, the fragrance filling her whole being. She wore her red rose with her hair clip and her eyes gleamed.

FIFTEEN

Dikwelle Hamine slowly finished her cup of tea and placed the empty cup on the bedside table. The window was open and the peacocks had already started to dance on the woodapple tree to the song of the rising sun. With difficulty she got up holding her stick, hobbling across the room and then sank into an armchair. She heard Tilakawathie scraping coconut in the kitchen. The sound of the coconut scraper came in short bursts like cutting a tree with a handsaw. Tilakawathie was making hoppers for breakfast. Loku Mahatmaya came back from feeding the cow and calf with fresh meadow grass.

'I feel exhausted. I've no energy to do that kind of work any more; going to the vegetable garden first thing in the morning, working there for a couple of hours, weeding or staking runner beans. Those aubergine and chilli plants need so much attention.' Dikwelle Hamine looked at her husband, her eyes pale.

'It's pointless and you're silly trying to do all these things when you're ill. You must realise we are getting old and you should go back to bed and rest. Let the onions and beans grow on their own' Loku Mahatmaya said.

Dikwelle Hamine was chronically exhausted. Sometimes she slept all day and then she couldn't sleep at night, waking up at midnight and staring at the night sky for hour after hour. The smell of food made her feel sick. She imagined a detritus of rotten vegetables, decaying fish and maggot-infested meat. Her round face and plump body had thinned into a series of sharp wrinkles. Her sleeping habits changed, her eyes were watery and droopy. Within a few weeks Dikwelle Hamine had turned to a skeleton. She refused to go near the kitchen and kept the bedroom windows closed. Tilakawathie was left to do the housework and cooking.

alone. The vegetable plot had been abandoned to stinging nettles. Bindweed twined among the runner beans and flowered along the fence. The cow managed to get through the broken stile and trampled the banana plants. Monitors and iguanas made colonies in the undergrowth of mimosa, bracken and sweet potatoes. Loku Mahatmaya was baffled by his wife's strange illness.

An Ayurvedic physician was called who treated patients with herbs and applications of oils and ointments. Loku Mahatmaya's summons was urgent but he readily accepted the diagnosis.

'It's only irritable rheumatism, not to worry Loku Mahatmaya but there seems to be a slight problem of unbalanced wind, bile and phlegm. That's why the patient is off her food. Dikwelle Hamine will be back on her feet soon.'

He prescribed several medications, an arishta, a fermented concoction of liquidised herbal ingredients, sugar and honey and peyava, a herbal powder that contained fourteen different herbs mixed with hot water. The news of Dikwelle Hamine's illness spread through the village like a bush-fire and the villagers poured in to Maha Gedara offered helping hands while others prayed for her recovery. They helped in the making up of herbal mixtures and drinks as instructed by the physician. Roasted coriander, ginger, liquorice, cumin and several other herbs had to be ground with a six sided herbal grinding stone, while someone else had to boil twelve types of dried herbs in a large earthenware pot to prepare a concentrated liquid. In spite of all efforts Dikwelle Hamine showed no sign of improvement, withdrawing completely and refusing to speak to anyone.

'What's the point in just writing an occasional letter? Rupa lives at the other end of the world and I want to see my daughter again,' she muttered. Day by day her condition worsened and she groaned in pain. The swelling which had begun on her toe spread along her legs and the physician was called back. Loku Mahatmaya was confused.

'The patient has to be bathed in herbal water. She's got all the symptoms of rheumatism with a weakened blood condition. Plenty of mandarins and pomegranate juice, thin rice porridge and herbal medicines will clear the system. The oils must be gently massaged on to the skin. Within a few days of taking the newly prescribed arishta the symptoms should disappear like dew under the sun.' The physician was confident and beamed as though he could resurrect the dead. Everybody in the village started talking about some kind of evil spirit cast on Maha Gedara, with Dikwelle Hamine the last victim and Rupa the first.

It was Rukmali's idea that a magic ritual spell of 'Huniyam' or a devil dance should be performed to get rid of the evil spirits. A Huniyam 'cutting ceremony' and devil dance were organised. 'Huniyam Yaka', the demon who cast the bad spell, held a burning torch in one hand and a sword in the other. He rode a scarlet horse and held a blood-viper between his teeth, which dripped blood down his chin and cheeks. The demon coiled several snakes round his waist and shaded his head with a venomous hooded cobra. The ceremony was elaborate and various sacrifices had to be offered to the demon. The magician tried very carefully to exorcise the spell without causing harm to the patient. At the final stage he stood in water and cut an ash pumpkin. It was believed that if the magical ritual was properly performed and the bad spell was 'cut' there would be blood stains at the heart of the pumpkin, proving the bad spirit had at last departed, having accepted the sacrifice.

The devil dancing ceremony was even more decorative and elaborate. A marquee was erected with a circular arena in the centre. The hall was festooned with coconut and areca nut flowers, betel leaves, yellow pineapples and the core of a banana tree. It was a non-stop dusk-to-dawn performance with the beating of demon drums and loud melodies on the flute. The audience was served with tea, coffee, biscuits and sweets. Dikwelle Hamine lay on a mattress overlooking the arena. The priest was the principal performer and wore a costume of red and white. He chanted Buddhist hymns for several hours amidst flares, flames and the incense fumes, which lit up the arena and perfumed the air. The priest begged all demons to appear on stage, eighteen in all. The beating of the drums ended and after a few minutes silence the priest called out the demons. They erupted in a fury and with a tumultuous blaring of drums. The staccato beating increased until the audience was deafened. The first demon suddenly jumped from behind the screen wearing a mask with long teeth and sporting a red costume. He wore a scarlet garland with a string of bells and more bells on his ankles that tinkled when he circled round the arena, laughing with the audience. Then he began to dance to the rhythm of the drum, spinning round and round, leaping high in the air. When he left the stage the second demon appeared and then all the eighteen demons jumped and danced into the arena in their distinctive costumes of green, blue, gold, yellow, orange and purple, all handcrafted with peacock feathers, beads, sequins, silver and gold bands. Each demon carried a particular object, a pot of red-hot coals, a burning flare, blood red flowers, a human skeleton or steaming joss sticks. Finally the priest confronted the demon that had entered the body of Dikwelle Hamine. The demon demanded a human sacrifice and the priest refused angrily. They argued for a few minutes in a musical dialogue, kneeling, shouting, name calling and dancing. At last the demon accepted the offerings of cooked food, sweets and fruits and promised to leave. A wicker tray of food on a triangular stand was left outside the compound. Through the night air came the hoot of the departing demon, accompanied by a mounting crescendo of snapping twigs and the performance ended only when the sun rose.

'I think it's time to take our mother to a doctor in Matara. Everything we've done so far has been a complete waste of time. I don't trust that Ayurvedic physician or his medicines. I am worried mother is very ill.'

Loku Mahatmaya agreed with Rukmali so they made arrangements very quickly. Soon the news spread and the neighbours gathered. With the help of several people but still with difficulty they managed to carry Dikwelle Hamine to the waiting car. As it drove slowly away the neighbours watched in silence. During the twelve mile journey Rukmali spoke only a few words. Loku Mahatmaya stared at the narrow tarmacced roads, the black trees and the darkening clouds. Dikwelle Hamine lay very still. Heavy rain curtained the windscreen and made the driver stop several times. Rukmali sat next to her mother, her mind hollow and empty. The fields at the side of the main road were bursting with turbid water.

When they arrived at Dr. Wickrama's surgery the rain had stopped and the sky cleared. Loku Mahatmaya trembled, not knowing what was to happen. He felt as if he would collapse. The smell of disinfectant crept into his nostrils, bringing tears to his eyes. Two nurses carried Dikwelle Hamine on a stretcher into a ward. Dr. Wickrama was never still, tending to patients who sat on wooden chairs and benches, marking their footprints on the dusty cement floor, waiting for their number to be called. Loku Mahatmaya sat in a corner and listened to the broken voices and the passing wheel chairs. The waiting room was packed, the air filled with whispering and the rattle of instruments on passing trolleys.

'The doctor's not there, he's had to attend an emergency. A critically ill patient has just been admitted,' a raised middle-aged voice commented through the chaos of the waiting room. Loku Mahatmaya imagined there would be a red alert and that he would have to admit himself or that he would collapse in the waiting room and die on the spot. He stretched his legs, putting his arms into a death-like posture, his hands on his chest and his eyes closed. A few minutes later he realised he was still breathing.

The doctor examined Dikwelle Hamine, who seemed even weaker, her hands and legs ice cold. Her blood pressure stayed high, her pulse was fast and irregular. She was given an injection and put on a saline drip. Dr. Wickrama alerted a nurse to make sure the patient was undisturbed. Dikwelle Hamine moved her lips and tried to say something but instead she fell into a deep sleep.

Although Rukmali was there, Dr. Wickrama motioned to Loku Mahatmaya alone.

'How long has she been ill?'

'Just four weeks'

'What have you been doing all this time?'

'An Ayurvedic physician gave her medicines and oils. We also had a devil dance ceremony to get rid of the evil spirits troubling her.'

'Your wife's very ill. I've just given her a couple of injections. We'll see how she is in a little while. We also have to do some blood and urine tests, her blood pressure's high.'

'How long she's going to be here, doctor?'

'It's difficult to say at the moment.'

'Please make her well again soon doctor,' begged Loku Mahatmaya with tears in his eyes.

'She's comfortable, I'll let her sleep.'

A few hours later Dikwelle Hamine had not woken and there was a green tag on her door.

'Nil by mouth/Do not disturb.'

'You should go home and try to get some sleep father. I'll stay the night if necessary. Mother is comfortable now and she'll sleep for a long time.' Rukmali said to Loku Mahatmaya as he rubbed his weary eyes. Loku Mahatmaya found it almost impossible to leave. He was scared and confused like a bird that had lost its feathers. A sudden pain, piercing as a needle, started at the back of his neck, penetrated his head then spread through his body. He kept blaming himself for not taking his wife to the hospital earlier. He was haunted by the doctor's words 'Your wife is very ill.'

It was just after midnight when Loku Mahatmaya opened the door to find a chimney lamp flickering on the lounge table. Tilakawathie and Ranhami the next-door woman had fallen asleep. He walked into the room where Rupa used to study and noticed the books on the table covered with a layer of dust.

'Why haven't we tidied up this table?' he wondered and took up a book. The bookmark fell on to the floor. 'Education for Wisdom' was printed in red on the thin cardboard strip. A tear fell from his eyes and dropped on the page. He went to the bedroom where his wife had lain for the last few weeks. The warm smell that lasted for forty years was there, impregnating every fibre from floor to ceiling. Soon an echoing emptiness possessed Maha Gedara and the bedroom. Sooty, the black and white cat, was sleeping contentedly on the bed. She jumped down and started to miaow, purring at his feet. The continuous tapping of an owl on the roof tiles shook Loku Mahatmaya. He remembered the 'demons and evil spirit.'

In the middle lounge at Maha Gedara was a bed by the window. It was covered with a reed mat with an all-over purple design, only recently woven by Dikwelle Hamine. The women who visited her when she was ill used to sit there looking concerned. Tilakawathie had left some food and a flask of coffee on the dining room table before she went to bed. Loku Mahatmaya drank some coffee but did not feel like eating anything. Listening to the endless tapping and flapping of the owl he lay on the bed until he fell asleep.

He saw a beautiful woman dressed in white, her face covered by a veil standing outside by the open window with a betel tray in her hand. A gleaming smile was on her face; she offered the tray to Loku Mahatmaya. As he tried to pick up a betel leaf from the tray he saw a coiled snake hissing in the centre. The betel leaves suddenly turned into blood red verbena flowers. The woman removed her snow white veil. Her face was red, her teeth black and she wore a garland of scarlet hibiscus. Loku Mahatmaya realised she was a witch and ordered her away. The woman disappeared. Loku Mahatmaya was awake now but he had forgotten where he was. He listened to the chiming wall clock. It was five and the birds had begun to sing. The arrival of another day came with the cock crowing. Was his nightmare some warning of his wife's impending death? Terror shook Loku Mahatmaya like a sapling in a storm. He packed a leather bag with Dikwelle Hamine's hospital clothing, his hands shaking. Night dresses, bed jackets, sheets, towels – a couple of each should do. A pair of slippers, a comb, a mirror, talc and some underwear.

'If Dikwelle Hamine had died during the night there would be no need for all this!' Loku Mahatmaya thought. Then he emptied the bag and packed just a couple of white sheets in case they had to cover her corpse.

'I'll pack the bag. You go and get ready,' said Tilakawathie and Loku Mahatmaya felt relieved.

When they arrived at the hospital the atmosphere seemed normal, smiling nurses, busy doctors and breakfast time. The smell of porridge, coffee and disinfectant lingered along the corridors. During the night Dikwelle Hamine had been transferred to the

Intensive Care Unit. She lay on a bed, her body covered with a white sheet, her eyes closed. A nurse tried to moisten her dry lips with a liquid, which dripped down her cheeks. Tearfully they watched the saline drip hooked into a vein. Rukmali, pregnant with her second baby, was exhausted.

Within three days Dikwelle Hamine showed some signs of improvement. Her chipolata-like fingers and swollen legs gradually went down and wrinkles appeared. She was diagnosed as having some complex kidney problem. On the fifth day she was well enough to sit up in bed.

'I feel I've risen from the dead,' Dikwelle Hamine said to her husband.

'God bless you. Perhaps you can come home soon. The rice fields are flowering orange and the cow has given birth to a beautiful ginger calf who dances on the meadows.' The villagers believed rice flowering with large orange blossoms was a sign of prosperity. It would take a long time for Dikwelle Hamine to fully recover. Her eyes were sunken and her face was pale. 'Dr. Wickrama was a god-send. He pulled me back from the grave'. Dikwelle Hamine hummed happily as she hobbled around in the garden with the help of a stick, the sun shining golden on her face.

SIXTEEN

Rupa watched and listened to the omens of winter, to the endless whistling wind, the days upon days of torrential rain, the tail end of autumn and then a sudden brilliant snowfall. The autumn celebrations of red, purple, orange and gold leaves had fallen within a few weeks, the listless trees were reduced to gaunt skeletons. The sun rose late and set early. Dew drops turned into icicles.

It was five o'clock in the afternoon when she got back from college. The sun had gone and the moon shone. The deep grey sky foretold an imminent snowfall. The air was striated with freezing fog, every hair root swelled with goose pimples. The doors and windows were closed beneath the flimsy veil of cold. A haunting emptiness squeezed and coiled round her whole being burned her nostrils and made it difficult to breathe. Gusts of freezing air poured like water through a hole in a dam when she opened the bedroom window. A weeping willow with its drooping, arching branches glared at the open sky. Rupa knew Aruna would be late that night. She sat in front of the black and white TV, numb and unable to stir herself towards the waiting housework. Now Hunter had gone Croydon Tech seemed completely dim, a miasma of dimness enveloped Rupa. Overnight heavy snow was forecast. Light white showers had started half an hour before and gradually became heavier. First there was a fine dust of sugar-like crystals mixed with clouds and mist, then random white slivers, followed by thin feathery flakes, finally continuous, piling up on the window ledge.

The sky was confused and the moon hidden away, white marble-like broken clouds shimmered through the stars, a shower of pearls on the waiting sea. Leafless trees held the white crystals between angles of twigs and saplings. Like a naked woman covering her body with white silk the earth slowly began to cover herself with a layer of soft snow. Through the frightened grey clouds the flakes were petals of sky blossoms. The dimmed street light flickered beneath clouds of clotted snow. A car slithered and skidded down the road, its engine revving and Rupa heard the muffled rumble of a passing train. The church spire loomed in the glowing darkness over the whitened treetops. Rupa felt a desperate need to go back to Ceylon and be with her parents again but she had no strength and no fare for her passage. Every penny Aruna provided went on bills.

'I still can't believe how my relationship with Kumara ended. I never thought he would disappear forever. Why didn't he come to the graduation ceremony? Why were we so stupid? Is he still alive?' The pale shadow of Kumara intensified in her mind. All night it snowed. The morning sun shone, reflecting a brilliant glow on the fallen snow. Layers of white crystals on sloping roofs had started to slide down to the ground. Squawking gulls circled round the frozen sky. The pavements had merged with the main roads. The streets were abandoned except for an occasional snow plough or a grit lorry. Black smoke rose from the chimneys and tangled with the clouds. More snow was on the way and everyone stayed by their fires. Rupa and Aruna huddled under the blankets.

'Time's going slowly and we were in England for a long time, longer than we had originally expected. I had a letter from home today, Aruna. My sister's had a baby boy. They haven't named it yet; they won't until the horoscope's been cast. The baby's name has to be given at a propitious time taking into account the time of birth, the star sand the first letter of the name must be given accordingly. My mother hasn't been well for a long time. I often wonder when we can go back to Ceylon!'

'It is not worth rushing back Rupa. I don't think we could go back soon even for a short holiday. The fares alone would be huge. It will take at least another three years to sort out everything before we can go back for good. I've got to really learn my job as a motor engineer. I'm intending to start my own motor business in Ceylon so I must know how to do it. Experience matters a lot Rupa. We also need money to take back a new car and British-made household appliances to set up home. It'll cost a fortune if we try to buy these things at black market prices over there!'

'Now my studies at Croydon Tech are coming to an end, I think the best thing is for me to find a job next summer.'

'I saw some children's toys at Hamleys in Regent Street the other day. Electric train sets, racing cars, talking dolls and Lego sets. They're so beautiful I wish I could have them for myself. If you go to Selfridges's sale you'll go crazy Rupa. Cutlery, crockery, bone china, Kenwood food mixers, Pyrex dishes, cut glass, washing machines; everything at rock bottom prices! If we have all this modern equipment, you'll be able to manage without servants! You know something else Rupa, a lot of people go back to Ceylon overland these days. They buy an expensive Mercedes and go in the car to save on airfares and shipping. We could do the same thing.'

'Surely it would take a long time to travel overland by car from England to Ceylon!'

'It's not so difficult as you'd imagine Rupa. From Dover through Europe, The Middle East, Afghanistan, Pakistan, North India and then down to South India and across to Ceylon. We can manage comfortably in six weeks!'

'It sounds very exciting, a real adventure but it may not be so easy as you may think, Aruna. It'll take the rest of our lives to earn the money you need.'

'Once I go back to Ceylon I'll never come to England again Rupa. We may even need to sell this house to buy the machinery!'

'What do you mean Aruna?'

'If I'm going to open a motor parts factory in Ceylon I'll have to send a couple of container-loads of machinery to begin with.'

'Surely it would be better if we could let out the house and see how things go?'

'Don't be silly Rupa! No point in leaving anything in a foreign country. No matter how long we have lived here we're still foreigners!'

'My parents are counting the days until we go back home Aruna. I'm getting fed up of the routine of life in England.'

Aruna tried to make it up to Rupa by taking her to Paris for a week. They visited the Louvre and as many museums and art galleries as they could fit in and of course the Eiffel Tower. It took Rupa's mind away from her loneliness. They walked along the frozen streets of Paris, breathing the cold air and ate French food cooked with cheese, olives and wine, so different from English and Asian meals. At the Louvre they gazed in awe at Leonardo's 'Mona Lisa', Raphael's 'Madonna and Child', Angelico's 'Coronation of the Virgin and the sculpture of the Venus de Milo: they drew Rupa's mind from her melancholy thoughts to the eternal harmony of the Renaissance. Hand in hand they wandered round the galleries like medieval lovers in a painting by Rossetti.

Back in London Rupa dwelled on the possibilities in their future but secretly remembered the excitement of her time with Hunter.

There was a Sunday one-day Test with the West Indies which Aruna watched avidly on TV. Rupa poured tea from a blue stripy Woolworth's teapot, opened a bottle of silver top milk and added some to both mugs.

'I've made a pot of Ceylon tea,' she said, handing over the mug to Aruna, sunk in the armchair, his eyes fixed on the screen.

'Lovely, Rupa.'

She sat beside him on the settee waiting for the break.

'We had an invitation from Chandra for an almsgiving at the Buddhist temple, there's a memorial service for her mother's death anniversary.'

'When is it?'

'Next Sunday. There'll be about twenty including the four monks.'

Rupa and Aruna decided they would go.

The London Buddhist temple was in Chiswick, a converted three bedroomed house with a large garden. Downstairs was a small library and there were religious activities of various kinds going on. Upstairs was a shrine room filled with fragrant flowers, joss-sticks and a seated statue of Buddha. The temple was run largely on the donations of visitors. Chandra had cooked a meal of rice, meat, fish and vegetables. She offered food and drinks to the monks who sat cross-legged on the cushioned floor, wearing saffron robes. Everyone had a meal afterwards. After the service, which was mainly chanting, a monk preached about the transferring of merits to the dead. In his right hand he held a beige fan. The moon faced Buddha look-alike monk was someone Rupa had seen before.

'I think I know him.' Rupa whispered to Aruna. 'It's the Rev. Hemasiri, the head of our village temple.' He looked at Rupa and smiled. Rupa approached him and said 'Rev. Hemasiri, I didn't know you were here. When did you arrive in London? I'm so pleased to see you.'

'A week ago. I never intended to stop in London but at the last minute I decided to come here for two weeks. I'm on my way to New York for a religious conference. Your parents didn't know I was coming here.'

'How are they?'

'I haven't seen them recently. Your mother was very ill. She was in hospital for a long time. I visited her after she came home.'

'I knew my mother was unwell but they never told me how serious her illness was.'

'It's better if you can go and see them sometime. They are very worried about you. Rukmali brought her new-born baby to the temple.'

'Please tell them I'm well.'

Rupa invited the Rev. Hemasiri for a meal if he stopped in London on his return journey. Chandra and her husband Jayanta had moved to Oxford, to a spacious flat in a stone-built detached house in the suburb known as 'North Oxford' where dons and research students lived cheek-by-jowl with city denizens. Chandra explained that Jayanta was doing the first year of his doctorate and that as a physics student, he had to spend long hours in the new concrete and glass research buildings in Holywell Street, opposite the weathered walls of medieval Magdalen.

'I get very bored stuck in the flat on my own, why don't you and Aruna come and stay for a couple of days?'

'We'd love to, wouldn't we?' Aruna agreed with the barest of glances at Rupa for approval. And so it was arranged and the next weekend they took the tube to Paddington and arranged themselves in front of the sprawling mammoth announcement board and searched up and down the lists of departures until finally they found 'Oxford via Didcot.' As the train was due to leave from platform fifteen in seven minutes they hurried along to find the carriages packed to capacity and were forced to spend the journey jammed in a corridor. With a hoot and a whistle and the peremptory waving of a green flag the express gathered speed and the glum backs of rickety tottering blocks were behind them and the slightly marshy terrain of Oxfordshire soon spread its welcoming arms of lush green foliage to greet them. When the train finally steamed into Oxford station they found their friends waiting and in the foursome with its constant chatter and surge of excitements Rupa found her doubts being sidelined. They were soon in Jayanta's scarlet mini, shooting through the half empty streets until a sudden squeal of brakes announced their arrival. The flat was on the first floor and after a quick snack Jayanta suggested taking Aruna for a drink so the two wives could enjoy a trip together round the shops.

'The winter sales have started and women's clothing is going very cheap. I went there yesterday and bought a pair of shoes less than half price! The shops were so crowded because some of the things are going at give-away prices.'

'I could do with a few skirts and blouses Chandra, most of my clothes are too tight.'

'I'll take you to the indoor market, you can buy marvellous food, there's one stall which only sells cheese.' They bought some Danish Blue, Mini Brie and Applewood cheese. At British Home Stores Rupa found the exact skirt she wanted in red with a matching blouse but after a couple of hours they both felt done-in and were glad to retreat to Chandra's flat. Chandra bustled about in the kitchen and quickly put a meal together. When they had eaten they set off to see some of the sights. They went to Trinity College and had a cup of tea with a vanilla slice in the restaurant. Then they visited the Bodleian Library.

'I often come to this library, just to sit and read a book, then I go out and do a bit of shopping and go home. I don't really care what time my husband gets back. I just get on with my work.'

Chandra seemed well used to the Oxford atmosphere. Rupa's mind drew her back to the past and held her there.

'You look very worried Rupa!'

'I just wondered if anyone I know is here among those students.'

'There are so many foreign students in Oxford Rupa. It's just possible you might find somebody who studied with you.'

Rupa was irritated that there was no Kumara. She looked around but saw only the gleaming spires and the dreaming blue sky.

SEVENTEEN

Another English spring arrived and a hot summer followed. It was mid July, the temperature in the eighties, the earth hard and dry without a sign of rain. The trees drooped and shrubs shrunk in the heat, the fields were brown and the ditches dry. There was a drought in many places and the water supply to the houses and gardens was soon restricted. Herds of cattle and sheep moved to the lowland valleys searching for water. Some reservoirs had dried out entirely exposing acres of burnt earth. Although Rupa was used to a hot climate she found the still air with no humidity extremely uncomfortable. The nights were sticky and Rupa felt breathless and she couldn't get to sleep. Instead she dozed in the mornings, some days not getting up for hours after Aruna had left.

'I just don't understand Aruna, I'm always tired but I can't sleep at night. I've no energy and my legs ache.'

'This unbearable heat brings all kinds of illness. School children catch measles and chickenpox. A strange flu-like illness is spreading all over the country. So many people are off sick in our factory. It's a killer disease for old people and hospitals are on alert. It's usually only in winter that they get flu epidemics like this.'

'I know I'm used to tropical heat, but we always get cool mornings and evenings in Ceylon. I never thought a country like England would get this kind of heat and drought.'

'I think you should go to the doctor Rupa. Try to make an appointment with Dr. Lawrence tonight. I'll come home early.'

'It's not necessary Aruna, this feverishness will go away when the weather's a bit cooler.'

Rupa tried to hide her illness from Aruna as long as she could, she didn't know why. She lost her appetite and the smell of fish made her sick. Tea and coffee were equally tasteless. Her lips cracked, her skin darkened and she lost weight. Finally she agreed to see the doctor that evening and told him her symptoms.

'Tomorrow morning go to outpatients at St. Helier Hospital. They'll take blood and urine samples. Come and see me in four days,' smiling Dr. Lawrence gave her a blue chit. Rupa came out as if nothing was wrong with her. Aruna looked puzzled.

'What did the doctor say?'

'He didn't give me anything. I've to go to St. Helier tomorrow for a blood test.'

'I'll drop you off on my way to work.'

That night Rupa went to bed feeling strange, tired and restless. Sweat poured down her face and the mounting tension in her mind kept her awake. Aruna had fallen asleep. She lay listening to the rhythm of his heavy breathing and the chiming of the wall clock, the night was warm, the window in their bedroom open. She turned on one side, then turned again and put her arm round Aruna. She threw the quilt to the bottom of the bed, feeling uneasy and uncertain. She knew that what Dr. Lawrence told her that evening was right, even before he had seen the urine test results. 'Possibility of a pregnancy.' Rupa knew she was pregnant and wondered why Aruna had not suspected her symptoms. Was he worried? Or didn't he want to know that she was pregnant? Why couldn't she talk things over with Aruna? Rupa didn't know how he would react if she told him.

Sunken deep in her thought she remembered home and the Vesak Festival. The religious ceremony of Vesak was on the fullmoon day of May. It was believed that the Buddha was born, enlightened and died on the identical day of the month. Vesak was celebrated with blazing streetlights and spectacular giant pandals illustrated with Buddhist stories. Adults and children brightened their homes and gardens with coloured lights and candle-lit Vesak lanterns. Rupa and her friend Dingihami made Vesak lanterns with split bamboo sticks. Loku Mahatmaya bought green, yellow, blue, red, purple, orange and pink crepe tissues for Rupa. The old man who lived near the rain forest had a bundle of bamboo sticks tied in bindweed waiting for Rupa and Dingihami. He gave them some wild nuts gathered from the forest. Rupa and her friend cracked the nuts with cobbles and ate the creamy middle. Then they walked home carrying bamboo. A paste was made by mixing flour and hot water and used for sticking the coloured paper. Dingihami stayed the night at Rupa's house to light the Vesak lanterns. In the evening after returning from the temple they lit the candles and hung the Vesak lanterns on every tree in the garden. A line of lanterns brightened the front of the house and the girls watched their colour, stars under the moon. Her face tight against the pillow Rupa tried to sleep. Her tears and sweat mixed together and the night was quiet.

'Rupa. Rupa, you're having a nightmare, go back to sleep,' Aruna touched her and got nearer. His body was warm and Rupa fell into a deep sleep.

EIGHTEEN

Three months of drought came to an end, the sky was confused and dense black clouds darkened the days. The wind was cold. As a fine rain touched down, the earth woke again. Withered trees came back to life and slowly turned green.

Seagulls, crows and black birds circled round the sky, giving warning of a storm. Heavy rain fell, accompanied by lightning and thunder. It rained for four days and nights and then there was freshness in the air, the smell of clay cooling after being baked in the sun. While the dusty trees were washed in rain, thirsty wild animals played in the blue meadows and water-filled ditches.

Now Rupa was three months pregnant her whole life had changed. Although she always wanted to be a mother she just couldn't believe that the day had finally come, her breath and her mind were entangled with the unborn baby, a stranger entirely. When she thought about that her loneliness would end she was suddenly afraid, then strangely delighted. Rupa's thin body was gradually becoming plump, the times of irritable morning sickness, cream crackers and black tea were over.

'If we were in Ceylon my parents and my sister would have helped me. Here we have to do everything ourselves, you have to go to work. I'm very worried Aruna.'

'When you live in a country like England you don't have to worry Rupa. Medical facilities are better here. Everyone who works with me is very understanding and they'll help me. I can always come home if you need me.'

'Childbirth isn't an illness these days, Aruna, unless I have complications. I know you're busy and you don't even have time to breathe. You're tired when you come home in the evenings. If we live somewhere near my relatives it'll be a great help. That's why I keep thinking about home.' The news that he was to become a father increased the tensions in Aruna. He became irritable and depressed, which saddened Rupa. Did he not want to become a father so soon? Or perhaps he had never wanted a child! He said nothing. Although Aruna saw babies in some vague way as part of a marriage his depression worsened. Rupa made sure that Aruna always got a meal in the evening. During the short time he spent at home he just watched TV mindlessly. He never asked Rupa how she felt unless she forced him to listen to her. He gave all his time to his own thoughts, sometimes sleeping whole nights on the settee. Rupa went to bed, assuming that he would come later but often she woke up feeling cold and alone.

In his mind Aruna started to blame Rupa for his depressions. If they had to occupy themselves for the next three or four years bringing up a baby, all his hopes would be ruined. Aruna had some kind of suspicion and fear about Rupa's pregnancy.

'This isn't the right time for a new addition to our family. Rupa will spend all her time with the baby. Babies fall ill, they cry. Some parents have to suffer, even having to give up their jobs and have sleepless nights. It's an end to freedom in life and a complete waste of time,' he thought secretly.

'Who wants to stay at home and spend all their time looking after babies and children? I'll be too old to start my own motor business by the time we go back to Ceylon.' These entwined thoughts bothered him constantly but Rupa had woken up to her imminent motherhood like a water lily in the sun.

Aruna had a mild toothache for about a week and it got worse with headaches and a slight temperature, during his lunch break he sat in the canteen anchoring his head in his hand, sipping a glass of coke when his works manager approached him.

'You don't look well Aruna. Is everything all right with you?'

'It's my wisdom tooth. I've had this pain for about a week.'

'Haven't you seen a dentist?'

'No. This pain comes and goes. I don't like dentists, the sound of the drill terrifies me.'

'I think you ought to go home and go to bed. Don't come back to work tomorrow if you aren't well.' Aruna readily agreed.

When Aruna came home Rupa was out. The small room next to their bedroom had been completely tidied up and the wardrobe was waiting for the baby's things. Her needlework box was open on the bed with cotton reels, coloured buttons and needles in separate sections. Two thin pieces of pink and blue material were laid out with a pair of scissors on the top.

When Rupa came back at about four o'clock Aruna was on the settee with a cushion pressed against his cheeks.

'I didn't know you were coming home early today Aruna. I spent the whole morning tidying up the baby's room, then I went out for a walk and did some shopping. The room was dusty and I left the window open to let some fresh air in.'

'This toothache is killing me. I couldn't do anything at work today. I took two aspirins and the pain's just bearable. What did you buy from the shop?'

'I was thrilled to bits when I went to 'Mothercare'. That money you gave me yesterday to buy a nightie and a housecoat, I spent on baby clothes. I've enough nighties already. That blue towelling housecoat will do for the hospital. I've already packed it in the suitcase. Look at these Aruna!' Rupa emptied the shopping bags onto the coffee table. A pink and blue smocked baby dress, a white shawl, a pair of booties, a bar of Johnson's baby soap and a tin of talc. She touched everything softly as if she was touching her baby. Then she pulled out a red box in the shape of a pig from a Woolworth's bag.

'What's that?'

'It's a moneybox. I'm going to save some pennies for the baby.'

Aruna laughed. 'A few pennies collected in a small box won't go far Rupa.' He looked away in pain, pressing his cheek against the cushion.

'You're not well Aruna. Why don't you go to bed and have a good rest? If you haven't had anything to eat you must be feeling hungry. I'll heat up some soup for you and make you an appointment to see the dentist.'

'I've never had this kind of toothache before. I feel like my head's inside a hot oven.'

'The trouble with wisdom teeth is always very bad. Try to get some sleep Aruna.' He went to bed. Rupa decided to make some fresh soup with potatoes, leeks and chicken. She put a steaming bowl with two buttered slices of toast on a tray but Aruna had fallen asleep.

'I brought some soup and toast for you. Soak the toast if you find it's hard to chew.' Aruna was still asleep. She put the tray on the dressing table and sat on the stool. When she looked at the mirror she realised how quickly her body was changing. Her face was full, her lips dark and deep lines appeared on her neck. Rupa remembered how when she was twelve she had stayed in a boarding house run by a middle-aged woman with a young servant girl called Indo. The girl was eighteen with a bright oval face and sparkling eyes, her waist was thin, her breasts full with golden brown skin and long black hair. When she walked towards the well in the evenings to fetch water, she held a clay vessel against her waist. Her breasts swayed from side to side, as though they were trying to push through her blouse, which was fastened with safety pins. Indo's parents were desperately poor and she had to work as a servant to support her family with what little money she earned. Her smile and her physical beauty always attracted men. Indo was having a secret affair and when she became pregnant, her body suddenly changed. She hid behind the outside lavatory and ate salt and sour mangoes to avoid morning sickness but the lady of the house eventually found out that Indo was pregnant.

'Get out of this house and my sight, you slut. I took you because you were a beggar woman's daughter. Now you're returning evil for good. You're the kind of nymphomaniac who could destroy a whole village.' The lady grasped Indo's shoulder and pushed her. Indo fell and hit her head against the kitchen wall. She cried and her long tangled hair covered her face. Twelve year old Rupa watched Indo crying, her tears troubling the earth and sky. The following morning Indo tried to commit suicide by drinking insecticide from a bottle she found in the shed. Fortunately the mixture was diluted and she survived. When she came out of hospital the first thing the lady of the house did was to send a letter to Indo's mother summoning her to come and take home her disgraced daughter. Rupa remembered how Indo left with her mother, carrying a tattered cardboard suitcase. Rupa never knew what happened to Indo or who was the father of the baby. Rupa looked at the picture on the wall behind the dressing table and tried to find the innocent beauty of Indo in Leonardo's 'Mona Lisa'. Aruna had woken and Rupa was sitting on the bed.

'Your soup is getting cold, Aruna. It's time to take two more aspirins.'

'It doesn't matter, I don't feel like taking anything hot anyway.' He sat up in bed and sipped a few spoonfuls of soup.

'I made an appointment for you to see the dentist tomorrow morning at ten o'clock. Can you manage the rest of the soup?'

He took the aspirins and finished the soup. Then he turned on his side and fell asleep. Rupa had not seen Aruna so down with any illness. Although trouble with a wisdom tooth could be very uncomfortable it still seemed out of character for Aruna to make such a fuss. Rupa was worried in case there was a problem at work and that was why he'd come home early that afternoon. The following morning he seemed a bit better but he still went to the dentist. The decaying wisdom tooth had to be removed. He stayed at home for four days nursing a painful jaw and then went back to work. In retrospect Rupa felt that this apparently slight incident was some kind of turning point in their relationship.

Without telling anyone except Hunter, who she had needed a reference from, Rupa had applied to London University to do a part-time degree in history. The morning a letter came with 'Birkbeck College' and its crest embossed on the stiff white envelope Rupa snatched it from the mat and locked herself in the bathroom to read it. She tore the letter open and when she realised it was the offer of a place her heart suddenly surged and she felt faint and had to sit on the edge of the bath. Holding the letter in her hand and trembling slightly she took it to show Aruna, who was cooking a breakfast for them in the kitchen. When Aruna read the letter he put it down and looked angry.

'I'm so pleased, I never thought they would accept me. Now the problem is managing the baby.'

'The whole thing is rubbish, you're crazy Rupa! I'm sick of listening to you going on about your classes. You can't have everything; babies and education! You should have some common sense and choose one, not both.'

'When I applied for this course I never knew I was going to have a baby.'

'That's your problem!'

NINETEEN

It was a mid-day in autumn when Rupa arrived at York railway station. The wind was cold, the leaves on the trees yellow and orange with the occasional blazing red. Falling leaves from the sky-high poplar blew like frightened birds, dispersed and dropped slowly. Waves were glazed in a silvery light as the Ouse flowed reluctantly beneath the bridge. Along the footpaths through the hefty Roman walls and the ancient gates Rupa walked towards the Minster which rose in the sky from the mists of the Renaissance, a giant with its spires, towers and stone walls.

Trembling slightly she entered the Minster through the huge double doors. The church with its exquisite carvings, stained glass, resplendent naves and Gothic altars was almost empty. Hundreds of candle flames flickered in a dark corner. Rupa lit two herself, knelt and then prayed for her unborn child. She closed her eyes for a moment; her nostrils quivering with the strange smells then she peered into the darkness echoing with the spirits of the departed in their lonely stone tombs. Above the dome came a roar of thunder. Rupa felt some power move deeply within her being. She felt no longer alone, as though Kumara stood next to her, holding a white lotus. The Minster was absolutely silent. Only Chandra and Hunter knew of Rupa's growing interest in Christianity.

'Why don't you come to the Buddhist temple anymore Rupa?' Chandra had asked.

'I've not changed my religion but I like to go to a church instead. The singing of the hymns soothes me just as much as listening to Buddhist chanting.'

'Have you told Aruna about your views?'

'No, I don't think he's bothered anyway. He doesn't care about me or my religion. I've no idea what he's got in his mind,

Chandra.'

'Rupa I always thought that you were being influenced by someone and you were converting to Christianity secretly.'

'No-one's influenced me. I was never allowed in a church when I was at home. My parents were strong Buddhists. Jehovah's Witnesses were the only people who ever tried to convert me since I've been in England. I learned how to think independently from Hunter, the tutor who taught me English.'

'If you're thinking of changing your religion don't forget it's a huge step Rupa. You should speak to the head priest in the London Buddhist Temple about it. I'll come with you, if you like.'

'Just forget it, Chandra.'

'You're going to be a mother soon. You don't want unnecessary trouble, do you?'

Rupa remembered how the river Yamuna in India flowed beside the Taj Mahal, surrounded by a breeze, the symbol of eternal love and how when she entered the Buddhist shrine in the Temple of the Tooth in Ceylon she felt the same immediate sense of serenity. There seemed to be an echoing power of God in York Minster referring to that sense of inner harmony.

Rupa was now seven months pregnant, she had put on weight and her breasts were full and deep. Her whole being was getting ready for the baby's birth. As the weeks passed by, Aruna seemed to be showing a spark of interest in the baby's arrival, even decorating the baby's room. Rupa visited the maternity clinic regularly.

'I went to the clinic this morning, Aruna. The doctor said that the baby had turned to the right position so there's no problem. A nurse from the hospital comes there every day and next week she's going to show me how to bath a baby.' Rupa went on excitedly but Aruna said nothing.

The following Saturday they went to Mothercare and bought a pram and a few more baby things. Rupa put them on the shelves in the baby's room and soon the air was filled with the soft smell of Johnson's baby powder.

As the pregnancy continued Aruna noticed a strange beauty growing in Rupa. Although she was preoccupied with the birth and often tense, her slow walk, loose clothes, shiny hair and elegant fullness brightened their home. When they went to bed that night he felt her skin, her breasts and her whole body warmer and softer than before.

'Seven months have gone, Aruna. I can feel the baby's movements. Put your hand just above here.' Rupa took his hand and placed it on her stomach.

'Unbelievable! It's moving and kicking very happily. I hope it's a boy and not a girl.'

'I don't mind Aruna. Whether it's a boy or a girl, it's our baby.'

Although Rupa's physical shape was changing quickly this was the first time Aruna felt that the baby there was waiting to be born. He felt as though this invisible being moving in Rupa's womb was closer to him.

In Eastern society the birth of a baby boy was always very welcome but a girl was regarded more a trouble than a blessing. Parents had to start saving for her dowry long before the girl was grown up. Soon the baby would see the sun. For the mother childbirth is inevitably painful. The pain that goes through bones, veins and flesh is knowledge; a life about to begin. Tiny beams of light from the furthest star brightened the darkness from birth to death. Rupa had seen a film at the clinic, which showed the reality of childbirth and the fulfilment that followed. Through a veil of anxiety images of the baby's arrival delighted Rupa.

TWENTY

The news of Rupa's pregnancy came to Maha Gedara and spread round the whole village on the same day.

'I just don't understand them. Everytime she writes a letter to us she says that they're intending to come back soon. They don't keep their promises so I don't believe them. I don't know why they live in a foreign country like gypsies, never coming home and settling down for good. This is the time she should eat well, for herself and for the baby. Those English people live on bread and potatoes. She has nobody there to provide fresh fish from the sea and rice straight from the fields. How quickly they've forgotten our customs. When a girl is pregnant she should come home and stay with her parents at least for the first few months! Aruna has to work. Who's going to look after her when she's got morning sickness? They just don't care about anything, do they? I don't think they are capable of bringing up a child without our help.'

Dikwelle Hamine was glad about the pregnancy but irritable with Rupa for not coming home for the birth.

'God bless her, God bless her'. Loku Mahatmaya announced portentously.

The following morning Rukmali and her husband came to Maha Gedara with their sons, Damit and Lal, to share their happiness, eating a celebratory meal together. The smell of cooking spread as far as the paddy fields and once again it was like the New Year celebration at Maha Gedara.

A meal was ready on the table. Milk rice, fried red onions, freshly cooked fish, jackfruit pickle, treacle cakes, curd, banana and mangoes.

Dikwelle Hamine served some food for Damit and said, 'This child is always ill and thin as a pin. If you eat everything I'll give you some cashew nuts to take home.'

Little Damit ate two spoons of milk rice and a treacle slice. Dikwelle Hamine looked on anxiously.

'You don't have to worry mother. Childbirth is nothing these days, particularly in Western countries with all the latest medical facilities,' Rukmali said.

'English people don't eat spicy food like us. Rupa would love to eat some rice and curry and woodapple cream,' said Dikwelle Hamine

Creamy middle of woodapples mixed with treacle is delicious. Loku Mahatmaya thought the milk rice meal cooked by his wife that day equally mouth watering.

After lunch Rukmali and her family left and Loku Mahatmaya went for a walk along the rice fields, carefully moving the stiff fallen stems onto the path. He looked at the vast stretching green rice fields.

'That rain we had yesterday was good for the growing rice. This year we'll have a good crop,' he mused.

The grass beside narrow paths had grown knee high and as he wandered past a ditch a large white tortoise suddenly jumped into the water, splashing his feet. The honey mango tree across the field was full and white with fruit and the whole village baked in the sun. A peacock tripped daintily on a branch of the mango tree, its shrill cry echoing across the fields. Ratti the cow was eating grass under coconut trees. She called her calf and gently licked its face. The calf made a huge jump across and came jumping back to its mother. Ratti bent her head and pushed the calf aside with her horns as if he was a naughty child. Then she called it again and licked its grubby neck with her coarse tongue. Loku Mahatmaya cut some grass and gave a handful to the waiting cow.

'Here you are girl. You must eat well, that little calf needs good milk from you.'

Ratti chomped happily, happier than Loku Mahatmaya did when he ate his wife's celebration meal of milk rice.

If you walk from Maha Gedara a few hundred yards along the red road you will see a large pond at the margin of the fields. The

Lilymarsh Pond, home to turtles, frogs, water snakes and monitors was covered with lotuses and blue water lilies. Tilakawathie picked some lilies from the pond and tied them into a bundle. Then she picked some jasmine and arranged all the flowers carefully in a wicker basket and sprinkled them with water. The flowers were ready to be taken to the temple. Dikwelle Hamine and Loku Mahatmaya went to the temple and made a ritual Puja at the shrine, offering flowers to Buddha, transferring merits to the gods. They lit a hundred coconut oil lamps and joss-sticks around the sacred Bo tree and made a vow to Skanda, the god of war. They promised to bring Rupa and her child to Kataragama temple one day and bathe them in the nearby holy river.

In the evenings Rukmali's son Damit sat under a mango tree and stared at the aeroplanes, talking about Rupa coming back with a baby. He made cardboard aeroplanes and threw them to the sky. He drew pictures of imaginary flying tree frogs chasing aeroplanes and fixed plastic windmills and airports in the garden. Although Rukmali tried to console her mother, when she thought about Rupa's life in a foreign country and the possibility that they might never return she became anxious.

On Sunday Rukmali and a friend went to an astrologer to hear Rupa's horoscope. They had to travel by bus to Galle, thirty miles away from home and then walk for half an hour to a remote village. The astrologer and his family lived in a small palm-thatched house. As they entered the compound the smell of joss-sticks poured from the adjacent open hut made of fresh coconut leaves and matted floor. The astrologer was dressed in native white clothes. With his finger he sprinkled a few drops of holy water on to Rukmali's face and asked them into the hut where they sat on cane chairs. Pictures of Buddha and the gods Skanda and Vishnu were hung above the burning incense sticks. Creamy yellow arecanut flowers were arranged in a clay vase. An oil lamp flickered on the rickety table. Rukmali gave him a ritual handful of betel leaves, the gift of a towel wrapped in brown paper and Rupa's horoscope.

'This is my sister's horoscope.'

'Where did you come from, madam?'

'We're from Matara. My sister went abroad a few years ago and shows no sign of coming back. Is she going through some kind of bad spell in her life?'

The man looked at the rolled-up horoscope and referred to a table of stars and planets' movements from the date of Rupa's birth.

'The holder of this horoscope appears to be born with considerable good fortune and merit. Although illness can occur during the first seven years of her life, the period from the age of twenty to thirty two seems to be moving ahead with no major problems. Venus is in house number seven, which is ideal for a happy marriage and for good children! The most significant character in this horoscope is that all the four main houses are occupied. A safe return to her birthplace is guaranteed. To tell you everything one hundred percent accurately I must read her palm.'

'Will there be any problems at a childbirth?'

'The moon is in a very powerful position but there seems to be a slight problem! An intermediate obstruction from Jupiter, Sun and Mars. Minor effects are not very good but are not in anyway harmful.'

'Is there anything we can do about it?'

'Yes, perform a ritual Puja to the god Vishnu. Offer a curtain for his shrine at the temple, stitched with a blue elephant in the middle. Then carry out a ritual pouring of milk from an earthenware pitcher at the foot of a sacred Bo tree to transfer merits to all the gods. This is a very positive horoscope and there's no danger at the expected childbirth.'

Rukmali felt relieved and gave him fifty rupees in a folded betel leaf.

Good fortune had returned to Maha Gedara again. Rain fell in time for both seasons of the year. The rice fields flourished and Loku Mahatmaya had bumper crops. After her illness and until recently Dikwelle Hamine had to walk with the help of a stick.

'I feel a lot better now. I don't feel dizzy anymore and I can open my eyes in the morning. I should be back to normal when I've taken another hundred vitamin tablets.'

She called the next-door woman's son, Dasa.

'My vegetable garden is a complete wilderness! No one bothered to clear it when I was ill. Can you pull out those bindweed and stinging nettles? Double-dig the earth and prepare seedbeds. There's plenty of composted manure in the cowshed.'

Dikwelle Hamine took a handful of soil from her vegetable garden and crumbled it between her fingers. She imagined runner beans twining in the cane obelisks, clusters of hanging pods, rain washed tassels of sweetcorn flowers and purple tubers of yam. Then she sighed.

TWENTY ONE

Rupa felt unusually tired and uncomfortable. Her knees and ankles swelled, her stomach got bigger and bigger, she started with back pains when she stood, even for half an hour. She only felt better when she stretched her legs. She tried to sleep at the edge of the bed, turning on her side. Whenever she got out of bed she felt jittery, as though some catastrophe was about to overcome her.

'I feel very strange this morning. My back aches and I feel numb.'

'Drink your cup of tea and eat the toast. Don't do any housework or go out, just stay in bed. I've got to go to work now but I'll be back at lunchtime.'

As Aruna left, the door slamming behind him, Rupa felt alone and afraid. She got out of bed and paced up and down in the bedroom, holding her stomach with both hands.

It was a sunny spring morning. A colony of black birds and sparrows were feeding on the grass in the back garden. Rupa looked through the window at the birds in the stone bath five or six splashing their wings simultaneously. When there wasn't enough room for everyone, another bird flew down from the sky and chased the others and got into the bath. They opened their beaks and squeaked fluttering their wings and feathers. There was a confused squawking and splashing, a fine rain of water mizzling in the air. Sparrows chirped on the budding branches of the cherry tree. Suddenly the whole flock flew away and disappeared over the empty horizon. The busy London road the other side of the bridge seemed quiet for once. She heard a double decker turn the corner, the brakes squealing. Overhead was the thunder of a Concorde as it faded in the wind, the air was filled with the scent of hyacinths.

Rupa heard the distant cry of a child. The sunshine warmed her and the verdant shrubs made secret promises. The squirrels looking for nuts ran along the ground then scaled the single poplar. In front of the house the narrow road was almost deserted. A young woman in shabby clothes urged a battered pushchair in the direction of the shops. Hand in hand an elderly couple hobbled along to the Post Office. An old collie with a stiff tail limped behind the couple. A line of pigeons swooped down on the slate roof. A child who was crying a few minutes ago caught up with his mother, who slapped him angrily and his cry increased in volume. Rupa felt a sudden shiver. There were goose pimples all over her body and the beginnings of a pain in her stomach. It was nearly twelve and Aruna should be home soon. Listlessly she turned on her side and fell back to sleep. Rupa was half awake and the clock on the table was ticking, the sounds around her were louder than usual. School children were going home early, perhaps they had broken up for half term. The quiet road was suddenly busy to the point of chaos. Children were calling mothers, laughter, pushchairs, car brakes, barking dogs, all combined to break the midday silence. Rupa was woken by sounds of movement in the house. She heard the front door being opened. 'I'm so pleased you're here Aruna. The pain seems to be getting worse.'

'Shouldn't we get to the hospital quickly Rupa? In case the baby suddenly comes out and I don't know what to do!'

'Don't worry Aruna' Rupa laughed. 'Babies don't suddenly come out in the way you think. The pain isn't continuous, I feel very thirsty.'

'Would you like some tea?'

'No, I feel a bit sick, I'll have some water.'

Aruna seemed confused and felt he couldn't move himself. He brought a glass of water, it fell on the carpet and the glass was broken. Then he rushed down to the kitchen and brought a dustpan and brush to clear the broken glass. He tried to wrap the broken glass in newspaper and cut his thumb. Rupa walked down to the kitchen and brought a mug of water and a plaster for Aruna's bleeding thumb.

'We'll see how I feel. If the pain gets worse we can always call the ambulance. Make sure you take that suitcase with us.'

Half an hour later a red light flashed incessantly accompanied by the insistent ringing of the bell and then Aruna opened the door for the ambulance men.

Rupa lay in bed wearing a green hospital gown with 'Mayday Maternity' stencilled in blue on the back. The woman in the bed next to her was about to give birth. She was breathing heavily, her eyes were tired, her face red. The woman pushed two pillows to the back and sat up on the bed, desperately trying to move her legs, wiping sweat from her face with her fingers. Rupa looked at her, worried and anxious.

'Nothing to bother about. I've got five already. This is my sixth. I'm used to labour pain. Just try to breathe heavily. It helps make the pain bearable. I never had any problems before so there shouldn't be any problems this time.'

Through considerable discomfort and pain the woman smiled slightly.

'I'm frightened,' said Rupa. 'The pains I had at home seem to have gone. The water bag's burst but now they say they are going to wait at least another twelve hours. The doctor was going on about doing a Caesarean. This is my first baby, if you didn't guess!'

'It doesn't matter how many children you have. It's always a special occasion. The pain a mother's got to go through at a birth is sweet and sour. It's harder work than anything. You only realise the beauty of it when you see your baby's face for the first time. I remember how I got ready for my first child fifteen years ago. I hand knitted all the baby clothes. My mother was so excited she did the same! Now I just use all the other children's cast-offs. Mother's love is the most important thing.'

The woman stroked her huge stomach. A few minutes later two nurses put her on a stretcher and wheeled her off to the labour room.

Rupa felt afraid. The next morning when Aruna came to see Rupa she was still lying on the bed.

'I don't understand this Aruna. All the pains I had yesterday have gone but I still feel uncomfortable. You remember that English lady who was in the next bed. She had twins last night.'

'What did the doctor say?'

'They check me and the baby every half hour. I think it's going to be a Caesarean tonight.'

'In that case I'll go to work today and come straight back at tea-time.'

'It's not worth you taking any time off yet. The hospital will phone you at work if they have to.'

Rupa remembered how the English woman's husband had brought flowers and kissed his wife and how unfeeling Aruna seemed. It was eleven. Aruna had been and gone. The bed next to Rupa remained empty. She felt she was alone in an uninhabited world with a baby just about to be born. Nurses in blue striped uniforms and doctors in white coats shadowed up and down the maternity ward. The smell of disinfectant lingered in the air. At last the curtains were closed and the lights dimmed. There was a yellow vase on the table filled with roses. Chandra had brought them that evening.

The ward was uncannily quiet; the sound of a falling leaf would have disturbed the silence. Rupa remembered her mother and wondered about Aruna, who would be sleeping after a day's hard work. If she had arranged for the birth in Ceylon they would have made such a fuss and the whole family would be around.

She stared at the ceiling, in a dream of vague thoughts shaken with the sound of light footsteps. Perhaps the night nurse was doing her late round. Rupa closed her eyes pretending to be asleep; she dozed off, dreaming, briefly woke and finally fell into a deep sleep.

She dreamed of trees covered in an abundance of yellow and purple blossoms, the nipples of the hills curtained with a thin layer of mist, in the distance lecture halls and tutorial rooms, the library a fortress, the abode of Saraswathi, goddess of wisdom. Rainbow coloured carpets hung from the rim of sky down to the earth. She walked along dew-covered melting clover paths, pink and blue parasols moving in the wind and rain. She listened to their laughter to the rhythm of castanets and the echo of wood pigeons above the campus hills. Falling petals were their laughter, raindrops their tears, freedom was their poignant memory, the morning sun and the scented nights their hopes. From the sandy banks of the River Mahaweli the wind echoed with songs of the past. Raindrops fell over a rainbow, clear as diamonds. A distant voice was calling her from the other side of the river. It was a familiar voice but broken in the howling wind.

When she woke up from the dreams the ward was empty as the Sahara desert at dawn. A sharp pain started from her back, spreading over her entire body. Her arms and legs were numb. One minute she shivered and the next she was boiling hot. The pain lasted for a few minutes, receding and suddenly returning. Rupa felt thirsty, her lips dry. Slow moving contractions quickly changed into endless pain. A nurse tried to make her comfortable.

'It's unbearable,' Rupa said, sweat pouring down her cheeks.

'We'll look after you, Rupa. Stretch your arms and legs and try to take a deep breath when the pain comes.' The nurse checked the baby's heartbeat and Rupa's pulse and blood pressure.

'Now it's time to take you to the labour room, Rupa.'

A few minutes later a porter came with a stretcher and they took her to the brightly-lit labour room. Rupa felt calmer once she realised she was surrounded by medical instruments and gadgets. She was still sweating and there was a salty taste on her lips. The clock on the wall seemed to have stopped yet the second hand still swept round. It was one forty five in the morning. Smiling the doctor gave her an injection into her leg.

'The baby is slowly moving down and it's in the right position,' the doctor told the nurse. Rupa struggled with the labour pains and asked for some water. 'In a minute,' the nurse said. The pain gushed like sea waves caught up in a hurricane which spread all over like a bushfire. She closed her eyes and held her fists tight. She found difficulty in breathing as she tossed and turned. Finally she was given an oxygen mask.

'I can clearly see the baby's head,' Rupa heard a nurse talking. After a few seconds her waist and stomach tightened, the pain flamed. A magical power seemed to emerge from deep within and began to fight pain such as she had never experienced before. The frightening storm submerged, golden sands of endless shores were covered in sun; the umbilical cord was separated followed by relief of weight as the afterbirth was expelled. It was two twenty eight. The child who had been merged within now flowed out into the world and melded with it like a blossom on a stem. The baby cried. A nurse washed away all the birth stains. Warmly wrapped in a white towel the baby was handed over to Rupa. 'It's a beautiful girl.'

Rupa's heart leaped. After the deluge on the first day of spring the screens of winter opened wide. For Rupa it was enlightenment, a perfect rose in her hand. The baby had a round face, dark hair, long fingers and even fingernails. Rupa kissed the baby's soft cheek and felt her warm breath. For a moment she forgot that it was only just born.

When Aruna arrived at the hospital in the early morning Rupa was asleep. The baby was sleeping in a carrycot, covered in a soft white blanket so only her face could be seen. He bent down and looked closely. The baby's breath melted him. He held Rupa's hand and sat in the chair next to her bed. She had woken with a tired smile on her face.

TWENTY TWO

The days and nights seemed to be moving faster than ever. Talking, walking and whispering - every sound in the house high and low was quietened so as not to disturb the baby. When Lisa was asleep the house was filled with a soft silence, deeper than her breathing. Ten in the morning was always bath time, the yellow tub with its pictures of pink and blue ducks and hopping bunnies half filled with lukewarm water and Rupa was ready in her plastic apron. Lisa smiled and played, kicking and splashing. Rupa talked and laughed, feeling as if she, too, was in the bath. Leaving splashed water on the rubber sheet Rupa dried the baby and wrapped her in a Mothercare towel. With a soft pink puff she dabbed talc from her neck to her bottom and dressed Lisa in a babygrow. Then it was feeding time and the baby fell asleep to the sound of her mother's heartbeat.

'I'm amazed to see how you manage with Lisa and how quickly you've got used to this routine Rupa.'

'The first few weeks I found it very hard going Aruna, I didn't know how to organise myself with a baby. I didn't even have time to wash my hair or even eat. Now the problem is that Lisa doesn't sleep much and cries a lot. The doctor thinks that she is not getting enough milk from me and we may have to introduce Cow and Gate. I feel exhausted.'

'I'm getting fed up with this job, same place, same work and same people everyday. This isn't my own business and I've to kill myself and all for someone else! The real problem is I don't have enough capital to start my own business in Ceylon. Its just impossible to think of.'

'Our situation has changed and I don't think we should just rush into things, Aruna. I'd love to go back to see my family but we have no choice! All I can think about is how to bring up Lisa without too much trouble.'

'The political situation in Ceylon is very bleak at the moment. The new government's altering all the export and import regulations. To buy a loaf of bread, a pound of dahl and some dry fish you've got to stand in a long queue from morning till night! Not the best economy, even for a third world country! But that's how it is.'

'I see what you mean, Aruna, but we must stick to our plans and go back when we're ready. We just have to live with what little we earn.'

'Nonsense! You don't think about what you say, Rupa. You can't do a job because there's no one to look after Lisa. Babies are expensive! We live in a society where people only care about money. How we live and the way other people see us is important. We've got to keep up the family image and not land ourselves with too many children.'

Rupa knew that Aruna was not entirely truthful and that his mind was turbulent with strange, secret fantasies. He never did what he said, nor did he ever divulge his plans. His ideas and reality always seemed to be in conflict. At times he overflowed with plans and then for days he would sit hunched in an armchair, staring at the wall. When he woke up he was always irritable. Rupa was alert, watching his increasing mood changes carefully.

'Why are you looking so depressed, Aruna? Our problems aren't a life and death struggle! Things don't always happen just the way we want. I think this country still has opportunities if you work hard.'

'Earning money isn't easy, Rupa. At the end of the day everyone deserves some peace. There's none of it when you have to spend all your time with a child. If we can get some kind of help with the baby then you can concentrate on what you like.'

'Don't talk rubbish, Aruna! I don't need anyone to help me. I know it's hard work but Lisa's my child and I want to look after her. I don't think people should work like machines, not the way you think anyway! I know things don't appear by magic but we have to allow enough time and wait and see how things develop.'

Lisa woke up and started crying like a cicada. Rupa went upstairs quickly, tying her long hair into a bun as she ran. Aruna left for work, forgetting to eat his cornflakes.

Aruna looked miserable when he came home that night. Apart from talking about how Lisa had stopped crying after taking ten ounces of Cow and Gate, Rupa got on with her housework. They had a quick meal of rice and curry during which neither of them spoke. She washed up and sterilised Lisa's bottles. Aruna sat in front of the TV and fell asleep until Rupa finally woke him just before midnight. After taking her two a.m. feed of her mother's milk Lisa had fallen asleep in her cot with its pictures of bears and rabbits having a tea party and eating porridge and honey. The silence in the room was melting into tiny drops when she smiled in her dreams.

But for Rupa sleep no longer came easily. However exhausted she felt she would lay and stare at the ceiling, her mind filled with images of disaster, trains crashing and avalanches, volcanic eruption, monsoons and earthquakes. When finally she slept the horrific images would go on and on and turn into livid nightmares until she woke, sweating and terrified but she had no comfort from Aruna, always with his back to her, hunched and silent. It was eight and Aruna was still asleep. Unusually for him he stayed in bed till late on Tuesday morning. Rupa noticed that Aruna was losing interest in his work and his odd behaviour made her uncomfortable and angry. She had enough on looking after the baby. The prospect of Aruna staying at home after losing his job was something she just couldn't cope with, she became so anxious she decided to wake him.

'Aren't you going to work today?'

'No, we don't have much work in at the moment. I don't think there'll be a problem if I have a week off.'

'I don't blame you Aruna, better have a few days holidays and rest when you can. You don't look very well!'

'I'm sick and tired of the whole thing. I think the way we live is useless. We just live for the day.'

'When I was at home on my own before I had Lisa I felt just

the same, desperately lonely, like living alone in a desert. Life in the west is so stressful! You remember that old man who lived in Thicket Crescent? He was dead and nobody found out for three weeks. When the foxes started to howl at night on his patio a neighbour wondered what was wrong and phoned 999. The next morning they broke down the door to find his decomposing body by the fire in his lounge! I was horrified when I heard about it. Let's go back to Ceylon, Aruna! It's impossible to plan everything years ahead. We'll go there first and then find a way of earning our living, you might even get a job.'

'Don't talk about jobs Rupa! I'm not a man who likes to work for anybody. I'll find a way of earning money but it has to be my own way and I don't need your advice.'

'I'm not trying to advise you, Aruna, I'm only telling you how I feel. I think it's better for you to do something rather than sit in that armchair and think all the time. You don't even care about Lisa! In the mornings I take her out in the pram for some fresh air but I think we should take her out more often, both of us together.'

'We can go somewhere with Lisa today.' Aruna suggested. Rupa was pleased and they decided to go to Kew Gardens. Within an hour, with a pack of cheese and onion sandwiches, a flask of coffee and a nursery bag full of the baby things, they were ready to set off. On their way to Kew Aruna was irritable, his driving bumpy and jerky. His sudden braking shook Rupa and Lisa. The Kleenex tissue box and the A to Z of London fell on to the back seat and Lisa started to cry.

Rupa sighed with relief when Aruna finally parked the car in one of the long streets of imposing Victorian houses behind the Botanical Gardens. She shushed the baby and jigged the pushchair up and down to keep her quiet. When they came to a clearing she set to and laid out the picnic things. She poured coffee for them both. Aruna sat with his back against the gnarled bark of a tree, Rupa looking at him earnestly.

'It was nearly four years ago when we first came here Aruna, I remember it as though it was yesterday. Nothing seems to have changed. Can you remember the friendly old couple we met?' Rupa talked on but Aruna said nothing in reply. Once again the trees were full of magenta blossoms. The morning sun lay on the grass. Birds sang on the budding branches then arrowed away in flight to the blue sky. A workman passed on his petrol mower.

'Isn't it a beautiful day?' He said, stopping his machine.

'Yes it is, isn't it?'

He started his mower again and sped away, cutting the grass in a strict vertical pattern. They sat on the benches under a cherry tree covered in blossoms and the ground was pink with fallen petals. Lisa began to cry so Aruna rattled a toy with a line of coloured birds.

'Lisa's feeding time's half an hour late, that's why she's crying.' Rupa took a bottle out of the nursery bag and tightened the teat. Lisa immediately stopped crying, stretched her arms forward and gurgled happily until Rupa gave her the bottle.

'I forgot to telephone work to tell them I wasn't coming in today. Our boss hates it when someone's away without notice. I'll have to tell them a lie, I'll say I've got bad diarrhoea.'

'Aruna I thought you had taken a couple of days off. I don't think it's a good idea not to go in without telling them. We've got enough problems at the moment and the last thing we want is for you to lose your job. There's a phone box outside the cafe. Shall we phone them now?'

'Don't you interfere with my work! If I lose my job it's my affair and nothing to do with you.' He was so irritable, Rupa was secretly angry but she said nothing while he sulked in silence.

The days they spent together were no longer enjoyable for Rupa. Increasingly Aruna would either stay silent, sitting with his head bowed and stare morosely ahead then suddenly jump up and go out of the house without a word of explanation. Sometimes he would return within minutes, as though he had tried to make a phone call but failed to get through. At other times he would be gone for two or three hours but still he would not say anything as to where he had been. Rupa began to wonder if there was another woman but somehow she didn't think this was the explanation for his secretiveness. His eyes always seemed cold and hard, his body taut like a coiled spring. Rupa never thought of either herself or Lisa as a possible cause for the changes in Aruna. Although she had to spend a lot of time on the baby Aruna wasn't at home during the day to see what was going on.

Sometimes when Rupa was feeding Lisa, Aruna stroked Lisa's head, even kissing and cuddling her; then he seemed to be very close to his daughter. Slowly but inevitably his secret fantasies made him more tense. He seemed unable to concentrate. Some evenings when Aruna came home Rupa was tired and had fallen asleep while Lisa was still suckling. Lisa's sleeping habits had changed and she had begun to cry at night, then Rupa cradled the baby on her knees and sang lullabies. Aruna's sleep was disturbed. Breast-feeding and constant sleepless nights exhausted Rupa. Her face was haggard and she lost weight. Her shiny skin darkened. At times she would hardly keep her eyes open. She wrote home less and less.

Lisa's continuing problems made Aruna's quick temperedness grow and it was with difficulty that he controlled his temper.

'I think Lisa is starting a cold. She's been restless for the last couple of days. She finds it difficult to breathe and suck. I've not been able to bath her for three days.'

'Rupa, I don't know how you manage with all these sleepless nights! Let's take Lisa to the doctor tomorrow morning. I can go to work a bit late.'

Rupa tried to feed Lisa but the baby wouldn't stop crying. If she fell asleep from exhaustion she'd soon wake up, cry to be fed and so it would go on. Rupa put the baby on her knee and fell asleep. Aruna wasn't used to looking after a baby but he thought he should have a try but when he held her she cried even more loudly, her whole body writhing in anguish. Finally he laid Lisa on the bed and woke Rupa.

'This is impossible Rupa! I don't think anybody brings up their children the way you do! You have no sleep, you don't eat and you're coming, apart at the seams!'

'I can hardly throw the baby away or just let her cry when she's ill.'

'Babies have to be trained from the day they were born. You're spoiling her Rupa! I think a baby's behaviour completely depends on her mother's common sense.'

'I did take her to the doctor yesterday. He told me to try Calpol but it doesn't help with her cold. Doctor Lawrence told me that some children seem to cry for no reason at all. You seem to think I don't know how to look after the baby and it's all my fault.'

Rupa and Aruna continually worried about Lisa's restlessness. Housework was abandoned and piles of washing grew in the bathroom and they lived largely on sandwiches. Aruna looked very fed up but he was always willing to go out for fish and chips. Rupa thought that Aruna was just ignorant about babies. When Lisa finally fell asleep her cheeks had turned red. Rupa felt helpless and burst into tears.

Childhood is always vivid. The sun is singular. The moon brightens the world of dreams. Eyes sparkle like diamonds and glitter beneath the stars. Raindrops and snowflakes are pearls. Thunder, lightning, rain, rainbows, clouds and snow light up the imagination. The rotation of days and nights puzzle them. Darkness disappears in the swift twilight. The scent of sal flowers in Lumbini, the place where Buddha was born, spreads to the end of the sky. Angels in Bethlehem sang through silver clouds. The river Neranjara dried to a sandy bed as far as the eye could see. The cold seasons ended, snow covered isolated villages, fields, valleys, lakes and magenta hills were soaked in sunlight. Water lilies stretched their petals. Ducks, swans and gulls flapped their wings anticipating the arrival of spring followed by a hot summer. The gap between the seasons narrowed. There was some peace between Rupa and Aruna when at last Lisa stopped her continual crying and began to smile.

TWENTY THREE

Everyone at Maha Gedara was smiling in delight at the news of the birth of a baby girl.

'Childbirth is always a worry. Thank god Rupa and the baby are well.' Dikwelle Hamine sighed with relief.

Loku Mahatmaya was in bed with a bad cough.

'God bless her and the baby!' he said in a croaky voice. Along with the precise time and place of birth, Rukmali sent a hundred rupees and a handful of betel leaves to the astrologer for him to cast the baby's horoscope. Within a few days she had the long rolled up strip of parchment with everything neatly written out in longhand. The astrologer suggested a few letters for the beginning of baby's name 'A' 'P' 'T', but the baby had already been named.

'A good horoscope! Powerful stars are together and there are no disturbances to interrupt the child's education and health. The first eighteen months aren't very good for the parents but it is not significant and doesn't seem to be a problem.' Rukmali said.

Since he had become ill Loku Mahatmaya grew thinner and thinner until he had no strength for his usual work. Ratti, the cow with the calf, had to be given to Rukmali's family. Rukmali was pleased that at last she could get enough milk for her children.

'This is a strange illness. Every evening I feel feverish, cold and shivering. This cough never goes away. I just can't sleep at night.' Loku Mahatmaya's voice was so low Dikwelle Hamine could hardly hear him. He started coughing again.

'Day and night all I do is sit by that cooking fire and boil herbs then strain them and make herbal medicines. I get a headache when I sit too long by a hot fire. It's all pointless, as you don't seem to be getting any better. Last night you were coughing non-stop. When we don't have the energy we used to have, even medicines can't cure all illnesses. I think you've got all the symptoms of that horrible mosquito illness, shivering and a temperature in the evenings. Mosquitoes breed in that Lily Marsh, it could even be consumption!' Suddenly her tone grew strident.

'I was awake all night and I decided to go to the balcony at four in the morning. You wouldn't believe what I saw! A long line of red and green flashing lights with a blue tail went across the sky. There were no stars. For a moment I thought I had woken from a dream and rubbed my eyes. I looked at it without blinking until it disappeared into the rain forest. I realised immediately what it was. Those two men in khakis cut that two hundred year old Banyan tree by the canal yesterday; it was ordered by that long faced village headman. The goddess who lived in the tree had to go and it was her leaving that I saw.'

'That Banyan tree was always the home of the goddess of rain. You're right. Sadly she had to leave,' said Loku Mahatmaya.

'When I had a cough like this before, ginger, coriander, wild asparagus and liquorice drink always cured it. Even ginger, lemon and honey worked. I don't know what's wrong with me this time. I must ask Dasa to bring a car tomorrow so that I can go to Matara and see Doctor Wickrama.' Loku Mahatmaya's cough stopped him talking.

'I'll come with you,' said Dikwelle Hamine.

'I must get something for my backache. You remember the narrow escape I had when I was ill, I almost died. Thanks to Dr. Wickrama, my life was saved. You don't want the same thing happening again!' Dikwelle Hamine became agitated.

'I can't bear to lose my cow, Ratti. She's like a child to me. In the evenings the whole area round the byre is empty. I miss that little red calf so much. I remember how she used to wait for me, chomping and shaking her head, when I took some grass for her. I hope she's all right at Rukmali's.' Loku Mahatmaya put his palm against his chest, as he coughed and wheezed tears trickled from his rheumy eyes. .

'Don't worry about Ratti. You're just not well enough to look after cows anymore. You can't even look after yourself.

I suppose this is what happens to everybody when they get old. I remember when I was ten my uncle went somewhere in the dry zone, to an elephant jungle in Hambantota. There were only a few people living in chenas and it was a wilderness with elephants and wild buffaloes. He was a forest ranger. He came home with a cough but he could never go back again. Unfortunately it was too late when they found out he had TB. It's a deadly disease you know! He died within the week.' Dikwelle Hamine was careful not to go near her husband, if she couldn't avoid proximity she held her breath. Secretly she believed he had malaria or TB or both.

The following morning Loku Mahatmaya asked Dasa to bring a car and they got ready to go to the doctor. Dikwelle Hamine opened her ebony wardrobe and took out a green silk sari for herself and the national dress, a white long-sleeved cotton top and a white wrapover sarong for her husband. As she opened the wardrobe door, a blouse she bought as a New Year gift for Rupa, still wrapped in brown paper, fell on the floor. The driver of the car was someone they had always known so Dikwelle Hamine offered him some bananas, biscuits and a cup of tea before they started the journey to the doctor's. Ranhami, the next-door woman, with her son Dasa and Tilakawathie stayed at home. 'We won't be long but don't forget to feed the dogs if we're late.' Loku Mahatmaya spoke as he got into the car.

They were lucky that Rukmali had asked one of the nurses to get a ticket for Loku Mahatmaya and they had no. 4 and didn't have to stay too long in the waiting room. When they were called a nurse directed them into a small room. Dr. Wickrama, wearing a white shirt with folded sleeves, blue trousers, dark framed glasses and a stethoscope round his neck, sat in a cane chair. Monotonously a ceiling fan flapped above like a hawk about to catch its prey. Green curtains framing the side-window had yellowed in the sun. They blew in and out of rusty metal bars. There was a picture of Dr. Wickrama standing in front of a snow-covered Red Square, when he was a student at Moscow University. A large brown spider was spinning in the sticky yellow cushioned middle of its web. In a corner of the picture its hairy legs moved to the white wall. Loku

Mahatmaya and Dikwelle Hamine sat on wooden chairs by the doctor's table. Dr. Wickrama moved his glasses slightly down as he looked at them. Loku Mahatmaya began to speak.

'I've this nasty cough, it never goes and I feel feverish, doctor.'

'How long have you had this cough?'

'I think for over a month.' He looked at his wife and she nodded.

'Have you taken anything?'

'Only some herbal medicines and 'kasaya' which we make at home boiling fourteen types of herbs.'

The doctor examined Loku Mahatmaya's chest.

'Do you smoke?'

'Never.'

'Do you drink?'

'Only an occasional glass of toddy. I suppose it's good for health!'

Dikwelle Hamine interrupted.

'Not occasionally doctor. We always have coconut toddy at home and he never misses it a day!'

Dr. Wickrama laughed.

'You have phlegm in your chest and a throat infection Loku Mahatmaya. I'll give you some tablets and a syrup for three weeks. Remember to come and see me again if you're still not well. You must have plenty of rest and don't do any heavy work.'

'I don't do any heavy work doctor. I've even had to give away my cow and calf.' Loku Mahatmaya continued, coughing.

Within two weeks Loku Mahatmaya felt better but he was still tired. He managed to walk around in the garden and do some occasional weeding but most of the day he sat on his armchair talking to the two dogs, Tommy and Ticky. Loku Mahatmaya and Dikwelle Hamine never called each other by name. Instead they would make some kind of calling signal like 'Are you there?' or 'Can you hear me?' After an early midday meal Dikwelle Hamine sat on the cement floor of the veranda weaving a reed mat with green and magenta designs of deer. The two dogs curled up and slept one on the coir doormat and the other next to the armchair where Loku Mahatmaya was resting. After a short nap he called his wife. 'Can you hear me!' Dikwelle Hamine rolled up her half-woven mat and Tilakawathie walked in with some black tea and inch square lumps of jaggery, a sugar-like dark brown sweet made of evaporated palm juice.

Loku Mahatmaya took off the muslin cloth he had wrapped round his head into the shape of a turban and placed it on the armrest and said, 'I sent Coronalis a message with Dasa and asked him to come round this evening.'

'What for?'

Dikwelle Hamine finished her cup of tea and put the empty cup on the teak table.

'It's impossible to continue working in the rice fields with just paid workers. We have to give them food and pay their hourly wages. On special days like sowing and reaping I'm completely tied up and I can't do anything else! Unless I'm watching they don't do the job properly and at the end of the day they go home counting their money. We're short of cash and in poor health at our age. I thought of asking Coronalis to take over the work in the rice fields, at least for a few seasons.'

'That's a good idea!' Dikwelle Hamine said.

'Tilakawathie and I find it very hard, cooking meals and making tea for the workers. They expect to be entertained as if they were at a wedding! We've to offer them milk tea with sugar and meals on time. Black tea with jaggery is no longer acceptable. If there's the slightest problem or delay their faces turn sour. Those days when people used to help their neighbours have gone. They just don't care about family values, all they're after is drinking and gambling money. But the thing is I'm not sure about Coronalis. His father was always faithful to the Maha Gedera family. I vagucly remember Coronalis having some alcohol and drug problems when he used to work with his father!'

'Coronalis has given up all his bad habits since he became a family man. He's well mannered and I've never seen him drunk. He's a strong young man and I'm sure he'll carry on with farming without giving us any trouble.' Loku Mahatmaya had no worries in handing over the rice land to Coronalis. The old farmer who was Coronalis's father became paralysed after a stroke and had to retire early. Since then Loku Mahatmaya decided to have the work done by paid workers because he was not keen on giving his land to a tenant farmer. He believed that Coronalis wasn't the kind of man who would go strictly by the book and demand that Loku Mahatmaya give him full tenancy rights over more than half the crops.

Dikwelle Hamine sat by the window and spoke while she was pedalling her Singer sewing machine. She was making up a dress for Tilakawathie. The machine came as part of her dowry and she treated it like a child. She made curtains, pillowcases, chair covers, blouses and dresses with the machine. Because it was the only machine in the whole village she sometimes had to sew things for neighbours. The machine was highly polished in black with a varnished table and metal pedals. There was a gold trademark at the right hand corner and 'Made in England' lettered in shiny gold. Once a week she cleaned it from top to the bottom with an oilcloth and no one could tell that it was forty years old. When she was pedalling the cloth crept under the needle faster and faster showing perfectly made stitches above the hem and Dikwelle Hamine shook her head to the front and back and moved her hands faster even than the working machine.

'Now it's time to find someone suitable for marrying Tilakawathie. She's eighteen and we can't keep a young woman at home forever. A respectable man possibly with his own house and someone who can earn his own living would be more than sufficient.' Dikwelle Hamine stopped pedalling to snip the end of a thread.

'Kapurala the matchmaker is always at the Post Office. He doesn't seem to have much work these days. I'll mention it to him tomorrow.' Loku Mahatmaya said.

'We're not going to live forever. We must do everything we can for her while we're alive. Although she's not our own daughter, she runs this house. What we really need is someone who can keep an eye on Maha Gedera and the land and who's not living far from us.'

'I think the matchmaker has lost interest in his job recently. He doesn't run up and down the country like he used to do.'

'Why?'

'He has made so many mistakes that he's not very popular anymore. Oh! I forgot to tell you something, you remember Gunapala, a son of a businessman who was proposed for Rupa. In the end it was our matchmaker who found a wife for him, a girl from a rich family in Colombo. Within three months his marriage had broken down!'

'What a shame! Gunapala was such a handsome man,' replied Dikwelle Hamine.

'The marriage was arranged without the consent of the girl. She was given a huge dowry. The girl had left him and gone to live in America. God knows why! The matchmaker had the blame from both sides. The girl's father was a wealthy man with all kinds of connections. The matchmaker is frightened to go anywhere near Colombo in case he gets beaten up!'

'Fate cannot be stopped by anyone. These things are meant to happen. See what has happened to our Rupa. She's not even living in her birthplace!' Dikwelle Hamine sighed.

TWENTY FOUR

Another spring was in the air with its aromatic days. Rupa and Lisa were playing in the garden. Lisa laughed as she rattled her wriggly-jiggly funny faced green train. She tried to run along the gravel path with her pull-along dog, fell over and began to cry. Rupa carried her into the house and Lisa squawked her squeaky duck. Rupa had collected a cardboard box full of empty kitchen rolls, Weetabix picture cards, plastic and rubber toys. Lisa spent hours and hours playing on the sitting room floor until finally she fell asleep with her grubby yellow teddy bear with red floppy ears. Desperation to see her parents grew and grew in Rupa.

As months changed to years, Lisa grew to a girl and Rupa thought it was time to go home for a visit. When Aruna came in that evening they were both irritable for different reasons. Aruna with difficulty was concentrating his mind on practical realities and Rupa on her own frustrations. Finally she spoke.

'Lisa is nearly three now and my parents aren't well. I had a letter from my father today. It's unusual for him to talk about their illnesses and his sadness about handing over the rice lands to a tenant farmer. I think, Aruna, that it's time to go back.'

'You must be joking Rupa, I don't think I can make it this summer?'

'Can't you take your holidays in August? Surely they'll understand if you tell them we're going home.'

'I think it's a complete waste of time and money. It will cost a lot more than you think.'

'You always say that, Aruna, I think it's pointless the way we live in a foreign country with no hopes whatsoever. It's impossible to plan everything months ahead.'

'I think the best thing is to send Lisa to Ceylon for a while.

It would be better for her in every way. She'll at least get some tropical air and they'll look after her with no problems. She can run around freely in the gardens without having to be wrapped in heavy woollens! You can work and earn some money and after a year or two we can either go back to Ceylon or have Lisa back here.'

'I wouldn't dream of doing that, Aruna. We can send her to a nursery when she's three. The day-nursery near the clock tower is very good.'

Aruna's harshness angered Rupa. She just couldn't be separated from her daughter. Aruna was irritated by Rupa's closeness to Lisa. His ideas about bringing up a child were different to Rupa's. Apart from providing food, clothes and a bed to sleep in, he thought children should grow like wild plants. Rupa noticed his irritability. The tense atmosphere between them came to boiling point. Lisa, wearing a blue smocked dress, ran up and down from the kitchen to the lounge holding a string attached to the neck of her black spotted yellow rubber dog.

The apparent calm of Rupa and Aruna's home life was completely deceptive, beneath the surface was a deepening fissure. Aruna's returns became irregular, sometimes it was late at night and Rupa and Lisa were already in bed. Aruna's dinner, left on the table, had gone cold but he had eaten somewhere else anyway. The spicy pork chops and rice cooked by Rupa had to be reheated and used the following day. Rupa didn't know where he had been but there was always the strong smell of alcohol on his breath. She didn't question him. At least for the time being, she would leave things to simmer. Rupa constantly thought about Aruna's suggestion of sending Lisa to relatives in Ceylon and so enable her to work. When she imagined how Lisa would grow up with aunts, uncles and cousins while her parents lived in England she became desperate and confused. A few days after it came as a surprise for Rupa that Aruna had decided to take a week's holiday and that they would all go to Scotland. The atmosphere improved somewhat and Rupa began to wonder if the troubles were at an end. She awaited Aruna's homecomings with some considerable excitement. Sometimes she read a book or sat by the window until she heard the steady hum of his blue Peugeot and then the slamming of the car door.

It was a Friday afternoon and they were getting ready to leave early on the Saturday morning. The Peugeot had been serviced and its tank was full; the suitcases, Lisa's food and bottles were packed.

'I've put two blankets and an electric heater in the boot just in case the bed and breakfast place is cold, Aruna. Edinburgh is colder than London and I don't want Lisa to fall ill.'

'The guest house is centrally heated so it shouldn't be a problem, Rupa. They'll give us extra blankets if it's cold.'

'Everything's ready. One last thing I have to do tomorrow morning is to take Lisa's teddy.'

Saturday morning arrived with the cooing of a wood pigeon signalling the approach of another warm day. They started at seven. Rupa, who had never been to Scotland, chatted incessantly to Aruna and Lisa but neither of them seemed to share her excitement. During the long tiring journey Aruna kept himself busy, driving as efficiently as a cabby who wanted to finish early. Sitting in the car seat for a long time Lisa was uncomfortable and cried to sit on Rupa's lap. When Lisa was sick Rupa went to the back seat and tried to play with her, rattling, shaking and showing red and yellow plastic toys. Lisa was quiet for a while when she was given a bald rubber doll with a belly button and a thumb in its mouth. Lisa pulled its thumb and tried to put her own finger into the doll's mouth but it didn't fit in. She laughed and tried again. Aruna had to stop the car in almost every service station to give Lisa a break. The scenery changed abruptly from golden fields of rapeseed to the murky waters of the River Aire. Rupa wistfully remembered Hunter's 'Beautiful North' when they made a brief stop by a bridge where a line of grey metal arches spanned the black polluted waters. She held Lisa up to watch the slow procession of coal barges, each with a great shire horse helping to pull it along, heavy rope stretched taut between the harness and the barge. The winding road from North Wales to Scotland seemed never ending. Although winter had gone and it was mid spring, snow still tipped the grey mountain tops and lay like a wall of mirrors reflecting the sunshine in glossy clouds. Lowland mountain fastnesses stretched as far as the eye could see, carpeted in magenta blossoms. The foot high heather plants with their fine leaves and clusters of flowers were covered in snow during winter. Now the spring sun shone they had grown again. They drove along the valleys between black mountains of rock slate and approached a huge plateau, away from any human habitation. They drove past a long stretch of hilly grassland where cattle and sheep herds grazed like still stones. The sudden thundering rumble and the hooting was from the Aberdeen Express, creeping round the bends and tunnels and all the way the railway line was parallel to the road. At last they came to a farmland area with a treeless landscape and boundaries of slate fences. The aerial view from the crest of the road was a frenzied tapestry of vivid shapes and colours.

When they arrived at the Travellers Inn guesthouse they were exhausted after ten hours of travelling. The warm generously proportioned room was welcoming with a double bed in the middle and a single in one corner. The walls were white and there were thick brocade curtains at the windows. In a cupboard by the bed was an electric kettle and on top a tray with sugar cubes, milk powder, tea, coffee and two cups. Neither of them was hungry and for once Lisa seemed content. Rupa made some tea while Lisa played on the floor and Aruna lay on the bed and fell asleep. Rupa chattered away to Lisa while she got her ready for bed. As soon as her head touched the pillow she fell into a deep sleep and Rupa sighed with relief.

'Your tea is getting cold, Aruna. It looks as though the journey's knocked both of you out. Let's just hope she sleeps through.'

'I'm going to have a shower. There's plenty of hot water.'

Aruna had his cup of tea and went to the bathroom. The blue tiled floor with its gleaming white bath and shower was very impressive. The water was heated by an electric geyser fixed to the wall.

'It was a long drive but I feel much better now.'

Aruna came back with a bath towel wrapped round his waist, his hair still wet and streaky. He put on his sarong then dried his hair. During the night Lisa cried occasionally but Rupa managed to calm her by taking her into the double bed. Aruna had some sleep but shifted uncomfortably with Lisa and her teddy packed between them. He realised that this was to be the pattern of the whole seven nights in Edinburgh. They visited the castle, which stood like a looming giant on top of the hill.

Ramrod stiff Scottish guards kited out in kilts and sporrans stood sentinel by the raised portcullis. They reminded Rupa of the life-sized models stood outside tobacconists' shops but when she whispered her observation to Aruna he merely grunted. A group of English schoolchildren were in front of them. Suddenly one of the boys pulled off a girl's beret and threw it in the air. It landed on one of the spikes stuck in the wall and the girl began to cry bitterly, out of all proportion to her loss. The teacher grabbed the errant boy and shook him.

'Now look what you've gone and done,' she hissed. 'Poor Tracy's in tears and it's all your fault! Go to the gatehouse and explain what's happened to one of the guides.' The boy's face was red with embarrassment as he shuffled off to the gatehouse.

'Do you know, Aruna, I rather wish I'd grown up here instead of in Ceylon! The children are so free, not frightened of anyone really. Nobody arranges their lives and their marriages, they can make up their own minds.'

Aruna sniffed. 'That's just your problem Rupa. You think you can do just what you want even after you're married. I spent a lot of time working out our future but all you want to do is stay at home with Lisa like the English. You're beginning to forget where we're from and how things are done in Ceylon.'

'It's you who doesn't care and you who forgets how things are done in our own country.

They spent a rainy day in Glasgow but to Rupa it seemed no more than a mass of stone tenements and roaring trams. By the time they returned to Edinburgh the tension between the two of them was mounting.

'There's nothing much to see except sky scrapers and packed streets.' Rupa said disappointedly.

'It's not so simple as you think and it isn't easy to see everything in a day with a two-year-old. I'm not a magician. There was a really good Motor Exhibition but how could we go with Lisa?'

The child was becoming unsettled, her eyes and nose running, her face red. Rupa knew that there was a lot of work and trouble ahead if it developed into a full-blown cold. The tension between them ebbed away but Rupa knew it would return. The more they pushed the arguments away the more they seemed to return and each time with more bitterness.

Rupa was glad when the holiday was over and Aruna finally went back to work. She wondered what the rest of their life would be like. Would it be nothing more than arguments and the spaces between them? Rupa insisted Aruna should go to Ceylon with them for a holiday and tried to persuade him while they were still in Edinburgh.

'It's better Aruna, if both of us can go with Lisa, otherwise the neighbours and our relatives may wonder why I am on my own and not with my husband.'

'I neither know nor care what your villagers think! Either you go with Lisa or just don't mention it again.'

Aruna's anger overflowed and Rupa finally burst into tears.

TWENTY FIVE

A few days after Rupa and Lisa had gone to Ceylon for six weeks' holiday Aruna left his job without giving notice. He phoned in to say he had glandular fever but never went back. During the first few days he didn't go out of the house but sat in his armchair, staring ahead. Some days he slept until late afternoon. He never cooked anything but an occasional meal Rupa had left in the freezer. A week later there was not even a loaf of bread in the house. Then he started to go out in the evenings and eat his meals at a restaurant or a pub and return home after midnight. Some days he never came home at all and spent the night in a guesthouse. When he realised his money was running out he used up some of Rupa's 'emergency household money' that she had hidden. Although he sent applications for jobs he never bothered to go if he was called for interview.

'I must find a way of earning money before she gets back. What's the point in earning a little money just for our living? My Peugeot's an old crock. When did I last do any repairs to the house? It must have been before Rupa came to England, five six years ago? I can't remember. Bills! Telephone, electricity, gas and tax demands piling up on the writing table. If Rupa was here somehow she would have paid those bills before the red reminder. I went to the bank yesterday and they agreed to give me a loan and one bigger than I expected. She won't be told about it. It's my money and I'll spend it, but not on bills! So many people have become millionaires by the age of forty. They can enjoy their lives! I don't want anyone's advice and Rupa only talks about education. Why do some people sacrifice their lives looking after their children? I don't think our parents had sleepless nights or killed themselves for their families. The children's future depends on their parents' wealth. I want to start my own business. When it's well established I will open branches all over. If I had a son I could hand over my business to him one day. Women are only good for babies and housework. Their knowledge doesn't stretch beyond a kitchen spoon! The man who listens to a woman is an idiot. They are the ghosts of humankind. If I tell my ideas to her or anybody else they'll certainly try to spoil the whole thing. It doesn't really matter whether I eat or not as long as I can do what I want.' He paced across the room, paced back again and looked out of the window, his eyes wild and strange. Then he sat in his armchair and stared at the ceiling light until he fell asleep, but not for long. Why was he behaving like a lunatic? Was it the separation from Rupa and Lisa? Had his mind tangled up with the insoluble family problems? He just didn't understand. Things were not very good at home between Rupa and Aruna and they never seemed to get any better. Suddenly he felt there was a black cloud rushing towards him. He closed his eyes and thought he was going to die. When he peeped again he noticed that the bedroom curtains had not been drawn since Rupa had gone.

'The doors and windows of this house haven't been opened and I'll keep them tight shut. The air is dirty and the atmosphere is polluted. Between the sky and the earth there's a layer of thick air mixed with dangerous chemical elements of lethal dust. If I open the window the wind will blow with germs unhealthy for human life.'

Aruna paced the room again and stood by the window looking at the distant television centre, a tall building with an illuminated tower on top. He imagined how the fast flying birds vainly beat their wings against the concrete pillar and dropped down to the ground with a sound, sosh, sosh!'

'TV antennas are sticking out to the sky from every roof and there are broadcasting stations everywhere. They send secret messages from spies. America, Russia, Ceylon, Germany and England all these countries belong to secret organisations.'

Aruna found difficulty in breathing. He tried to squeeze his nostrils between his fingers. He felt as if his lungs were about to collapse. Starting from the lungs his whole body system would fail and leave him dead. He held the radio on the writing table with both hands then smashed it against the window with his full strength. There was the sound of an explosion and the fragmented glass spread all over, tinkling palely. He noticed an enormous hole in the wall between the window frames, bits of broken glass all over and the curtains blowing in and out with the sudden wind. He saw everything through the hole, the black tarmacced road and lowering dark clouds.

'That enormous dark green heavy vehicle is stationary, a council dustbin lorry. No, it's not stopped, now it's moving, wobbling up the road, towards my house with its roaring noise. There's a gang of men, they're aliens in yellow clothes on the pavements and they are collecting the rubbish from metal bins. The rotator at the back of the lorry squeezes the rubbish with its metal forks like rolling bundles of hay. These men are university graduates like Rupa. Within a minute the lorry will have stopped in front of my house. They are the secret agents and liars riding a bin lorry full of dirt and rubbish.'

He slammed the bedroom door as loudly as he could. There was strewn glass over the chair, carpet, books and the stack of bills on the table. He closed his eyes and lay on the bed.

More and more Aruna was out of reality as the confusion in his mind increased. Even the slightest thing he began to see in the kaleidoscopic wind tunnel of his mind. He found the most mundane things hard to believe and impossible to understand. Inevitably he became helpless and at times completely unaware of what was happening. His fantasies were more and more complex and resolving the impasses impossible. His mind struggled and then fell into a morass. He grew suspicious of everyone. When he tried to run away his mind collapsed. He realised that the only way to win the fight with the ghostly monster pursuing him was by hiding and suddenly confronting it. When he went out the people, the animals, the scenery, everything seemed unnatural. Like a snail slowly moving its head out of its shell occasionally he crept out, but when danger signalled he threw himself into a shelter, remained hidden and then moved on furtively.

He built an inner world of labyrinthine complexity and willed it to work. He made his plans but at their heart was his burning hatred for women in general and Rupa in particular. Like a mongoose drumming its tail on the ground, planning to hypnotise a venomous snake, he plotted and planned in secret having not the slightest idea of what would come out of it all.

'Mummy, Mummy,' Aruna seemed to hear Lisa calling her mother, knowing full well they were in Ceylon. The house with its closed doors, drawn curtains and slivers of glass, had the sour smell of stale food. A cold wind occasionally blew through the broken window flapping the damp curtains and dusty books on the table already wet with rain. The branches of the apple tree shook in the wind.

'Lisa… Lisa…' he called his daughter. He stared into the night, vaguely remembering where they were.

TWENTY SIX

The view from the aircraft was like a collage, the sea was above and the sky below. The horizon was a blue and white straight line, neatly drawn. Through mountains of white cloud the aircraft descended, an hour and a half late when the VCIO landed at Colombo airport. Rupa couldn't believe her eyes when she saw the endless ribbon of coconut palms, silver sand beach, the glittering blue velvet Indian Ocean and Ceylon, the Pearl of the East. After a long sleep Lisa had woken and she cried when the aircraft abruptly thundered, shook and touched down. It was just after nine in the morning and as they came out at once they felt the rising tropical heat. After the immigration check, they walked through the reception area, passing a line of duty free shops and then they came to the luggage collection point. Lisa was thrilled to see how the luggage moved along the carousel and wanted a ride. Rupa raised her voice and said 'No! You can't do that Lisa!' The airport was like a moving sea, passengers carrying travel bags, suit cases, holdalls and children. Women in glinting silk saris, khaki uniformed porters, taxi drivers waving name cards, the roar of passing trolleys and the echoing of announcements calling transit passengers to the Singapore flight; through the flow of passengers rushing out at last they came to arrivals. Rukmali, her husband and their children, Damit and Lal, were waiting. Arrivals, as always was flooded with smiles, tears, kisses and laughter.

Back at Maha Gedara Loku Mahatmaya and Dikwelle Hamine had been getting ready for weeks and weeks. They woke early, feeling the strength they had so long lacked, they talked about Rupa and Lisa. With a piece of cloth Loku Mahatmaya cleaned the dusty books on Rupa's table but some of the book covers were scorched because they had been left in front of a window for seven years.

Four days ago Dasa cut an enormous bunch of bananas from the garden but they were green and needed to be ripened so Dasa dug a hole under the rambutan tree, placing a layer of dried coconut leaves at the bottom and on the sides. The bunch of bananas was wrapped in hay and buried under a sheet of wood, a tiny hole pierced in the middle for air. He covered the top with soil. Once the bananas were hidden underground they had to be kept there for three days. Every morning and evening Loku Mahatmaya blew smoke from a charcoal flare into the ground through the small hole on top. The day before Rupa's arrival Dasa came to dig up the bananas. Loku Mahatmaya stood and watched, his eyes filled with tears.

'They're ripened! They're yellow! Just like an orange parrot.'

Loku Mahatmaya cried. Dikwelle Hamine rushed to see the perfect bunch of bananas ready, completely yellow.

'I made some cashew nut toffees yesterday. I must make some treacle slices this afternoon. They are delicious with bananas.' Dikwelle Hamine touched the softening bananas as she talked. Loku Mahatmaya looked at the wood apple tree covered in white fruits.

'I picked some ripe wood apples this morning. The honey mangoes will be ready by tomorrow.' Dasa climbed the mango tree, picked some ripening mangoes and put them in the wicker basket, which he carried on his back. Loku Mahatmaya took them upstairs and spread them on a gunnysack under the bed. Every morning he pressed the mangoes with his thumb to check whether they were ready to eat.

On their journey from the airport to Matara Lisa seemed tired and uncomfortable with the soaring heat.

'I must have travelled hundreds of times up and down this road but I feel very strange today. The heat is unbearable, the trees and even the people look withered.' Rupa took off Lisa's shoes and clothes and left her with only her cotton pants.

'We haven't had rain for months. There's a shortage of water. The drought is worsening and the people who live in towns get power cuts everyday. You must be very tired, Rupa! Let me hold Lisa.' Rukmali tried to take her but she wouldn't go to a stranger.

During the last seven years Rukmali's son, Damit, had become a grown child. Lal, her second son, was four. Their van drove through the crowded streets of Colombo; bicycle bells, bullock-carts, tooting horns, Leyland buses, ice cream vendors and clouds of dust. Everything was sticky and dusty, the air sultry and all hands were damp with sweat. The rainless earth was burning. During the hundred-mile journey, all the way along the beach, the breeze was slightly cooler. On the horizon the sea and the sky massed as night fell.

It was pitch dark when finally they arrived in Maha Gedara. As it was a special day the two-leafed solid front door was open wide. The glow from the ceiling lamp on the veranda spread as far as the king coconut tree in the garden. Only occasionally you could see the front door of Maha Gedara open. Once a week Loku Mahatmaya opened every door, cleaned the cobwebs and dust from chairs and fanlights with a coir broom and shut them again. Dikwelle Hamine sat outside on the cement step, her smile could be seen from a distance. Rupa at once noticed that her parents had aged during the seven years. Dikwelle Hamine's face was deeply wrinkled, the skin under her eyes sagged and darkened. She was shrunken, hunched and pale and her hair was grey. Loku Mahatmaya was thin and drawn, his ribs prominent, walking with the help of a stick and occasionally he coughed. Tommy, the fifteen-year-old dog, had gone deaf, one eye was blind and he hobbled behind Loku Mahatmaya with his tail bent between his hind legs. Ticky, the other dog, had died. As she entered the house she smelt a mouldy dampness. The house hadn't been repaired for a long time and patches of green fungi had grown on the white walls. There was a crack in the concrete ceiling over the veranda. The bed and wardrobe in Rupa's room were left untouched. Lisa was tired and had to be put to bed straight away. When she pulled a pillow from the almira a gang of red cockroaches fell to the floor, creeping under the bed and vanishing into the drawers. Rupa realised that her parents had lost all interest in the house. Rupa was devastated when she learned that Tilakawathie had left two months before. Nobody in the village knew where she had gone. There was a rumour that she was living in a chena in the northern dry zone with some unknown family. Dikwelle Hamine was furious about the whole affair.

'I just can't believe it. Tilakawathie is a member of the Maha Gedara family,' Rupa said.

'I don't want to hear about that vesi. We gave her food, skirts, blouses, saris, gold necklaces and bangles with no thought of the cost. She wasn't even too old for marriage! Only very recently we'd spoken with Kapurala the matchmaker about a marriage proposal for her. She couldn't wait, could she! Whether she's alive or dead I just don't care.'

'Don't be so nasty about her mother! She looked after Maha Gedara and she cared about us all. I just can't fathom her suddenly going off. We'll never find anyone better than Tilakawathie.'

'There's nothing we can do about it. We never had any argument, no kind of row at all. But she did become stubborn. She didn't do any work in the vegetable plot and every afternoon she went to bed, pretending to be ill. She didn't have much to do in this house, especially after the rice fields were given to the tenant farmers. All she had to do was make something for us to eat. It was no big deal for a young woman of eighteen. I'll never have her back over my doorstep and what she did was a disgrace. The humiliation caused by her is quite unforgivable. I don't want to spit on the sky, it'll drop on my face. I couldn't tie up that cow to a tree with a rope!' Dikwelle Hamine continued talking and then suddenly went quiet. However much she denied it Dikwelle Hamine couldn't bear the loss. Tilakawathie helped with the cooking, the housework and the gardening. When Dikwelle Hamine was convalescent after her long illness Tilakawathie nursed her. Rupa remembered how they made Vesak lanterns together and secretly went to the rain forest to cut bamboo. Tilakawathie cooked an early meal on Vesak day and they went to the temple in white clothes. Rupa only vaguely remembered the last New Year they spent together at Maha Gedara. Tilakawathie was wearing a green dress with a yellow floral pattern. Rupa went to the kitchen hoping this was a dream, then she began to worry about the missing Tilakawathie.

Within a week the two-year-old parrot had flown from its cage.

It woke everyone in the house, with its gibbering and singing and called Tilakawathie 'sister, sister.' When it had flown away once before, it returned in the evening and sat on Tilakawathie's shoulder. But this time it never returned.

Tilakawathie had left home one Sunday afternoon when Loku Mahatmaya was out visiting Rukmali's family. After lunch Dikwelle Hamine had her usual hour's snooze. When Loku Mahatmaya came back about four, he assumed Tilakawathie was weeding the vegetable beds. When she didn't return at dusk Loku Mahatmaya started to worry, then panicked and searched the gardens, the fields and even inside the well in case she had drowned. Loku Mahatmaya wondered if she had been bitten by a cobra and was lying dead or in a coma. Dasa went to every house in the village trying to find some clue as to her whereabouts but no one had seen her. Loku Mahatmaya had her listed as a missing person but so far nobody had come forward with any news, only rumours that she had been seen in some distant market with a man. Tilakawathie's dusty teak wardrobe had been moved to a corner of the storeroom. When Rupa opened the door the peppermint smell of mothballs poured out into the small dinghy room. Tilakawathie had packed her belongings neatly on the shelves. The green voile dress with faded flower spray prints was folded and laid on a top shelf. The night before Rupa left for England she gave her a black leather handbag and it was hung up onto a hook. Rupa opened the bag and there was a white handkerchief with a blue flower and the initials T.W. cross-stitched in red by Tilakawathie. The handkerchief was folded with a few cloves and cardamoms inside. Rupa felt that the whole village was empty.

Once again the vegetable plot was abandoned, weeds were everywhere and bindweed overhung the banana plants and tangled the croton hedge. The margossa tree in the corner became a bats' habitat at night. Peel, pips and half chewed mangoes, jackfruit, cashew nuts and browning bananas mixed with their black droppings under the tree; covered with flies it gave off a rotting stale smell. Loku Mahatmaya began to miss the early morning song of the green parrot and the fresh cup of tea from Tilakawathie and the pain in his heart grew.

It was a year ago since the next door woman Ranhami had died. Ranhami helped Dikwelle Hamine with the housework, house minding and cooking. She sat by the hearth for hours and hours boiling herbal medicines when someone was ill. Sixty-year-old Ranhami's death had come as a shock to everyone. She had a fit and collapsed while she was drawing water from the well. Loku Mahatmaya gave twenty-five rupees to Ranhami's son, Dasa, to take her to the hospital. Twelve hours later she died without regaining consciousness. The small house where she lived belonged to Maha Gedara. Dasa and his family with two children had by now moved into her house. The village near Maha Gedara had only a handful of families. Rocks, hills, streams, trees and people all belonged to the village margined with paddy fields. The villagers were used to a self-sufficient rural lifestyle and lived their infinite lives. Long footpaths wandered through woodlands past the village, through bamboo marshes and citrus hills where the peacocks danced. There was a stream where the villagers swam under the scorching sun. The air was heavy with pollen and the fragrance of wild flowers, bormbu shrubs with scented white blossoms, satin and banyan trees going on and on.

TWENTY SEVEN

Everyone at Maha Gedara, together with Rukmali's family, was getting ready to go to Kataragama Temple for a ritual Puja dedicated to Skanda, the god of war. The journey had to be started at five the following morning so as to be there at ten for the ceremony.

'I'll make a packed lunch for everyone. We can eat our meal somewhere by the river' Rukmali said.

'I don't mind bringing some fish and onion fry, some savoury rolls and bananas. We need a few limes for the Puja but don't bother to buy them from the market. Our lime tree in the back garden is drooping with fruits.' Dikwelle Hamine roasted some limes on a charcoal fire and put them in a clay pot. When Rupa was pregnant Dikwelle Hamine and Loku Mahatmaya had made a vow to the god Skanda to bring mother and the child for a Puja after bathing them in the holy river Menik Ganga. The promise had to be kept promptly before ill fate should befall them. Rukmali was very busy; lunch packets of rice and curry were ready, wrapped in banana leaves and packed tight in a wicker box. Drinking water was poured into empty plastic medicine bottles provided by Dr. Nimal's wife. They were in the van early and soon on their way to the temple.

On the two-hour journey from Matara to Kataragama they had to drive through the dry zone where the driver had to be cautious without sounding the horn because of the wild elephants crossing the road. People who grew fruit and vegetables in chenas would bring their crops to the roadside and sell them from the cadjan huts. Onions, aubergines, sweetcorn, chillies, mangoes, bananas, roasted peanuts and cashews, pots of curd made from buffalo milk and treacle were displayed along the makeshift stalls. No one seemed to care about flies or dust. They bought what they fancied and Loku Mahatmaya paid for everyone. The five-month drought had come to an end and the water level in the river had increased. The torrential downpour in the highlands caused the lower levels to flood. Turbid water gushed over the banks, the river flowed fast with walls of rolling froth.

'I don't think anybody can bathe in the river today. Just get a handful of water and wash your face. Remember to wash Lisa's feet in holy water.'

Dikwelle Hamine gave everyone a roasted lime. The swollen river roared. Rupa was so frightened that someone brought her a bucket of pale water. They wetted their hair with lime juice and water for ritual purification. Everyone dressed in white and approached the temple across the bridge. Rupa, holding a tray of jasmine, followed Dikwelle Hamine. The rain had stopped and the sun was burning. Lisa and Rukmali's children enjoyed digging holes in the scorching sand.

They watched fire walking, men and women walking over a bed of burning embers. The temple grounds shook with the constant blowing of conch shells and drum beats.

Past memories came back to Rupa suddenly, she remembered the day she had come here with Aruna. It was the first day after their wedding.

Rupa paced through the door into the temple holding Lisa's hand. The room where the god Skanda lived was dim. The coconut oil brass lamp in the middle provided a faint light. Thousands of incense sticks were burning with a smoky aroma. A red screen protected the area around the god's statue. A young woman sat praying on the floor, clasping her hands together. She was making a vow to the god begging for the birth of a son. Rupa, wanting to see the powerful creator, robed in red and garlanded, peered through the rood screen. For a second she shook with fear when her eyes made contact with a looming figure. She couldn't see the god, but only the red turbaned priest chanting Pali and Sanskrit hymns with trays of food offerings in his hands. Perhaps the god was hidden behind him? The woman continued to pray and salaam, believing the god was looking at her. When the Puja ceremony was over, everyone was given a handful of ritual food, a banana, a slice of milk rice, chunk of coconut or some sweets.

Rupa looked at the screen.

'O mighty god!
I am not making a vow today.
God Skanda I ask a boon of you,
To grant the wish I asked of you.'

As she came out her ears were filled with the tintinnabulation of the temple bells. Having only two more weeks of their holiday left Rupa decided to visit some of her university friends but she didn't know where they lived. Rupa had lost contact with them since she left the university eight years before.

It was a Sunday morning. The door to the ground floor flat next to the Lazarus Studio in Kandy was closed. It looked deserted with overgrown grass in the front garden. Rupa knocked on the door once and then again. A dog barked and barked but still no one answered. She knocked again, this time louder. She heard the dog running up and down barking, approaching the door, scratching and then retreating.

'Is anybody there? Is anybody there?' She rapped on the dusty window, tracing with her fingertip a loop on the grimy pane. Then she sat on the cracked doorstep, hoping someone would see her. Ten minutes after a drowsy looking old man opened the door. The dog barked non-stop wagging its tail harder and harder.

'I'm Rupa. Does Milan De Silva still live here?'

'I've never heard of anyone in that name!' The old man gave a toothless smile and then looked vaguely at the sky.

'Do you know, about ten years ago a family lived here with their only daughter called Milan? She was a university student.' The old man thought for a minute touching his ear lobe.

'Oh! I know that young lady. She lived in Rome for several years and back again. She lives in Colombo Road now.'

'Can you tell me exactly where it is?'

The old man smiled, rubbing his eyes. He held the white dog with bald patches which was trying to jump out and sniff Rupa as she stood waiting.

'Go straight on about a quarter of a mile. Turn right at the first crossroads to Lake View Terrace. Our little lady lives at number four. It's easy to find, there's a big avocado tree by the gate.'

Milan was a fervent Catholic and Rupa remembered her intention to visit the Vatican City when she was a student. It looked as though she had realised her wish. Rupa felt relieved, she had no doubt that it must be Milan who lived at number four. The old man had given precise instructions, a house with a garden, a large avocado tree in the front with dense green foliage drooping with heavy fruits. Rupa saw a woman in the garden walking towards the house, wearing a long blue skirt and a loose white blouse. She came to the front door when Rupa opened the gate. She looked at Rupa's face inquisitively.

'Don't you recognise me, Milan?'

The elegant woman with a winning smile frowned in puzzlement, then smiled' 'I do recognise you! You're Rupa! You've changed so much. You're thin and your hair is shorter. Please do come in.'

Ten minutes later Rupa was sitting comfortably in an armchair and a young servant girl brought a tray of cakes, bananas and fresh orange juice. After they had a drink they were both delighted to be able to swap stories about the last seven years.

'A year after I left the university I got married and went to England, that's how I lost contact with all my friends. Lisa, my daughter, will be three next birthday.'

'I went to Italy and lived in Rome with my brother for four years. I travel all over the world as a missionary. Last year I went to London for a month. Next month I'm going to Delhi for a couple of weeks. Where is your husband and your daughter?'

'Aruna's in England. I came with Lisa for six weeks' holiday. Lisa is with my sister's family. She doesn't like travelling in hot weather. Have you any idea where those two sisters from Kandy are now? Irangani and Chandrani I mean. I'd very much like to see them again.'

'They're both married. Chandrani lives in Canada. Our friends seem to be scattered all over the world.'

'Milan, have you heard anything of Kumara? I completely lost contact with him. I've no idea what happened to him.'

'I often wonder about you and Kumara, Rupa. I think he also had gone to England.'

'England! How did you find out, Milan?'

'About a year ago I bumped into him. I think it was just before Christmas. We couldn't talk much, I was in a hurry to catch a train to Colombo.'

'Where did you meet him?'

'On the campus. He walked in as I was leaving the library. He asked about you, Rupa. Unfortunately I didn't know your whereabouts.'

'I wonder whether he still lives there.'

'I've no idea but that was the impression I had.'

'He must be married now I suppose. There are so many Asians living in England. It's impossible to find somebody in those countries unless we have their telephone number or their address.'

After lunch with Milan Rupa left feeling as if she had lost something for the second and final time.

The Temple of the Tooth with its golden roof stood by the Kandy Lake guarded by a white wall. Lines of Buddhist Pilgrims worshipped in front of the glaring sacred shrine. Thousands of coconut oil lamps flickered, jasmine, marigold and temple flowers opened and the Kandyan dancers' ankle-bells and drumbeats shook the sky to its end. Rupa took off her shoes at the entrance and walked up the damp steps. As she offered a tray of white lotus to Lord Buddha, she felt as though Kumara was holding her hand. It was only ten years ago since Rupa and Kumara made a vow in front of the same altar, promising to meet when they passed their final exam. Carillons were ringing in the shrine, the campus mountains were fading in a distant mist as Rupa turned away like a camel in the desert who had lost its sense of direction.

Rukmali had found out from a friend that Deva, the Harvard educated executive who had proposed to Rupa, committed suicide during an attack of mental illness, apparently overdosing on his medication. Rupa found it hard to believe the changes over the seven years of her absence: meeting Aruna, Lisa's birth, Hunter the tutor, unforgettable memories of Kumara and her whole life in England ran parallel in her mind. Maha Gedara was ageing alongside Loku Mahatmaya and Dikwelle Hamine. Loku Mahatmaya had lost interest, the cinnamon land had become a wilderness of mimosa and a rash of nettles creeping under the palm trees. Bindweed, like morning glory shaded the scrub with their white flowers. The upstairs shrine was disused and the door closed since Tilakawathie had gone. The weather-beaten bronze statue of Buddha was black and greasy. The marigold offered by Dikwelle Hamine three weeks ago on a full moon day had withered. Now Rupa's six weeks' holiday was finally at an end.

'Six weeks has passed like a single day. Lisa doesn't follow me round and play happily. I don't have any housework or cooking. Aruna must be impatient for our return. Soon it will be winter in England and the fires will have to be lit. Lisa will find it difficult to get used to our life in England again.'

'Rupa, neither your father nor I have the energy we used to have. I'm tired and he's always ill. Please try to come back soon and next time bring Aruna. God bless you.'

Dikwelle Hamine took the fall of her blue sari in her hand and dried her tears. Rupa's eyes were focusing on the calendar on the wall. How fondly she remembered the last days of her holidays from the university and the anticipation of a new term.

'Everybody was so happy during the time Rupa was here. Damit and Lal have had such good times playing with Lisa. How long is it going to be before you come back again?' Rukmali's voice was heavy with sadness.

Finally the day had come for their departure. For Rupa it was so different to the day when she first went to an unknown country to meet her husband when they were only just married. She felt like cancelling her flight and staying at Maha Gedara but Aruna was on his own and they had to go back. Rupa had some vague fear about their future together but she could not put a name to it.

'Don't spend too much money on travelling, my daughter. If anything happens to me Rukmali is here and she'll sort it out.

Spend your money on this little girl's education.' Loku Mahatmaya thinks he hasn't got much time left.

As they said their good-byes at the airport Loku Mahatmaya stroked Lisa's head and Rupa burst into tears. Lisa, wearing a pink cotton dress, ran up and down the passenger lounge carrying a child's handloom bag. She threw her shoes up in the air and then laughed suddenly and with all the spontaneity of innocence. After check-in their luggage was trundled away and they went into the departure lounge. The air-conditioned hall was like a wall dividing them from the heat of their homeland. Loku Mahatmaya stood waving forlornly until Rupa and Lisa disappeared among the moving crowd. There was an announcement asking the passengers on the nine thirty London flight to come to gate three as their aircraft was boarding.

TWENTY EIGHT

As the weeks and months merged, memories of Rupa's holiday in Ceylon faded like a jet stream in an electric storm. Aruna found a job in a postal sorting office. His shift changed every week and if he had a few days break after a week on nights he slept eighteen hours a day or slunk out of the house on his own.

'Why did you leave your last job Aruna? I thought you were happy at A.C. Motors.'

'A.C. Motors? You don't know what they did when I was ill with glandular fever! They actually sent someone from work to see me. Fortunately I wasn't at home that night. He put a note through the door asking me to contact them urgently. Did they think I would have answered the door even if I had been in! Bastards, trying to poke their noses into my affairs!'

'I didn't know you had glandular fever Aruna. Did you send them a medical certificate?'

'No, I didn't see the doctor. What I don't like is secret messengers coming to my door to check my whereabouts and peep through the letterbox. I made sure all the lights were turned off at night and my car was parked in the garage. This job I'm doing now, driving a Royal Mail van isn't what I want either.'

Aruna wasn't interested in giving any house keeping money to Rupa and he simply ignored her. She couldn't pay bills on time and the telephone was disconnected. Due to the rate of inflation the cost of food and basic household goods had shot up. She knew it was going to be a problem when the gas and electricity bills came in December and also McKays, the shop, which used to sell cheap clothing for women and children, had closed down.

Lisa had a place in nursery school from January, five days a week from eight to one. Rupa found it impossible to find a suitable part-time job. All the jobs like cleaning and catering seemed to have been filled. Although there was a vacancy for a school 'dinner lady' Rupa didn't think she could cope with it. She realised that finding a job and earning money wasn't as easy as being a student. Her applications for jobs were rejected out of hand. Being a mother of a young child wasn't helpful either. Three months later, Rupa was still searching for jobs, scanning ads in shop windows, local papers and employment agencies but she ended in despair with no prospects of any job. When Aruna found out what Rupa was doing he said, 'I thought you were going to study history at Birkbeck College, Rupa?'

'No, I gave up on that idea. Survival comes before everything else Aruna!'

Rupa was called for an interview for a job on the assembly line at Philips Electrical. She passed and was asked to start the following Monday. The middle-aged manager had travelled in Asian countries so at least they had some common ground for conversation, tea and rubber plantations, cinnamon and coconut oil production, tropical weather even. Although the pay was poor, what little money she earned came in handy and she could collect Lisa from nursery on her way home from work. Everything in their lives had fallen into routine.

Ten months working in a factory seemed ten months too long for Rupa so she started to look for something better. She couldn't understand why no one wanted her, even as a clerical assistant. She had no previous experience and she spoke with a slight accent, but surely it would be no cause for concern in such basic work? She always expected the thin letter of rejection a few days after an interview and that was what she always received.

'We regret we are unable to offer you this vacancy but we are happy to keep your correspondence for future reference.' When she went for an interview at 'Oaklands Furniture' in Croydon the manageress who interviewed Rupa told her that they only took school leavers with a British education.

Rupa felt so excited when she was offered a very basic job at the General Nursing Council. The strict atmosphere in the office, staffed and managed entirely by women, reminded her of her boarding school days watched over by the Catholic matron. No one spoke or laughed while they wrote up the personal details of nurses in heavy leather-bound ledgers. They had to write with their heads down, as if they were in an examination room. Ten pounds and six shillings a week was her whole salary, which she used on food, clothes and travelling. Two and six pence worth of luncheon vouchers a day was just enough to buy fish and chips from a café. It was a long traipse from Croydon to Portland Place by Greenline bus. She arrived promptly at eight thirty. The bus went through the streets with their shops and offices of Streatham, Brixton, Oval and finally passed Trafalgar Square and Regent Street. Rupa's journeys were as regular as the tick tock of her alarm clock.

Rupa was two months pregnant when she decided to tell Aruna. He acted as though he had been struck by lightning, seeming frightened and confused at the prospect of an addition to their family.

'I'm not worried this time, Aruna. Lisa isn't a bother anymore. I can look after her and the baby without any problem.

Rupa felt more confident but Aruna fell silent. He began to spend more time sunk in deep thought and extravagant plans. Soon he began to see family life as a nightmare of panic and noise. Rupa's nerve began to crack. She became depressed and started to blame herself.

'I sometimes feel it's better if Aruna never comes home at night. He doesn't speak to Lisa and he doesn't want to know about anything. All he does is sit in the armchair and go to sleep or talk as if the world was ending. I haven't seen my friend Chandra since she moved to Edinburgh. Aruna thinks it's entirely my fault that I'm pregnant. If I try to discuss anything with him it always ends up in an argument,' Rupa thought with a kind of burning fury, baffled by Aruna's behaviour.

'What were the real reasons for Aruna's rapid changes of mood? His personality seemed to have cracked down the middle, his moods moved up and down like a yo-yo. The only woman he was ever really close to was his mother. He cried hysterically the day the news of his mother's death arrived.'

Day by day Rupa and Aruna got used to living separate life styles. Rupa did not know his whereabouts or even when he came home. She stopped making regular evening meals because she never knew when he would be home. Sometimes she would fall asleep while reading bedtime stories to Lisa. When she thought about the birth her feelings were numb.

'Why are you always looking so depressed, Aruna? Tell me someone who hasn't got problems! We have to accept things as they come or we'll go mad.'

'Nothing goes right in my life, Rupa. Someone up there is watching me like a hawk, just waiting to disrupt my plans. I've put in an application to start a business in Ceylon to import motor parts but I had no reply, not even after ten weeks!'

'Nobody is watching you. I think you're straining your mind Aruna. Please don't get obsessed with these things. Do you really have to start this business you always talk about? If you can find a reasonably paid job that should be enough to support us.'

'It will take at least a year before I sort out myself properly but I have decided to go somewhere away from London to find a way of earning money. Further up north the cost of living is low and renting business premises is easier than in overcrowded London.'

'You're not going yet, are you?'

'Yes I am, very soon. I've already made up my mind.'

'You never told me that you're looking for a job away from home, Aruna. I think it's better if you can wait, at least for a few more months until I have the baby. I don't feel secure on my own with Lisa and it's not fair that you're trying to get away while I'm pregnant.'

'You shouldn't worry about it, Rupa. It doesn't matter where I work. I can come home when you need me and when I have spare time.'

Rupa was baffled when she heard Aruna's intention to find a job away from home. Why was he trying to go away while Rupa was getting ready for the birth? Was this one of his secret plans when nothing really happens but goes on and on? She felt like crying aloud to the hollow sky but there was nobody to listen. She couldn't have any hope now, not for anything but still the child would have to be born.

Rupa went to bed that night with tears brimming in her heavy eyes. She kept awake the whole night, listening to the rhythm of teeming rain on their bedroom windowpane. Finally the clock struck five. Birds in the woodland grove had already started to sing tweed---too---tweed---too---tweed---too---. It was the beginning of another windy day. She put her arm round Aruna to get close. His face was overshadowed with weariness and the tension in her mind was growing. A frail thread of uncertainty and sadness separated them. It was so hard to pull a carriage with only one horse. An unguided missile in a war zone is dangerous. The doors and windows were still closed against the night but it was already dawn. They breathed in each other's warm breath and felt the other's soft touch under the eiderdown. The crescent moon was fading while the morning star trembled.

TWENTY NINE

'Rupa this is the right job for me, I have to work hard and put all my effort into it. When I find somewhere self-contained to live and get everything sorted out, we can all move! There's nothing to worry about. I'll come home every weekend.'

Aruna slung his green canvas travel bag over his shoulder and his car keys rattled. Rupa looked away, she had nothing to say. She touched her chin with her left hand. It was another gloomy Saturday afternoon.

'Can you bring me a pretty doll, daddy?' Lisa kissed him and waved as he closed the gate. When Aruna left home and went to his new job in the north Rupa's daily routine completely changed. After she left the General Nursing Council on maternity leave, time crawled by. In the mornings she was busy getting Lisa ready and then she walked with her to school. She had to prepare for the birth but the excitement this time was less and she really wanted the day to come quickly. The foetus inside was growing into a healthy baby and seemed to need little attention. During the day she was alone at home in the brewing silence as she waited impatiently for the weekend.

Things seemed to have got better again between Aruna and Rupa. Lisa looked forward eagerly to Friday evenings when Aruna would arrive with chocolates, toys and new clothes.

'I've done so many temporary jobs in the past Rupa. At last I've found a job where I can use my know how. It's with a big motor company and I've got the foreman's job.'

'Since Lisa and I came back from our holiday in Ceylon so many things have gone wrong Aruna. A trail of problems one after another. It's hard to believe that good fortune has finally come to our family.'

'Nobody interferes with my work anymore, not like the place where I worked before, no one knows where I live. I've got a room in a big terrace house in Newcastle belonging to an old Indian man called Abdul Rashid. There's a gas fire and a washbasin in my room. The toilet and kitchen are in the basement. I share them with another tenant who has a bad stammer. I can't understand a word he says! After a day's work I can sleep comfortably because no one's there to peer through my keyhole.'

'You don't know how worried I was Aruna. You looked so unhappy and I didn't know why. I thought your irritability was connected to some illness. Lisa is no bother to me, she's happy with her toys and books. I do feel very lonely on my own though.' Rupa believed that Aruna's depression and her tension would gradually ease and fade away because things were moving in the right direction. His foreman's job was at Ferguson Motors, a large company in Newcastle. Now Rupa had to manage alone. Everything during the week and over the weekends fell into place and all the gaps were filled. One day began and ended with little difference to the next.

Rupa gave birth to a son in the early autumn. They named the baby Shane. Aruna was delighted because it had unexpectedly joined a missing link in the family. Aruna had it in his mind that it was going to be another girl. The birth of a son was regarded as an asset to an Eastern family and that was what Aruna had always wanted.

With two children in their family and her husband always away from home life was not as easy as Rupa had imagined. Although the General Nursing Council was prepared to take her back after three months somehow she couldn't stand the prospect of returning. The children have to be fed, they fall ill and expect an enormous amount of attention from their parents. Being a single mother and discovering all it entailed was a nightmare. The imaginary super mother with a mechanical body and clockwork mind collapsed rapidly in the face of reality.

As time went on Rupa began to feel more and more lonely and tired of her unchangeable routine. She had great support from her neighbours, an English couple called Flora and Anthony who visited her regularly. They had three children of their own and Lisa and Shane played in their large garden. Rupa's children had the opportunity to let off steam in the playroom of their house with a huge electric train set. The trains ran beneath tunnels, over bridges and through signals to the children's delight. Rupa and Flora went shopping together and did baby sitting for each other.

Then after only a few months the couple sold their house and moved to Wiltshire in the West Country and Rupa began to feel that no one could replace them. Anthony and Flora's new detached house was near Salisbury Plain, with a separate playground for children in their large garden.

Stonehenge was only four miles from their new home and they took Rupa and the children there one day. It reminded Rupa of the ancient ruins at Anuradhapura in Ceylon. The huge slabs of black stone stood like giants in the middle of the plain, staring at the empty sky as though they were worshipping the sun and praying for their ancestors who had lived during the Iron Age.

'Rupa, you're very welcome here with the children anytime. They can play and run around with our boys.'

When Flora spoke Rupa felt a great surge of relief.

The complexity of their lives following months of disagreement added to the burdens of the young family but the situation finally improved. The transformation that occurred after the birth of a son was incredible. Every weekend Aruna brought some presents for the children and seemed to enjoy watching them play. Rupa couldn't believe it when he took her out shopping and asked her to choose what she wanted. He bought her a Jones portable sewing machine, a dress and a jacket. They felt a kind of closeness that they had never possessed before.

'I think, Rupa, I have done enough for the others and now it's time for me to start something of my own. I've learned from Fergusons how to manage a business properly. Now I feel confident and should get out as quickly as possible.'

'What do you mean, Aruna?'

'I want to become self-employed. I'm thinking of starting a

small business, repairing vehicles and selling parts. You may not have realised but this is a kind of business where I can make a lot of money Rupa.'

'You can't start a workshop just like that .You need money for it.'

'It shouldn't be a problem. I can get a bank loan. I saw Fergusons general manager last week and explained everything. He was impressed with my ambitions. They might agree to give me a personal loan, provided I'm prepared to buy stock from them. They're very large wholesalers Rupa.'

'I think it's a good idea if you can make it Aruna. Don't you think you should move back to London?'

'No way! Start a business in London? That's not what I want. It'll have to be somewhere in Newcastle where land and business premises are affordable.'

'I don't really care what you do Aruna, it's much better for the children if we are in one place.'

'I'll have to get the loan approved before anything else. It'll take some time to become established. Don't forget that I'll have to pay back the borrowed money with interest. We'll see what happens next anyway.'

'Whenever you propose to do something it worries me no end. The last thing we want is more trouble. What happens if your plans don't work?'

'We'll sell this house.'

'Sell this house? Do you think we should move to Newcastle so soon?'

'We may be able to get a council house or rent somewhere.'

'I don't like that idea. We wouldn't have the freedom we have now. Here at least the children have a garden to play in and nobody calling to collect rent. Don't you think the bank will give you a larger loan!'

'Don't panic Rupa, I'm only talking about a short period, most probably a year, when I have to invest all my capital. Once I start to get a reasonably good income we can easily buy a large house with a garden wherever you like.'

The following weekend Aruna decided to sell their house and see the estate agent.

'Aruna, this is the house where we lived since we got married. The children are used to the area and to their schools. We never had any trouble from our neighbours. I don't really think it's a good idea. You're so selfish! I'd rather go back home with the children. I can't take the stress anymore, having to move house, coping with new neighbours, new schools and everything else.'

'Don't worry Rupa. I guarantee it's not going to be a serious problem for any of us. People move house to improve their life style. You've got to take a risk and make a move forward and start something new in your life sometimes.'

'I don't believe you! The whole thing is a load of rubbish. We're not going to improve our life style moving to a council house. We hardly survive each day as it is and I'm very tired. You just don't care about us. All these mad ideas of yours will end in trouble. Why don't you leave me and the children alone and find a way of doing your business without selling the house? We'll end up homeless with just a sleeping bag, begging on the streets!'

'Believe me Rupa, the most sensible thing we could do at the moment is sell this house and put the money into my business. You won't say no when I buy a five bedroom house with a large garden.'

Rupa felt angry when the estate agent started to telephone her to make appointments for viewing. Newly married couples, retired people with pets and families with young children came as prospective buyers. Rupa hated them all. They checked every corner of the house: built in cupboards, wiring, general construction, roof slates and any cracks in the walls. They asked her about the garden shrubs: honeysuckle, buddleia and lilac for summer and yellow jasmine and mahonia for winter flowering. They made offers to include the furniture and carpets and tried to knock down the price. Rupa didn't want to sell the house to anybody but within two months a sale was agreed at the asking price and contracts were exchanged. The lucky new owners were a young couple, the woman expecting her first baby in three months. Soon the completion date was only a week away. Rupa was full of regrets and her hopes flowed like floodwater down a drain.

It was a midsummer evening and the sun was warm. Geranium and petunia beds were in full bloom. Lisa and Shane were playing in the back garden. Lisa pushed a go-cart backwards and forwards while Shane sat there. He made the starting sound of an engine – broom---broom---broom---. Rupa emptied her drawers into cardboard boxes. The wardrobe was bare. The floor rugs were rolled up. The pictures were down and there were lines of grime on the yellow walls in the shape of the picture frames. Black clumps of floppy cobwebs gathered in corners where the furniture had stood for years. As the china and glassware was safely packed in tea chests, the tinkling sound spread all over the house. Lisa and Shane watched forlornly as their broken toys were thrown into the dustbin.

A removal lorry stopped in front of the gate with 'Pickford's Removals' on the side. The belongings of the new owners of number sixty one had arrived.

THIRTY

Rupa stared blankly out of the dirty windowpane, through the yellow wilting nets smelling of mildew and out onto the rough asphalted surface of the back road. Here and there the uneven patterns of cobbles lay exposed and puddles gathered over blocked drains to form a stream hurrying along the gutter. In the yard over the road, purple flannelette sheets hung on a washing line, so sodden had they become that they held still in the face of the chuntering wind. The once so proudly kept up back-to-backs had fallen on hard times. No longer were the front steps outlined in yellow or grey donkeystone after the paving stones had been given their weekly scrub. The respectable working class had long departed to the far flung estates of neat Airey semis and multi storey blocks. All that remained were the remnants, the very old, along with incomers from Pakistan, India and the West Indies, who worked briefly in the cotton mills before they finally closed. There were families with numerous children but with no sign of a father.

It was just before noon on Saturday. The smell of fish and chips wafted temptingly on the wind and the last drops of rain seemed to have fallen. The sky had a washed out empty look and even the clouds seemed bedraggled. In the tiny front gardens all attempts at cultivation had been abandoned and even the weeds fought to survive against rising mounds of broken rubble, discarded bottles, tyres, masses of waterlogged newspapers and even an abandoned pram.

Rupa and Aruna had moved to the three bedroom back to back in Watford Terrace which criss-crossed with Langton Avenue and Benville Lane. Dozens of streets spread out over the slow rise of Dunscome Hill where, until a year ago, the red trams had rattled and jostled their passengers into the city centre to do their weekly shopping in the thrust and bustle of Kirkgate Market. Although the market remained now there were stylish green buses which swept down Rhymber Hill, hooting their impatient horns.

As soon as they had moved in Rupa realised Aruna had made a disastrous decision.

'I hate this house, Aruna, it's cold and dirty and depressing. Someone's even stolen the front gate! Lorries use the road as a short cut and if I let Lisa out of my sight for a minute she'll end up under their wheels. What on earth did you think you were doing, bringing us here? Have you no sense of responsibility at all? Why on earth didn't we stay where we were?'

'You've got to be patient, Rupa. We don't have to stay here if we're not happy. This house isn't ours so we can leave at a moment's notice. You'll soon get to know the neighbours.'

'You mean we've to pack all our things in cardboard boxes again and move from one place to another like gypsies! You're never at home, you don't see what's going on in the neighbourhood. Some people look very rough, the men have got terrible looking tattoos and some of the women might even be prostitutes! I don't know how safe it is for me and the children to be here on our own.'

'You worry unnecessarily Rupa.' And with this he put on his coat and hurried out, slamming the door behind him.

The run down area where they lived was only two miles from the city centre. The rows of terraced houses were more than a century old and the streets were narrow and cobbled. Some houses had tiny front gardens while others had no garden at all. Rupa noticed the huge difference between the clean London suburban houses they had left and her new home. Some of the families seemed enormous and yet they lived in tiny houses. No one went to work and they lived on their pensions or on Social Security. Poverty wasn't the only reason for the broken marriages. There were many addicted to alcohol, especially amongst the men and after the pubs had closed at night Rupa heard their ribald laughter as they passed beneath the bedroom window.

Rupa couldn't believe how quickly the children seemed to grow up in those mean streets. They left school at fifteen and seemed to go straight into married life. Eileen, the next door neighbour was friendly enough. She had been married and divorced four times and now she lived with a twenty-five year old called Jamie. He had only recently come out of Armley Jail after serving a two-year sentence. He seemed quiet enough and always had a pleasant smile. Jamie, who had worked as a miner, was the only son of a retired headmaster. He was, it was whispered, some kind of drug addict. In the evenings his personality changed abruptly, there were constant arguments and fights with Eileen, which sometimes went on all night. Once Eileen dragged him along the road after pushing him violently through the doorway. She left him in the street and hurried back locking the door against him. Soon he began to curse and sent a volley of obscenities at the door until he finally kicked it in with his considerable strength. Surrounded by the splintered panels he sat on the step and cried helplessly like a child, begging Eileen's forgiveness. Eventually she opened the door, 'Come on love, in, in!' She gave him a perfunctory kiss and ushered him inside, holding his hand. On several occasions she dialled 999, but by the time the police arrived with their flashing lights and blaring sirens the situation had calmed down.

'It's only a misunderstanding, sorry to have bothered you,' Eileen smiled. On another occasion Eileen had locked and bolted her door when Jamie arrived home late at night blind drunk. He smashed the window with a brick and stormed into the house, quite unable to control his rage; systematically he smashed down four doors. Eileen dialled 999 but when the police came she told them it was either an attempted burglary or malicious damage by 'a person or persons unknown'. Terrified, Rupa lay awake all night. The following morning Eileen knocked on her door.

'Eeh love, a'm right sorry about the noise last night.'

'I must have been fast asleep, I didn't hear any noise, Eileen. Those huge container-lorries go up and down the road day and night. Would you like to come in?'

'No I've got to go to do some shopping, I've run out of milk and bread. Jamie isn't a bad man, you know. He doesn't like disturbing anybody. His mother's in the LGI with pneumonia. He's worried about her and he soon gets into bad moods.'

'Don't worry Eileen, I don't take any notice of these things.'

Eileen was a rough looking woman. Her voice was croaky and she coloured her permed hair raven black. Her lips were bright carmine with lipstick smeared on heavily and her eyebrows and lashes masked with deep blue mascara. Occasionally she wore a brown wig. When she went to the working men's club at night she wore chinking costume jewellery, tasselled earrings, broaches and necklaces in flashing silver and marcasite. As she came out of the door the air around her was perfumed with her musky aroma. Once it was past midnight when Eileen chased Jamie along the road. She was wearing black underwear, a suspender belt, nylon stockings, bedroom slippers and her undone bra straps hanging behind her shoulders. It was like an act from a soap opera and the night was freezing cold. Six foot tall Eileen was frightened of no one. Until recently she had run a brothel in Chapeltown, Leeds notorious red light district. She was always very kind to Rupa and the children. One day Rupa met Eileen at the newsagents. Eileen was buying tobacco for her pipe.

'Hang on a minute Rupa, I'll walk home with you,' she bellowed. Eileen's voice shook the small shop and its customers blanched at the sound. Rupa stood outside next to a Labrador dog which was waiting for its elderly owner, then they walked home together.

'Rupa, I can see that you're not used to this area. Before you go to bed at night make sure you lock your doors and windows. This isn't a dangerous place, but if your door is unlocked a drunk could just walk in. They're out of their minds, you know. Last night about two, Gerry was drunk and lying on our steps with his packet of pork sausages and a bottle of cider by his side. Jamie gave him a cup of coffee and then he staggered home. The slightest problem, you let me know, Rupa! Those men and boys who live around here are scared of my big mouth, to say nothing of my brother. Now he really is a hard man, fifteen years in Dartmoor for armed robbery! Between you and me the last man who crossed him got mysteriously shot, shot dead I mean! I don't like those punters who try it on with our girls! I'll teach them! I know all the big people, even in the police.' Rupa listened, wide eyed.

Jackie was another neighbour, a single parent with a four-year-old child, who had been to prison for serial shop lifting. During the Christmas season the shops were bursting with goods and crowded with customers. Jackie seized the opportunity to grab everything in sight. When Jackie gave Rupa's children some brand new toys for Christmas Rupa was pleased but soon became anxious in case they were stolen. Finally she decided to avoid her neighbours.

Rupa noticed how Western society treated people with psychiatric problems. In the East the mentally ill were ignored and pushed down to the bottom of the social ladder but in England they were regarded as 'sick' and various treatments were available. The man had been at the head of the British family for centuries. The situation was rapidly changing with increased employment possibilities for women. Women could also claim family allowance and Social Security. People in the East, particularly women, still lived in a tightly controlled social system. Single parenthood was not recognised at all and the woman who 'made a mistake' became taboo for the rest of her life. Rupa thought that it was all so unreasonable. There were day hospitals and 'drop ins' in the UK for the mentally ill to learn to live happier lives. Although unemployment was high it didn't seem to be a problem for Rupa's neighbours because most of them had never wanted to work. They had created their own world away from everyone. Certain minor crimes and many odd kinds of behaviour were acceptable as a regular part of society. Some were used to life behind bars. In spite of the available help most of those with addictive personalities remained addicted. Rupa wasn't used to this kind of society and soon began to feel desperate.

THIRTY ONE

There was a slight breeze and a leaf from Sri Maha Bodhi, the sacred Bo tree, fell on her shoulder. The sun was about to set in a crimson sky diluted with pale lemon. A rainbow arched towards the darkening lake. The flickering coconut oil lamp reminded her of the brief time gap between the lives of a stillborn baby and a man who lives to ripe old age. Here and there a pilgrim prayed with hands clasped together or paced up and down the temple path. When a bird flew from branch to branch the leaves rustled. She sat cross-legged by the golden wall, her eyes touching the floor and the flags above her were white and yellow. She wore a faded saffron robe with her head shaved. Holding a rosary in her hands she was meditating, counting the beads again and again, an emblem of the endless cycle of birth and death. A candle of faith which had burned for two and a half thousand years was still shining, a light in the darkness of this unknown world. No one knew who she was or where she came from. The missing Tilakawathie had been ordained as a Buddhist nun and now she was known as mother Sudharma.

Loku Mahatmaya and Dikwelle Hamine had reached old age. It was a long time since Rupa and Tilakawathie had left home. Maha Gedara was the house where Loku Mahatmaya was born. As their old age was passing quickly and quietly they enjoyed the tranquillity of their togetherness. The 'elephant rock' at the edge of the fields was a solid black rock with a cave hidden beneath and curved in the shape of an elephant. When Loku Mahatmaya was young he used to climb the rock with his sisters and friends. They decorated the rock with wild flowers and clusters of red lantana berries, an image of their childhood, a bejewelled tusker in a procession. Loku Mahatmaya remembered the smooth-surfaced stone slab called a 'washing stone' which belonged to the village dhoby family. They used it when they washed stained clothes, striking them against it. One day on his way to school along the red clay road he climbed onto the stone with his heavily muddied feet. When he realised that the washerwoman was watching him from top of the hill, twelve-year-old Loku Mahatmaya was terrified and ran away, forgetting his pencil case for which he never returned. When the dhoby woman paid her weekly visit to Maha Gedara, she had brought the pencil case with her and told everyone what he had done. His mother told him off severely. A few years later the washerwoman died but Loku Mahatmaya felt humbled whenever he saw the disused washing stone. Loku Mahatmaya realised that Rupa and Aruna would never return to live in Maha Gedara as his wife always expected.

'I don't mind where they live, as long as they care about their children's education. What's the point in their coming back to Ceylon when the children could have a better education in England? Our country isn't peaceful anymore. There's always trouble - riots, curfews and strikes. The schools and universities are closed most of the time and the children's education is continually interrupted.'

Although Loku Mahatmaya was pleased for Lisa and Shane, Dikwelle Hamine listened to him and sighed.

All the rice fields belonging to the Maha Gedara family were now cultivated by tenant farmers and some of their cinnamon lands were abandoned and overgrown. They had enough rice to eat but little was left for selling. Bonemeal fertiliser was no longer available and the farmers said that this was the cause of the poor crops. Due to heavy monsoon rain or prolonged drought crops were ruined or the farmers were unable to cultivate their fields for the two consecutive seasons of the year. Dikwelle Hamine used to grow aubergines and runner beans alongside the paths between the fields but since the farmers took over they grew their own vegetables and only a small proportion was given to the Maha Gedara family. Some insecticides they used were harmful to wildlife: parrots and sparrows were becoming rare in the fields. Loku Mahatmaya used to grow a special variety of rice for their own use but now they had to accept that the farmers chose the variety.

'I'm not used to eating this tasteless rice. It smells like mouldy straw when it's cooked and it's completely uneatable! These days everything is done for money and not for quality. Those tenant farmers have no idea about what to grow and the government doesn't give them proper advice either. Anyway there's nothing we can do about it. We're getting old and our health isn't good.' Dikwelle Hamine sat on the reed mat and rubbed some herbal oil on her swollen arthritic knees.

'I don't have the energy I used to have.' Loku Mahatmaya trudged along, chewing his betel nut mix.

Loku Mahatmaya was a strong man when he was young and everyone in the village was frightened of him. He went for moonlight walks, while the rest of the village slept, carrying a shotgun over his shoulder, spare bullets in his pocket and a torch in his hand. Occasionally he shot at the empty sky, confusing the wild animals and waking the neighbours. Everybody knew he was guarding his territory and Loku Mahatmaya had no enemies.

Davith was a well-known thief who lived by stealing from other people's gardens. He used what he could and the rest was sold to the village market stallholders. Once at two in the morning Loku Mahatmaya met Davith walking down a path carrying a load of stolen bananas and coconuts.

'I can't believe you still haven't given up that business Davith.'

'God help me, Loku Mahatmaya. I'm a poor man with a family. Can you believe it, my wife's pregnant again. Her stomach is swelling fast. She's got morning sickness and all she can eat is bananas. I swear by the God Skanda, Loku Mahatmaya, I'll never touch anything belonging to you.'

'It's time for you to sort yourself out Davith! Why don't you work in my paddy fields? I'll give you enough rice to feed your family.'

'I'm a poor man Loku Mahatmaya, but at night this whole village is mine. I don't do any harm to anybody, I don't even kill a fly! But I must feed my wife and our children.' There was a strong smell of alcohol all round Davith. He had emptied someone's hidden pot of toddy and when he spoke his voice was slurred. In the mornings Davith worked as a rubber tapper and the rest of the day he slept in his shed on a wooden bed with a mat on top. At night he went out stealing from gardens, he even dug up yams from vegetable plots. If he ever got caught he always had an excuse ready. On another occasion Davith told Loku Mahatmaya that he had been out shopping, forgetting it was past midnight. Davith, his wife and their three children lived in a palm-thatched mud hut, the floor of which was smoothed by applying a mixture of clay and cow dung. The attached shed with its sloping roof was used for cooking, storing firewood and drinking water with just enough room by the door for his bed. His wife and children slept in the main hut on floor mats. The dog slept in the shed under his bed on an old gunny rug. A bamboo screen was hung at the front to protect them from the wind and rain. The only piece of furniture Davith possessed was a wooden bench with black fingerprints all over it. The bench originally belonged to the temple and had been given away by the priest. The palaini hedge around their compound kept off the wild animals. The family used canal water for drinking and bathing. Amazingly the villagers seemed to have accepted them and their way of life.

Dikwelle Hamine and Loku Mahatmaya enjoyed their evenings together, telling each other stories about their past.

'It's so sad to see what's happening to those good old village headmen like you, who used to live like gods. Now they have to struggle in their old age,' said Dikwelle Hamine, a sarcastic smile on her face.

'Hhh! What else is there to say about those golden days! We climbed trees, turned rocks upside down and went hunting. When I made a loud hoot from the top of the red hill my friend Raja got my message and gave an even louder hoot from the sand valley a mile away. We lived like kings of the valley and forests! You have no idea about our life in this village before I brought you to Maha Gedara fifty years ago.' Loku Mahatmaya started to tell his wife an amazing story with great excitement. 'I never forget that night. It was pitch dark when I travelled back from Matara. It rained non-stop and the road had turned to a muddy field with water streaming down and puddles all over. I had to push my bike all the way up the hilly roads. I must admit that I'd had a couple of drinks that evening! I staggered half way down the hill and when I was right in front of the tamarind tree an enormous rope dropped down from the hilltop. I stopped at once. The next thing I remember was someone tall like a ghost with a funny face coming towards me. Considering it was late at night and I was on my own with not a soul in sight I was a bit shaky.

'Who are you?' he shouted and shone a torch on my face. I closed my eyes but I recognised his voice straight away, it was Agris Appu, the criminal well known for killing for the merest pittance! 'It's only me Agris' I said. He shone the torch once again. 'Oh! This is Loku Mahatmaya. You can go now. Mind it's very slippery down the hill,' said Agris. I had to push my bike for another mile or so. It was on the same day that a woman who died in childbirth was buried by the side of the road. As I walked past her grave I felt very strange. Have you heard that when a dead body is buried the devil Maha Sohona pays his visit to the grave on each of the first seven nights?'

Dikwelle Hamine, looking at the dark corners of the house said, 'My mother never let me go near a grave on my own for the first three months because devils cast spells, particularly on pretty young women.'

Loku Mahatmaya continued. 'Then I heard a noise kra---ss, kra---ss, kra---ss, the sound was a bit similar to when you cut wood with a hand saw. I had a torch with me but you mustn't shine a torch at a ghost and never try to run away either. It was torrential rain and I was drenched like a dog, which has fallen into a pool of mud. The sound started to come directly from the grave in a continuous crush. I couldn't see anything because there was a pandal in the front and the area around the grave was decorated. I knew that anyone who had the devil Maha Sohona's spell would not be able to walk more than seven steps forward, then he takes you for his sacrifice. Fortunately it suddenly came to my mind just like that, a mantra I had learned from my father. 'Orm---orm---namo---namo---yum---

yum---hum---hum—' I started reciting. I was confident and definite that no devil could cast spells on me against that mantra. Whatever it was I laid my bike flat in the middle of the road and went near the grave and shone my torch. Then I saw two sparkling green eyes staring at me.' Dikwelle Hamine listened without blinking her eyes and with great enthusiasm.

'Do you know what it was? It was a large black cow which had come there to eat the tender coconut leaves decorating the woman's grave!'

Loku Mahatmaya and Dikwelle Hamine laughed together. Dikwelle Hamine completely believed the ghost stories. She told Loku Mahatmaya how she walked home one dark-moon night from his parent's house. She was carrying eight-month-old Rukmali and only the fireflies lit her way. All the way to Maha Gedara, through the forest paths and fields, a ghost followed her stamping the ground.

'You know that dead valley between the hills? Every evening at dusk you can hear a baby crying,' said Dikwelle Hamine. 'One day it was about seven when I walked alongside the canal in the twilight. I saw the vague outline of a woman dressed in white walking up and down on top of the hill. She was carrying a baby on her shoulder in a rather strange way. I knew it was a ghostly figure and I rushed home without looking back. At that time of the evening everybody should keep their young children indoors. You can tell when this evil spirit is about, the air smells sour.' Dikwelle Hamine shrugged and shrieked. At the edge of the rain forest there were huge gnarled fig trees near the dead valley. When the branches grated against one another they made the noise of a trombone. The villagers believed that it was a supernatural sound connected to some hidden power. Loku Mahatmaya thought it was the evening goddess who appeared through the forest showing everyone her new born baby.

When Dikwelle Hamine was young everyone in her village admired her beauty, her knee-length abundant hair, beaming face and her pale brown skin; a glimpse of it remained in her wrinkled face. Once a native 'viridu' singer who went round the village reciting panegyric songs composed on the spot, came to her parents' home. He had seen young Dikwelle Hamine picking marigolds in her garden and sang a song for her describing her as a woman of priceless beauty like a shining moon. Dikwelle Hamine and Loku Mahatmaya could vaguely remember how they met at a village fair and how they fell in love. When she took part in a New Year's celebration as a native dancer Loku Mahatmaya waited for an opportunity and sprinkled some scent over her. 'Undoubtedly it was a charm made by you to change my mind and not a perfume. If I had the faintest idea that it was going to end up like this I would never have taken part in that New Year's celebration.' She only said this when she wasn't happy with her husband.

'Rubbish, it wasn't a charm at all! The bottle of sandalwood scent was given to me by Santhi, the flower man who used to make bridal bouquets and he was the man who arranged those white roses on our wedding day.' Whatever Loku Mahatmaya said Dikwelle Hamine believed that he had made some kind of charm to make her fall in love with him.

In the evenings they sat on the bench under the gardenia tree, gazing at the spirals of the vanishing sun. They often talked about their respective ages. Loku Mahatmaya said that Dikwelle Hamine was only four years younger than him while Dikwelle Hamine believed that he was thirteen years older than her. Loku Mahatmaya had never had a horoscope. Mice had eaten Dikwelle Hamine's parchment horoscope years ago, so neither could remember exactly how old they were.

Rukmali's sons had grown up, their youngest son had won a Commonwealth Scholarship to Canada. They also had a daughter called Manohari, who studied at the university. Loku Mahatmaya and his wife didn't go anywhere beyond the village except to see a doctor. The deep sadness in their mind about Rupa had gradually faded away. They listened to stories about their past as if they were melodies of a vena played in the dark. Rupa's bookcase in the corner of the veranda was full of dust and cobwebs. The Sinhalese – English encyclopaedias with their red leather covers were colonised by cockroaches and moths. Dikwelle Hamine had not forgotten the proposal for Rupa from Gunapala, the son of a wealthy businessman. She thought it would have been better if Rupa had lived in Ceylon. England was a far away country and when she remembered Rupa's departure, the sadness in her mind erupted, stirring and flowing like waves. She felt as if some alien had abducted her daughter. Deep in her mind Dikwelle Hamine believed that Rupa and the children were living in some strange world with artificially lit nights and days under an endless dark arch with the stars un-nailed.

THIRTY TWO

Lisa was in bed, off school for two days, with flu and a chesty cough. She had vomited several times. There was a rapidly spreading epidemic and half the school's classes were empty. At least it was Friday so Lisa could stay in bed over the weekend without missing any lessons and Aruna would be home soon. Rupa was sitting on the edge of Lisa's bed. In a corner of the bedroom the old convector rattled, spluttered and hummed manfully but gave out little heat. You could feel the draught creeping in under the door. By now they had a dog, a Border Collie called Elsie that ran up and down drumming on the stairs and thrashing her tail against the rickety banisters. The telephone rang.

'You stay in bed, Lisa. I'll be back in a minute.' Rupa ran down with the dog following her. It was Aruna.

'Rupa I won't be able to come home tonight. I've to work over the weekend. Since I started my own business there's just so much unexpected work, I don't have a spare minute! After all, if this is going to be our livelihood I've to put all my effort into this workshop. Today and tomorrow workmen are installing new machines. I'll definitely come home next Friday.' Tears brimmed in Rupa's eyes.

'For heavens sake Aruna, we've been waiting all week, counting the days until Friday. It's really not fair you asking us to wait another week. Lisa isn't well and I kept her at home, she's got flu. I was going to cook a nice meal for us tonight. I thought you would be home early.'

'Take Lisa to the doctor.'

'I've taken her to the doctor already. He gave her something for her temperature and a bottle of cough mixture. She's got to stay in bed and have plenty to drink. She's been vomiting. I do think you should at least try to come and see the children. They don't understand why you suddenly cancel your visits home.'

Lisa came down coughing with watery eyes and red cheeks.

'You must stay in bed Lisa. Don't run up and down when you're ill. Why did you take your socks off? Your feet will get cold.'

'I don't want to stay in bed mummy. Can I stay downstairs with you and Shane? What time is daddy coming?'

'Daddy isn't coming home today. He's got a lot of work to do.'

Rupa asked Lisa to lie on the settee and put her socks on; then she covered her with a soft woollen rug to keep her warm. Rupa felt Lisa's forehead with the back of her palm.

'You have a temperature Lisa. Benelyn syrup hasn't cleared your chest either. I think its time for you to take another dose of medicine. This house is damp and it's not good for your flu.' Rupa gave her a Panadol with a glass of Lucozade and stroked her head. A few minutes later Lisa fell asleep. Shane sat on the floor and tried to make 'Thomas the Tank Engine' with his Lego set. When he looked for his biscuits the plate was empty. Elsie wagged her tail and licked her whiskers.

The wind blew in sheets of showery sleet. Ice crystals drummed and gathered on the window frame like perfectly cut marbles. The swollen window couldn't be properly closed and the water leaked through the windowsill flooding the kitchen floor. When Rupa put an aluminium pail underneath the sill drops of water dripped down with a dull metallic sound. The dust spotted rainwater was rusty brown. Rupa wiped up the floor with a mop but it was still damp. She avoided talking about Aruna's absence and soon got used to it but Rupa found it hard to accept that she was ignored by her husband when she so desperately needed his company. She didn't bother to cook a meal because Lisa couldn't eat and Shane wasn't hungry. Instead they had eggs on toast and a glass of milk for supper.

Rupa and the children had fallen into a different lifestyle. Lisa and Shane occasionally played in the back street with children from the neighbourhood. After dinner they went out for walks with the dog but they didn't stay out for long. On weekends they went to the park and Rupa watched them play. In the evenings there were board games or books to read while Rupa was busy with her housework. As time crawled by Rupa began to feel increasingly lonely.

The workshop belonging to Aruna was only a mile away from Newcastle town centre. For the first six months he worked day and night sorting out the business. He started repairing motor vehicles and soon huge amounts of unexpected work began to pour in. He bought spare parts wholesale and re-sold them at a considerable profit. He was able to employ a foreman and eight workers. The machinery and the tools they needed to do the repairs were on the ground floor of the building. There were two sales departments with storage facilities attached to the workshop. The car park was big enough for several large vehicles and a dozen cars. Aruna was planning to extend his business to include repairing agricultural vehicles. There was a flat above the shops so Aruna moved out of his shared accommodation. During the day it was busy with cranking, welding, roaring engines and the sound of drilling. At night the silent machines with dripping grease under their heavy hoods hovered like grey ghosts. What little spare time Aruna had was spent at the 'Dick Turpin', a local pub and the working men's club. He met several people he had known at his old jobs and they had meals and drinks together. Sometimes they played billiards and darts or watched TV until late.

When Rupa was interested in Christianity she learned that Friday was a special day and she stopped cooking or eating meat on that day so they ate fish and chips instead. But for Rupa and the family it was a special occasion because it was the day Aruna came home for the weekend. Their routine changed abruptly and for several weeks Friday passed with no sign of Aruna. Days of the week came and went and Friday became just another day. Aruna's visits became irregular and the memories they brought became a sad song in Rupa's heart. Rupa told Aruna that she was prepared to live in Newcastle.

'It's only a business place Rupa, you must be crazy trying to live there with children,' he said.

'You're so unreasonable Aruna, I shouldn't have to beg you every week for housekeeping money. Unless I keep going on you just forget. I find it impossible to pay the rent regularly and I'm four weeks behind. From the first of January my rent's going up. Fortunately the landlord understands my situation. If I can't manage the arrears all in one go he lets me pay by instalments.'

'You never told me that you're behind with the rent Rupa. If you remind me next week I'll pay the lot.'

'I don't know how many times I've told you but you never listened. When Shane was littlc I could use Lisa's clothes for him. Now it's not so easy as you think Aruna. I need extra money for the children's clothes and books. Last week I bought some second hand books and toys from Marsden market. I often have to buy things from charity shops. If you can't come home and see the children, you should at least think about what they need.'

'I think about everybody. That's why I work so hard.'

'No, Aruna, you're totally self-centred, you only think about yourself.'

Two weeks later Aruna settled Rupa's rent arrears but he wasn't prepared to talk to her about anything else.

'Mum, why do you wash clothes by hand? Gemma's mum and dad bought a washing machine. They wash all their clothes in it'

'We need a lot of money for a washing machine Lisa, they have to be repaired when they break down and we don't have that kind of money.'

'Dad's got some machines in his workshop. Do you have to have a lot more money than he's got to buy a washing machine for us?' Lisa looked at her mother's face.

'No, your dad's machines are expensive. He uses them for repairing cars and vans when they break down.'

'One! Two! Three! Only three months to go for my birthday.' Lisa jumped, hopped and laughed.

Her eyes sparkled like stars and her smile was innocent. She jumped up and down and ran from the lounge to the kitchen. Elsie, who slept under the dining table, got up and chased Lisa, barking and wagging her tail.

Jamie had his weekly wages on Friday. Eileen met him after work and they went out to the working men's club. He had spent his money generously and Rupa heard them coming home late arguing and both very drunk. Saturday afternoons the pair of them went to Sainsburys to do their weekly shopping.

'Would you like to go shopping with us Rupa? We're going to Sainsburys. Jamie'll pay the taxi.'

'I'm all right Eileen. We don't do weekly shopping. I can always walk there if we want something.' Rupa wasn't keen on going shopping with them because they would usually start to quarrel in the supermarket. Once Rupa went shopping with them and she would never forgot the awesome row Eileen and Jamie had in the shop.

'Jamie have you taken a tenner from my purse?'

'Course I 'aven't, Eileen, you know me!'

'That's the trouble you lying bastard, I do know you. Hand it over!'

Jamie backed away down the pet food aisle with Eileen following hot on his track. She snatched a tin of cat food from the shelf and hurled it at his head. It missed by a mile but sent a handful of shoppers' skedaddling out of the way. There was a bang and a crash as piles of tins and packets cascaded down, mostly on the 'exotic fruit and vegetable' display. A purple cabbage was thrown up in the air and passion fruit strewn on the floor. An old woman pulled back her trolley in mortal terror, her purse dropped and coins scattered everywhere. When a store detective approached them Eileen rapidly calmed down.

'Sorry lad but it's all your fault, you'd better make sure these tins are stacked properly in future! It would have caused a serious accident if these tins had fallen on my feet.'

Rupa quickly exited, pretending that she had seen nothing. Eileen was unusually quiet on the way home by taxi and Rupa felt relieved when she finally arrived home.

Why was Aruna trying to get away from his family? From the day Lisa was born he had changed into a different person. How long could Rupa carry on single-handed? She felt as though her life was caught between a troubled marriage and two dependant children. A woman who found herself in an unhappy marriage should not have to suffer such festering pain. The institution of marriage in the Western world had been crumbling for decades. Rupa felt her body was coiled round and knotted together by Eastern and Western cultural strings. She was left to float helplessly in the sea caught up in the rough waves turning towards the shore like falling walls. She could die at any moment. She had to break the strings, stretch and swim to some sanctuary. She had no one to tell her problems to. Rupa began to notice how some people lived their lives hiding their psychiatric problems and inhabiting their mad world until they finally died. She was frightened to think about Aruna's recent changes, which only she could see. Rupa trembled as she saw how Aruna increasingly avoided the three of them. She felt like a fish being borne out on the tide into the open sea, utterly helpless to change direction.

One morning Rupa stood by the stove, stirring porridge for the children's breakfast when Eileen pushed open the door and ran in, waving the previous night's 'Evening Post'.

'Eeh Rupa lass, I've just seen t' paper. Jamie 'ad it stuck in 'is jacket pocket; silly daft drunken bugger nivver thought to tell me. Look!' With her ringed callused fingers she pointed to the two-inch high headlines. 'RIPPER KILLER BELIEVED TO HAVE SLAIN ANOTHER YORKSHIRE WOMAN.'

'There's some loony out there, e'es done in four women, so far all of 'em 'ave been on the game it says a couple in Chapeltown, one in Woodhouse and one over in South Yorkshire. It says 'single women should not go out unaccompanied after dark' so don't you forget, I don't want you to be his next victim!'

Rupa felt grateful for Eileen's concern and she promised to be careful. She watched the lunchtime news on TV and as the weeks went by 'The Yorkshire Ripper' became the focus of nearly every conversation amongst her neighbours. It was early November. The days were shorter and the misty nights of Leeds were freezing. The summer insomniac sun seemed to have sunk into its annual hibernation. Winter had finally come. Rupa walked along the quiet street of Woodland Grove, surrounded by giant oak trees, overhanging shrubs and heaps of fallen autumn leaves. She thought she heard someone following her and tried to run. The pavements were icy, leaves decayed in clumps, she slipped and grazed her knee and her elbow. Fortunately no one was there. Rupa felt relieved when she met two policemen walking up Harehills Lane. It was only early evening when Rupa, laden with shopping stood at a bus stop in Chapeltown Road. The whole area was silent and deserted as a graveyard, dark as death. It was bonfire week, two days before Guy Fawkes' day and the occasional crackle of fireworks could be heard in the distance. The following morning it was on the front page of the 'Yorkshire Post' 'Woman's body found in playing fields.' Everyone was shaken and Eileen called again.

'Stupid girl, that Wilma, I knew her very well. She didn't know her job properly, that's why she got killed. It doesn't matter how experienced you are, it's silly to go into the red light area that time of night when a killer's about. At least the girls should go in pairs and not on their own. I know that junction in Harehills. It's notorious. The very first thing I told our girls was not to get into a car without thinking! Poor lass, she had a young family to support. I'm so sorry for 'er kids.' Rupa made them a cup of tea as she was speaking.

'I was at a bus stop in Chapeltown Road, yesterday evening, on my way home from shopping. It was only six but the whole area seemed haunted. I was so frightened, I tried to run, then slipped and hurt my knee. It was only in yesterday's paper; it said that the ripper may have moved out of the Leeds area. I make sure we're in by seven and all our doors and windows are locked. How did you get to know that woman who got killed, Eileen?' Rupa had goose pimples on her arms.

'You don't know me Rupa, Leeds is my home. I know every inch of that red light district. I don't have to ask anybody where the turning is to join a junction or how to find a nightclub or a bar anywhere in Leeds. The thing is Rupa, you mustn't let anyone see that you're a stranger in the area, even if you haven't a clue about where you are. Those girls have to know exactly what they're doing when they get involved in the game. It's a business and they don't have to fall in love with the man. The goal is to earn as much as you can. Most girls I know have families to support, but there's never been anything like this before! Marijuana, heroin, LSD, cocaine: they're freely available these days. I told my girls how to understand a man just by glancing at his face. They shouldn't be frightened to ask one or two tricky questions. They've got to be tough, not delicate and sensitive. Then they've to ask the man about the cash! If the man doesn't like to discuss money, look for someone else!'

Rupa couldn't believe how brave Eileen was, standing like a heroine in front of her, a goddess to help you when you're in trouble. Eileen hated men who used women like old footballs. She looked at them with a sickening feeling. If you shake an apple tree, a shower of fruit falls on the ground. If you dug out Eileen's past and her involvements your mind would land in an endless tangle. Like a weaverbird entering it's nest through a tiny hole Rupa went in and closed the doors. The strings had been loosened in the carefully woven nest. Eileen was a tough woman. Rupa felt some kind of coward in front of her. In her world no fear seemed to exist. Like a bird stretching its wings in the empty sky she could move around in society. No one knew who Eileen really was or even her age. She told Rupa that she was thirty-nine but Jackie had told Rupa that every Thursday morning Eileen went to the post office to cash her pension book. Rupa didn't know how true this was but one thing Rupa did know was Jackie fancied Jamie.

Rupa could not remember a single day without some kind of trouble, row or an argument among the neighbours. A middle-aged loner who was an alcoholic had died in his flat and by the time it was discovered by the Social Services, his body had decomposed beyond recognition. Twenty one year old Jason Brown died only a week ago, having mixed alcohol with his medication. Rupa heard of some trouble between two families in the middle of the street. It was Eileen who phoned the police but when they arrived the two families were sitting together having cups of tea. How frequently the sirens of police cars and ambulances wailed through those otherwise silent streets.

THIRTY THREE

Long winding Domestic Street and the cobbled cul-de-sac of Domestic Terrace merged at a narrow junction. The black pillared and porticoed mass of a former Methodist church was festooned with banners announcing 'The world's cheapest carpets'. On the opposite corner was a transport café. It was just after one p.m. on a Monday afternoon when Aruna walked through the back streets of terraced houses, untended and gloomy with overflowing dustbins, washing lines, broken toys and worn out furniture piled in the tiny back yards. A depressed white dog barked abruptly and growled on a step where the door stood open. The dog's barking became incessant.

'Quiet, Sheba,' a woman snapped.

Aruna was slightly shaken but the dog didn't approach him. He passed a parade of shabby shops and a dinghy post office. There was 'Bobby's Sandwich Shop', closed down and boarded up. 'Paragon Brothers', the second hand furniture shop, too small for its contents had stacks of dubious looking beds, rickety chairs, flimsy wardrobes and colourless rugs spilling onto the pavement. Aruna noticed the sign 'Domestic Café' red lettered on a peeling board. The entrance to the café was at the side, opening straight onto the pavement where a line of cars straggled along the curb. He walked in, looked around and saw a woman serving the waiting customers. There were about eight tables in all, each with four bare wooden chairs. The space between was just enough for someone to pass. The tablecloths were plastic squares of pale blue. Each table had salt and pepper cellars, a soggy tomato sauce bottle, vinegar, a sugar bowl and an ashtray. The oblong window on the Domestic Street side was half covered with a tatty grimed net. The red tiled floor was clean but chipped here and there. The walls and the ceiling were greasy and yellowed with tobacco smoke. Aruna ordered lunch, the standard meal of fried eggs, sausages, bacon, black pudding and chips. He sat at a corner table drinking his mug of tea, waiting to be served. A few minutes later a woman wearing a green apron arrived with a piled plate of food, a fork and a knife.

'Sorry, it's been so long.' She smiled and put the steaming meal on the table. Every item was uniformly coated in thick brown gravy.

'I've so many regular customers. It's one of those days I've been busy like this since the morning.' She gathered a pile of empty plates then hurried back to serve a man with a rich brocade of maritime tattoos covering his hands and arms. Aruna didn't know what to say so he stayed quiet and ate his food. Anna, the owner of the café, was of Polish origin, slim with her hair combed back neatly and tied up in a yellow ribbon with a bow. She walked rapidly up and down, smiling at everybody while she served meals and cleared away. An old man with arthritic hands who couldn't cut his bacon called loudly. She came and quickly cut the meat into manageable slices. Bill, a burly lorry driver with a sagging beer belly, sat next to Aruna, exhaling a heady aroma of alcohol and stale tobacco, his breath slow and stertorous.

Within a few weeks Aruna got used to having regular meals at the Domestic Café. He always sat in the same corner, speaking to no one, paid his bill and left abruptly. 'Are you all right there? Would you like anything else?' When Anna spoke to him her voice was sharp and abrasive. As the weeks passed by she began to chat to him and eventually involved him in long conversations. One January morning he arrived for his breakfast in a thickening fog. Although the café was warmed by an electric fire a thin layer of ice had settled on the outside windowpane and the sides were dripping with condensation. One customer had just finished his breakfast and two others were tucking into fried eggs on toast. For once Anna wasn't all that busy. 'Not a very nice day!' She announced breezily.

'It's freezing and the fog's getting worse. It's going to be like this all day.' Aruna rubbed his cold hands and sat at the table next to the fire.

'I'm so busy I don't have time to go out. Sun and rain don't bother me at all, but if the weather's bad I don't get many customers.'

'Do you usually get a lot in Anna?'

'Not that many, but I open at seven for breakfast and meals are served all day. When you run a business you've got to be efficient. Most of the people who come here are regulars. Because I don't charge much some locals who can't cook their own food come here for meals, not just drivers and factory workers. Some of them I've known for years. Making cups of tea all the time isn't an easy job.'

'Do you manage everything yourself?'

'Maggie does the cooking but I've to do everything else. If I'm not here I've to get someone else to take over.'

'I can't imagine how anyone could run a business like this seven days a week.'

'I don't open on Sundays. That's the only break I have to do my housework, check the accounts and relax in the bath. Everything I need I get delivered so that's not a problem but if I'm off even for a few hours all hell breaks loose.'

Aruna went back dreaming of Anna's efficiency and her smiles. At night her image kept him awake and he became obsessed with her. For hours and hours he secretly enjoyed thinking of her perfection. Like a sudden flash of lightning, sexual desire spread from his mind to his body and his whole being. Anna's soft auburn hair and darting blue eyes flowed like a field of pampas grass. Her laugh reminded Aruna of an angel's song. Her long tapering fingers were always busy. She was a perfect woman who single-handed, ran a café where a stream of customers poured in ceaselessly. He wanted to hold her hands, touch her soft breasts and feel his body pressed against hers, then kiss her alluring lips and cheeks. On the following morning Aruna arrived earlier hoping Anna wouldn't be busy. 'You're early today, Aruna!'

'I've got to be at a motor wholesalers at nine. The roads aren't good round here and I want to avoid the rush hour. How do you get here so early in the morning Anna?'

'I don't have to travel. I live upstairs in my flat. It's comfortable enough. I've to work hard but I suppose my business isn't too bad. Men from the quarry and drivers from the bus depot never miss their meals. I haven't got much room for entertaining but I give them generous helpings and they're soon satisfied.'

Two drivers walked in. 'Morning Anna.'

She went to serve them their breakfast.

Anna appreciated Aruna's generous tips and soon began to notice the difference between him and other regular customers, even telling him something of her past.

'I was only twelve when we emigrated from Poland. My father had left my mother when I was very young. I can't remember anything about him. All I remember of my childhood is being with my mother. She never told me anything about her life. I often wondered if my parents were refugees during the war. I remember how I sat on a bench with my mother one day in York Railway Station, waiting for a train to Newcastle.' Aruna interrupted.

'I've never been to York station. I always travel by car but I've seen sign posts to the station often enough.'

'It's one of the oldest stations in the world, it's at least a hundred years old. The original buildings are still there, they're beautifully kept up. I remember my mother was staring at the dome and the arching glass roof, her eyes looked strangely empty. I sat watching the pigeons and the trains as they slowed down and stopped. Crowds were getting on and off the trains like sea-waves. They streamed in and out of the station with piles of luggage. Non-stop expresses went through the station thundering and echoing. The vast building looked like a standstill railway guard watching the throng of passengers. There were some flashing lights above, like the building's great eyes! I noticed there were tears in my mother's eyes. I became worried in case she was ill and I asked if she was all right.'

'Anna, your father was a train driver,' she muttered tearfully.

Then the Aberdeen express arrived with full steam up and we got in. She never said a word about my father again.' When Anna talked about her childhood Aruna listened patiently. Suddenly his own memories poured out with images of Rupa and the children but then they disappeared quickly like bubbles in a whirlpool.

'This used to be a small teashop run by my mother. She sold sandwiches, buns, sausage rolls and teacakes. I helped her make cups of tea. She died four years ago, it was a terrible shock. As she got older she couldn't do much but she was always about to keep me company. She taught me how to run the café. I can't bear to think about my mother's death but I try to carry on as usual; in my mothers own words it's my 'destiny'. Since she died I've lived in the flat on my own.'

'In spite of your mother's death you seem to be managing to work efficiently Anna. Haven't you any other relatives?'

'No, not here or in Poland. I was born in a poor country. Winter's very long there and sometimes we had snow for months on end. Everyone has to struggle to survive in a climate like that. According to my mother we were Roman Catholics going back for generations. I can remember going to church every Sunday morning. Because we lived in a Communist country she got brain washed into accepting Communism. She wished England was a country that was ruled by the Politburo! We Poles are a very hard-working lot you know.'

'Do you have strong beliefs like your mother?'

'No, I'm no bloody Commie! Communism seems to be on the way out and if mother was alive she'd have had heart failure! I'm a cradle Catholic and I really believe my religion. I can vaguely remember living with my mother in a dinghy room. We were very hard up and she didn't have enough money, not even for food. I had one dress, which I wore every Sunday when we went to mass. It was green with white lace frills and it had been given to me by a friend of my mother. She always bought me a packet of tiny sweets on our way to church. I loved those sweets with a cumin seed in the middle. The statue of Christ and the altar always appears in my dreams. I still can hear the sound of the church bells and imagine the sweet smell of the church that will never leave me.'

'If your mother was so poverty stricken how did she manage to come to England and settle down?'

'I simply don't know anything about it Aruna. I've no idea how she managed to get the fare even. It was a secret she kept until she died. It's possible my father may have provided the money, he's a complete mystery to me. I may even have been illegitimate. I've never seen my birth certificate.'

'All my relatives live in Ceylon. Haven't you got any friends Anna?'

'You're lucky Aruna, at least you've got family and relatives somewhere. I don't really have much time for friends. Just after my mother's death I was so lonely I started a relationship with a bus driver who came to my mother's teashop every day. After a while I found out he was married and it all ended in disaster. One day his pregnant wife came to my café looking for him. I asked him not to come anymore and I heard that he got himself a transfer and they moved away. I must admit that he was a nice guy and we had some great times.'

After the meal Aruna went back quietly to the counter. He looked round, no one was waiting to be served and everybody was preoccupied with their food. Anna looked at him and smiled.

'Would you like to go to the pictures tonight Anna?'

'I'd love to. I haven't seen a film for ages.' Anna didn't seem surprised by his invitation.

'What time can I pick you up?'

'It has to be after six. I need time to close up and get ready. Half seven is fine.'

'I'll see you tonight.'

Aruna looked round in case anyone heard their conversation but no one seemed to be within earshot. He went back to work feeling like winning a fortune. He walked up and down his workshop with a new energy. Uncharacteristically he chatted to his workers. He went home early, allowing himself time for a shower, a shave and to change his clothes. Aruna looked at his watch impatiently, even checking the time with the speaking clock.

It was half past seven when he stopped his Peugeot in front of the Domestic Café. Anna came out in a lemon-green dress and a matching jacket. She got into the car wearing a broad smile.

'You're in time Aruna!' when she kissed his cheek he felt strange, somehow overwhelmed. Soon the car was filled with the fragrance of 'Blue Grass'. There was a brief silence.

'It's a beautiful car Aruna, so comfortable.'

' I know. I've an obsession with Peugeots.'

He adjusted the side mirror with a flourish. 'Where do you want to go? There's a good film at the Ritz, *Gone with the Wind*.'

'I don't mind. It's been a busy day for me on my feet in that bloody café. It's nice just to sit down and relax for a couple of hours.'

On their way to the cinema they chatted casually as though they had known each other for years. They had balcony seats near the aisle and through the showing Aruna could think of nothing but this perfect woman sitting next to him.

'That really was lovely! This is quite a posh picture house, I don't mind coming here again, Aruna,' she said as the film ended. During the journey back she noticed how confidently Aruna held the steering wheel. When he took a wrong turning she asked, 'Aren't we going home Aruna?'

'I feel a bit hungry, Anna, wouldn't you like to go somewhere and have a meal?'

'That's a good idea but please not the same kind of food I eat every day! Just a snack will do for me Aruna.'

They went to the 'India Garden' with its flashing fluorescent yellow green awning and brass meshed wall lanterns. A waiter in white stood at the door wearing a turban, bowing as he ushered them in. While they were looking at the menu with its embossed gold lettering, a waiter brought a dish of savoury popadams.

'I've never been to an Indian restaurant before. I don't really know what to order,' she whispered. They discussed Asian food for a few minutes, tasting the popadams and drinking some red wine. Finally they ordered a mild chicken curry with yellow rice for Anna and a hot Madras mutton vindaloo with biryani rice for Aruna. They had mango with pineapple cream for dessert. When Aruna dropped her off she kissed him on his lips.

'It was a very enjoyable evening, Aruna, I'm not used to such treats!' She invited him to her flat on the next evening and as Aruna drove away, he kept touching his still wet lips, feeling like a million dollars.

Within a few months Aruna's daily routine had entirely changed. He no longer needed to go to Leeds for meals cooked by Rupa and he began to live like a bachelor again. He visited Anna regularly, some evenings waiting impatiently until the café was finally closed. She provided him with free meals in return for the outings and Aruna was well satisfied, indeed he couldn't quite believe the sudden fortune that had so opportunely fallen his way. He compared Rupa with Anna, setting Anna's beauty and efficiency against Rupa's. He couldn't imagine Rupa running a café without him to help her.

It was half past eight on a warm mid-summer Saturday night when Aruna and Anna walked into the five star Wellington Hotel close to the Tyne. The sun's silvery slough fragmented through a grey haze. The incessant squawking of gulls quieted as they flew towards their cliff-top nests. They were already well known to the receptionist in the glitzy entrance hall carpeted in red and cascades of white lilies in every corner, wide corridors, green stairs, the opulent bar and the vast billiard room with a balcony leaning over the Tyne. While the river flowed slowly towards the estuary they enjoyed the grey blue evening from the penthouse suite, the great silent river hidden in the darkness: it broadened, twisted then turned away to the north. The road's bends and slopes followed the river and ran parallel towards Tynemouth. A line of streetlights glowed as midnight chimed and the flow of traffic over the bridge began to lessen. They could see in the distance the rim of the town merging with the silent cloudless sky. The city looked like a field crushed by falling stars. The large bedroom was lavish and spotless with an en suite bathroom. The bed covered with a creaseless spread in red and green brocade stood near the window. The night was cool so Aruna turned off the air conditioning. Anna lay naked under a thin cotton sheet like a mermaid in a crystal stream. When they made love he finally penetrated her moist softness, which he had so long and feverishly awaited. Her slim body with its flawless stomach, soft pointed breasts and firm thighs reminded Aruna of one of the maidens in a fresco in the Ajanta cave paintings. They wanted the night never to end. Clusters of stars shone in a moonless sky. The bright streetlights of the short summer night disappeared at sunrise. The Wellington Hotel and the River Tyne were veiled with a brittle brightness. The lonely Tyne, hidden in the dawn, had finally woken.

'I don't understand why you've lived in England for such a long time on your own, Aruna. As far as I understand it Ceylon is a beautiful island with tropical sunshine. I read somewhere that it's a natural paradise with long beaches, lines of palms, waterfalls and tea plantations. If I were you I would want to go back and enjoy the easy life there.'

'I've no intention of living permanently in England Anna. When I get some real money from my business I can do what I want. Although my country is okay to read about freedom there is limited by caste and tradition. Since I've known you, Anna I've lost interest in a lot of things.'

Their nights and days ended in bright colours and a new strength. Bill, the bus driver, a regular at the Domestic Café, glared at Aruna.

'I'll see her in my bed one day,' he whispered to Harry, the quarryman who sat at the same table.

'I bet I'll have her first,' Harry announced, stubbing out his cigarette with the air of a man who has accepted a challenge.

Rupa felt as lonely as the invisible river Saraswathi at Bharat, where it joins the two rivers from the sky. As she lay in bed lonely in Leeds she dreamed of the Ganges, India's holy river, which helps the ill and vulnerable by purifying their spirits. The river was never lonely, bearing it's fathomless waters over thousands of miles like a gathering of hair from the God Shiva until finally it merges with the river Yamuna at Sangam, the eternal meeting place where dreams are realised.

THIRTY FOUR

Rupa was getting the children ready for school when she heard a knock on the door. The dog ran downstairs barking.

'It's only me, Rupa,' Eileen shouted through the letterbox. Rupa opened the door.

'Did you listen to the wireless this morning?'

'No, I'm just sorting out Shane's school bag.'

'That Ripper bastard was finally caught by the police!'

'Where?'

'Somewhere near Bradford I think. They caught him red handed, in a car with a woman. There isn't much on the news yet. All they said was a man has been arrested in connection with a serious crime and he will be further questioned about recent Ripper killings.'

'Thanks Eileen, I'll buy a paper this morning.'

'Don't bother Rupa, I'll bring you my paper. You sort the kids for school, I'll see you later.'

Eileen went off in a hurry to the newsagents to buy her tobacco, milk and the paper.

Rupa walked to school with the children. On the way back Elsie started to wag her tail vigorously. Rupa saw Eileen was talking to Jackie through her window.

'Hang on a minute, Rupa, I've got the paper for you,' Eileen shouted. The dog began to get excited and barked loudly, wagging her tail at the same time. Rupa stood on the pavement outside her house.

'See you on Saturday, Jackie,' Eileen bellowed and waved as Jackie walked away. Eileen came to Rupa's with a rolled up 'Daily Mirror'. When Rupa invited her in Eileen handed her a plastic bag. 'I bought this pair of slippers from Littlewoods' catalogue. They're too small for me, will you try them on?' Rupa put on the fluffy pink slippers. They fitted perfectly.

'You can have them Rupa.'

'Thanks a lot Eileen, now I can get rid of my worn out old pair. These ones will last, they look as though they've got some go in them!'

There was no need for Rupa to read the paper. Eileen related everything about the Ripper while they sat over a cup of tea.

'I must dash now, Jamie's still in bed. I'm going to cook a really nice meal for him, shepherd's pie, chips, swede and gravy.'

'Isn't he well Eileen?'

'So the bastard says! I don't believe that bugger. He had too much booze last night and he's got a hangover. He'll sleep until I kick him out of bed. By the way Rupa would you like to come over to my place on Saturday night? It's my fortieth birthday, the big four O! I'm having a party and Jamie is paying for everything. Don't worry about the kids. They'll be alright with the dog. Just come round and have a drink with us.'

Rupa readily agreed to go though quite why she wasn't sure. Eileen put her black jacket on. As she was leaving the front door Rupa noticed Eileen's tall, broad shouldered frame. She was wearing a short red skirt, showing her long legs. She reminded Rupa of some kind of ancestral Neanderthal figure, her waist enclosed in a six inch deep skirt of leaves.

When Lisa came home from school Rupa said, 'It's Eileen's birthday party on Saturday and I've had an invitation.'

'A birthday! Can we come with you, mummy?'

'No, you can't. It's not a children's party.'

'It doesn't matter, she'll have some jelly and ice cream.'

'She only invited her friends for a drink.'

'You don't drink mum.'

'I'm not intending to stay long. Will you be all right Lisa? Don't answer the door to anybody.'

'Shane and I can play a game.'

Rupa bought a birthday card, 'Happy Birthday to a Special Friend'. A bottle of wine would be welcome at the party but Rupa had no idea what Eileen drank. How about a scarf? But again she might not like it. Finally Rupa bought a Terry's milk chocolate box, wrapping it carefully in green paper.

Since Saturday morning Eileen and Jamie had been preparing for the party. Rupa heard them going in and out constantly, slamming the front door every time. Rupa made some sandwiches for the children's tea, which they ate with potato crisps and jelly and ice cream to finish.

When Rupa rang the bell Eileen came to the door dressed in a loose silk dress, bead necklaces, flashy rings, coloured glass bangles and tasselled earrings.

'Come in Rupa love,' she croaked.

'Happy birthday Eileen! Sorry I'm late.' Rupa said, handing her the package.

'Ta love, you really shouldn't have bothered.'

There was a smoky aroma all through the house, a mixture of alcohol, tobacco and perfume. There were more guests than Rupa had anticipated, jammed into the overcrowded lounge, sitting or standing some twenty-two in all. Although most were neighbours with familiar faces Rupa only knew Jackie to speak to. Eileen's elderly mother was in the corner, squeezed into an armchair, holding a glass of champagne. Baby faced Jamie was serving drinks. There was a table by the window filled with crisps, sausage rolls and chicken drummers.

A sumptuously decorated cake with a dozen pink candles from Alan's Bakery round the corner dominated the display, a gift from Jamie. Bottles of wine, whisky, gin and lager were stacked under the table. Eileen opened a large packet of Savoury Bombay mix and said loudly 'I brought this specially for Rupa.' Everyone looked at Rupa, who sat next to the old woman, drinking orange juice and feeling uncomfortable. The cake was cut and the guests were rapidly emptying their glasses.

'I can't believe you're sixty today, Eileen, I'll be eighty five next June' the old woman said. Eileen reddened but no one seemed to notice they were so busy eating and drinking. Eileen was knocking back large whiskys and her cheeks were already a fiery hue.

'Don't take any notice of my mother. She's going senile,' Eileen announced in a strange whisper.

'I bet she's got her pensioner's bus pass!' Jackie muttered, then laughed out loud but everyone pretended not to have heard. By now it was half past nine and Rupa began to feel more and more uneasy.

'I must go now Eileen. Lisa and Shane are on their own.'

'Don't go empty handed, Rupa love. Take some cake for your kiddies.' Eileen cut two chunky slices of birthday cake and handed them to Rupa, folded in a tissue. Rupa felt a great sense of relief as she left.

When everyone had gone, Rupa heard Eileen and Jamie having yet another fight, banging on the walls and hurling crockery until there was a final crash as the wall unit toppled over, then silence.

Aruna hadn't been home for seven weeks. The children rarely asked about him and Rupa's rent was in arrears yet again. It had been a hot summer so Rupa found some relief in the September gas and electricity bills being low. Whenever she telephoned Aruna at work someone else answered and the message she got was that he wasn't there and nobody knew where he was. It was equally difficult to contact him in the evenings. Rupa became suspicious, just where was her errant husband? Trying to speak to him always ended in failure so she decided to say nothing to anyone for the time being. But inside Rupa's mind she began to blame herself for her own naivety. Why is she not confronting her husband? Rupa knew that if she were English she would go straight to a solicitor and get a court order for maintenance.

'Sometimes I feel like going to his workshop with the children and telling him what a bastard he is in front of everybody, or burn the whole place and then admit it was done by his neglected wife, who's struggling to survive. I don't care about him or how he lives anymore. All I want is for my children to grow up safely without noticing their father is always away. If I have a row with him it will end up in a terrible divorce, which isn't the right thing according to our culture. Living in a foreign country as a single parent is hell.'

Rupa became more and more suspicious of Aruna's behaviour and at times became helplessly depressed. She even wondered whether there was another woman. Whatever the reality she didn't want to face it.

Anna got used to Aruna's unusually quiet behaviour. He kept his secrets carefully hidden. She was never invited to his flat because it was only a business place, but he visited her regularly in the evenings. They sat together and watched TV then spent the night together. It was a Sunday and Aruna wanted to go to Birmingham for the motor show. Anna didn't want to go because she was so far behind with her housework. When Aruna returned at five they had an early tea, then sat in front of the TV. 'You look very tired Anna!'

'I'm exhausted, I did all my washing this morning and I gave my flat a real clean. My feet are aching, I hope it's not going to be a busy day tomorrow.' She picked up a blue ribbon from the couch, gathered her hair to the back and tied it in a ponytail.

'You're a hard working girl Anna, I've never seen any woman with such determination.'

'Aruna, I want to tell you something. I don't want to disappoint you so please don't misunderstand me. I don't think our relationship is going to last long.'

'I don't understand what you mean Anna.'

'I think it's something always hidden in myself Aruna. I can't live with a man or have a long term relationship, however much I want to. I get depressed, bored and I even become suicidal at times! I can't do anything to stop myself. I'm sorry, it's just the way I am, Aruna.'

'But I love you Anna, I felt desperately close to you from the very first day I came to your café. You may be under pressure from your work but I can always help you.'

'Do you remember that day we went to 'The Omar Khayam' to celebrate the increase in your business turnover? We saw a cabaret spectacular, Middle Eastern belly dancing. You enjoyed it so much you didn't leave me alone all night. That afternoon I was getting dressed, combing my hair, sitting in front of my dressing table. You came to my flat straight from work. I saw you reading a letter sitting on my bed. I saw from my mirror that a photograph fell onto the floor near my feet. A picture of two beautiful children! You grabbed it and stuck it back in your pocket. I don't know why, I remembered my mother. I still have a photo album belonging to her. My favourite picture is of my mother standing in front of a cathedral, by a huge carved stone pillar. I was only three and she was holding my hand. My mother was a young woman with a beautiful smile.' Aruna was quiet as Anna continued.

'I was only sixteen when I became pregnant. Unfortunately it was an ectopic pregnancy and it had to be terminated. The theatre nurse told me that I had twins, a baby girl and boy. I was heart broken but my mother was so pleased for me. She never asked me who the father of my babies was. In fact it was the local vicar and my mother knew him very well. When I got pregnant I promised him I wouldn't tell anyone but I always wanted a healthy baby. I'm twenty five now and sometimes I watch little children playing in the back yards; for a moment I imagine they're mine.'

'Anna don't get so obsessed about things that happened years ago! Losing a pregnancy is nothing these days, no big drama like you think anyway.'

'My mother was poverty stricken because my father had abandoned her. I'm a Catholic and we believe in comforting the helpless. Faith can move mountains. I'd like to look God straight in the face on Judgement Day.'

'Don't you want to see me anymore Anna?'

'You can see me whenever you want Aruna, but I don't want to go to bed with you any more,' Anna burst into tears. When Aruna tried to console her she became irritated and screamed at him angrily. She threatened to commit suicide unless he left her flat at once. Finally she ran into her bedroom, slamming the door.

Aruna was shaken and confused to see how suddenly his relationship with Anna had ended. Was it just a bout of Anna's anger due to over-work? Would she change her mind? She might even apologise and have him back the next day. Aruna felt like a failure, humiliated by a mere woman. Had Rupa been in touch with Anna? Hardly likely, because his secret world with Anna was so well kept. He stood in his bedroom at two in the morning hurling his shoes and socks under the bed, dropping his jacket on the floor and then he lay on the bed like a fallen scarecrow. He had to go to work in the morning but he felt so tired. He wanted to sleep and never wake up. Aruna's feelings about the Domestic Café and Anna's bedroom poured out like a mixture of sour fruits.

Two days later Aruna went again to the Domestic Café for lunch, hoping that things might have cooled down. Anna welcomed him with a smile. He found out that she was now seeing an Englishman from Durham, who was going through rehabilitation for alcohol addiction.

'George had to give up his university education during his final year after a breakdown. He studied theology and now he's training to be a clergyman,' Anna said with a gleam in her eye. As he walked back to work along the damp back streets Aruna felt as though Rupa's shadow was trailing behind him.

Another day had ended and Aruna was back in his flat after work. He was getting ready for his evening out in the 'Dick Turpin'. The Domestic Café with its single tea-room, Anna, the woman who made unlimited cups of tea for her customers, had turned to a torrent of scalding water in Aruna's mind. He felt as if he had fallen from the sky and smashed against a rock; then he was floating down a turbulent river, holding onto an uprooted tree. Anna had rejected him and in no way could he accept the humiliation. Like a broken down engine endlessly turning over but unable to move, Aruna felt his life was over. The early morning sky was beginning to clear when he saw a squirrel jump from the leafless skeleton of a birch onto a damp wall and then down to the frozen ground. The sun fell on the snow, casting dark and menacing shadows.

THIRTY FIVE

It was mid December and Christmas was approaching. Young and old alike were looking forward to the break. The streets were decorated with yellow and scarlet bunting and figures made of coloured bulbs, winking and blinking in the evening dark. Lisa was expecting Santa and she knew that baby Jesus' birthday was due. She wrote an invitation for Santa on a card with a picture of her house drawn on the front, time schedules were given for both Santa and Jesus:

Christmas Eve

Jesus:

1. Go with Virgin Mary, meet the Pope and have breakfast in the Vatican City.
2. Private lunch at Buckingham Palace with the Queen, her husband and Prince Charles.
3. Attend midnight mass at Westminster Abbey.

Santa:

1. Copy down all the letters children sent.
2. Feed reindeer with enough food for two days.
3. Recondition sleighs to travel at supersonic speed, giving enough time to visit every chimney.
4. Roller skates, dress, doll, beanbag dog, make-up set for me, a bicycle for Shane and a large bone for Elsie.

Please don't forget us Father Christmas.

Christmas day

> You must be very tired Father Christmas. Please go to bed early. Let the reindeer run around under the trees.

Two weeks to go for Christmas and everyone's excitement increased. Shops were stacked to overflowing with toys, sweets, chocolates and all kinds of gifts. School children had broken up, shop windows, houses and streets were brightened with flashing colours and decorated trees. Rupa was given a four foot high artificial tree by Eileen.

'My mother gave this to me years ago, when we used to live in Scarborough. I only used it once. Your kids can have it if they like. It was stuck away in the attic but there's nothing wrong with it. It'd cost a fortune to buy a new tree Rupa!'

'Are you sure you don't want it, Eileen?'

'Of course I don't! We can hardly have a tree with Jamie about. The bugger'll fall over it when he's had a few.' Eileen laughed, showing her tobacco stained teeth and Rupa could smell the alcohol on her breath.

The tree stood in the corner of the sitting room and the children started to decorate it straight away. Rupa bought a set of lights and a reel of sparkling tinsel from Woody's in Leeds Market. Soon the tree was filled with cascades of shimmering lanterns, foil wrapped chocolates and a laughing Father Christmas. There was cotton wool for snow and a glimmering angel on top. Lisa and Shane were full of innocent joy, even Elsie ran up and down, sniffing, barking and jumping.

Aruna telephoned Rupa one Thursday night. 'I'm coming home tomorrow Rupa. My workshop is closed for two weeks over Christmas and the New Year.' For a moment Rupa was tongue-tied.

'You haven't been home for ages, the children will be very pleased. What time are you coming?'

'It'll be in the evening. I've to make sure everything is okay before I leave. My workmen are having a lunchtime party. No one will do any work unless they really have to, they're all too full of the Christmas spirit.'

'That's wonderful, we'll see you tomorrow. Don't drink too much Aruna, you have to drive a long way!'

Finally it was Christmas, the star of Bethlehem was already twinkling with only two more days to go. At last Aruna was at home with his family. Lisa and Shane glowed with delight at his presence. Rupa was feeling a strange happiness and became almost manic with activity. Her rented home, like a weaver bird's nest, became noisy all at once. The confused state of the house was like the interruption of joy when parent birds bring food for their fledglings – an incessant chirping.

It was a strange moment when Aruna opened the door. Rupa stood by the stairs. Shane and the dog ran down, almost tripping in their excitement. Lisa shyly peered round the sitting room door, cuddling her toy bunny. Aruna noticed that Rupa had lost weight; she looked strained and drained, worn out with her weariness. His son and daughter looked cheeky yet innocent and they had grown hugely. Elsie, the black and white border collie, had grown too. She licked Aruna and pawed him continuously, then she jumped up and down, drumming her paws, barking loudly and trying to grab Aruna's attention.

Rupa had already started to cook their dinner, a curry and fried rice. Aruna went to the kitchen and Rupa put the kettle on.

'What are you cooking Rupa?'

'I'm cooking a chicken curry, it's almost ready. You're probably living on take-away so I thought of making some Ceylonese food.'

'I'd love a curry, Rupa.'

Rupa made some tea.

'I brought some toys for Lisa and Shane. They're in the car. I thought that you may want to see them first.'

'I'm glad you brought some presents for them so I can wrap them up and put them under the tree.'

There was a sudden heavy downpour with sleet slashing against the windowpane. Lightning flashed and thunder followed; lightning zigzagged across the sky with continuous drum rolls of thunder. The dog was terrified and hid under the bed. Lisa and Shane closed their ears with their fingers every time the thunder crashed. Rainwater dripped through the yellow patch under the kitchen windowsill. Rupa put an empty tin under the leak and the red stained water pit-patted into it. When Aruna tried to close the swollen window a rotted piece of wood crumbled away. Only after an hour did the heavy rain finally turn to drizzle.

They had a meal together. Rupa washed up and cleared away as quickly as she could. Aruna had brought several bags of presents for the children and Rupa was delighted with the coloured pens and pencils, water colours, school bags, a few dinky toys, colouring books and chocolates. There was a dress for Lisa, a playsuit and a car for Shane. Lisa was given the dress and Shane the blue racing car as early presents.

Rupa wrapped the other presents, labelled them and put them under the tree. Lisa ran upstairs to try on her new dress with Elsie bounding at her heels. A minute later she came out onto the landing wearing the long sleeved green dress with yellow lace frills that she had so lovingly unwrapped.

'Mum...mum... come and see my new dress,' she screamed and then ran back down the stairs.

Rupa helped Lisa tie the bow.

'It's beautiful Lisa! Just the right size for you.'

'Thank you daddy, I'm going to wear it on Christmas day.'

Shane was busy playing with his car. Lisa sat on the floor writing a card.

'It's eleven o'clock and time for you to go to bed, Lisa and Shane. You can write your cards tomorrow morning Lisa.'

'Oh mum...we don't have to go to school tomorrow. I'm crossing off the dress from my Father Christmas list. I added a pair of black shoes instead.'

Elsie had already curled up on the rug for the night, the children were in bed and Rupa had made some coffee.

'I'm so glad you came home for Christmas, Aruna. The children always talk about going to see the lights in London. I'm frightened to go out at night and I haven't even taken them to see the lights in Leeds.'

'We can go to London tomorrow if you like!'

'It's a long way Aruna, the children will be tired.'

'It's nothing Rupa, only a three-hour drive! If we leave in the early afternoon we can be back by ten.'

'I can always ask Eileen to feed the dog and take her out for a short walk, she wouldn't mind at all.'

They agreed to go to London on the following day.

At night Rupa felt strange when Aruna was sleeping next to her. She was so used to sleeping alone in a cold bed with a hot water bottle by her side, she found it almost uncomfortable. Although Aruna had quickly fallen asleep breathing heavily, Rupa lay awake, hoping desperately that their marriage would work. It was incredible how the atmosphere around the house had changed within hours. Lisa was asleep with her new dress under her pillow. Shane would wake up in the morning looking for his new car. Even the dog seemed over excited. This was the happy family situation Rupa had always wanted. She put her arm round Aruna and moved closer to him feeling his heart beat and his hairy chest. She could smell the sweat of his tired body.

Every one was up early, the children full of the Christmas spirit, counting the increasing number of presents under the tree all wrapped in shiny paper.

Rupa made a cooked Ceylonese breakfast of string hoppers with fish. Lisa and Shane were excited about going to see the decorations, how they wished their daddy was home all the time!

The family set off to London in the late afternoon. Half way through the journey Aruna stopped at a service station on the motorway and they ate Kentucky fried chicken and chips. Lisa was very impressed to see how fast her father could drive. They arrived at seven and London was glittering. There was a sixty-foot high Christmas tree in Trafalgar Square brilliantly lit by a thousand yellow fluorescent bulbs, glowing in the chill mist. The banks of the Thames were wreathed in golden luminous drapes, which shone mysteriously on the ripples of the river. Big Ben struck the hour and even the pigeons were awake and peering through the stone lattices. Trafalgar Square with its fountain sprinkling like showers of pearls was packed to capacity with singing, laughing, drinking crowds; some had fallen asleep under Nelson's Column. No one seemed to feel the freezing wind or notice the long night.

At last Christmas was over. Eileen had piled up six cardboard boxes of empty bottles for the bin men. Rupa was beginning to feel some sense of falseness in Aruna's behaviour.

'I'm fed up of living on my own Aruna. It's not fair for the children. I feel desperately bored at times. I've nowhere to go.'

'I thought you'd settled down okay Rupa. So far you haven't had any problems, have you?'

'That's what you think Aruna! Eileen and Jamie, the next door neighbours, quarrel all the time and it's a terrible nuisance. The children seem to be sleeping with no problem but I just can't sleep when there's loud arguments going on next door almost every night! I don't mind where we live, Aruna, as long as our family is together.'

'Rupa, I think the schools in Leeds are better for the children. Newcastle's not a good place to live, although it's cheaper to run a business there.'

'Aruna, I don't understand you. Surely there are schools and families with children there! Don't you enjoy a good meal and time with the children when you've finished a day's work?'

'I'm very lucky Rupa, I can get a good meal at my regular café.'

'No wonder you're looking so well!'

'I don't really care what I eat or when, Rupa. My mind is always occupied with my business.'

'You're always away and you'll never get a chance to see the children growing up Aruna. Shane starts his new school next September. The landlord has increased the rent again from the first of January. I think it's pointless living like this Aruna.'

'We may be able to buy this house for next to nothing!'

'You must be joking Aruna! I wouldn't pay a ha'penny. I don't want to live here forever. I think it's time for me and the children to get out of the area altogether.'

'Listen Rupa, I came home for a break. Do stop nagging about the neighbours. I don't care who they are or what they do. But I am concerned about the children.'

'I've had enough of your manipulations. You don't mean anything you say and you don't care about us at all. You never even bother to phone. I've no way of contacting you because you are always 'unavailable'. You used to come home on weekends and now we have to look in a crystal ball to find out when you're coming home. You may try to build up a big business, but we have to live today.'

After half an hour Rupa realised that she wasn't going to get anywhere. She screamed.

'You're a selfish bastard who doesn't deserve what you have! If you're so concerned about the children why don't you take us to Newcastle? You've a flat there and we aren't allowed to stay there with you or even occasionally visit you. We aren't aliens with funny faces, I've had enough of your secrets.'

Rupa put her jacket on and went out. She walked aimlessly along the disused paths of East End Park, her mind shaking and empty. The main road was busy as ever with the constant hum of traffic. She sat on a bench where damp green mould flourished. There was a great mound of old tyres, soaking wet rotting cardboard and building rubble strewn on the grass patch in front of her. She didn't know why she was sitting there but she didn't move until her hands and feet began to freeze. She caught a bus to town, getting off at City Square. She walked along the alleyways off Briggate and along the narrow curved streets around the railway station. She wandered between the buildings, along empty pavements and shuttered shops, even Kirkgate Market was closed. When she arrived home two hours later Aruna was gone. The house had an air of abandonment. Lisa sat in a corner of the lounge, patiently painting a picture with watercolours. Shane had fallen asleep at the wheel of his car. The dog lay next to him, curled up. The fire had gone out. Rupa locked the door behind her and shivered as though the next world was converging on the one around her.

Aruna was back in his flat in Newcastle, sitting in front of the fire, trying to warm his cold feet. It was a two bedroom flat but he used only one room. The other was locked, full of junk: empty cardboard boxes, old suitcases, scraps of rolled up carpet, tools, cobwebs and dust. Aruna thought the flat was comfortable enough for Rupa, the children and the dog for a weekend if it was properly sorted. But he wouldn't want anyone to live there, not even Anna.

He went for a walk around the steel shuttered workshop, eerily empty but still heavy with the smell of grease. He returned to his room, confused and desperately wanting Anna. He sat in the armchair, recollecting the specially poignant moments with her, his mind relaxing and then he felt completely exhausted. Like a wall of water pushing its way down through a burst dam, confused feelings clouded his mind. He couldn't control the pain and the desire for Anna. The five-star Wellington, naked Anna, a perfect sculpture, her underwear strewn on the floor, the smell of her soft skin, the view from the balcony with the bright sky and the silvery Tyne and the sleepless nights, were insistent mirages. He felt like breaking into the Domestic Café, kicking over the chairs and tables and forcing his way into Anna's bedroom and into her. Then he thought about Rupa and the spoilt Christmas holiday. If only he hadn't married Rupa Anna might have accepted him. Bachelor life is completely free so the marriage somehow must be ended. His interminable rage made him feel like grabbing Anna with his sinewy hands and throwing her into the Tyne from the hotel balcony but somehow he couldn't take revenge on a woman. Instead he sought his prey like a king eagle, dangerous as a lion in heat. He grabbed a bottle of wine and with his tight fists smashed it against the table. The bottle crumbled with a terrifying bang. The broken green glass lay all over the table, the bed and the floor; some shards were stuck on the blue curtain. Aruna didn't realise that he had cut his finger. Blood sluiced down to the table and mixed with the spilt wine. Like an enemy invading a fortress he surrounded the Domestic Café, his rage and anger upsetting what little was left of his equilibrium.

The following morning Aruna went back to the café. Anna had only just opened after the holidays. No one else was there and she was cleaning the tea room, the floor was still wet. Aruna saw an aspect of Anna's attractiveness, which he never noticed before, her soft pale face, her pearl bright teeth and her hypnotic smile which would torment even a saint. Her long silky hair was tied back with a pink ribbon. She was wearing a dark blue blouse with a low cut neck from which her breasts were trying to escape. His desire for Anna took over his psyche like a volcano about to erupt.

'Happy New Year Aruna. How are you?'

'Fine, thanks.'

'We had plenty of snow here it was freezing cold and all I did was stay in and watch TV. I went to midnight mass on Christmas Eve.'

'I was in London last week. It was cold but no snow. I have a problem with sleeping.'

'Why? Is it something to do with your business? People don't want to repair their cars over Christmas. They spend all their money on food and drink. Everyone's penniless until they get their January pay, some people are even in debt. Not many people bother to go to church anymore. Not to worry, soon you'll be busy again! I don't expect many customers for another fortnight. Most of my regulars are on holiday.'

Aruna stirred sugar into his tea and sipped slowly but said nothing.

'What's wrong with your finger Aruna?'

She said pointing at his bandaged finger.

'I cut it.'

'How did you manage to do that?'

'I tried to open the tool box in a hurry and pulled the tools out cutting my finger with a sharp blade.'

'What a thing to do!' She shrilled, then shrugged.

Bill the bus driver with his beer belly opened the door.

'Happy New Year Anna!'

'Happy New Year Bill! Did you have a nice Christmas?'

'Smashing! Plenty of drinks and food! My wife had to set the alarm and get up at four in the morning to put the twenty five pound enormous turkey in the oven. Oh! The smell of her cooking was gorgeous! I'll tell you a secret Anna, her's isn't so good as the food you serve!'

They laughed loudly which irritated Aruna. He couldn't remember the smell of Rupa's cooking. Aruna finished his breakfast and left without speaking to Anna. He went back to his flat feeling something of a loser yet again.

At night his tension mounted. He felt as though he was going mad, like some kind of alien from a distant planet. He paced up and down like a zombie, thinking he was running along on wheels. He took some sleeping pills but still woke after only a few hours with a fuzzy head. He felt completely exhausted. The Domestic Café, Anna's smile like the opening of a Himalayan orchid, the decaying kitchen window in Rupa's house and her dimpling cheeks, the workshop, the Wellington Hotel, innocent Lisa, mischievous Shane and Elsie wagging her tail.

Aruna had a dream – he was sleeping with a woman who was hugging him and getting closer and closer to him. But then she tried to strangle him. Her blood red fingers dug into his shoulders. He could see the hands moving inexorably towards his neck. Her tangled spiky hair fell over her face. Aruna failed to recognise the woman who seemed to be wearing some kind of disguise. In mortal terror he tried to scream but he couldn't open his mouth, his lips were stuck together and he found it difficult to breathe. The walls in his bedroom turned black and began to cave in. In the pitch darkness something was threatening him. He felt his heart pounding. At last he opened his eyes and looked at the alarm clock. He heard the tick-tick-tock but could see nothing. His hands shook as they were stretched towards the light and finally he was able to press the switch. It was six a.m., a long and lonely January day stretched ahead. There was no sign of light through the half drawn curtains. He felt like a ball of wax thrown into a fire, his whole being seemed about to melt.

The following morning he had his breakfast at the Domestic Café as usual. He handed a ten pound note to Anna, who snatched it with a broad smile. Her affair with the alcoholic clergyman had ended abruptly. She couldn't resist mentioning to Aruna that her twenty sixth birthday was near. At once he offered to take her out for a meal and she accepted gladly.

On her birthday they went to the Omar Khayam for the evening meal. After they had eaten they decided to go back to her flat, both already quite drunk. As it was Saturday night and neither had to work the following day.

'You're beautiful Anna I want you desperately,' he whispered in her ears. He entwined his fingers with hers. When he felt the touch of her lips and her face his body was hot as molten lava but she stayed as cold as ever. He moved closer to her. Anna's hair ribbon fell to the floor.

'You're a married man with children, Aruna. I've found out your big bloody secret and no way am I seeing you again. I need freedom in my life and if I want a man I want one who's free too and who doesn't tell me a load of lies.'

She burst into tears. As he reached out to touch her naked body, 'Leave me alone,' she shouted, 'Go away'.

Aruna was red with anger and confusion.

'Divorce isn't a big drama if two people don't get on,' he said but she stayed silent. Whatever she said, in his mind Anna was still an angel, a treasure from heaven, a faultless virgin! Aruna's fantasy world glowed even more fiercely, like a floating comet in unending skies but soon the skies darkened. It took a long time for Aruna to realise that his affair with Anna was finally over. The woman who worked behind the curtain of the Domestic Café and the spectral temptress who haunted his dreams had finally and irrevocably merged.

* * * *

Alice was of Rumanian origin. She was five feet nine and with a flat chest. Alice looked older than her thirty-five years, her cheeks hollowed out when she smiled. She had a vivid scar above her lip and her right thumb and forefinger were stained with nicotine. Aruna met her at the 'Dick Turpin' and soon they were drinking together. Within a couple of days she had invited him to the council flat that she shared with her eight-year-old daughter, Tina. Tina's father had been a Russian soldier. The child had been conceived on their first night together and Alice couldn't even remember what the soldier looked like.

Aruna liked Alice's company but he had no idea why. She wasn't fussy like Rupa or watchful like Anna and she was always available. Her flat was untidy with rubbish bags piled by the kitchen door. But soon Aruna began to dislike Tina's inquisitiveness and the late hours her mother allowed her to keep. She jumped up and down on her mother's bed like a clockwork doll showing the soiled palms of her feet. On one occasion she gobbled down Aruna's take away before he realised what was happening. One night she sauntered into their bedroom while they were making love but Alice said nothing. Their relationship ended as abruptly as it began when one evening Aruna went home to find his wallet was missing.

THIRTY SIX

Lisa was ten and Shane was seven. It was clear that Aruna would never come to live with them. Rupa saw her past as a miasma of spiralling emptiness with livid shadows in-between.

Damp black fungi flourished underneath the kitchen window where water dripped constantly. There were even damp patches on her bedroom ceiling. The bell push above the front door had rusted because the landlord wouldn't do the smallest repair as the whole block was due for demolition.

Drugs had become a serious problem in the neighbourhood with pushers openly selling their wares on every street corner, even in daylight, dealers sitting in flash Cadillacs, sneering at the police and playing loud abrasive music on their car stereos.

Along with the freezing winter wind harsh poverty crept through the kitchen window. Rupa decided to look for a job, any job, just something with a ten pound note in a brown envelope on a Friday night. When Rupa told Eileen that she was looking for a job she was very pleased.

'At least you've got the sense to earn a few extra pennies. No one around here seems to want to do anything. God! We didn't waste our time when we were young. Don't worry Rupa, we'll keep an eye on the kids if you have to go out to work.'

Rupa noticed that underneath Eileen's heavy make-up wrinkles were beginning to appear. The Ripper trial had been going on for weeks and at last it was nearly over and everyone was waiting for the jury to go out. As Rupa had expected Eileen started to bang the door-knocker loudly. It was in the afternoon while Rupa was making sandwiches for the children's tea, expecting them back from school any moment. Elsie went mad, jumping, barking and thrusting at the door.

'It's me again Rupa. I've got some good news for you.' Eileen spoke from behind the door. When Rupa opened it the dog pushed herself out and pawed at Eileen.

'Come in Eileen.'

'That Ripper bastard has finally got his just desserts. Ee's been locked up for life.' Eileen waved the 'Yorkshire Evening Post', laughing triumphantly.

'I heard a bit about it on last night's news. It's a horrifying story,' said Rupa.

Eileen stood in the entrance hall twisting the paper in her hands as she scanned the middle pages. The dog sat at her feet looking up.

'Just listen to me Rupa, I'll read the best bits for you.' Rupa sat on the stairs and listened patiently.

'Peter Sutcliffe, possibly suffering from paranoid schizophrenia, believed that he heard the voices of God. He was caught by a constable in the act of committing yet another crime. When he was young he had worked as a gravedigger, even digging up newly buried women's bodies which he ogled obsessively. He was a sadist who killed women for the sheer pleasure of it. Yesterday he was jailed for thirty years.'

Rupa thought that not even Maha Sohona the demon who visits graves, digs the bodies up.

'What do you think of that Rupa? You must be pleased that you're not one of his victims! I must go to the washerette today. That bugger Jamie's piled up his dirty washing again. Working down a mine, you can imagine what his clothes are like.' Eileen muttered as she hurried away.

Rupa was called for an interview for a job in the accounts department at Harris Carpets, really no more than a school leaver's job, adding columns of figures and sending out circulars. She doubted if she had got it. The manager she saw seemed very off-hand and kept looking at his watch as though he was due to somewhere else.

Lisa had been nagging her to go to W.H.Smiths to buy a book and a few sheets of coloured paper for a school project on dinosaurs.

Somewhere at the back of her diary Rupa had jotted down a couple of possible titles. The branch she was looking for was somewhere on Commercial Street, she was sure just past the Leeds Library. It was housed in a quaint nineteenth century building with a series of stone arches enfolding the bow windows.

Rupa pushed open the swing door and through an arch she saw the shop proper with its tall presses of books and low tables of sale items and remainders. Suddenly she felt relaxed, back in a world of books and the leisure to study whatever she chose.

She remembered her student days as she wandered over to the remainders and began leafing through a few of the somewhat shop-soiled volumes on offer. One title caught her eye. 'Rites of Winter' by C.J. Hunter. She picked it up and looked at the fly-leaf. 'C.J. Hunter was born in Leeds. After reading English at Balliol College, Oxford he researched modern poetry under William Empson at Sheffield and taught in a variety of colleges. He is now completing his doctoral thesis on post-war English poets at Leeds University.'

Her heart gave a leap. There was a minute photograph of Hunter, who looked exactly as she had known him plus a few grey hairs.

Then she read the opening poem.

In sleep I dream the gratitude I know
I cannot say
Now you are in a latitude where palm
trees hold the sway
There are always things between us that
keep getting in the way
And stop me from expressing the things I
mean to say
In a night of wind and weathers love will
not go away

Rupa looked at the price. Originally seven pounds, fifty pence, now down to four. She counted the money in her purse and totalled it to three pounds, sixty and she needed her fare home. She glanced at the spine. 'Chatto Younger Poets' and in one of the almost blank first pages she saw the publisher's address. She snatched a pencil stub from her pocket and jotted it down. When she got home she would write to Hunter, care of the publisher and hope he'd get it.

When Rupa came to Vicar Lane she saw the huge ancient building with its domes and towers stretching to the sky, Leeds Kirkgate Markets, in gold lettering above the stone arch of the entrance, glittering like a signpost to the stars.

As she walked into the great building, shaded by the awe inspiring dome she felt she was under the protection of her guardian angel. The stalls stood in lines, crescents and circles and the stallholders welcomed their customers with beaming smiles. It was like a kingdom, a territory of their own.

She bought some Smarties for the children, ten tubes for a pound. Soon she had lost herself in the tumultuous streams of buyers and sellers. She walked along the narrow centuries old cobbled ways. Rupa found herself pushed up against shopping trolleys and men and women loaded with baskets and bags and mothers with babies in pushchairs. There were separate stalls for fish, poultry, bacon, cheese, eggs, greeting cards, pet food and china on every side. She bought a bottle of glue from Woodys for Shane to stick Weetabix cards in his scrapbook. Then she came to the back of the market which reminded her of an Eastern fair where there were gaudy displays of fruit, vegetables, flowers, dried fruit and nuts.

One stall sold only exotic food: aubergines, mangoes, lychees, bananas, kiwi fruit and pineapples, even fresh coconuts in their brown hairy shells. Rupa bought bananas and aubergines at affordable prices.

She came out in Dyer Street and returned to the shopping plaza, with its grand Victorian arcades carved with designs shining like sapphires set in gold. Finally she approached City Square and waited for the 62 Circular to East End Park. The bus stop was in front of Trinity Church and at once her eyes lit on the statue of the Black Prince on his horse, his dark figure full of masculine strength, glowing in the winter sun. Rupa felt she might almost be a muse, listening to the voice of an unknown prince. The green and yellow bus arrived, slowing down and pulling to a stop. She got on, her spirit glowing, the last passenger in a long queue, still gazing at the statue.

Rupa arrived home to be welcomed by the dog waiting by the door. It was half past two and Elsie started her short sharp barks, demanding her afternoon walk. Rupa quickly put her on the lead and walked her down to the park, almost pulled along by the dog and quite unable to keep up with its pace. They played for about twenty minutes, Rupa throwing a tennis ball and Elsie catching it and returning it. Then they walked back, Elsie panting and Rupa sweating all the way home.

On the way back from the park Rupa bumped into Eileen.

'Have you heard what happened in Chapeltown last night?

'No I haven't Eileen.'

'Those bloody riots have started again. Whole streets on fire and looting all over the place. Must dash, I'm late.'

Rupa felt hungry but decided to wait for the children and sat down for a cup of tea. Elsie lay on the rug but her feet soon became unsettled and ran to the door at the sound of footsteps. It was Shane and Lisa and at once the house became noisily chaotic with their scattered shoes, socks and school bags, the dog jumping and tripping over them. They ran straight to the kitchen for a glass of Vimto.

Rupa had bought a large stand pie from Leeds Market for fifty pence. To go with it she made some chips and a salad. The dog had some Pedigree Chum and the children's leftovers. After the meal Lisa went to her room to work on a project. Shane sat on the floor in the sitting room with a pile of picture cards in an empty ice cream box, a bottle of glue and the scrapbook.

Rupa finally decided to write the letter to Hunter she had been composing all day in her mind. She spent half an hour re-constructing the beginning. The last time she wrote to Hunter was many years before, asking for a reference when she applied for a place at Birkbeck College. She kept thinking of giving up the whole idea but finally she made up her mind to write the letter.

18 Watling Terrace

East End Park
Leeds 9

Wednesday 9th January

Dear Mr. Hunter,

I went to W.H. Smiths today and I was so surprised to find your book 'Rites of Winter' on a shelf. I am writing to you care of your publisher and hope you will receive this. I am glad to tell you that I also live in Leeds now. We had to sell our house in London and move to the North about three years ago, because of my husband's business in Newcastle. I have two children, Lisa and Shane. My husband doesn't live with us anymore. I wanted to buy your book, but I didn't have enough money so I read some of your poems standing in the shop. I am trying hard to find a job, any job to earn some money, but so far I am unsuccessful. Tomorrow I am going for another interview, at Sun Alliance Insurance. Wherever I go they turn down my application, even for the most basic clerical job.

Rupa.

The next two weeks passed quickly and Rupa was still looking for a job until one Thursday morning when she received a letter quite different to the usual run of rejections. Sun Alliance Insurance had offered her a clerical job in their home insurance renewals and policy drafting section. She read it carefully twice. It was definitely an acceptance.

'We are pleased to offer you a job in our Fire and Accident Department from Monday 28th January. Please complete the enclosed acceptance form and return it as soon as possible.'

Although the starting salary was very low there was a free lunch and the flexible working hours came in handy. Rupa discussed the difficulties she had with her two young children on the phone with Mrs. Jenkins, the kindly staff supervisor. She could start work after the children had gone to school and return at half past four. It was only a bus ride away to the city centre where their office was situated. The only problem was that the children had to be on their own for about an hour before she came back and the dog was used to an afternoon walk. But Elsie would soon get used to the routine and Eileen would keep an eye on everything. The first few months would be a bit difficult but soon everything would fall into place. As it was an office job, she might need some new clothes but she could buy them when she got paid. Rupa was fed up with asking Aruna for money. Although he occasionally sent some, it was irregular and she had to spend it on food and she was still always behind with the rent.

The following day once the children had gone to school, Rupa opened her wardrobe and emptied it to see whether she had enough clothing to start her new job. Some skirts and blouses needed ironing. Suddenly she thought she could smell gas. She pushed everything back into the wardrobe and rushed downstairs. All the knobs were in the off position on the fifteen-year-old gas cooker. She couldn't open the kitchen window because she wouldn't be able to shut it again. When finally she opened the bathroom window cold air pushed in with the drizzling rain. Then Rupa called Eileen next door who was there in seconds, Jamie having gone to work.

'I can't smell anything Rupa. Why don't you call the Gas Board? Just in case! For your peace of mind! That's what the buggers are there for, it's their job.'

Eileen knew where the gas main switch was in the meter cupboard outside. She turned the lever to the off position. 'It's done and you're safe! The buggers from the gas board'll come and sort it out for you. I'll be at home all morning and come round Rupa if there's any problem.'

Rupa phoned the Gas Emergency Service. Now the gas supply to the house had been turned off and it was no longer a red alert but they would be there within the next few minutes. Rupa didn't have an electric kettle so she'd always boiled water in a large milk pan and until the gas was reconnected she couldn't make herself a cup of tea. She sat in the lounge in front of the spluttering coal fire, waiting for the Gas Board, wondering at Eileen's ability to get things done. Then the doorbell rang. Elsie ran to the door with her usual loud bark and Rupa followed her. Rupa opened the door and the dog pushed herself out sniffing and wagging her tail. The man who stood at the door couldn't be from the Gas Board – no yellow oilskins or heavy boots. Rupa was stunned for a second and then she recognised the stranger, it was Hunter.

'Mr. Hunter er, I'm so glad to see you! Do please come in. I'm sorry the house is in a mess. The Gas Board are coming to check on a possible leak.'

Hunter smiled and followed Rupa into the sitting room. At her invitation he sat in a faded green armchair, stretched his legs and warmed his hands in front of the fire.

'Rupa, I brought you a copy of my book, 'Rites of Winter'. He took it out of his briefcase and handed it to her with a smile.

'Thank you so much. I'd love to read it Mr. Hunter,' she smiled as she turned the pages. Then there was another knock at the door. This time it was the man from the Gas Board who told Rupa there had been a leak down the road and what she had smelt was a whiff from there. It was all sorted out now and he turned the gas back on.

'I can make you some coffee at least,' she began to relax. She found an unopened packet of malted milk biscuits she had intended for the children's tea and tipped them out onto a plate and put it on the small glass-topped table in front of the fire. Hunter noticed that Rupa had changed over the years, her face lined with marks of strain. It was amazing how much a young woman could be changed by motherhood.

'So you're a single parent now!' Hunter said nibbling a biscuit.

'Have you found a job yet?'

'Just yesterday. I'm starting a clerical job for an insurance company on Monday. I thought you might like to come for a meal one night.'

'I'd be delighted! I'm on my way to see my course supervisor. He lives around here. Normally I'd see him in his office on campus but he's recovering from a knee operation so I said I'd go to his house.'

They chatted inconsequentially for a few minutes and then the children and the dog were suddenly in the kitchen and Hunter said he must be going.

'What about Friday night, say about seven?' Rupa asked.

'Lovely, I'll see you then.'

He smiled and waved as he walked down the narrow pavement. Rupa felt relief washing over her like a great wave.

THIRTY SEVEN

Rupa heard the chiming of the clock at midnight and again half an hour later. She was sleeplessly struggling with a headache. Through the darkness she could see a faint light on the window and she opened a drawer in her bedside cabinet where there was a bottle of herbal oil given by her father when she left for England. She opened it and with her forefinger massaged some oil on her forehead and neck. The poignant aroma spread through the bedroom, a mingled fragrance of sandalwood, cinnamon, citrus, asparagus, mint and cardamom, which soon spread over the whole house. It was the melancholy smell of her childhood at Maha Gedara. Rupa felt only a temporary relief from the herbal oil. She could never remember such a blinding headache.

'It's pointless taking painkillers for a headache. It only makes you feel worse. You need some fresh country air. Go to the Yorkshire Dales for the weekend.' Diana, who worked in the office had said that afternoon. But was it true? How can someone find the remedy for a headache so easily? Rupa lay still, her eyes tight closed, trying to force herself to sleep.

This is a crippling nuisance of a headache. I don't think it's caused by my office job, sitting down from nine to four, at the same desk, the same chair; sending out home insurance renewals in white Sun Alliance envelopes and drafting policy endorsements with additions and deletions, a quick lunch on the mezzanine floor and then back to work. The building is enormous with thirteen floors. The lift hums, stops then hums again up and down all day – perhaps I'm becoming phobic. I can't always manage to walk up thirteen flights of stairs. The aerial view from the top floor is like a landscape by Constable. Church spires, the market buildings, the dome of the Corn Exchange and then the sprawl of the inner city.

The arcs of vapour trails left by vanishing jets billowed among the clouds. The Concorde makes the sky tremble.

Rupa felt the urge to jump on a plane and go - it mattered not where – just so long as Lisa Shane and Elsie the dog were with her. Leeds with its strangely shaped buildings, lines of cars and buses and the River Aire, were all packed together while the open spaces stretched to the countryside beyond. At the Sun Alliance the decorators were painting the reception hall in yellow and the rest of the building in sea blue, orange, green and deep pink.

The painted walls are too bright, the newly laid carpets soft to the touch of my feet. The air conditioning would soon cool the pouring sweat generated by the summer heat.

The burning pain started from her nostrils and spread inexorably to the touch of her body.

The cause of the headache might be the smell of paint and the chemicals that the workmen carried with them everywhere. The vague sense of aimlessness cannot be overpowered by any mental mechanism.

Rupa pondered her long distant training in Buddhist meditation. She remembered that the doors and windows in the office were slightly open while the decorators were working. Within a week or two her headaches would disappear with the fading smell of new paint.

Rupa knew that her double bed was large enough for two, but still she slept on one edge. The only warm section of her bed was underneath, in the shape of her own body. She didn't want to stretch her arms and legs so she curled up instead. The cold wind was tapping on the windowpane and Rupa was still wide awake. These insomniac nights must end. The command punched through her mind like a drum beat as she got out of bed to realise it was snowing heavily. The moon shone in a corner, sprinkled with snowflakes and the snow-washed night sky glowed while the leafless skeletons of poplars shivered. There was a blanket of quiet everywhere and the winter night was haunted by the emptiness. The house was freezing, the world outside her home like a desert full of white blooms. Rupa tried to close the window but still the cold air pushed in through the widening gaps. Lisa and Shane were fast asleep. Elsie was sleeping quietly, curled up in a corner of Lisa's bed. The smell of fresh paint had sunken into Rupa's mind. The fresh but unbearable smell would flow all over her body like a lightening flash. Although Rupa was tired she came home in the evening with a strange happiness, eager for the waiting children and the dog, her mind brightened by some invisible light.

Their marriage ceremony began by the tying of his little finger to her's with a golden thread, which now was strangling her. The thread had grown out of all proportion into a noose all round her body and then coiled like a snake. The tight knot had rooted like bindweed inside her and the pain of the inflamed wound was spreading. Livid scars were formed in the shape of a noose. These scars would only change their shapes when time had run on.

It was a Friday and Aruna was not coming home. Saturday, Sunday, Monday, Tuesday, Wednesday, Thursday. He might never return. A widow is a woman who is taboo in Eastern society just like an infertile woman was a bad omen. If you meet her at the beginning of a journey you should go back home, have a cup of tea and start out again or even postpone your trip to another day. Tthhh! Tthhh! Tthhh! You should spit on the ground three times. A dog shaking its head flapping its ears or the chik, chik, chik, chik sound of a gecko hidden among the roof tiles were also bad omens. Children without their fathers or wives abandoned by their husbands could bring bad luck and were also taboo. At a wedding, a funeral, an almsgiving, a devil dance or a girl's menarche both parents must participate. Doesn't Rupa belong to Eastern society any more? A deep unreachable anxiety was growing in her mind.

The breeze and light snow had turned into a blizzard, the streetlights dimmed and hidden. The gale-force wind blew the world upside down and it seemed as if it would snow forever. The wind shivered between the rows of terraces, forcing itself against every door and window.

When the morning came the sun was hidden behind banks of grey cloud. Even the birds were confused, flying across the sky numb as blown leaves, all sense of direction gone. Why was Aruna gradually fading from Rupa's mind? A mirage, the lost traveller's only hope. The ants smell honey, stick to it and die. Rupa must find an oasis where she could assuage her hunger and thirst. The road ahead lay through barbed wire and quicksand. The end of a marriage is a disaster but was it anyone's fault?

The next day started with tired yawnings. Lisa and Shane had woken early to get ready for school. They needed toothbrushes, toothpaste, towels, shoe polish, socks, pens, pencils, books and the door key. After Lisa and Shane had gone silence reigned again then Elsie barked furiously at the voices of passing children and at the postman's footsteps. When he had pushed the letters through Elsie ran to the door and back to the kitchen, carrying the mail between her teeth. When Rupa entered the office that morning inevitably the paint smell would strike again. She turned to one side but she still could not sleep and tried rubbing herbal oil on her forehead again.

This awful headache is still going on. My eyes are on fire. I feel so lifeless. My head feels like a lead weight. When I go out the cold wind will burn my nostrils and spread all over my body.

Rupa knew she must be ill and when she took her temperature she confirmed it. She telephoned her office and they suggested she stay in bed and keep warm. What relief... Elsie carried 'The Times' to the kitchen when the boy pushed it through the letterbox. The headlines were also about the snow and the resulting chaos. Also 'Jean meets her brother after fifty years', the story of a reunion on the second page with a picture of two children holding hands and a picture of them fifty years on, redolent with smiles. Jean had lived in a displaced persons' camp in France for six years and then moved to England for a new life when she was eleven. Her brother ended up in a concentration camp and after the war he lived in France. Jean managed to trace her brother through some international charity.

Rupa read the story and remembered meeting Hunter. She cried and then smiled. Pearls of showers shone in the sun. She felt like singing and dancing in the rain but then darker memories overwhelmed her. She remembered Kumara. Where was Kumara? She had been a young student when she knew him but now she was a mother looking older than her age. For years after she had sent him messages through the clouds but all too soon the ravaging winds had blown them away.

For once the house and the neighbourhood seemed strangely quiet. Apart from the sound of some little children pushing their tricycles on the tarmac in the back street and an occasional mother calling the whole area was still silent. Rupa lay in bed looking out of the bedroom window, watching the shape-changing white and grey clouds. A huge silvery cloud rode in the azure like a ship at anchor. Although her headache was slightly better her whole body ached. The fan heater Rupa had recently bought at a garage sale was emitting a continuous hum and the room was warmer. Rupa could hear the heavy breathing of Elsie, sleeping under her bed.

Hunter was supposed to be coming for dinner the following day at half past seven. If Rupa was not well enough to go out Eileen would do a bit of shopping for her. She closed her eyes, tracing vividly the foundations of her past. She managed to get a couple of hours sleep but her hot water bottle had gone cold. She got out of bed and Elsie immediately stretched her legs, crawled out and ran down the stairs.

Rupa went to the kitchen to make a cup of tea and to fill the hot water bottle when the telephone rang. 'Who's phoning me at this time, eleven in the morning?' she wondered. It was Hunter.

'I thought you'd have gone to work Rupa, but I dialled your number in case you were there, I don't know why!'

'I didn't go to work today. I'm not feeling well so I stayed at home.'

'What's the matter Rupa?'

'I had a blinding headache all night and now I feel feverish.'

'Did you take anything for your headache?'

'Just Panadol, I've some herbal oil for headaches as well.'

'Did you have a rest this morning?'

'I managed to get some sleep, it was so quiet after the children had gone to school.'

'It's my day off today, Rupa. I'd like to come and see you, if it's all right with you.'

'It's fine with me, I feel a bit better now. When are you coming?'

'In about half an hour. I know you're ill Rupa. I'm only coming to see you so don't make a fuss about anything.'

Rupa couldn't believe Hunter was coming to see her, no one except Eileen had ever visited her when she was ill. She hadn't even had a wash in the morning and had only just woken. Quickly she went to the bathroom, washed and got dressed, then she went downstairs and added some coal to the fire just as the door bell rang.

Rupa opened the door to find Hunter stood on the step wearing a blue cord jacket.

'Do come in.'

'Sorry I came at such short notice.'

He kissed her on the cheek. She felt his moustache with a strange tingling sensation. Elsie started barking, moving her legs backwards and forwards towards the lounge. Hunter sat in the armchair and Rupa on the settee. They both went quiet for a minute and then he spoke.

'How do you feel now, Rupa.'

'I feel a lot better than I did last night. I think I'm coming down with flu. Would you like a cup of coffee Mr. Hunter?'

'I'd love it, if it isn't a bother.'

Rupa made a pot of coffee. As she offered some to him a strange felicitous feeling glowed within her.

'I'm so glad you came. When I'm on my own I get obsessed with things and it makes me worse.'

'How did you become a single mother, Rupa? I remember you telling me a bit about yourself when I used to teach you in Croydon. I had the feeling that you were happily married and looking forward to going home.'

When he mentioned Croydon Tech, she remembered how close to him she felt and suddenly she felt uncomfortable.

'Things gradually changed in my life over the last twelve years. I never expected to end up with two children on my own in a foreign country. I don't need to tell you that this is one of the roughest areas in Leeds. Although we moved north Aruna, my husband, never lived in this house. He started his business in Newcastle and he's got a flat there.'

'Why don't you all go and live there?'

'Because he doesn't want us to! I've never even been to Newcastle.'

'Doesn't he come to see you or the children at all?'

'Occasionally. The children are used to life without a father.'

'How do you manage on your own?'

'With great difficulty. I'm working now so hopefully things will improve. Aruna's business is well established and he earns good money. He lives alone but it's business first and family nowhere. His behaviour's weird. I've been suspicious about what he's been up to for a long time – other women certainly but that isn't the whole problem. I don't think he can live with anyone, he gets paranoid whatever the situation and then he's got to move on again. Now I'll be rejected in Eastern society for the rest of my life. A woman whose marriage has ended is always at fault and she's considered a bad omen! Wherever I go I'll be ignored. I'll be an outcast and even women I've grown up with will whisper behind my back and even stare at me in the street. They'd rather not see me at all on 'auspicious family occasions' like engagements and weddings because I may bring bad luck to their future lives! But I'll be welcomed with smiles at a funeral. They live out their superstitions as much as they always did.'

Hunter laughed. 'But you live in England Rupa! Do you really care about all those things? I think you're a bit hysterical. We don't bother with 'auspicious moments' in Leeds or in London. I'm sure you are capablc of sorting things out efficiently.'

Rupa burst into tears so that even the dog was frightened and hid behind the settee.

'Come on Rupa, you're a grown up woman with two beautiful children and a lovely dog. I understand your problems but the most difficult period of your life is over and things should improve.' Hunter sat next to Rupa and put his arms round her shoulders.

'I'm sorry to see you're so upset. As for me I've been married and divorced since I left Croydon Tech!'

Rupa was astonished but said nothing.

'My marriage only lasted for six months and I don't have any children. Linda, my ex-wife remarried and now she lives in America. She's a tutor in the English Department at the University of California at Santa Barbara.'

'Do you still see her?'

'Not really, I've seen her only once since we got divorced but she does phone me occasionally. She seems to be busy with her life, she has a child now. Her husband's a marine architect. It's sad my marriage didn't last but I think we weren't suited to each other – she expected a very expensive life style. Our views on everything were poles apart and we always ended up arguing. I didn't leave her, by the way, she left me.'

Rupa couldn't believe how any woman could reject and leave a man so understanding as Hunter. It was half past one and Rupa decided to make something for their lunch. When Hunter said that it wasn't fair for her to do things when she was ill Rupa insisted he ate something.

'Don't feel bitter about your husband's peculiar behaviour, Rupa. He was born with his strange mentality and unfortunately he seems to hate women.'

The afternoon seemed to pass at inordinate speed and neither of them wanted it to end but finally Hunter rose to his feet.

'I must go now Rupa. I've to see my tutor this afternoon. Don't go to work tomorrow, have the rest of the week off! I'll come and see you when you're feeling better.'

When Hunter had gone Rupa realised how close to him she felt. A strange happiness hovered over her whole being and Aruna's weird ways began to slacken their hold.

* * * *

Another Christmas arrived. It was a cold December day with crisp air and a twilight that was receding rapidly. One bedroom window was open wide. Lisa and Shane were leaning out, watching

Santa's sleigh as it progressed down the road accompanied by a group of carol singers. Rupa's children waved at Santa with his long white beard, who was smiling and waving at everyone. While the sleigh pulled slowly down the street coloured flashing bulbs brightened the night sky. Lisa knew that their mother was going to be late home that evening because she had gone shopping. It was a Friday and the shops stayed open until nine. Shane was still hungry, in spite of having emptied the biscuit tin earlier, so Lisa made some jam sandwiches. They ate most of them and Elsie finished the rest. Rupa arrived home, weighed down with two large carrier bags full of food, an hour late because the bus had broken down. Eileen had dropped in to make sure the children were all right. 'Don't be naughty, mummy should be home soon,' she told them. Lisa was reading and Shane had gone to bed. The window was still open and the house was freezing.

Since Rupa had started work, the children matured rapidly and their daily life fell into a fixed routine. They left home in the morning with their school bags on their shoulders. They had lunch at school and stayed until half past three when school finished. Rupa arrived home at half past four. When either child was ill she had to take time off. Eventually the children began to ask questions about their father so Rupa told them that he was busy at work and he couldn't come home. Sometimes she stayed silent, numbed by the weight of her depression. Rupa vaguely believed that there was a light at the end of a dark tunnel. What she did need was time to come to terms with what had happened. She did all her housework after the children had gone to bed. During the short winter days and longer winter nights she hardly saw her children in daylight. Aruna no longer even paid the rent. He knew that Rupa was working so he considered it no longer necessary. He believed that if he spent too much on his family he might go bankrupt so Rupa had to go without. At the end of the year a profit sharing bonus was paid to the staff at the company where Rupa worked so she managed to buy some new clothes for herself and the children, a fridge freezer and even a washing machine.

As you go along the motorway just before Newcastle town centre, turn left at the crossroad to Sandhurst Road. After about a mile you will see a large road sign on the right and a white name board with black lettering and a red arrow pointing to 'Harjan Motors' which was Aruna's workshop. He had bought a piece of land next to the workshop. Most of his profits he spent on further improvements to his business. In spite of it becoming such a success Aruna suffered increasingly from attacks of migraine. He hated Anna for leaving him but somehow he blamed Rupa more for marrying him in the first place.

On the last Sunday before Christmas, Aruna telephoned Rupa and told her that he was coming to see them but only for the day. Lisa and Shane jumped up and down in excited anticipation.

'Guess what dad's bringing me! A necklace,' Lisa announced gleefully.

'A Lego set and a Monopoly set for me' Shane shouted. When Aruna walked in empty handed Shane and Lisa looked at each other in bewilderment.

'They must be in his car. Mum'll put them under the tree,' Lisa whispered. Rupa heard the whispering but she knew that Aruna had brought no presents. Glumly Rupa made tea. As she handed over a mug of tea to Aruna, Rupa said, 'Aruna, I think Lisa and Shane are expecting some presents from you. Haven't you got anything for them?'

'No.'

'Then I'll put something under the tree and pretend it's from you.'

Suddenly Aruna's anger escalated. He pulled a bundle of notes from his wallet and threw them on the table shouting, 'Lisa, there's fifty pounds on the table. Can you buy something for you and Shane tomorrow?'

Lisa took the five crisp blue ten pound notes with some trepidation and ran upstairs clutching them and calling to her brother.

'Shane, Shane, Shane, we're going shopping with mummy tomorrow.'

Together they made a list of things they were going to buy for Christmas.

During lunch Aruna said that he would be going soon. He had to be in Newcastle and it was too risky to leave business premises unattended for a long period of time.

Even before clearing the kitchen Rupa began to speak.

'I do think Aruna, it's time for you to do more for the children. They are not babies anymore, now it's a different situation. They've started to ask why daddy's never at home.'

'I know my business has become a bit of a headache for everybody, including you, but if I involve you in my business I'll go bankrupt, I know it. Now interest rates have gone up it's difficult to get a bank loan. I'm just not far enough on with my business not to be hit by high interest rates and the recession. People just won't spend money. Really big businesses are still doing well, they can afford to sell motor parts cheaper and do repairs cheaper than we can.'

'Do you think its all my fault these ups and downs in your business? All I do is run round like a squirrel up a tree and down again, hoping to find a hidden hoard of nuts. You just don't listen to me. I'm fed up with everything.'

There's nothing I can do about it. I just don't have money.'

'I'm not asking you for money Aruna, I don't want to live here the way we do, with doors and windows closed day and night.'

'Are you asking me to invent a house for you with open doors and windows?'

'Did I ask you to sell the house in London and move us to a slum? I don't like to see the children grow up in a rough estate full of alcoholics and drug addicts.'

Aruna stamped his foot with burning fury and hurled his cup of tea across the room. It smashed against the kitchen tap. Broken china fell onto the sink, the rest onto the floor while a stream of tea poured down the kitchen cupboard. When Lisa heard their argument she ran upstairs and slammed her bedroom door. Elsie her tail drooping, hid under the bed. Shane was terrified and closed his eyes pretending to be asleep, laying on his bed and closing his ears with his fingers. Aruna stood up, then marched out of the room and across the hallway. The last Rupa heard of him was the resounding slam of the front door as he left. She brushed away her tears and went upstairs to comfort the children, feeling her marriage was finally over.

THIRTY EIGHT

Jane who lived across the road in Sefton Avenue, was a close friend of Eileen, Rupa's neighbour. Thin and long faced, forty five year old Jane often smiled and showed her squirrel-teeth. She worked part time as a barmaid at the Lord's Tavern in Briggate. Jane was going to marry Michael who was sixty, three weeks on Saturday. Rupa also had received an invitation to their wedding. Michael was completely bald and Jane told everyone that he had thick brown hair until recently when he was given chemotherapy for prostate cancer. He had a tattoo of a naked woman with large breasts on his right arm and this was his fifth marriage. He was the father of eleven children and he boasted of five grandchildren. Until recently he had worked for the council as a dustman.

'I've no choice but to marry Michael, he's so much in love with me he's threatened to commit suicide if I don't give in,' Jane told Rupa. When Rupa passed all this on to her neighbour, Eileen laughed.

'Don't you believe Jane's mad rubbish, Rupa. The bugger's only got two years to live and she's after his pension. All four of his ex–wives are alive and they're queuing at his door on Thursday mornings when he gets his giro! Now he's on long term sick and the social pay him a bit more, some kind of disability allowance! You know she tells everyone about Michael's thick brown hair, its all a pack of lies, I've known him for ten years and he always was bald. What difference does it make anyway?'

'I've had a wedding invitation, too, Eileen. Jane's just a neighbour, not a friend. I don't know what to do. I feel a bit uncomfortable going to the wedding on my own, I don't know what to wear. I don't have money to buy new clothes.'

'Don't you worry Rupa. Jane and Michael are friends of ours.

I'm going with Jamie to the Registrar's office and then on to the reception. You can come with us. Not a big problem, eh, there'll be a lot of fun so don't you miss it, Rupa!'

The wedding was scheduled for half past eleven in the morning and there was to be a reception later on at the Lord's Tavern. Everyone in the neighbourhood was getting ready.

The last three weeks had gone quickly and finally it was Jane's wedding day and a fine sunny July morning. Eileen was wearing a purple frilled silk dress and matching dusky pink shoes, gold tassel earrings, three necklaces, a ring on every finger, bright red lipstick and her hair permed and black. Rupa wore a blue dress with a single string of pearls. She had stopped wearing her gold jewellery, which she had worn at her own wedding, because it symbolised the scars of her broken marriage. Even her wedding ring she kept buried deep in her needlework box among the hoard of discarded buttons.

At quarter to eleven Jane arrived in a limousine with her eighty two year old uncle, her only living relative. The car belonged to the bar manager, who hired it out for special occasions. The old man climbed out of the car with the help of a stick, he seemed confused as he looked around. Jane was wearing a long cream dress, shiny with sequins and beads and she tottered along on five inch stilettos. She wore a single yellow rose in her hair and held a matching bouquet in her ringed hands. She emerged from the crowd with a serene smile, her eyes flashing. It was half past eleven and the crowd started to look round for the groom, staring at each other in puzzlement. The aged uncle sighed anxiously; he had come a long distance by coach the day before from Glasgow and now he felt exhausted as he sat in the waiting room, yawning, almost dozing off. The woman receptionist came out and asked about the delay. The bridegroom was late due to a traffic jam, everyone presumed.

At twelve fifteen Michael arrived alone in a taxi. He got out in a hurry, leaving the driver with his hand out. Michael fumbled in his back pocket but seemed to have forgotten his wallet.

'Bugger it! My wallet's in my jeans at home. I'm not used to these bloody trousers,' he muttered, glaring round. Jane realised that there was a problem and ran to pay the taxi, forgetting for a moment that she was the bride-to-be. Her silk dress caught in the wind and ballooned into a fantastic shape and everyone started to laugh uproariously.

Michael was wearing formal black trousers, a maroon jacket and tie with alternating bands of green and pink. A strong smell of alcohol surrounded him as he went into the Registrar's office. The registrar seemed confused and stared openly at Michael's strange outfit, then he smiled politely and asked the couple to sit down. As they were exchanging vows Michael began to stammer and he was unable to continue.

'Its not so easy to r.r.read a load of j.j.jargon without m.m.making a m.mistake,' he finally managed to get out.

'Its all right Mr. Smith, take your time and try to relax,' the registrar repeated the vows even more slowly. Finally Michael and Jane became lawfully man and wife, the event duly being witnessed by Eileen and Jamie. It was only two days before the wedding when Michael bought Jane's ring at a pawnbroker's in Albion Street for a few pounds. Even as the couple were walking out of the office a row broke out.

'I never wanted to go through all that l.legal g.g.gibberish. I only s.signed because you f.forced me to, J.Jane,' Michael shouted angrily, wiping a thin thread of spittle from his lips.

'Haven't you forgotten that you threatened to commit suicide if I didn't marry you Michael?'

'M..m..marry you, you m.must be d.daft!'

Eileen interrupted.

'Stop mucking about you two now. You've only just got married! Shut your great gob and behave yourself Michael.' She frowned at the couple, her frown like a thundercloud.

Rupa was frightened and stood behind Eileen, wondering what was going to happen next.

'Are you all right Rupa? Those two have forgotten that today's their big day! The bugger hasn't given up the drink, not even on his wedding day!' Eileen patted Rupa's shoulder reassuringly. As Jane walked down the steps she slipped on the highly waxed surface and fell arse over tip. She tried to stay upright by grabbing hold of a banister but failed abysmally, displaying her pink knickers to all and sundry as she rolled down the steps, her rose bouquet tangled in her train. She kept one shoe on but the other flew through the air and somehow wedged itself between the bottom rail of the banister. With difficulty she smiled and pushed on the errant shoe.

In all there were forty guests, mostly Jane's friends and neighbours. The elderly uncle couldn't quite manage the party. He felt dizzy so a doctor had to be called. Everyone was served with a single glass of champagne, a handful of roasted peanuts, a sausage roll and a slice of wedding cake. Wine was proffered by two of the staff who worked with Jane at the Lord's Tavern. Tea, coffee, extra food and drinks had to be paid for by the guests. Reluctantly Rupa bought a slice of cheesecake and a cup of coffee. Eileen and Jamie were satisfying their thirst with innumerable whiskies. An hour later another even worse row broke out – this time over a woman. Jane began to feel uncomfortable and slightly irritated. When Rupa tried to push her way to the side of the gathering her hand encountered Michael's vast stomach. Suddenly Michael disappeared into a corner, kissing Sharon passionately and pressing her up against him, the next minute Jane was dancing with Jamie and kissing him. Eileen's angry look kept Jamie well under control. Then a glass of whisky got spilled on Jane's evening dress so Rupa grabbed a handkerchief from her handbag and dabbed at Jane's dress.

'Don't make a fuss about it, it's only whisky, it won't show a stain, Jane.' Eileen laughed at Jane's red eyes and at the tears cascading down her cheeks. Abruptly Jane straightened her dress and ran to the toilet to wash off the whisky. The dress was on hire from Blessings and it had to be immaculate when it was returned.

'That Michael's a bloody bastard who can't leave women alone and an alki to boot!'

Everyone heard Eileen's loud croaky voice, except Jane who was fortunately still in the toilet. Eileen had finally run out of money so she borrowed fifteen pounds from Rupa.

'I guarantee I'll pay you back on Tuesday when I cash my giro but remind me anyway on Monday night, Rupa.'

Eileen was quite aware of her little lapses of memory when she was 'under the influence'. There was a large table in the corner of the hall covered with a green tablecloth and a posy of pink carnations which was meant for the wedding gifts.

'Have you got something for them Rupa?'

'I didn't see their gift list, Eileen, so I bought a set of stainless steel cutlery.'

'That'll do. They never had a list, Rupa but I know Jane, she expects something from everyone. Jamie brought some booze and cigars from us, that's what Michael wanted.'

Rupa noticed that there were wrapped bottles already lining the table.

'Someone's been nicking our presents. Haven't you noticed that four bottles have gone walkies Jane? I've asked Peter to keep an eye on the table.' Michael suddenly blurted out.

'Peter acting responsible! That's a joke. Bottles don't fly. How dare you suspect any of us!'

When Eileen screamed Jane dragged him to one side.

Michael was already shaky on his feet and he had begun to stammer again. His voice shook up and down the crowd like a wind chime. Apart from Rupa everyone started hugging, kissing, dancing, drinking and singing 'For auld lang's syne' in a ragged chorus. By the time it was ten thirty Rupa felt she'd had enough but the party showed no signs of ending. Quietly she slipped out of the pub and stood at the bus stop where she could still hear the distant hubbub, punctuated by the crash of breaking glass.

THIRTY NINE

The overnight snow had begun to thaw with the morning sun. The verges and paths were squelchy and the wind shivered over, what settled snow remained on roofs and branches. The watery sun hovered beneath the thinning grey clouds of the Newcastle sky. York Road was empty as the tundra on that particular Sunday morning. Shuddering and alone, Aruna paced along slippery pavements, the shape of his soles and heels patterning the fallen snow. He passed the terraces, slipped into an alleyway and skirted back Morning Terrace from where the church spire behind the sloping roofs was just visible. Surreptitiously he tapped at the door of number twenty eight. A woman opened it and beckoned. Aruna shook the snow from his shoes and as he entered a wave of warm air enveloped him. The house was Mary O'Keefe's, who was known as 'Irish Mary'. Soon he was sitting in front of the glowing coal fire in the front room. His shivers and goose pimples melted before the smoky fumes that surrounded him. Mary was plump as a barrel at forty-five and only five feet tall. She combed her shoulder length hair into an untidy tumble, gathered at the back with a tawdry silk hair-band. Her skin was mottled with spots.

'I've an allergic reaction to artificial heat. I can't wait till summer comes when I can open the windows again.'

Mary squeezed a tube of acne cream and rubbed some onto her skin. Her large wobbly breasts and round buttocks were only just covered by a flimsy blue night dress with pink ribbons hanging loose from the low cut neck. Her nightie was 'see through' clear as a reflection in still water. She looked like a sculpture by an inexperienced amateur. Aruna felt as weary as someone who has undergone a major operation, his face was drawn, his eyes heavy with sleep.

'You look tired Aruna!'

'I'm exhausted. I couldn't sleep last night.'

'I've got some fresh bread. Would you like some toast?'

'I can't eat anything but I would like a cup of coffee.' 'I ground some beans last night. I'll make a pot.'

Mary went to the kitchen. Soon the smell of freshly brewed coffee spread throughout the house. Aruna took off his jacket and hung it over a chair. The fire was turning into a pile of ash and cinders so Mary banked it up and jabbed at it with a heavy brass poker. A cloud of smoke disappeared up the chimney and the coal began to burn with a vivid orange glow. They drank their coffee in silence. Mary went to the door to bring in the two pint bottles of milk, which rested on the step. When she came back Aruna had fallen asleep.

'You really are tired, Aruna! Why don't you come to bed?'

When Aruna opened his eyes, Mary was sitting next to him undoing his shirt buttons. Aruna threw his shirt towards a chair but it fell on the floor, he left it and followed Mary upstairs. Mary turned the electric blanket off as they slipped under the quilt. Aruna felt as if he had been embraced by a warm sea current. They made love so passionately that beads of sweat rimmed their foreheads. Their bodies cooled but the sheets were wet with the sweat of their incendiary passion. The sun had disappeared but at least the snow on the trees was gone, leaving the earth sodden.

Mary had given up her job on the rhubarb farm when Aruna had made his offer of making her his housekeeper. They sat up in bed chatting casually, Mary smiling with all the enjoyment of an addict.

'Mary, you said you're originally from Belfast didn't you, when did you come to England?'

'It's a long story Aruna. My parents were immigrants. They were poverty stricken so just after the war they came to England looking for work. I'm the youngest of a family of nine. My mother worked as a cook in an old people's home until she died. My father worked 'on the lump' on building sites. He was a terrible drinker and my mother knew he went with other women as well. They rowed non-stop so we all left home as soon as we could. I started as an auxiliary nurse when I was sixteen. Then I went to train as a nun – imagine me in a convent! It was as strict as hell so you can believe how long I stuck it. One morning I just packed my bags, hopped over the wall and thumbed a lift to Leeds. I lived in a bedsit for a few years then I moved here and managed to rent this two bedroom house, but I can't afford to buy my own furniture. Every stick in the place is from some charity or other.'

'I'm sorry you had such a rough time Mary. I'll help you re-decorate your house. Get rid of this rickety bed and that worn out settee to start with!'

Impulsively she pulled a front door key from her pocket.

'Here, this is my spare, Aruna, you can have it!'

'Ceylon Daily News Cookery Book', a title of Rupa's that somehow had ended up with Aruna. Perhaps she had given it to him to help him manage quick meals on his own. Aruna had never opened it, pushing it behind some old account books. When Mary was tidying up his flat she found the book covered in dust.

'Aruna I found this in your bookcase. This is exactly what I was looking for. I can cook English and Italian food with no problem, but I've no idea how to cook a curry.'

'You can have it, Mary. Someone gave it to me but I don't want it.'

Mary took it home and studied the recipes. She bought some curry powder, garlic, desiccated coconut and chilli from an Indian grocery shop. She cooked chicken curry with pilau rice and a wattalappam, a treacle pudding just as the book said.

Within three months Mary's house had been re-decorated. A new Axminster was laid in the sitting room, where the walls were brightly painted in eggshell blue. The bedrooms were carpeted in green and there was a new king sized bed, still in its plastic sheeting.

'The bedroom must be a special feature in this house Aruna,' Mary said with naïve delight as a van full of new furniture pulled up outside. 'I've never slept in such a comfortable bed, Aruna! When we were young we never had beds. I remember sharing a mattress with my older sister. My parents always had second hand furniture from the Sisters of the Poor. Some of the mattresses were stained with pee.'

'Mary this dressing table set and the double bed are a special gift from me.'

She looked at the label dangling from the mattress, 'Parker Knoll'. She arranged her room with her make up laid out on the dressing table. She kept her gold jewellery in a secret drawer in the dresser. There was a framed photograph of Mary wearing a black cloak, sitting on a wall in front of a cloister, taken when she was at the convent. The cookery book sat next to it with Rupa's name written in Sinhalese. Mary prided herself on being very 'broad minded'. She told Aruna, 'Of course, men need women, I don't care what they do the rest of the time as long as they're good in bed.'

Mary was not family conscious like Anna so he felt relieved, fearing no outside involvements or interference.

'There are some beautiful houses with large gardens just up the road. Someone like you Aruna, you should live in one of them! I'll come and do all your housework and the garden,' Mary often said. Aruna stayed silent.

Six months had gone in a flash. It was Monday morning. Harjan Motors was always busy at the beginning of the week with the wholesale deliveries and new orders to be sorted out. By the time Aruna arrived at Mary's house for lunch it was already half past three. Mary was ill in bed so there was no meal ready. When Aruna went upstairs she was groaning plaintively.

'What's the matter, Mary?'

'I've been sick all morning and I don't feel well. I can't stand the sight of food and the smell of it makes me sick.'

She ran to the toilet. Aruna heard she was making loud noises, pretending to vomit.

'Shouldn't you see your G.P.?'

'I'll just have to wait and see for a few more days. I do think Aruna, this is the time you should be with me, its more important than rushing back to work.'

'But you know Mary, Monday's my busiest day of the week. I haven't had anything to eat. I don't ever stop. I can call the doctor for you.'

Mary started crying hysterically and then she began to roll about on the floor.

'What exactly is wrong with you? It could be what you ate. Have you taken something for indigestion? Two people are off sick today and next Monday's bank holiday. I've to be there and I really must go now.'

'I think I'm pregnant Aruna!'

'You told me two days ago that you've reached the change of life and you're safe. Today you're telling me a very different story.'

'You don't care Aruna, do you?'

Abruptly Aruna put on his jacket and left.

Mary heard the door click and knew Aruna had gone. Quickly she got up and ran to the bathroom to look in the mirror. She turned round and then turned again. She checked her body in every detail for any of the usual signs of pregnancy. There were folding lines on the neck but they were pale and not dark. Her nipples are no darker than usual. She squeezed them but there was no sign of milk.

I can't breast feed the baby if I have no milk, she thought. It was impossible to see any difference in her normal quite distended stomach. She put on a maternity dress and imagined what she would look like in a couple of months. Mary had been collecting maternity dresses, 'Mothercare' bras and knickers for years and she kept them ready packed in a suitcase and perfumed with rose pot-pourri.

At the same time Aruna was entering the Domestic Café. Lunchtime had passed but Anna was still there her face decked with a smile.

'I haven't seen you for ages, where have you been all this time Aruna?'

'I was busy with the business,' he lied casually, sitting at a corner table with his tray of food. There were some faces Aruna had not seen before. The café looked different too but Aruna couldn't work out the reason. There were no reflections visible in the windows, so dirty were the oblong panes. The teashop had not been decorated for years and the wallpaper was beginning to peel. Even the cutlery wasn't properly washed. The white ceiling had turned yellow with cigarette smoke and under the table by the window stains from dropped food marked the tiles. But Anna's smile and the air from the heater was warm and welcoming as always.

FORTY

Mrs. Fermie was a middle aged Austrian who lived with her Scottish husband in a large Victorian house in Moortown with a cascading blue wisteria arch at the front. When she walked into the office in the morning wearing a long pleated skirt and a white silk blouse some brief summer fragrance wafted in with her and remained all day because her whole wardrobe was suffused with a rich lavender pot-pourri.

'My niece was coming for tea yesterday so I made some cakes and shortbread biscuits. There was a lot left and it's a shame to throw it away. My husband doesn't have a sweet tooth so I brought some for your children instead,' she handed Rupa a carrier bag with a biscuit tin inside, smiling all the while.

'Thank you Mrs Fermie. Your home made biscuits are delicious. You can't buy anything like this in the shops.'

Mrs Fermie would bring something for Rupa's children every Monday; biscuits, cakes, chocolates or some apples from her own tree.

'The days of my childhood I spent in Austria were unforgettable, snowy hills like a picture post card. I even remember Hitler coming to my school and visiting our class. He gave me a pen because I was a bright child. By the millennium we'll be starting to get old and it'll be time to hand the world over to our children. Rupa, you really must think about your children's education. I've a grown up married son who's a doctor so he's no problem, but your children are still young. I don't know whether I should tell you this, but I often wonder about the rough neighbourhood you live in.'

'I know it only too well, Mrs. Fermie. Touch wood, so far we haven't had any real trouble from the neighbours. I've tried to discuss this with Aruna but we always end up rowing.'

'Rupa, If you need any help don't forget we're always here. Bringing up two children single-handed isn't nothing.'

She added reassuringly as she straightened a few wisps of grey hair.

It was a dark afternoon in early autumn when Lisa met her brother at the school gates at half past three. The sky was clouding over and a fine drizzle blew in the wind. She held his hand as they walked down Oakland Avenue in the homeward flow of children, mothers, pushchairs, dogs and cars pulling out. The Avenue ended at a junction with the main road where a lollypop man was waiting to cross the children. They swarmed across in a mass but within minutes the crowd had dispersed and Lisa and Shane were walking alone down a narrow path beside an orchard bordered by overgrown hawthorn hedge. There were apple, pear, greengage and cherry trees, some still heavy with fruit and their branches occasionally drooped over the hedge. The area seemed abandoned to the approach of winter, an Eden for every swooping bird and skittering squirrel. Shane jumped and tried to pick an apple from an overhanging branch.

'Shane, don't steal anything belonging to other people,' Lisa shouted.

'Nobody wants them Lisa, they'll fall and rot anyway'. When Shane jumped up again and pulled a branch a shower of red apples fell into the hedge and eagerly he snatched a few.

'Look, Shane there's a lot more under the hedge.'

'Let's leave them for the hedgehogs.'

'I want to go home now.'

They held hands and rushed away, running and running until they came to a small parade of shops. Lisa, her fingers stained with ink, tugged a few pence of saved up money from her pocket. They went to Goldings and bought two ice cream cornets and a chewing bone for Elsie. They dropped their school satchels on the ground and sat on a wall to eat their ice cream when it began to rain. It was half past four by the time they arrived home. Lisa took the house key attached to her neck chain and opened the door.

'Elsie, we've got something for you' Shane shouted, but there was no sign of the dog. They called her again, Shane running upstairs to see whether she was asleep on his bed and then they checked under the furniture but still there was no sign of Elsie. The children became frightened, not knowing what to do.

'Call Eileen' said Lisa and Shane somewhat shakily ran next door. Eileen came to find Lisa crying.

'Shall we call mummy?' said Shane.

'Not yet we'll have to find out what's happened.'

Again they searched but still no Elsie was to be found.

Rupa was about to leave the office when she had a telephone call from Eileen.

'Rupa, this is Eileen. The children are all right but the dog seems to be missing. Not to worry for the moment, she may have got out somehow and run to the park or somewhere. I'm only phoning you because Lisa and Shane are panicking and they asked me to tell you.'

'Elsie's quite clever, Eileen. She knows the way home from the park. It's unlikely she'd run into the road either. I should be home within half an hour but it depends, only if I get a bus straight off Eileen, could you please stay with the children until I get there?'

'Don't worry Rupa, I'll be here, see you later.'

When Rupa came home the children seemed to have calmed down although they were still in a state of shock. The salmon sandwiches Rupa left in the fridge for their tea hadn't been touched.

'These kids of yours are real cowards Rupa, they wouldn't even let me out of the room!'

'Thanks for your help Eileen. The dog has a name and address tag on her collar along with our telephone number. I'll phone the police.'

'If you don't get anywhere give us a shout, Rupa.' Eileen left but came back after tea. Rupa was the last person to leave the house in the morning and she was positive she had locked the door and that the dog was there. Eileen had knocked on the neighbours' doors to see if anyone had seen a black and white Border collie, but no one had.

'It could be one of those bastards who lives around here has taken the dog and expects you to pay for her return. After all it's only a dog and don't you say you'll pay a penny Rupa!'

Rupa telephoned the police and gave them a description of the dog. Then she phoned Hunter but he had gone to Oxford for a seminar and wouldn't be back for two days.

'I don't think anyone in their right mind would try to kidnap my dog and demand a ransom from us Eileen.'

'What you don't see is Rupa, the bastards aren't in their right minds.'

'I still can't believe this is happening to me.'

'Don't forget Rupa, Jamie and I are next door. Just bang on the wall, if you want us. I'll make sure that bugger's not on the booze tonight.'

After Eileen had left Rupa began to worry that if someone had kidnapped the dog. Soon they would be telephoning, a man with a strange voice demanding money she didn't have. Did Eileen suspect someone in the neighbourhood and wasn't letting on? Rupa wondered. Whatever Eileen had said if someone demanded a sum of money she would somehow have to find it to get the dog back. But Rupa didn't fancy meeting a stranger secretly with cash in her hand. The kidnapper might ask for a huge sum and what then? If Hunter was about she could have borrowed money from him, little though she wanted to. Reluctantly Rupa telephoned Mrs. Fermie and told her about the dog.

'Don't be silly Rupa, no one's going to ask you for a ransom for a dog! If you needed any money I'd be happy to give it to you but the most important thing is the security of your home.'

'I'll pay you back as soon as possible. I can go to the bank tomorrow and borrow some money if necessary.'

'But you haven't borrowed any money from me Rupa! Nothing has happened yet except the dog is missing. Do let me know if you need any help.'

Rupa for a moment felt relieved. Lisa was waiting by the phone but it never rang. Rupa telephoned the local dogs homes, in case someone had taken her there. When she telephoned the police for the third time they realised her panicky state and told her that someone was coming round straight away. Within fifteen minutes a police car stopped in front of the house, no uncommon scene in the area. A constable and a W.P.C. came in but by now it was dark and the sky was heavy with rain. They had a look around to see if there were any signs of forced entry. The kitchen window wasn't fully closed but no one had tried to open it further.

'Has anyone except you and your children got a key to the house?'

'No.'

'Did you lock the door properly before you left the house this morning?'

'Definitely. I always double check it.'

'Was it still locked when you came home?'

'I think so, but the children were back first and they can't remember.'

'If the dog is found we'll let you know straight off. Don't worry too much at this stage, it may be someone's looking after her and you really have to allow at least a couple of days. One thing we have noticed was you have a Union lock. If someone had found out your key number they could easily buy a duplicate. If they got into your house looking for money and valuables the dog may have somehow got out. But we can't see any signs of attempted burglary. Why don't you change the lock straight off and put on a five lever mortise deadlock?'

'I can't have the lock changed tonight.'

'Well, make sure you bolt it properly when you're in. If there's any problem dial 999. Don't open the door to anybody you don't know.'

When they left Rupa felt better but some kind of fear began to haunt her. She didn't want to discuss things with the children so she went to the bathroom and wept secretly.

Eileen and Jamie called. 'Any news Rupa?'

'The police told me to change the lock but the landlord couldn't care less about security.'

'Eeh, Rupa, Jamie'll do it for you, 'e learned joinery when he was in the nick and he's really good at it.'

'Thanks Jamie, I'll give you the money if you could buy the lock and fit it for me tomorrow.'

'Don't let your landlord get away without paying for the lock. You better get some money off that old tight wad!'

It was nine but there was still no phone call and no news about the dog. Shane had gone to bed and he didn't want anything to eat so Rupa woke him up and gave him a glass of milk. Lisa had fallen asleep by the telephone but Rupa managed to give her some biscuits and send her to bed. Ten, eleven, twelve; the hours passed and still nothing. Rupa couldn't sleep. Everyone kept saying it was only a dog but Elsie was like Rupa's own child. She felt a sharp pain like a ball of fire spreading through her body. Although she fell asleep several times she woke a few minutes later with a burgeoning sense of anxiety. In the early hours she fell asleep out of sheer exhaustion, then suddenly woke up in terror when she heard a tapping at the door. The time was ten to four. She felt like dialling 999 but something told her not to. Eileen next door wasn't on the phone and Rupa didn't feel like disturbing them by banging on the wall at this time of the night. Then she heard the sound of the knocker three or four times.

'Who is it? Who is it?' she shouted but no answer came. She looked through the window at the moonless, starless, pitch dark night and the still falling rain. Rupa couldn't see a thing. Now it was ten past four. Then there came a scratching and a continuous scrabbling on the door. Rupa listened and knew it was the dog. She went downstairs and there was no sound of anyone except the dog. 'Elsie, Elsie,' she shouted and she heard the dog calling her. Rupa knew it was Elsie's bark. With the excitement all her fear had gone and Rupa put the key in the lock and opened the door. Elsie jumped in and Rupa shut the door quickly. The dog was soaking wet so Rupa dried her with a towel. Elsie started running round jumping and licking everyone. She jumped onto Lisa's bed and pulled Shane's bedding off, wagging her tail non-stop. Lisa got up and hugged Elsie. Shane jumped up and down in glee they all laughed and ran to the fridge and ate the salmon sandwiches, sharing them with the dog.

The following morning Jamie fitted a Regency security lock to Rupa's door and managed to close the swollen kitchen window. When she offered to pay him Eileen said, 'It's all right love, he didn't pay 'owt for it, his mate gave it to him, it 'fell off the back of a lorry', if you know what I mean.' Rupa was delighted.

'You never know what kind of bastards live around us. I knew that poor dog hadn't disappeared for a day by the sea! But I gave everyone the message that you're as poor as I am and it'd be a waste of time.'

'Thank God, whoever took the dog brought her back safe and well. Thanks Eileen, you've been so kind to me and the children.'

Eileen was convinced that the dog had been kidnapped but by who they would never know.

Rupa had taken a day off to recover from her ordeal when Hunter arrived unexpectedly.

'I got your message Rupa, I'm sorry I was away in Oxford and only came back late last night.'

'We lost our dog for a day, but we've got her back now. The whole thing was a complete nightmare. The children were terrified and I had to call the police. They suggested that I should improve my security! Jamie next door changed the lock for me this morning. Eileen still believes that someone stole the dog and was going to ask for money to return it.'

Rupa and Hunter were relaxed now and it didn't feel strange any more when he sat next to her or if he kissed her intimately. But there was always some kind of fear and guilt in her mind because she was still married. Aruna had left her with the two children and it was hard to accept that it was final. She was very confused and began to wonder if she would ever be able to make sense of her agony.

'Rupa, I think it's time for you to make a move out of this area. Where I live in Alwoodley people don't kidnap their neighbours' cats and dogs. You pay rent but the landlord doesn't do a single repair.'

'That's what my friend Mrs. Fermie always says. This area's becoming worse now and weird things happen all the time. What about my children's schools?'

'Well if you move to a better area the schools there will be better, too. Do you know Rupa, since last May the law's changed and women can apply for a mortgage? Divorce is easier than ever and women can apply for promotions on the same terms as men!'

'It was only last week I found out about these changes. I saw a circular in the office about the mortgage thing for women.'

'I'm sure as an insurance underwriter you'll be able to ask for a loan to buy your own house.'

'I'll go and see my head of department tomorrow. Would you like another cup of tea?'

'I'm fine Rupa, I've to be back on campus before lunchtime. I'll give you a ring tonight.'

Rupa went back to work. The next day the superintendent came to see her and asked about the missing dog.

'I'm terrified of living alone with two young children Mr Hopkins. I desperately want to move out of the area.'

'If you need any help, do let us know Rupa.'

'Am I entitled to apply for a mortgage with Sun Alliance Mr Hopkins?'

'I can't see why not! Go down to the finance department and ask for a form.'

Within six weeks Rupa's mortgage application had been approved and she was looking for a house. It was a quiet morning when she walked past the gates of Roundhay Park and a cuckoo called from the top of a poplar. The bird's song mingled with the chiming of St. Mary's church bells. Somehow another spring had come.

FORTY ONE

One Friday, a fortnight later, Hunter came to Rupa's for an evening meal. After they ate together the children wanted Hunter to play Scrabble while Rupa cleared the dishes. The atmosphere in the house was so quiet that even Elsie had fallen asleep. Lisa and Shane were tired when the game was over so Rupa sent them to bed. Hunter sat on the settee reading Rupa's 'Evening Post'. By the time she came down it was half past ten. They sat in front of the fire with a cup of coffee.

'Rupa, it's so nice to have a meal with your family. I really enjoyed it.'

'We hardly go out in the evenings. I'm just pleased you came, it makes a change for the children.'

'Now you've sorted out your mortgage you've got something to look forward to Rupa.'

'I don't know what kind of future I've got. I often feel like going back to Ceylon but the one thing that keeps me here is the children's education. My life is so messy it's difficult to say what's going to happen next.'

'I can see what you mean Rupa, but if you really mean to go back do think twice. Once you are there you might end up in an even messier situation, Eastern culture being what it is.'

'I know only too well the shame and disgrace which follows me. Here I'm just held down by my past but there I'd be an untouchable.'

'Rupa, you haven't changed much during the years since I first met you at Croydon Tech except that I was your English teacher then!'

He held her hand, Rupa was quiet and then Hunter kissed her passionately. She was suddenly caught up in the wave of his hypnotic touch and moved closer to him. As he kissed her again she felt numb, as light as a melting flake of snow. Half an hour later they were still together and her eyes shone brightly.

'Things change like the wind,' he whispered in her ear.

Hunter left just before midnight and Rupa went upstairs feeling a strange sense of elation. She lay in bed trying to recollect what Hunter had been telling her, re-living every moment in her imagination. He even said that one day he might marry an Eastern woman! Had Hunter really meant that bit about marrying and did he mean Rupa by his comments? How would the children react to him? How could she tell her parents, or would it be better to keep them in the dark? What about Chandra and her other Ceylonese friends? Would they accept such a change? She had given up pondering Aruna and his mad ways. He chopped and changed and all Rupa knew for certain about him was his unreliability and his contempt for his family. She remembered Kumara, the one friend from the old times she really cared for and had tried so hard to contact but with no result. Was Hunter serious or was he just trying to be kind? Suddenly she felt a sense of panic at this thought and then she remembered his quiet re-assuring tones and his unforgettable touch and how her loneliness disappeared when she was with him. 'Things change like the wind', wasn't that the unceasing whisper?

There had been no word from her parents for weeks and Rupa had begun to worry. She decided to write a letter to them, late though it was. She must tell them that she might be moving soon.

For the last couple of months Eileen and Jamie had been unusually quiet so Rupa presumed that things were better between them. No sooner had this idea crystallised in her mind then she heard the eruption of a furious argument through the plaster lath of the wall. Again and again she heard the phrase 'the dog, the bloody dog' in Eileen's rough nasal tone, followed by a crash and the sound of breaking glass and a howl of anguish from Jamie, as though Eileen had gripped his testicles and was refusing to let go. Then came the sound of running feet and the slam of the front door, more running and a second slam. Rupa peered anxiously out of the window. She saw Eileen wrapped in a bath towel, chasing

Jamie down the street with a sweeping brush in her hand, Jamie wearing only his y-fronts. They disappeared round the corner and Rupa continued to watch out of the window but after a further half hour neither had returned and Rupa decided she might as well go to bed but at half past one the fight began again. Rupa heard the sound of hurled cutlery and crockery. She was terrified in case one of them killed the other but she didn't want to call the police. She was trembling, not knowing what to do when she heard the dog running up and down the stairs. Finally Elsie calmed down and settled beside Rupa's bed and there was silence again next door. Eventually Rupa managed to fall asleep.

The following morning Rupa found a folded note on the doormat.

'Rupa love, I am going to my mum in Bridlington for a couple of months but I may never return. I managed to take all my belongings in two suitcases. I wanted to tell you that it was Jamie and his mate Andy who stole your dog. They had been planning it for months, ever since you started working. The bastards got a duplicate key made. Sally, Andy's girlfriend kept the dog in her room. They were going to ask five hundred quid ransom from you and divide it between them. Now you've got your dog back and the bastard got what he deserved, well a bit of it anyway. Love, Eileen.'

A few days later there was a council skip parked outside and two men in yellow overalls were loading up the broken furniture and rubbish from next door. Eileen and Jamie had finally split and the house was vacant.

FORTY TWO

October the fourteenth was a special day for Rupa and her family. They were packing their belongings and moving house. The sounds of the preparations added another dimension to the already noisy and over excited children's calling and Elsie's barking. Rupa had to hand over the key by noon on the following day. Apart from their own belongings, some kitchen utensils and a few items of old furniture they had nothing to take. Rupa's and Eileen's houses were now empty, haunted by memories. Fifteen Hornbeam Avenue, Roundhay was to be their new home, a three bedroom terrace house near Roundhay Park. There was a large back garden abandoned to weeds and brambles by the previous owner, an Alzheimer's victim who had moved to an old people's home. In the front garden a lone magnolia tree stood sentinel. Autumn had come in a whirl of vivid colours and the leaves on the trees were lush and dense. In the early afternoon of the following Sunday Rupa and the children were looking at the birds' nests in the overgrown ivy knotted along the fence. Shane was counting them and searching for eggs when the dog began to bark, a certain sign that someone was at the door. Elsie ran to the front and they all followed to find it was Aruna. The children and even Elsie were excited, although Rupa felt some disquiet but eventually she relaxed and wondered what had brought him.

'Dad, come and see the birds' nests,' Shane shouted.

'Would you like something to eat Aruna?'

'No, I had a meal at a service station.'

Aruna looked round while Rupa made some tea.

'The house has been neglected and needs a lot of repairs. The garden is a complete wilderness,' he said disparagingly.

'I don't mind that Aruna. Now we're in, the decorations and all the rest can wait. I can start on the garden in spring.'

Although there was some tension Rupa spoke to him in carefully measured tones, determined to keep the peace at all costs.

'The only problem is the schools aren't very handy, Aruna.'

'Yes, I thought it must be a long way. How do they get there?'

'Lisa can walk in twenty minutes but Shane'll have to go by bus. He's asking me to buy him a bike. Where I work isn't near either but now the children are a bit older it shouldn't be a problem.' Aruna didn't stay long but before he went he gave Rupa enough money to buy the bicycle. Rupa felt relieved when Aruna had gone. She realised that their marriage had ended irrevocably. A state of intense, sadness and uncertainty permeated her whole being for several days.

Since they moved their life style had greatly improved. Most of her neighbours were either out at work or retired. Although Rupa didn't come home till late afternoon it didn't matter. After school the children had fallen into a routine of reading and doing their homework until their mother returned. When Rupa looked back it was as if she had reached an oasis and she could see a camel wobbling uncertainly across the desert sand, a mirage on a desolate track perhaps. She remembered Maha Gedara and the rhythm of the seasons, harvesting time and the sun soaked rice fields. Bleakly she thought how Maha Gedara had declined over the years as her parents had aged.

Aruna's visit had brought painful memories back to Rupa. She spent another night trying desperately to sleep. At five in the morning her bedroom window was opaque; she opened it to see the clouds moving rapidly as if they were hurrying home. Dense fog shrouded the trees in Roundhay Park and the solitary magnolia in Rupa's garden had become a bare skeleton. The milkman's float suddenly screeched to a halt, shaking and jerking with its overload of jammed crates. The milkman snatched four red-topped bottles and dumped them on the doorstep of number fourteen, swung the four empties into the clattering crate, then chugged slowly and purposefully away, the mournful sound of the engine dying in the distance. Elsie was asleep stretched on the fireside rug. Rupa sat on the sofa with a cup of coffee and remembered last night's dream.

'She was pregnant again. Aruna was critically ill in an intensive care unit, his arms and legs paralysed. He was breathing stertorously while his body lay limp. Rupa watched helplessly as a line of blood moved along a transparent tube and into his body through a wrist vein. His heartbeat showed on the monitor, the irregular rise and fall noted by a watching nurse. When Rupa touched his ice cold feet a drop of blood fell on the white sheet. Suddenly an aeroplane crashed into a ball of fire and the dream ended as the whole scene was engulfed in a dense pall of smoke.'

Rupa was overwhelmed by a sense of terror but soon she regained her bearings, realising it had, after all, only been a dream. She felt helplessly lonely as she listened to the rumble of a passing train. She tried to recall how she sat by the Thames with Aruna only a few days after she first arrived in England. Blossoms were falling onto the feathery ferns along the bank and drifting into the water. Now her children were settled in England but what did it really matter whether they grow up under an Eastern or Western sky?

* * * *

When Rupa came back to the office after lunch there was a note on her desk. 'Rupa, phone Christopher Hunter.'

She thought it was unusual for Hunter to phone her at work. She phoned the University English Department and the girl said he hadn't been in so she tried his home.

'I'm phoning from the office, I got your message, are you all right?'

'I stayed at home today, Rupa. My mother died suddenly in the early hours of this morning, at the nursing home.'

'I'm very sorry to hear that, Chris. I remember you telling me that she hasn't been well for some time.'

'But I never expected her to die so soon, Rupa' his voice was shaking.

'Is there anything I can do to help you?'

'I just need some time to come to terms with mother's death.'

'When is her funeral?'

'Next Monday at half past two. I'd like you to come.'

'Of course I'll come. You'll have to tell me how to get there. Chris, I'd like to go to the chapel of rest if it's all right with you. In our country the body is kept at home until the funeral so all the friends and relatives can gather to pay their last respects.'

'That's fine, Rupa. Can you meet me in Burley's undertakers in Cookridge at half past eleven on Monday morning? I'll give you the exact details later.'

Rupa finished work early and decided to pay a quick visit to Hunter on her way home. She took the Alwoodley bus from City Square and got off at the health centre. Then she walked down Benhill Grove an oak lined avenue until she came to a group of six houses and a small block of new flats. There was a straggling wood across the road, struggling to survive against the encroaching tide of speculative buildings. As she entered the block she could smell new wood and fresh paint. Number three with the polished door was on the ground floor. She rang the bell and a stranger answered.

'Is Chris in?'

'Yes, do come in, you must be Rupa. I'm Steve, a friend of Chris.'

Rupa had never seen Hunter in such a state before. He lay on the sofa, his eyes red, cigarette packets scattered on the floor and a tumbler full of whisky on the glass topped coffee table.

'Are you all right Chris?'

At first he said nothing so Rupa thought it's best to leave him alone so she spoke to his friend while she sipped a glass of orange juice. By now it was six. Rupa looked at her watch.

'I'd better be on my way home. The children are on their own. They're not young anymore but they still expect me to make an evening meal for them. I'll see you later Chris.'

'Thanks for coming Rupa,' he managed to get out.

Hunter had seemed quite together when she spoke to him earlier but now he was stricken. He must be in shock, Rupa reflected. His mother was very old, so why had he not been more prepared for what must inevitably happen? As she mused about the strange depths of his grief she wondered if he had any brothers or sisters, she could not recollect his ever having mentioned any.

Over the weekend Rupa kept to her normal routine, doing the weekly wash and the weekly shop, ironing, pottering about in the garden, making sure the children did their homework, talking over the happenings of the last four days, especially with Lisa who she told about Hunter's mother's death.

'He'll be very lonely, mum,' Lisa said with a newly discovered maturity. 'Why don't you marry him?' Rupa felt herself blush.

'He hasn't asked me but if he did what would you feel about it?'

'It's your life, mum. I'll be off to university next year and Shane won't stay a child forever. The less said about dad the better. You should follow your feelings,' Lisa smiled enigmatically as she slipped on her new blue denim jacket and opened the back door.

'I've got to pop to the library to collect a few books on comparative religion I ordered. I'm going to try to speed read them over the weekend and use the stuff in an essay I've got to hand in midweek. Miss Parnaby thinks I might get a place at Durham, her old university, to do comparative religion and theology. All our relatives in Ceylon are so boringly practical, they're all going to be lawyers, doctors or businessmen. It's all so predictable, get your qualifications, find a marriage partner of the same caste and with the right horoscope!'

Rupa smiled at her daughter. 'Well you are the one person whose future I don't have to worry about! I'll make a salad while you're out and leave it in the fridge for you so you can help yourself when you feel hungry.'

When the door closed behind Lisa, Rupa sat down at the kitchen table. She was astonished by Lisa's comments but at the same time a great weight was lifted from her mind.

On Monday morning Rupa put on her best clothes, borrowing Lisa's smart black shoulder bag to set them off. She didn't know who, if any, of Hunter's relatives might be at the funeral and what ideas they might have formed about her if, that is, they even knew of her existence. She had no idea how to get to the chapel of rest so she booked a mini cab, which dropped her off just after eleven. She saw Hunter stood outside the chapel looking haggard, a cigarette drooping from his lips. A few minutes later the funeral director arrived with the keys to the chapel. A small outbuilding of grey weathered stone. He spun the key ring on his finger in a business–like way, humming a tune and with a broad smile on his red face. He didn't seem the kind of man who could look miserable, however hard he tried.

When the solid oak door opened Rupa was feeling slightly anxious. She entered the chapel with Hunter by her side. The coffin was under the window resting on two black metal struts. The lid stood upright against the white wall with 'Rosemary Hunter Aged 76' scrolled in copperplate on a brass plaque. The room was redolent with the odour of death, a numbing cold that seemed to emanate from the grave itself and centre on the still body. Rupa reached out and touched the hand, the flesh of the middle finger eerily white where the gold band of her wedding ring had been removed. She was wearing a pink silk dress with a velvet trim draped round the head and shoulders. A vase in the corner held a bunch of deep red tulips, the petals like wax. Hunter stood motionless in front of the coffin, muttering a prayer, only an odd word of which Rupa managed to catch. Finally he stooped to kiss the pale shrunken face and motioned Rupa to follow him outside. When the undertaker had driven off Hunter wiped his forehead and almost smiled.

'That was terrible. I'm so glad you came, no one in my family's bothering, they don't, you know these days 'dead is dead' it's as curt as that. Would you like to come for a coffee at Betty's, it's just round the corner.'

The bijou café managed to survive on a regular clientele of shoppers and pensioners; about a dozen were grouped round small glass topped tables, munching scones and ginger cake with their cups of tea. Rupa and Hunter found an unoccupied corner table and a waitress brought a tray with a small metal coffee pot and the customary 'plate of cakes'. Rupa poured the coffee while Hunter lit a cigarette.

'I didn't know you smoked.'

'I don't usually, only when I'm under stress, I never get addicted fortunately.'

'How do you feel?'

'Very guilty. I've only been able to visit my mother regularly since I moved back up north. Before that I phoned her and sent a weekly letter but I could only see her in the holidays. It was a good job I happened to be in Leeds at the end. The matron of the home phoned about six on the night my mother died. She said she'd sent for the doctor and things didn't look good, she'd know these things, it's her job. I went and just sat by the bed holding her hand. She recognised me I think, but that was about it. There was a nurse who kept popping in and she was there at the end, she was trying to give my mother a drink when she called me over.

'I think your mother's gone, Chris,' she said and she had. Without a single word, she died so quickly. The nurse opened the window, she said it was 'to let the soul out', it was an unforgettable experience. I felt as though I was at the doorway to the next world. The next thing I knew was that I was crying my eyes out. I kept crying for a while, then I began to feel a bit better. I stayed around until they took her body away, then I phoned your office. When I first saw her the day she died she smiled at me. I wondered if it was the same smile she had on her face the day I was born. Somehow I know it was. Her hands smelt of lavender water, it was something she always used.'

They arrived at the crematorium at two. The coffin was in the chapel in front of a yellow screen, with a bunch of fifty red roses from Hunter laid on the top. A priest gave a very brief address, then abruptly the curtains were drawn and the coffin slid out of sight. There were only a handful of mourners, none of whom Rupa knew. They sat in silence while a recording of Beethoven's 'Cavatine' was played over the loudspeakers. For a few seconds there was a hushed expectation, then the mourners stood and filed out, nodding politely at the priest who smiled and occasionally shook a relative's hand. The next cortege was waiting and the mourners weren't encouraged to linger. Hunter spoke briefly to a few of the mourners but no one seemed close to him.

After a few minutes only Rupa remained with Hunter.

'This wouldn't have been my way but she left instructions in her will so I had no say.'

As they walked down the narrow lane to the wide open gates, they noticed Brenda Williams, a poet and close friend of Hunter's, who had come to the funeral and was standing by a lichen covered tomb staring at the empty sky. When they approached her she seemed suddenly to waken, as if from trance.

'I've written a couplet,' she said in a subdued tone.

Your blue wasted gaze was left to my sight.
Immeasurable in the heart of light.

She turned to Rupa.

'It's only in the East that people know how to respect the dead and dying.'

FORTY THREE

Lisa rushed in with her friend Allison, waving a sheet of paper and shouting.

'Mum! Mum! I've got it! I've got it! A place at Durham to study Theology and comparative religion.'

'I'm so pleased Lisa, what grades did you get?'

'Three A's and a B,' Lisa smiled, her eyes gleamed and ran upstairs.

'Shane, Shane, I made it!'

She ran downstairs again with Elsie following, barking and pulling at her skirt.

'Mum, we're going to the pub tonight, to celebrate. Don't worry, we won't be late.'

'Lisa, I don't like you walking home on your own at night.'

'Allison's dad'll give us a lift home. Allison's got four A's.'

'Well done Allison. Congratulations! Will you be going to the same university?'

'I've got a place in Cambridge for English.'

'Brilliant! When does your course start Lisa?'

'It'll be early October, but I'm going to find a summer job and earn some money.'

'So you're going to be away from home! Shane and I will have to get on with our lives.'

'Shane's all right mum. He'll be busy studying for his O' levels.'

'But I'll feel very strange without you at home Lisa.'

'I'm only going to university, not the moon! You'll have plenty to do mum. You can always brighten up the garden. Why don't you go out with Chris? Dad isn't going to come back.'

'How do you know?'

'I just know, don't be so naïve mother.'

Lisa and her friend Allison changed into their new denims. Suitably arrayed in make-up, jewellery and 'wet look' yellow shoes they went out giggling and whispering to each other, leaving spirals of perfume around the stairs and the hallway. Rupa sat in the lounge and thought over what Lisa had said. But did she really want to remarry? What would she say if Hunter proposed? What about getting Aruna to agree to a divorce? Hunter wouldn't hang around. He might even look for another woman. But would it matter? All these questions were hypothetical – Hunter might never say a word. But Lisa was right, as Aruna hadn't come back in twelve years he was hardly likely ever to. Even if he had wanted to start again Rupa would not want it – her mistrust of him was total.

Rupa had been trying to get in touch with her old friend Chandra for a long time but without success. After Rupa moved to Leeds she never got round to writing. Chandra's last phone number was in Edinburgh but when she dialled it there was a man whose voice resounded with a strong Scottish burr. He muttered, 'Sorry lass, you've got a wrong number'. She even wrote to Chandra's parents in Ceylon but no reply ever came. Finally in desperation, she wrote to Chandra's husband, Jayanta, c/o Edinburgh University Physics Department hoping he might still be there.

The telephone rang. It was Jill, Rupa's friend who lived in Abbey Road in St Johns Wood, near the famous 'Beatles Zebra Crossing.'

'Rupa, I've a spare ticket for the Chelsea Flower Show. Would you like to go with me?'

'I'd love to, Jill. I've never been there before. When is it?'

'Next Tuesday. I'm a member of the RHS and that's the first day when the show's open to the public.'

'The only thing is that I'll have to take a day off from work. I can't see any problem but I'll let you know definitely tomorrow night. What time do I have to be in London?'

'It doesn't really matter. I've got all day tickets. Try to get here early as possible, say between half ten and eleven.'

'That should be fine, the Leeds – Kings Cross intercity only takes two and a half hours.'

When Rupa told Shane that she was intending to go to London on Tuesday he said 'I don't mind mum, you don't have to rush back home. I'll feed the dog and take her for a walk. Don't bother to leave any food for me. I can get some take away on my way home from the library.'

On Tuesday morning Rupa was up early and on her way before seven wearing a navy blue jacket and a bag over her shoulder. The pavement and the grass were damp in the light drizzle. Although it was late May the wind was still cold. As she walked past the shops she heard the clock in the tower strike seven. A red bakery lorry was parked outside the supermarket, bearing the logo 'Londis' on the side.

A man was carrying crates brimming with newly baked crusty bread and confectionery. The smell was so tempting that Rupa felt hungry, although she didn't usually eat breakfast. She picked up a bus to town and it was twenty to eight when she finally arrived at Leeds City Station. The London Kings Cross train was scheduled for five to eight so Rupa sat on a bench on platform three watching the coming and going of the trains. A smartly dressed business woman with a black leather bag stood in front of the information board, constantly consulting her watch. A group of school children were waiting on the same platform, gangling adolescents wearing bright coloured anoraks and ski pants, shouting jokes and hurling insults at each other and generally making a nuisance of themselves. From their talk Rupa gathered they were going on a day trip to London 'to see the sights'. There was an announcement over the tannoy and finally the London train arrived and jerked to a halt. Rupa found a window seat well away from the children. Growing green fields, scattered farms and startling vivid yellow acres of rape seed appeared and disappeared as the train spun over the singing tracks. It was a clear bright day and Rupa watched the shadows of the moving trees reflected in the carriage windows. The greenery faded as the train began to pass through London's crowded outer suburbs with their concrete blocks of council flats and unending offices.

From Kings Cross to Victoria she took the tube to where she

was to meet her friend. Rupa could smell the dank sooty air of the tunnels as trains whooshed in and out of the station, starting back when a squeal of brakes triggered a brief yellow flash of current. When Rupa finally arrived at the meeting place she was late, hurried and out of breath.

The crowd at Chelsea Flower Show was like a swollen sea in a storm. For a minute Rupa and her friend Jill felt completely lost, then they found 'directions', which only added to their state of bewilderment. First they visited the show gardens: the poet's garden with its vivid back cloth of willow weeping into an overgrown pond and a tree house with a rickety ladder. Decadent Mediterranean and aristocratic Victorian gardens with lavender borders and vineyards. A worthy garden for the disabled with raised flower beds, a pollen free gravel garden for hayfever sufferers, chintzy cottage gardens where flowers and vegetables circled a hen house. Suddenly Rupa's eyes lit on the 'Garden of Harmony' constructed by Leeds City Council, where azure Himalayan poppies and the pastel hues of flowering trees, shrubs and ferns grew beside a stream running over ragged rocks. A wild life corner for butterflies, hedgehogs and a brown fox complete with pampas grass tail. Winning exhibitors displayed their bronze, silver and gold medals.

When Rupa and Jill entered the three acre marquee, where a sea of vibrant colours leapt into the light, they transversed displays of rare orchids, caressing roses, beautiful button-hole carnations and tropical exotica. Rupa felt dazzled and dizzy at the plethora of blooms and she was relieved when at last they emerged.

'Is there anywhere we can get a drink?' Rupa demanded, pushing a stray wisp of hair from her damp forehead.

'Look there's the refreshment tent'. Jill answered, pointing to a distant marquee. They had some unbelievably expensive sandwiches and a plastic cup of plastic coffee. Rupa sighed as she finished her drink.

'Don't expect things at Leeds market prices!' Jill laughed.

'I think I've seen enough, Jill. It's very beautiful but it has been a very long day and I've to get back to Leeds tonight.'

'It's only three. Why don't you come back to my flat for a cup of tea? It's only a short bus ride from Victoria.'

'That's fine, as long as I can get to Kings Cross by eight.'

They caught a bus to the Finchley Road and walked down Marlborough Hill to Abbey Road. Although St Johns Wood was in Central London the air was heavy with the scent of summer as a riot of catkins drooped their yellow lambs' tails over the green expanses before vast white houses with iron grills at every window.

'Old Tower Court was built to house Jewish refugees from Hitler in the 1930's,' Jill explained as she pushed open the tall heavy front door with its well polished brass ornaments. 'Some of them still live here, very old and very fragile,' she led the way into the flat, at first dark and mysterious but with the lights on a sanctuary of harmony, brimming with books and four exquisite cats purring their welcome. When Jill had made some tea they sat and chatted and Rupa outlined the strange turns her life had taken and suddenly the mantelpiece clock chimed seven and Rupa realised she must get a move on to catch her train.

They hurried to St John's Wood station and down the hundred or so steps and half an hour later emerged into the havoc of Kings Cross. The Leeds intercity was already on the platform and Rupa gave a sigh of relief as she settled into her seat and waved goodbye to Jill as the guard blew his whistle. The train surged into the night and rushed into the beckoning arms of the north.

As Rupa was rushing to catch the train a man pushed a blue and yellow flyer into her hand. She had stuffed it into her bag and entirely forgot it until she was rummaging for her ticket. Rupa was fascinated to discover that it appeared to be a strange birthday party invitation.

Texas Tickle Worldwide Productions Inc.
invites you to a birthday party at
68 Mulgrave Close, London NW8
To gain entrance please phone 071 526 000.
Copyright owned by George Tickle. Dustbin outside
feel free to kick it!
Countless numbers of guests are expected, but you

are very special.

Don't worry.

Party will run continuously for forty eight hours.

From 8 p.m. on the 31st May to 8 a.m. on the second of June.

Food and soft drinks will be provided. Special deliveries by Buckingham Palace.

TO CELEBRATE

45 years of being a complete idiot.

22 years of being the best lawyer in London.

36 years of being the best drummer.

3 years of being the longest sectioned patient in Islington Hospital Psychiatric Unit.

Please don't bring any gifts, flowers or alcohol.

BE HAPPY AND SMILE.

S.M.Dunhill B.A. Hons. Barrister-at-Law B.Mus.

Rupa wondered if he was a truly free spirit.

She arrived home just as it started to rain. The moon shone wearily and wanly through the laden chestnut trees and the wet glossy leaves of the magnolia shone in the night. Rupa opened the door but evidently Elsie didn't hear. By now she was partially deaf and blind in one eye. She lay fast asleep on the rug. When Rupa opened the door Elsie turned up her ears, slowly stretched her legs, yawned, hunched and with great difficulty got up. She was nearly seventeen and could no longer wag her tail, but she had a welcoming smile on her face.

FORTY FOUR

Although it was early April the night was still cold. Trees heavily laden with magenta and white blossoms drooped behind the thickening fog. The sky was cloudy with no sign of the sun. It had rained heavily the previous night with rumbles of distant thunder and now the pavements were gleaming wet. It was a Sunday and Aruna felt haggard and hungry. He walked towards the Domestic Café like a wound up toy. He hadn't been there for a long time. He walked past an area of wasteland between two blocks of back to backs. Although it was no longer used for dustbins, everybody still called it 'the binyard'. Children played hopscotch in the enclosed yards during the summer. Overgrown nettles and bracken had taken up the corners and turbid puddles had formed in the middle where the cement had cracked. The weathered green brick wall was covered in lichen and slimy snails and slugs. At the edge of the puddle there was a face down rag doll.

Aruna was shaken to see the front window of Domestic Café boarded up. From a distance he gazed at the graffiti on the outside wall. As he got nearer he noted the scribbled letters in white chalk against the blue paint of the front door 'Anna, Anna, Anna'. The café was empty and the letterbox covered with chipboard. The bottom half of the door was brown with accumulated dust but the paint was still visible where a dog had urinated and the step smelt sour. The history of the Domestic Café was now in the public domain. Aruna peered through the keyhole. All the tables and chairs had been removed. At the corner where Aruna used to sit for his lunch was a rolled over paint tin, a thin stream of white paint dribbled onto the tiles. Anna had gone so strangely and finally. Wendy, the hairdresser next door, was spring cleaning, vigorously mopping, dusting and sending everything flying as Aruna walked despondently into her shop.

'We're closed on Sundays!'

'I'm sorry to disturb you. Do you know where Anna's gone?'

'A 'aven't a clue, she must 'ave done a moonlight on Sunday 'cos when I came in the Monday morning café were all boarded up.'

The Domestic Café was up for sale. 'Humphrey and Clark'- the estate agent's sale board already weathering in the wind and rain.

As he turned away his desperation mounted. He hardly noticed it was raining as he walked past the gates of Beckwood Primary School and then he turned back onto Domestic Street, still searching for Anna. When finally he returned to his flat he felt suddenly alone. It was a long time since he had seen Rupa and the children. When he looked into the mirror he saw the inevitable beginnings of age, greying hair and obesity. He tired so easily these days. The children were grown up and Lisa was away at university. There was no way in which he could buy back his past or change his future. The Domestic Café, the Wellington Hotel and Anna's unforgettable smile, her long hair tied with a yellow ribbon: such ecstatic images filled Aruna's mind until, one by one, they disappeared and all he was left with was the oncoming darkness.

Aruna hadn't had anything to eat and began to feel hungry so he went to the kitchen and opened the fridge, empty but for the remains of a cut loaf and a small piece of cheese. He made cheese on toast and took it with two glasses of neat gin and went to bed. After a couple of hours unsuccessfully trying to sleep he got up and determinedly made his way to Mary's.

Her house was in the dark and he wondered if she was out. He opened the door with his key.

'Mary, Mary, are you there?'

'Who is it?'

'It's me Mary,' he went upstairs and found her in bed, her face covered with a sheet.

'Are you all right?'

'No.'

'What's the matter?' Mary was silent.

'What's the matter, Mary?'

'You know Aruna, I've told you before. I'm three months pregnant now!'

'Have you been to see a doctor?'

'No, a woman doesn't have to go to a doctor to find out that she's pregnant. I'm hungry Aruna.'

'Don't you cook anymore?'

'How dare you expect me to cook? I'm going to be a mother. It's more important to me to look after myself and the baby.'

'Would you like some tea?'

'No, it always makes me feel sick. Didn't you bring any Chinese take away?'

'The Money Tree' is shut on Sundays. Look Mary, there's something seriously wrong with you. You aren't pregnant. It's all a fantasy.'

'Are you telling me now that nothing has ever happened between you and me, that we never made love ever?'

'I'm not telling you anything. Stop talking rubbish, you're off your head. Why don't you get up and do something. I'm going downstairs to watch the cricket.'

'When a woman is bearing a man's child any man but you would be concerned. You know full well that I can't work anymore. If you're like this now what's going to happen when the baby's born? Just leave me to get on with it! You better start paying up now.'

'Paying for what?'

'Maintenance!'

When Aruna went to the kitchen he realised that Mary was lying to him. She had eaten an evening meal of Irish stew and chips and the washing up was still piled up in the sink. Glumly he sat in front of the television and switched on the Test coverage. Mary rushed downstairs, screaming and stumbling in her rage.

'Liar! Liar! You're destroying me and cheating me.'

'I'm not cheating anybody.'

'Have you forgotten you promised to move into a large house with me? A house and land which originally belonged to the Churchill family and you never even bothered going to look at it!

You promised to pay me double money if I'd be your housekeeper, you dyed-in-the wool liar.'

'I don't have any money to give you. I furnished this house for you. I gave you a job and put your life together Mary. What more do you want?'

'I don't care if you live or die you bastard!'

Mary paced up and down the lounge, her tangled hair falling across her face, her eyes incandescent with rage piercing his very soul. She stood with her hands on her waist and reached towards Aruna, grasping his collar and ripping it.

'Don't you hear what I'm saying?'

'I'll finish your problems for ever.'

Aruna snatched the clock off the mantelpiece and hurled it so it bounced off the television screen and fell against the hearth, the glass face smashing and the wooden casing cracked wide open. Aruna grabbed the 'Ceylon Daily News' cookery book from the table and tore it from cover to cover, the ripped pages strewn round the room like plucked chicken feathers. In frustrated rage Aruna repeatedly banged his head against the wall until he staggered away, blood pouring from his cut brow. Mary stood spitting at him and hurling obscenities. Then she picked up the phone and dialled three nines as Aruna kicked over a dining chair and stormed out.

Ten minutes later Aruna stopped his Peugeot in front of his workshop but he sat with the engine ticking over, unable to move. The workshop was dark and silent but in his mind the machines began to rev up, the wheels turning faster and faster, emitting a mindless hysterical banshee wail. Aruna stopped up his ears, his head resting on the steering wheel, even with his eyes tight shut there was a fiery crimson glare spreading everywhere. Finally Aruna started the car and drove around aimlessly.

By now it was late and heavy fog had descended. Around the Tyne it seemed darker than ever, the silence broken only by the hooter of a distant ship. Ridges of black water lapped against the bank and beckoned ominously. Aruna hadn't realised he was running out of fuel until the engine shook, jerked and juddered to a halt. The single streetlight flickered on and off, illuminating a boarded up warehouse. Aruna shook his head, climbed out and turned round briskly to open the boot, where he kept a jerry-can with a couple of gallons of petrol. Then he drove on to a filling station and afterwards blindly and aggressively, keeping one foot on the accelerator and one hand on the wheel, staring ahead, cruising on auto-pilot until he became suddenly aware of a police car's flashing blue fluorescence demanding he stop at once. He opened his door at the policeman's approach.

'Can I see your driving licence and insurance, sir?'

'Yes, I'll get them.' He searched the glove compartment.

'Where are you going sir?'

'I'm going home after a business trip.'

'Did you fill your tank at a Fina station?'

'Yes I did.'

'Did you pay your bill?'

'I suppose so.'

'You didn't and the matter's been reported as a theft. We shall have to arrest you.'

'I'm so sorry about it. My wife is very ill and my mind was concentrating on getting to Leeds to see her tonight. In my anxiety I must have completely forgotten to pay the bill. Can I give you the money now?'

'You don't have to pay it now, just take it to the nearest police station and report your payment within the next twenty four hours.'

Aruna had to sign the constable's entry book. He felt a great surge of relief when he was allowed to go.

Like a dying elephant staggering back to the jungle he arrived at his flat, exhausted, his eyes burning, his limbs twitching. In his sleep he dreamed of calling Rupa. When she couldn't hear him, he called again even more loudly. He followed her slight figure along a path with narrow bends, sometimes losing sight of her, then regaining it. Suddenly Rupa turned to a silhouette and disappeared in a freezing mist. The wind, the rain, the river, the sea and the birds fell silent together.

He woke shivering, the images of his long dead parents hovering before him. His father had been a village headman under the British raj. He had a long flowing white beard but his hair was thin and he always wore a tweed jacket and carried an ivory handled silver topped walking cane. Aruna remembered how his father had threatened to punish him for climbing mango trees and then his mother's dying words.

'I want you to live without bringing disgrace to our family, my son.'

FORTY FIVE

Rupa remembered the days she lived at Maha Gedara and her own student life when Shane was getting ready to go to Magdalen to study Classics in October.

'I can come home when I want to mum, Oxford isn't that far.'

'But it isn't the same for me Shane. We never know what will happen in four years time. I am so pleased. I'm sure you'll make some friends and you'll like it there.'

Jeans, shirts, underwear, socks, towels, bedding, books, shoes, toothpaste, toothbrush, soap, shampoo, pens, sellotape and an alarm clock. He packed the lot in a rough and ready way. Rupa felt as though her life as a mother was ending.

'But he'll soon be back for the holidays,' she consoled herself.

'Have you got everything? I'll send some more money if you need it.'

'I've got enough money mum. I'm going now. I'll give you a call when I get there.' Shane said good bye with mock cheerfulness but his eyes were red and his face drawn as he got into the car. Oxford was a long way off and full of the memories of famous people. As Rupa closed the door behind him a sense of emptiness swept over her. Elsie hobbled back to the lounge, lay on the rug and looked at Rupa expectantly. Lisa, now in her final year had returned to Durham.

It was a warm Saturday in autumn. Buddleia and honeysuckle were still in flower. As the night scented phlox and evening primroses wafted their subtle perfumes in the air Rupa remembered Kumara and their days together.

'If I send a proposal to Maha Gedara would your parents agree to their daughter marrying someone from a different caste?'

'You don't have to send a matchmaker to my house Kumara, you

can propose now!'

She laughed, he laughed and they both laughed together, but some sadness was in them. A cold wind suddenly blew and Rupa closed the kitchen door. Elsie was snoring and Rupa sat down with a mug of tea. She tried to remember her children's growing up over the years. How could she have guessed the strange role Aruna would cast for her as a wife only in name? She tried to remember the early days of their marriage – could it have turned out differently? She wondered at the changes in Aruna and what the future might hold.

The following weekend Lisa came home and Rupa realised how much she appreciated such brief occasional visits.

'I'm so pleased, Shane seems to have settled in Oxford. Now I'm left with my own life,' Rupa told Lisa spiritedly.

'I don't like you living on your own, mum. I'm finishing my course next June and I've been accepted for a postgrad course. We don't know what Shane's going to do when he finishes at Oxford but I don't think either of us will come back home for good mum.'

'I do feel lonely when I come back from work but I can always find something to do to pass the time and there's always Elsie to keep me company.'

'I think it's time for you to enjoy your life mum. You shouldn't worry about me or Shane.' Lisa added a log to the smouldering fire. Rupa listened to what she had said and began to wonder about her uncertain future.

Hunter had been busy writing a book on Ezra Pound's Cantos. He seemed to have recovered quickly from the shock of his mother's death. Rupa was expecting him for Sunday lunch. She cooked a traditional English meal of roast beef and yorkies. He arrived early with his finished manuscript when Rupa was taking the joint out of the oven.

'I didn't expect such a lavish meal Rupa, roast beef and Yorkshire pudding with blackberry and apple pie with custard for dessert! Lovely.'

'It's so strange and empty here without the children. I was up early this morning so I decided to cook something I knew you'd like. After the meal Rupa made a pot of coffee.

'I can do the washing up later.'

She piled everything up in the sink and they sat together.

'How do you feel Rupa?

'Very strange, with the children gone I still live like a hermit.'

'Why don't you start something new? Read some books or study English in your spare time.'

'I don't think I can make up my mind to study anything. The best part of my life's gone. It was wonderful to watch children grow like seedlings.'

'Open a new chapter in your life. Start from the beginning. You're not too old. You don't have to wait for the next rebirth. You can't run away from the past. You've got something you've never had before, freedom to work out your own future.'

'Chris, England's your home. I was born in an Eastern country and grew up in a village. Sometimes I feel completely lost and confused. I don't think I could ever settle down here on my own forever.'

'But you don't have to. What I meant by 'a new life' was you must get your confidence back Rupa and be positive. We make our own choices but society does influence us, more in the East than here. Your marriage to Aruna did a lot of damage, you always try to hide behind your own anxiety and you mistrust everyone. People aren't all the same, Aruna's an odd fish.'

'You're right but I can only trust my children and the dog.'

'Don't be too hard on yourself and don't think every man's another Aruna. I remember you were interested in Christianity. It doesn't matter what religion you accept – you can take a bit from one and a bit from another! Learn to trust people and don't dwell on the past.'

'I'm beginning to feel bored with my job. Mrs. Fermie, who was always so helpful and kind to me retired last Friday. I don't have to rush home to cook for the children anymore. Even Elsie's past going for walks. She's old and terrified of other dogs. She finds it difficult going up the stairs. She's happy at home wandering round the garden watching the birds.'

'I'm sorry if I seem hard going, Rupa. I want you to be happy.

Whatever the culture is you've got to adapt.' Suddenly Hunter held her hand and kissed her. 'I know life's not as easy as we expect,' he said then he kissed her again. Rupa cleared the kitchen and made some tea while Hunter worked on his manuscript. When she came back they sat down and relaxed together. Rupa felt more secure than she had in years. He put his arm around her and said 'Rupa will you marry me?'

She burst into tears, whether of anxiety or relief she didn't know. She felt numb and could think of nothing to say.

'I do understand, Rupa.'

'I'm so frightened of losing you, Chris, if anything ever went wrong. I'm not sure if I can ever be married again.'

* * * *

A year passed and Rupa was no further forward. Lisa, who had finished her degree, was doing her doctorate at Durham. The children had come home for Christmas. Rupa sat and watched them decorate the six foot tree. Suddenly she realised they were children no longer. They were young adults with their own lives and for all she knew their own lovers. She remembered the day how the umbilical cord was cut and they were separated from her. But it was all a long time ago. The clock on the wall in the labour room had said four fifteen. The air had been thick, her nostrils were burning and an oxygen mask was clamped over her face. The woman doctor in a white coat said, 'Don't worry, it's going to be only two stitches.' It all seemed so long ago. Rupa knew how quickly Christmas would pass and then she would be on her own.

It was a cold January morning when Elsie suddenly fell ill, refusing any food or drink. She had been to the vet's on and off for the last eight months. Rupa made her a comfortable place to sleep with a soft quilt by the fire. Now she had to ask the vet to call because Elsie was too ill to be taken.

'I'm sorry there's nothing I can do. We did everything possible for Elsie. Seventeen's a grand old age for a Border collie,' the vet concluded. By the afternoon her condition worsened. She had lost the battle and gave up; she closed her eyes finally in Rupa's arms. Elsie's lifeless body lay, her eyes half opened. Her face with its distinguishing white moon mark and her faithful closeness would be in Rupa's mind always. Elsie's body was buried in Rupa's back garden. She disappeared forever in the hazy sunshine and grey clouds of mid-afternoon. That night seemed especially dark and an unexpected change in the weather covered her grave in a soft silky cloth of snow. Rupa planted a pink star magnolia tree 'In memory of Elsie, the beloved family dog.'

Rupa was now entirely on her own and she thought about Hunter's proposal. 'Marriage' in Rupa's mind had become a word associated with pain and betrayal. She didn't want the additional scar of a divorce to add to her woes. Rupa tried to bring to mind Kumara's appearance but the space of two decades had blurred the image. She remembered the last time they were together was in the temple near the university when they both were young students. They had stood by the wall and watched the rising river down the valley. The rain had stopped, the trees were glossy and the bamboo on the banks were drooping. The black trunk of a fallen tree floated away turned zigzags across the river and disappeared under the turbid foam. She looked for Elsie and realised that she was no longer there curled up on the rug. The house was eerily empty.

The telephone rang and Rupa rushed to pick it up, expecting Hunter but it was her old friend Chandra.

'Chandra, I just can't believe it's you! It's been so long since I last spoke to you. I didn't even recognise your voice. Where have you been all these years?'

'How are you Rupa? I just got the letter you sent to Jayantha c/o the university months and months ago. One of his friends kept all our mail while we were away. I sent you various letters but I don't think you got them. We've been living in Australia for the last few years and only just got back. I wondered if you and Aruna had gone back to Ceylon. I phoned you during the day but there was no answer.'

'I'm out at work during the day. I live on my own now.'

'On your own! Where's Aruna?'

'The story of the last fifteen years isn't easy to tell in a few minutes. He left me and the children years ago.'

'I'm sorry to hear that Rupa. I just can't believe it happening to you and Aruna.'

'I know it sounds like some evil spirit had possessed us. Whatever we wish in our lives I suppose in the end its destiny gets its way.'

'How are the children?'

'Lisa and Shane are both at university and doing well.'

'Where's Aruna now?'

'In Newcastle. He's got a motor business called Harjan Motors.'

'I'm in shock about the whole affair, it's just not something I expected. I can't believe how much Aruna's altered. He's someone we thought we knew very well. I'm baffled by his change in personality! Newcastle isn't far from Edinburgh. I'll go and see him if you want.'

'Don't worry about me Chandra. I live like a weathered oak. My worst problems are over and I'm happy now.'

'I'm so glad Rupa.'

'How's your life, Chandra?'

'Not much different, except we're getting old. Jayanta's gone grey. Melbourne is a marvellous place. Houses are cheap and very spacious. We had a large garden with a lovely bottlebrush tree. We even had a swimming pool. The climate is fantastic with hot summers. But Jayanta wanted to come back. He likes Edinburgh University.'

'Are you still working Chandra?'

'Yes, at the university library.'

'I'm so pleased to hear from you, come and see me sometime. I don't have any Ceylonese friends. When a marriage breaks down most old friends fly away like birds.'

Rupa was delighted to have found her old friend again.

FORTY SIX

The double leaf front door at Maha Gedara was half-open. Chinky the dog lay on a gunny rug at a corner of the cement surround that protected him from drizzle. There was the smell of stale jackfruit, yellow segments with large nuts in the middle opened by crows and night birds. A large egret with its shiny yellow feathers and sharp black beak flew down from a treetop. The annona tree near the abandoned vegetable plot was still a bats' habitat where rotten fruit, rind and nuts were piled up under the tree, surrounded by a swarm of flies. At sunrise the screaming of the peacocks shook the rubber trees. There was a huge pile of tree stumps by the barbed wire fence: the stumps were soaked with rain and clusters of rust brown edible mushrooms rapidly sprouted from them. A peasant woman sat gathering them on a banana leaf. The rubber tapping had been abandoned for a few days owing to the heavy morning rain. Dasa was husking coconuts in the garden.

'I don't feel any better with Dr. Ratnam's medicines. I feel tired and dizzy. I keep shivering and my cough won't budge and I keep feeling sick.' Loku Mahatmaya tried to stretch himself in bed but he was still uncomfortable, however he shifted. Finally he covered himself with a green bedsheet.

'Whatever the cause is I've boiled some herbs with ginger, honey and puffed rice – that should sort it out.'

Dikwelle Hamine put a cup of herbal medicine with a slice of jaggery on a saucer and put it on the bedside cabinet.

Day by day Loku Mahatmaya grew weaker and every night fever scourged him, even getting out of bed became too much for him. Whenever Loku Mahatmaya fell ill, Dikwelle Hamine secretly believed that he suffered from some highly infectious disease.

Rukmali was getting ready to go to work. When she opened the door to leave she found Dasa sitting on the wall, wearing a turban.

'You're nice and early today Dasa!'

'I brought a message from your home.'

'Is there a problem?'

'Nothing to worry about. Dikwelle Hamine asked me to let you know that Loku Mahatmaya isn't well.'

'What's the matter?'

'Aches and pains, you know he always gets that kind of thing.'

'That's right Dasa, my father hates going to a doctor, all he believes in is herbal medicines.'

'He's had every variety there is: 'Peyava' 'Arishta' and everything going but he's still no better.'

'Don't go yet Dasa, have some tea, I'll try to drop round this morning.'

Rukmali gave him tea and bananas, which Dasa ate with relish, then rode speedily away on his bike. He slowed down at the hill and pedalled with all his might, his sweat-drenched shirt blowing up like a balloon.

As Rukmali entered Maha Gedara the pungent odour of herbal oil greeted her. Loku Mahatmaya lay on the bed, pale and frail. Rukmali put the back of her palm on his forehead and knew at once he had a temperature.

'Let's go to our place for a few days father. It's so easy to go to a doctor from where we live, its easier than here anyway.'

'I don't think it's necessary, child. When I last had a similar illness, I didn't go to a doctor. All I did was take some 'Arishta' and it went away with no problem. What about the dogs? I don't think anyonc else could look after them. They must be properly fed and they will miss me.'

'Don't worry about the dogs. There will always be someone here to feed them.'

Dikwelle Hamine agreed.

'That's right, you really had better see a doctor. Have you forgotten what happened to me! I almost died a few years ago, waiting like this. Did you hear me? I'll be ready soon. It doesn't do any harm staying with Rukmali until you feel better. Dasa'll keep an eye on everything.'

With difficulty Loku Mahatmaya sat up. He muttered in a low voice, 'Remember to take a few bunches of bananas and some king coconuts for the children.'

Reluctantly he agreed to go. Rukmali took some time off and decided she'd better take him to the doctor's. The doctor prescribed a course of antibiotics and vitamins but after three days the patient's condition worsened.

'Let's wait and see how he feels by tomorrow morning. Unfortunately today and tomorrow are public holidays. Tonight there isn't a single doctor covering Jayaratna ward. I don't think we can do much even if we admit him now,' Rukmali sighed. By midnight everyone in the house was confused by all the dithering. Dikwelle Hamine was talking anxiously non-stop. A list of items was hastily prepared: a bottle of honey, a jar of Marmite, herbal oil, a towel, a bowl and a sponge to give the patient a bed bath, a sick bowl, Horlicks, orange juice and cream crackers. Everyone was rushing to help and the neighbours had started to gather outside. 'Isn't there a doctor?' 'No, the doctor's away,' 'It's a public holiday,' 'What about the hospital in Colombo?' 'I know a friend of Dr. Simon,' everyone discussed the possibilities over a cup of tea.

'God help me, I don't know what's going to happen,' Dikwelle Hamine cried aloud.

'Be quiet mother, don't disturb the patient, he needs some sleep,' said Rukmali.

The following morning Loku Mahatmaya was finally admitted to Jayaratna ward.

'I feel a bit better now,' he said as he was helped into the car. Two hours later Loku Mahatmaya lay on a bed in room two, covered with a white sheet.

'We've taken an ECG but only Dr. Kodige can read it,' a nurse said.

'What time is the doctor coming?' Rukmali was worried.

'He's supposed to be here at nine. He'll do a ward round before he goes to the surgery,' a nurse replied.

By now the surgery was crowded with waiting patients. An

old man was coughing incessantly. A pregnant woman sat holding her stomach, her mother next to her clutching a cane bag full of clothes. A baby cried while its mother sang a soft lullaby. The queue stretched as far as the outside gates. A high level of tension mixed with the smell of Dettol, the air was thick and almost impossible to breathe. It was eleven and there was still no sign of the doctor. Loku Mahatmaya was groaning with pain and breathing with great difficulty. The nurse gave him an oxygen mask and said, 'We're not supposed to give a saline drip until the doctor comes.'

'When is he coming?'

'Dr. Kodige couldn't come to the morning surgery. We expect him about three this afternoon.'

By now some of the patients had left but others were still waiting. A mother undid the safety pins fastening her blouse and breast-fed her baby. Some patients were drinking 'Elephant brand' portello, eating biscuits, sweets, peanuts and packets of boiled chickpeas brought from street vendors. Some had brought flasks of tea and coffee. Loku Mahatmaya had developed a chest pain. His arms and legs were cold. Rukmali and her son Damit stood, confused and desperate.

'Is there any way we can take my grand father to the General Hospital by private ambulance?' asked Damit.

'We're not allowed to move a patient until he's been seen by a doctor,' the nurse said as she checked his pulse and marked it up on the record sheet. From time to time a nurse came to room two and checked Loku Mahatmaya's blood pressure.

'I'm not well child.' Loku Mahatmaya groaned. At half past five Dr. Kodige arrived, arrogantly waving his stethoscope, accompanied by a nurse. Rukmali's face brightened up at once.

'Please help my father doctor, he's very ill.'

'How do you know? Only a doctor knows a patients condition.'

Rukmali walked out of the room with tears in her eyes.

'I'm not a doctor but I know my father's very ill, he hasn't been treated since we brought him here this morning.'

Without speaking Dr. Kodige gave him an injection.

'The ECG seems to be okay. The patient is looking a bit pale. We may need to give him blood.'

Dr Kodige was short and fat. He wore blue trousers and a white shirt. He was a man who couldn't respond to a smile.

When Rukmali returned to his room Loku Mahatmaya lay staring at the ceiling. Suddenly his whole body was shaking, he jerked on to his side and screamed, clenching his fists. Rukmali shouted for a nurse.

'Heart attack!' Snapped the nurse, tight lipped. Rukmali ran to Dr. Kodige, who was in the surgery.

'Please see my father, doctor, I think he's having a heart attack.'

Dr Kodige was furious. The woman patient sat in front of him interrupted.

'I'm all right doctor. Please go if it's an emergency.'

Tut tutting all the way Dr Kodige strode to room two. He gave Loku Mahatmaya another injection and told a nurse to put him on a saline drip. Then imperiously he commanded, 'I would like to speak to this patient's next of kin alone.' Damit and Rukmali had entered the room together.

'Don't you understand Sinhalese? I don't want two people. Can one of you get out.'

He beckoned Damit with his forefinger. Rukmali was frightened and went out, sobbing.

'The patient is very ill. I still can't make out what exactly is wrong with him. We'll just have to wait and monitor his responses'.

Dr. Kodige gave an inscrutable smile. By now friends and relatives were gathering outside Jayaratna ward: among them were two doctors who managed to get to Dr. Kodige. At half past seven Loku Mahatmaya was admitted to ICU.

By dawn his changed respiration was noted ominously as 'Chain Stokes' breathing.

'Isn't there a doctor on duty?' Damit demanded.

'Loku Mahatmaya was admitted as one of Dr. Kodige's patients. We can't give him blood without the doctor's permission.'

'Isn't he coming in today?'

'He's taken some leave to watch the Ceylon – Australia cricket match on TV.'

An hour later a nurse came out.

'We phoned Dr. Kodige at home. He's prescribed some medicines over the phone and ordered a blood transfusion.'

A line of blood trickled into the dry withered body of Loku Mahatmaya but it was too late. His battle had ended. He died that afternoon.

Everybody in the village was preparing for Loku Mahatmaya's funeral. White flags were hoisted for five miles around Maha Gedara. There was a huge pandal decorated with orange king coconuts, yellow palm leaves and flowers. Loku Mahatmaya's body lay in a coffin, covered in white satin with elephant tusks at either side an oil lamp at his head and one at his feet. Masses of flowers arrived.

His body was to be kept at Maha Gedara for five days until Rupa arrived from England. The hundreds of mourners who came to pay their last respects were lavishly entertained with food and drink.

The night bird 'ulama' had cried seven times from the top of a mango tree in front of Maha Gedara the night before his death, which was taken to be a bad omen.

At half past four the funeral procession started out, the lead landau bearing the coffin. Drummers, pipers and saffron robed Buddhist monks processed behind. Loku Mahatmaya's body was cremated in an elaborately decorated twenty-foot high pyre, covered in white drapes.

Thousands of mourners from neighbouring villages gathered on the final day at the family cemetery. Two nephews carried flares round the pyre three times before setting it alight at the first sighting of the evening star. The pyre burned all through the night, lighting up the sky as more and more satin wood was consumed.

The drummers continued to beat out a dull melody and as the morning star faded the corpse was ash and the drumbeats stopped.

* * * *

Six months passed and Dikwelle Hamine was alone.

'I don't want to live in this desert anymore. If I had known that he was going to go first I would never have married him,' she lamented. Abruptly she left Maha Gedara and went to live with Rukmali. Dasa looked after the dogs, during the day they slept on Loku Mahatmaya's grave. Maha Gedara was now all but abandoned, doors and windows closed, the white washed walls weathered and turned green. The front steps were cracked and anthills appeared unhindered.

The villagers believed that the house was haunted; ghosts were hiding in dark corners while at night they peered through curtains. Bats flew in through a broken fanlight and nested under the roof tiles. Cobwebs were woven into a pattern of wheels. Rotten mangoes, bananas and wild berries heaved up in a corner covered in black fungus mixed with excrement of bats smelling stale and sour. An ebony linen chest on the upstairs was open, a tarnished copper key sitting in the lock, untouched, half empty, moth-eaten green silk rags decades old.

Under the mahogany bed a photograph lay upside down: in it she was smiling holding a bouquet of roses, a white veil draped over her neck and shoulders flowing above her black hair, he was smiling majestically. As the moon shone through the jackfruit trees the dogs barked. On the wall, the clock with Roman numerals had stopped at half past five.

FORTY SEVEN

Rupa was back in England after her father's funeral, but within a few days she became unwell and went to see Dr. Barnes, who had been the family doctor for years.

'How are you Rupa?' He greeted her with a familiar smile.

'Not very well doctor, I've just come back from Ceylon after my father's funeral. I can't sleep and I always feel tired and sick. I have constant headaches and I just don't feel like doing anything except sitting and crying.'

'Is your job stressful?'

'I don't think so. People at work are kind to me.'

'How are your children?'

'They are both at university and I'm on my own.'

He checked her blood pressure and found it was normal. After reflecting briefly he said, 'I'll give you a medical certificate for four weeks. You need a good rest and a break from work and everything else. You're suffering from depression due to stress. I'm not giving you any sleeping tablets. Don't force yourself to do anything, not even cooking. You must come and see me in a fortnight.'

Rupa was surprised but within a few days she began to feel more relaxed and her equilibrium was almost restored.

Hunter phoned on the Thursday night.

'There's a good play on at the Yorkshire Playhouse. Would you like to come with me tomorrow night?'

'I'd love to, what's on?'

'Ibsen's 'An Enemy of the People'.

'Where do you want me to meet you?'

'At the Playhouse, by the outside steps or in the lounge, Rupa.'

'I might pop in to see you tonight if I finish work early.'

When Rupa arrived at the Playhouse Hunter was sitting in the lounge his head buried in a book. Two tickets and a cup of coffee for Rupa were on the table in front of him.

'Sorry I'm late Chris,' Rupa said as she rushed in.

'Don't worry Rupa, there's plenty of time. The play isn't going to start yet.'

'I thought I was going to be late.'

'I'm glad you came, Rupa. You really need a change, something to cheer you up. How do you feel?'

'All right. I'm beginning to feel better. It's a lot for me to lose my dog and then my father. I just have to accept things as they are. My parents were so close to each other and I just can't believe that one of them's gone. It must be a terrible shock for my mother.'

'At least you managed to attend the funeral, Rupa.'

At seven the doors opened and they all filed in. When the lights were dimmed and the play began Rupa finally relaxed. Sitting next to Hunter she felt grateful for his warmth. At the same time she had a deep-down fear that he might be disappointed in her, but he seemed happy enough.

Rupa was enthralled by Ibsen's play, especially the final lines:

'Dr Spockman: It is this, let me tell you - the strongest man in the world is he who stands most alone.'

The play ended and the spectators swarmed out. When Rupa and Hunter came out into the open he suggested they went for a meal at the 'White Swan' in Briggate. While they were eating their meal of king size yorkies filled with minced lamb with a huge helping of chips, Hunter drank whisky.

Suddenly he said, 'Would you like to spend the night with me Rupa? You can come to my flat if you want.'

She blushed and dropped her knife on the floor.

'Would you like another drink of lemon Rupa?' Hunter enquired trying to sound re-assuring but looking slightly anxious all the same.'

'I've finished my thesis Rupa. Hopefully it will be published next year. What I want is you to be with me.' He bought another whisky and lit a cigarette.

'All I want is a book to read, a drink to enjoy and an Eastern wife!' He smiled a slightly drunken smile.

'Are you going to have any more to drink Chris?'

They both laughed.

'I know how you feel about your father's death, Rupa. None of us like to see our parents grow old, fall ill and die. When the end comes we go into shock and it takes a long time to get back to normal. Parents and children are part of us.'

'My father was born, lived and died in the same village. He loved his home Maha Gedara and the village he grew up in. I don't think he had the stress we have to go through.'

When Rupa remembered Maha Gedara was empty she felt as though her past no longer existed.

'I remember when, as children, we ran across the fields and with our sticks struck the rainbow's reflections in the pools.'

'I had a wonderful childhood myself, Rupa. Our houses were heated with coal fires. Every morning the milk woman came with a horse and cart, ringing a bell. My mother had a four pint aluminium jug, which she had filled with milk every day. She bought cutlery, crockery, pots and pans and baking trays from the 'pot man'. We knew when he was coming near by the sound of his horse and cart and the jingling of the pots. The poor horse stood there chomping oats while the women gathered to buy pots and pans. My father worked in a bank and my mother stayed at home but they didn't seem to have any money problems. I went for walks in the woods with my friends, picking buttercups and bluebells.'

Hunter's stories fascinated Rupa and reminded her of her own childhood, in many ways poignant and similar, although she grew up in a Far Eastern country. She felt as close to him as if they had grown up together. An hour later Hunter and Rupa walked hand in hand into his flat through a luminous mist.

On Monday the four weeks' sick leave ended. Rupa returned to work but somehow she never settled. The smell of paint, the air conditioning, the neat clothes and shoes suitable for the office, the non-stop ringing of telephones. The routine fire drills and rapid evacuations, Christmas dinners and parties, coffee at ten, lunch at twelve, tea at three and the opaque office air, everything had become stale. She started looking for a new job.

Within a few days she had a positive reply to her enquiry and the invitation to attend an interview at the headquarters of Leeds City Council's Department of Social Services at Merrion House.

When the day came Rupa felt much more confident than she expected. She sat in the waiting room with three other hopefuls. She was the last to be interviewed. There was a panel of three sat behind an immense polished oak desk, clearly the most senior was the woman who sat in the middle in a high backed leather chair surmounted by the city's coat of arms embellished in gold.

'You are from Ceylon originally and you have a degree in sociology I gather. How many years have you lived in England?'

'Twenty years.'

'Well you should have a good picture of things by now. Why social work?'

'I'm tired of insurance underwriting, the same kind of work everyday. I had problems of my own and I didn't really know where to turn. I'd like to be there for other women who end up in my situation and think I can be of some use.'

'How do you see your responsibilities as a social worker?'

'Well I don't see myself sat in an office but going round to peoples houses, sitting down with them at the kitchen table and listening to their problems. That's the most important thing – listening. I think if you listen hard enough you can help people to get through, because that's what life's about, getting through and surviving at the end of the day.'

'Let me ask you a question,' put in the diminutive man sitting on the right. 'If a woman tells you her husband is drinking heavily and attacking her violently when he's drunk what would you suggest?'

'I think she should leave him and take the children with her immediately. If there's no chance of his rehabilitation, then she hasn't got much choice but to go for a divorce, she has to help the children grow up.'

'Yes, that seems perfectly acceptable,' it was the woman in the large chair who spoke.

'We are taking more people from ethnic minorities. Do you

have a problem leaving your present job?'

'I'll have to give them four weeks notice, that's all.'

'Thank you Rupa, we'll send you written confirmation within the next few days.'

Half an hour later Rupa was back at her office desk feeling a burgeoning sense of happiness. She picked up the telephone and rang Hunter to tell him the good news.

'This calls for a celebration,' he announced and they agreed to meet for a drink that night.

During the first weeks of training for her new job Rupa learned how some unfortunates become 'street people' because of their psychiatric problems. Many tried to run away and hide when the police or drug dealers were after them, never staying long in any one place. They possessed nothing and moved with a carrier bag containing all their worldly possessions. One such was Tracey, a single parent looking after one child. Her two other children had already been taken into care. She was well known to the police and often had fights with her latest boyfriend.

'You're a young woman with a beautiful little girl, Tracey. I'm sure you'll feel much better if you don't get involved with violence and simply look after your child,' said Rupa naively.

'I'm not the nice woman you think. I became a prostitute when I was sixteen. Once I was nearly beaten to death but fortunately the police found me in time. I'm used to courts and prison cells. I don't have a place in society and I'm prepared to accept it. My daughter was born when I was in prison.'

Tracey smiled like a child, her voice was soft and she always kept her room tidy.

'You do have a place in society Tracey. We're here to help you,' but Rupa wondered what the place might be and if she could really help.

One afternoon the phone on Rupa's desk rang. It was a neighbour of Tracey saying that there was a fight going on between Tracey and her boyfriend in a locked room and with Tracey's three year old in there with them. Rupa decided to take a police escort and when they arrived with their sirens screaming Tracey wouldn't open the door so the police had to break it down. Her boyfriend's face was pouring with blood while the child contentedly sucked a lollypop. When the constable asked Tracey to get into the police car she smiled innocently and said 'What about my daughter? Surely you're not going to put her in care over a private matter like this? John here's not pressing charges are you John?'

'No, course not, it was my fault anyway.'

'There you are now,' Tracey said smiling again. Rupa nodded her assent and the police drove off.

Another client was twenty-five year old Natalie, a woman who had spent long periods in a psychiatric unit under section and who had three children.

'I had an abortion because I wasn't sure who the father was,' she said, as if discussing a visit to the dentist. The long term effects of heavy medication had left her looking perpetually pale and her hands had a persistent tremor.

Matthew had had a good upbringing and a private education. He became an office worker but he had a drink problem and ended up a street beggar, sleeping rough in Burley Park. Rupa, for all her good intentions, found many clients very difficult to help. At one time many would have been permanently institutionalised but now the 'care in the community programme' left them on the streets at the mercy of inclement weather and to the kindness of strangers.

FORTY EIGHT

Shane's graduation day was warm and sunny. Rupa and Lisa went to his room in Magdalen two hours before the ceremony was due to begin. Incredibly he had got a first. The four years had gone like the wind and now smiles were on all the students' faces as they put on their gowns and mortarboards, rolled certificates in their palms, friends and relatives falling over each other. Rupa remembered her own graduation and Kumara's inexplicable absence, but today her smile was the smile of a mother. By five it was all over. Shane had been accepted for a further year's study and after that it was 'wait and see'.

Rupa found it difficult to accept that Lisa and Shane returned only for short visits and they were no longer the brother and sister who used to come home from school with inky fingers, mud-spattered shoes, school bags slung over their shoulders. They were no longer the mischievous children who used to make snowmen and throw snowballs. When Rupa told them that it wasn't the Eastern custom to thank their mother after a meal Shane said, 'Mum, it's something I do automatically.'

'The food is delicious, is quite sufficient,' Rupa said, explaining that in the East it is the custom to provide a meal for everyone who appears at meal times.

On Monday Rupa and Hunter went to the Moderno Café in Lower Briggate for a poetry reading. When Rupa looked at the audience of a few dozen she thought they seemed to come from a different world to the one she lived in. The men wore jeans, pullovers and canvas shoes. They seemed to smoke incessantly while the women looked very intense, wore spectacles and carried huge volumes under their arms. The reading was to be given by Jon Silkin, a small wiry man with a huge beard. He wore a soiled sheepskin jacket many sizes too big.

'I'm glad to see so many of you here,' he began, his green eyes flashing a sardonic smile.

'I'll begin with 'Death of a Son,' people always expect me to so I might as well get it over with.' In a semi hypnotic gaze Rupa listened to the first poem and to the many that followed. When at last the reading ended she half-heartedly joined in the applause. She was relieved when Hunter suggested they took a walk along the waterfront where tottering Victorian warehouses were being turned into million pound penthouses.

'Did you enjoy the reading Rupa?'

'I did actually. Is this somewhere you go regularly Chris?'

'I go if I'm free. Are you happier now Rupa?'

'Well Shane's got his degree and a first at that, Lisa's doing well so I feel better than I have for a long time.'

'I've got to tell you something Rupa but you may not like it. From October I'll have to be in Oxford, at Balliol for a Post Graduate Fellowship.'

'I'm so pleased Chris, how long will it last?'

'Just the one year, you can come with me if you like!'

Although Rupa was pleased for Hunter his news came as a huge shock. The year was going to be a very long one. When Hunter started something he always worked very hard at it and he would never raise his head in Oxford. He had always been kind to her; when she was off sick after her father's death he was always there to share her grief.

'After all it's his future and what else can I expect?' she reflected.

Rupa was expecting her friend Chandra on the Saturday afternoon. A helicopter was lazily circling Roundhay Park. It came from the west and eventually disappeared over the horizon with a last tremble. Distantly a train rattled and thundered through the afternoon heat haze. From her school days the solitary line of English poetry she had learned 'The boy stood on the burning deck' – which Hunter was always so sarcastic about – came into her mind. Then another sound began to drift towards her, a slow steady mechanical roaring which she could not place until she recalled there was a feast in Roundhay Park, complete with big dipper, carousels and bumping cars.

The Edinburgh – Leeds express arrived in Leeds City Station at one thirty five, twenty minutes late. Rupa waited impatiently on the platform until Chandra, wearing a smart two piece emerged with a wide smile. Rupa noticed she was older and thinner, the signs of strain showing clearly in the lines on her face.

'I'm so pleased to see you, Rupa,' she said as Chandra pushed her way through the crowd. When they arrived at Rupa's house the meal in the oven was ready.

'I brought some home made pickle and apple chutney for you Rupa,' Chandra said, placing a parcel on the kitchen table.

'I'm so glad you could make it, Chandra, its weird how we found each other after so long.'

They had their meal then Rupa made coffee. She was surprised how quickly Chandra had done all the washing up for her.

'I'm sorry my husband couldn't come. He's busy with his research, some days he just won't stop.'

Chandra relaxed in the green armchair by the hearth and kicked off her sandals.

'So how are things with you Rupa? We haven't seen each other in fifteen years. We've been in Melbourne, Australia for some of that time. How's life with the kids?'

'I'm all right now but it was hell at the time.'

'I still can't believe that Aruna's done a bunk. You hear of this kind of thing happening all the time, but I just can't imagine it happening to you, Rupa.'

'It's all too boring to go over again, but I learned my lesson. I'm happy now, time goes like the wind.'

'Have you any new friends Rupa?'

'Not Ceylonese ones. Christopher Hunter, who is at Leeds University is a close friend, but he's off to Oxford for a year in October. He helped me to get through the worst period. He travelled in the East and said he'd always fancied Asian women.'

'So he fancies you then?'

'He wants to marry me.'

'If I were you Rupa' I'd not hesitate. I know Aruna is a friend of ours but there is no way I'd want to defend him over this. Dumping you and two kids in a foreign country's just about the worst thing a husband can do.'

'Some things got sorted out without too much bother. My degree helped me get the social services job. As for going through the palaver of a divorce with a liar like Aruna, I just don't know.'

'You ought to grab the chance while you've got it. Race is irrelevant these days, a lot of our university friends have inter-married.'

'I've not been well recently, Chandra. I've had bad migraines for the last six months. I keep feeling sleepy but I can't sleep when I do go to bed. I feel exhausted even if I haven't done anything.'

'Have you been to the doctor's?'

'A few times. The last blood test shows that I'm anaemic so I take iron tablets. It's not only that I get stomach pains as well and I feel sick at times.'

'You better get a referral and see a consultant.'

'I'm going to the doctor's next week. I'll see what he says.'

Chandra stayed the weekend, but before she left on Sunday she said, 'Remember this is England, Rupa, your friend Chris Hunter sounds very nice! Keep in touch.'

On Wednesday night Rupa's stomach pains suddenly worsened. She was alone, so in the end she dialled 999. Within ten minutes an ambulance arrived with its blue lights flashing and wailing siren. The two ambulance men, one young and one middle aged, seemed to know what the problem was at once. Before she knew what was happening she found herself being wheeled into casualty where an incredibly young looking house officer gave her a cursory examination and said 'Appendix, could burst, get her to theatre.'

She felt a gentle prick in her left arm and then her mind blurred floating, floating....

When she woke up she found herself on Women's Surgical. At midnight a nurse asked her how she felt.

'I'm in agony, it's so painful,' she said.

The duty doctor gave her an injection and in the strange world of a drug induced sleep she found herself in an open-air theatre. The play must long have been over because the stage was deserted, their ornate carved masks scattered over the boards. Rupa found herself sitting on a fallen tree trunk by the river with Aruna next to her.

'A crocodile's heading our way,' came a frenzied cry from the crowd, adults and children alike waving sticks to ward off the animal's approach.

'Sunio, don't go near the river, get back here,' a woman cried. 'Get back Sunio or I'll smack your legs,' she screamed.

The river roared by the waves washing over the banks, each wave bearing a huge crocodile. The scene changed and Rupa became a bride, but her wedding dress was moth-eaten. Then a scene of childbirth: blood and water filled placenta separating from the womb and a baby's cries. A child crawled towards her, smiling and showing his milk teeth, then school time arrived. Next came moving house packing her belongings in cardboard boxes and the removal lorry, empty boxes scattered in the back yard. Rupa was caught in a storm like a tree shaking in the wind. The wreckage of a ship was cast on the shore.

Rupa woke to find a nurse checking her pulse.

'You've got a temperature, I'll ask Dr Crabtree to take a look.'

The nurse shook the thermometer and recorded on the chart.

It was a Sunday afternoon, Lisa and Shane had been to visit her. The green curtains were drawn back. White clouds slowly turned grey. Rupa's temperature was still high; then came Chandra with a smile and a bunch of flowers. When Chandra started to talk Rupa almost forgot that she had had an operation. 'Problems in the Royal family, dinosaur skeletons and their eggs, cookery, gardening and comets in the sky,' Chandra's topics of conversation were endlessly varied.

'The Edinburgh Festival has finished and it rained cats and dogs for days and nights, still everything went well. You should try to come next year, Rupa.' Although the injections and tablets kept Rupa's temperature down she felt tired.

'I think Rupa, you should try to have a rest. Your eyes look droopy.'

Within seconds Rupa was asleep. Chandra sat beside her and read a paper. Rupa's mind drifted.

She passed along a pebbled valley and hills. The sky was empty but suddenly a great eagle flew across, as large as a Sea King helicopter in its dimensions. There were jagged spirals of colour in front of her. The kaleidoscopic lines grew smaller until they finally disappeared. Rupa woke up sweating but her temperature had gone back to normal.

'I must be off now,' Chandra said.

'Are you going back to Edinburgh tonight? You can stay at my house. Lisa and Shane are there.'

'I've already booked a day return and my husband'll meet me at the other end. All last week he was away on a conference at Glasgow University. He went with Ben and Kumara, two of his friends. You know what Jayanta's like! Every morning he leaves home at half past seven and he doesn't come back until late. He's a workaholic but I don't mind, he's very kind to me.'

For a minute Rupa thought she was still dreaming.

'Kumara! Is he an Indian?'

'No, he's Ceylonese.'

'What's his surname?'

'I don't know that much about Jayanta's friends, Rupa. As far as I can remember he arrived in Edinburgh recently from London or Cambridge, I think. He's been to our place once. Ben Hamilton, the other friend, is someone I know well, he's somewhat senior to my husband. It's twenty past six, I've got to go!' Chandra put on her jacket.

'Thanks for the flowers Chandra.'

'There are some beautiful carnations in my garden. I'll bring you some when I come next time.'

Chandra slipped her bag over her shoulder and said, 'We'll see you on Saturday Rupa. You're a lot better now and you should be able to go home soon,' then off she rushed.

'Who is this Kumara? A friend of Chandra's husband, I just

wonder' Rupa reflected her mind tingling.

Rupa was put in a separate room away from the other patients because she seemed to have developed some minor complication. At seven in the morning a cleaner came in her green striped overall, pushing a trolley with disinfectants, cleaning brushes, dusters, toilet rolls, plastic bags and buckets.

'Morning,' she entered the patient's room.

'Morning.'

She moved like a robot, cleaning every surface, polishing the windows and vaccing the floor then she re-loaded her trolley and off she went.

At seven thirty a nurse arrived in a neat uniform.

'Morning, Rupa.'

'Morning.'

'Have you done your walk up and down the corridors this morning?'

'Yes I have.'

'Slept with no problem?'

'No, I couldn't sleep at all. I felt feverish and had a migraine.'

The nurse gave her some tablets with a glass of water.

'Here you are, this should sort you out.'

She changed the bedding and re-made the bed, re-arranged the flowers in the vase and left.

At eight breakfast was served and the daily papers arrived. Half an hour later the empty plates were collected. With a shaking rattle and shuddering roll the trolley was returned to the kitchen, pushed by the same stout West Indian lady who had brought round the meals, her hair deftly bound in a turban aflame with scarlet parakeets perched on verdant palms.

At ten Dr. Crabtree arrived with the staff nurse.

'Good morning, Rupa.'

'Good morning doctor.'

The nurse handed over the patient's chart.

'How's my patient today?'

'I was sick this morning. I feel a sharp pain when I walk.'

'Don't worry about that, you'll feel better in a day or two, but you still have a fluctuating temperature. I'm changing your medication today.'

'When can I go home doctor?'

'It's still a bit early because of your unstable temperature. Today's Friday, I think you should be able to go home by Monday.' As always he left in a hurry.

Slowly Rupa began to feel better. She wanted to go home. The hospital smell fogged her brain. It was no different to the paint smell at Sun Alliance. She felt like running away to find if this Kumara was the Kumara she had known. She got out of bed and opened her suitcase. As she bent down her stomach twitched and she screamed out loud, her cry bringing a nurse.

'You don't have to get up, ring the bell if you need anything Rupa.'

'I just wanted to find a book to read,' Rupa replied, feeling guilty. Although the doors and windows were open in the dingy room, she realised she couldn't just run away. On Monday as Dr. Crabtree had said, she was to be allowed home.

Rupa phoned Chandra, 'I'm home now Chandra, I feel a lot better and I can look after myself.'

'I'm glad everything went well and you're home Rupa. Don't over do things, housework can wait!'

'I think Kumara, your husband's friend, is someone I knew at university. Is he Kumara Rangama?'

'I think so, I'll get his contact number from my husband if you like.'

All night it rained heavily. The following morning Rupa was looking at the giant acacia at the bottom of her garden, now after last night's storm, leaning towards the adjacent block of garages.

She heard Roy, her next door neighbour, calling over the fence.

'This is my favourite tree, Roy. I'm going to have to call a tree surgeon in to cut it down before it falls.'

The road by St. Barnabas was blocked. A tree fell across and the church spire only just escaped. By the way Rupa, there's a parcel for you. There was no answer when the postman knocked so I took it in.'

'Thanks Roy.'

It was a bouquet of orchids and freesias wrapped in rose decorated paper marked, 'Guernsey Fresh Flowers.' Inside was a short message from Hunter.

If the sun is absent
Let the moon and stars shine
Lie over where beneath
East, West and under any sky.

See you Wednesday.

FORTY NINE

Rupa couldn't believe that the day had arrived. She rubbed her eyes with her forefingers and tried to work out if she was awake or sleeping. Outside the trees were glowing with bright autumn colours and Kumara was coming. The sun peered through prismatic spirals of cloud from the distant horizon. An aeroplane slowly appeared and drifted across the sky like a silver dolphin. The sound of the plane came nearer and nearer until it was directly overhead. It passed away into the blue and white streaked firmament, the sound modulating into a plaintive *diminuendo* then melded with the morning's silence and stillness. In Rupa's mind was a whisper of the past and an invitation.

Rupa was at home recovering from the operation. She began to notice her house was full of books and ornaments dreary with dust but it didn't matter. She got up and washed, then sat on the sofa and drank a cup of tea. Slowly she walked upstairs to get ready. When she opened her wardrobe an aroma of tropical pot-pourri filled the air. She remembered the day she was preparing to see Gunapala, the son of a wealthy businessman, in the presence of her parents and the matchmaker. Today she didn't know what to wear but what did it matter anyway? She pulled an old skirt and a colour washed tee shirt. She looked at herself in the mirror in the bathroom as she combed her shoulder length hair. The pink bedroom slippers Eileen gave her would have to do.

She went downstairs and opened the patio door. The fuchsia in the tub was a profusion of purple pendulous flowers. Was she waiting for the Kumara she had known? Or was it someone else who pretended to be him? Was this just only a meeting of an old friend in a house in England? This wasn't a play and Rupa and Kumara were real people. It wasn't a frog prince story either, nor a Romeo and Juliet scenario nor a story from the Ramayana. She listened to the clock as it ticked the minutes away, slowly oh so slowly. She began to shake with excitement. Her feelings were somehow confused with her recent operation, Aruna, Hunter, Chandra and now Kumara she had been waiting for so long. Only an hour to go for eleven o'clock, but it seemed to be the longest hour she could remember.

Just before eleven the doorbell rang and she opened the door. He smiled. She smiled and invited him in.

'How are you Rupa?' He kissed her on her cheeks.

'I feel a bit better now, please do sit down.'

Kumara had changed so much. When he sat on the sofa and stretched his legs Rupa noticed how his hair had greyed and that he had grown a beard. When she had known him at the university he had been tall and well built but the years seemed to have somehow diminished his stature and he had lost weight. Certainly he was middle-aged and looked older than his years. When he smiled there was a warmth in his eyes but he looked weary and drawn. When he spoke it was as if he had gained strength rather than lost it but where before he had demurred now he spoke confidently. His voice had a musical lilt and its timbre was rich and resonant. He looked her straight in the eye.

'Would you like a cup of tea, Kumara?'

'We'll have something to drink later, just come and sit down by me.'

'Did you find the way all right?'

'Yes, with no problem. Motorways aren't all that busy on a Sunday morning! I left Edinburgh just before eight. I stopped at a couple of service stations.'

'You must be tired.'

'I'm used to long distance driving, Rupa.'

She sat next to him. He realised she was eager to hear his story, but for the moment he seemed unable to speak. Neither of them knew how to begin. Should it be with the end of student life? Finally Kumara broke the silence.

'Twenty six years is a long time Rupa.'

'My story is incredibly long, Kumara. I ended up in England as a single parent. Both my children, Lisa and Shane, are at university. Tell me what happened to you.'

He hesitated, swallowed and then began.

'I had this terrible accident, twenty-six years ago. My sister and I ended up in Colombo General Hospital in Intensive Care. My father was a careful driver but the driver behind wasn't. We were driving along the Kandy – Colombo Road when an overloaded pantechnicon right behind us tried to overtake. He must have been mad or drunk. He hit us and our car ended up in a ditch. Another lorry ploughed into us, somehow the driver managed to stop but we ended up sandwiched between the two lorries. Fortunately my father only had cuts and bruises but my sister and I were out cold and on the critical list. Samanta was in a coma for two weeks. It was incredible that we survived at all. I don't think I ever told you about my sister, Samanta. She was such an attractive girl but after the accident her face was disfigured with scars. She was seventeen and studying for 'A' levels at Kandy Maha Maya College. I had some head injuries but the worst injury was on my stomach.' Kumara opened his shirt and said, 'Look at this scar, Rupa.' There was a six-inch long blue-black twine-like scar and when she touched it she felt the coldness of metal.

'After the accident my father lost interest in everything. He couldn't accept that this had happened while he was driving. We could have both ended up dead. The doctors said that the type of plastic surgery my sister needed was only available abroad so my parents took a big step, they sold most of their property except our home and we all came here. I was in ICU on graduation day, then I was transferred to Navaloka Hospital. It was our father's determination that brought us back to normal. It took a long time for me to get really well. It wasn't just the injuries, due to the trauma I had lost my self-confidence.

Imagine – I was even frightened to go out of the house or cross the road! I had constant nightmares, which still terrify me. Eventually we all lived in Hammersmith. After two years, when I was really better I got a place at Cambridge. I did my doctorate at London and became an English lecturer. I hadn't forgotten you Rupa but I could never find you. I still visit Ceylon, at least once every couple of years. I always call in at the university and see some of our old friends. Once I bumped into Milan and she told me that you were married and a mother.'

'So somehow you managed a full recovery within a few years!'

'Rupa, whether it's physical or mental we just have to carry on with our lives! Painkillers just give passing relief. At times, I wonder how I didn't end up permanently off my head.'

'How is your sister now?'

'After a long period of various treatments and plastic surgery she began to look better. Most of her facial scars faded. She finished her education in England and married an Englishman. She is happy now.'

'I'm astonished Kumara, in spite of such bad luck you still managed to continue your education.'

'I never wanted to marry. When I was in London I had a Japanese girlfriend called Junko. I taught her English and French she always wanted me to go to Japan and stay with her family. She was the daughter of a businessman. She begged me to take her to Ceylon for a holiday. She lived in England for five years and she was keen to marry me but I didn't fancy living in Japan so it never materialised. After she left Junko kept on writing to me. You know what I'm like Rupa, not very good at writing letters to any of my friends. I visited Japan twice but I never went to see Junko. I've done a lot of travelling all over the place.'

'How are your parents?'

'Both of them are still alive but old.'

'Do they still live in England?'

'No, they went back to Ceylon after my sister got married. My father worked here as an accountant until he retired. They love their own country and they always wanted to go back once my sister was sorted out. I had my own flat but I got desperately lonely at times. I never thought we'd meet again Rupa.'

'I don't imagine your parents liked you staying single!'

'My mother wanted me to get married and settle down before they went back. She always wanted me to marry a woman from the same caste but in the end even she gave up. My life was so changed I didn't want any more problems.'

Rupa listened in silence to the answer to twenty-six years of unexplained events. She made some coffee.

'Would you like to eat something Kumara?'

'Don't bother Rupa, we can always eat something later. You should be resting and not entertaining me. Let's go for a walk Rupa, it's a lovely sunny morning.'

They went to Roundhay Park and to the 'Tropical World of Nature', where an exotic atmosphere had been created inside glass houses. Rupa felt strange holding Kumara's hand again as they wandered round listening to the birds and the roaring waterfall set amidst ranging palm trunks. It wasn't the walk they were used to along the sandy banks of the river Mahaweli ridged with lantana bushes, bindweed and wild azaleas, nor the days when they made garlands and bridal bouquets with cascading wild asparagus flowers.

When they came into the open again it was a warm day but warnings of winter's approach were everywhere. The grass verges had turned yellow and the leaves were falling. The iron gates of St. Mary's Church were open and the bell tolled incessantly. Some squirrels munched avidly at the fruits of a chestnut tree. The sound of wood pigeons echoed and re-echoed. They sat on a bench by the canal bank where a pair of black Tasmanian swans glided imperiously. In the middle of the lake lay a tiny island where they nested.

'Now, I've told you my life, what about yours Rupa? You have been with me all these years.'

'It's a story for later Kumara.'

There was silence.

'Are you well enough to go to London with me Rupa?'

'I'm fine, Kumara.'

The air between them became suddenly charged.

It was early evening when they arrived at the South Bank Centre by the Thames. The river was full of pleasure steamers with strings of coloured lights tied from stem to stern. The shore was packed with tourists jabbering in every tongue and even the air seemed busy with criss-crossing aircraft to and froing from Heathrow. The Queen Elizabeth Hall was the venue for a symphony orchestra and they had managed to get a pair of seats for the front row. The hall was dimly lit and rippled with conversations. They sat together, seeming to be listening to Britten's 'Sea Interludes' but lost in a shared unconscious paradise.

By eleven it was over and soon they reached Kumara's flat in Kensington. He drew the curtains and Rupa perched on the arm of the settee, vaguely aware of his presence. Distantly a clock chimed midnight. Rupa felt she had reached a crossroads between time and eternity. In Rupa's mind a voice which would not be stilled kept saying 'Which way, Rupa, which way?'